BRIAN MCBRIDE

TYRANT

Published by Irewolf Books
1830 Stony Point RD
Santa Rosa, CA 95407

This Irewolf Books first paperback edition May 2025.

Cover design © 2025 Beacon House Creative.

Printed in United States of America.
ISBN-13 979-8-9879749-3-3

To the Jailbirds —
for letting me tell your story

PRAISE FOR
THE MAMMOTH ADVENTURES

"*Mammoth* is not just a book; it's an adventure. This must-read is a page-turner steeped in the fog of the Pacific Northwest. Get knee deep in the mysteries of *Mammoth* alongside Tommy and the Jailbirds for an unforgettable journey."

– Morgan Hubbard, author of *Legends of Arcadia*

"*Mammoth* is everything good about the adventure stories of my childhood, scaled up to an older audience. And the characters! They're flawed, messed up, but at no point did I feel hopeless or despairing while reading their stories. Definitely worth the read – and the reread!"

– Brigitte Cromey, author of *Tales of Sea and Skies*

"An epic adventure for a new generation of readers, *Titan* blends the adventures of *National Treasure* with the mysteries of the *Hardy Boys* with characters that you can't help but root for and a plot that leaves you wanting more."

– Anna Augustine, author of *The Allura Novellas*

"*Leviathan* is another wild ride that continues a story that will not just tug on your heart strings, but immerse you into a world of adventure, intrigue, suspense and characters that somehow feel like home. With a killer plot that will keep you up late, this story is one for this generation to latch onto and gives readers not just relatable characters, but ones that are so real they could be us. It doesn't shy away from the searching questions our generation is asking and gives answers that will leave you filled instead of empty – all encapsulated in a story that will leave you with tears and a pounding pulse."

– Victoria Lynn, author of The Chronicles of Elira

"*Leviathan* is a breathtaking ride, a quest for truth where loyalty and friendship are found to be more valuable than gold and the most dangerous of secrets are worth bringing to light. The Jailbirds are my jam and I highly recommend this series to any mystery adventure lover."

– Laurisa Brandt, author of Birthright of Scars

THE MAMMOTH ADVENTURES

Mammoth

Titan

Leviathan

Tyrant

OTHER WORKS BY BRIAN MCBRIDE

Love and the Sea and Everything in Between

Every Bright and Broken Thing

Sons of Slaughter

We the Wild Things

101
Atlas Rock
Hollow Hill Road
Hollow Hill Bay
Lighthouse
the wall
Clark Estate
Morales
101
arinas
Museum
the Yard
Library
Crow River
the Boathouse
Mammoth beach
Silver Springs Trailer Park
Mayfield residence
Porter Pools
Lake Yellowtail
Aviary
101
Sommerfield State Park
N
W
E
S

REID
CLARK
LYDIA
CLARK
IMMY
ALVAREZ
MAYA
MORALES
JUDE
MAYFIELD
MARS
HIGHLAND
TOMMY
RHODES

TYRANT

BRIAN MCBRIDE

Irewolf Books
Santa Rosa, CA

Episode One

DEAD AND BURIED

"They'd walked through a door that
their parents had tried years ago to close,
lock, and throw away the key - and they'd
paid the price for it."

PROLOGUE

April 23rd, 1886

Death was a shadow in the corner of Othniel Cuvier's eye, ever present, ever haunting. Like sand through the hourglass, the seconds of his life slipped by. Running out, spilling onto the ground around his feet. There was little time left to do what needed done, and often he found himself regretting that he had not seen the truth in time, that he had been swept away by the man's deceit. If only he had recognized the truth, then perhaps he would not be preparing to flee death, perhaps his life would not hang in the balance as it did now. Perhaps…

Three blocks of wood sat on the desk before him, no longer than his index finger, no wider than his wedding band. Lantern light cast a dim glow across the parchment and the wood shavings strewn across surface. Hunched over, knife in hand, he imagined in his mind what he intended for those blocks of wood. His life's work, taken from him. But here he could etch it upon these blocks, prove to the world what he had accomplished despite their disbelief, their prejudice. Three fossils, three precious, hidden wonders. He grabbed one of the wooden blocks and carved out his vision. The movement of the small carving knife against his palm rubbed the flesh raw. Skin cracked, drew blood. Still, he continued into the night, carving out a message he prayed would echo beyond the grave.

Behind him, the door opened. He glanced over his shoulder to see his daughter slipping inside. She quickly shut the door to silence the busy sounds of the inn below. Shuffling across the floor, Katherine took the seat beside her father, watching as his blade bit into the block of wood.

He felt her eyes on him, her questions burning a hole through his heart. For a moment, she remained still, silent. Katherine understood what was at stake, though he'd told her little of his plan. Obadiah Hawthorne could take Othniel's life's work, he could pillage and destroy, but the man would not have his daughter.

"You could speak up," she whispered. "Tell the world what you've found. Tell them now before someone else gets the chance. There are those who would listen, I'm sure of it. Timothy, he…"

Othniel shook his head, sweat beading on his brow. "I fear I will not get that chance." He paused, glanced up at his daughter. Her brown eyes pleaded with him to put a stop to this madness, but she did not yet understand the forces at work, closing in around Othniel even now. The choices that Othniel had made – that he had been forced make – had spiraled far beyond his control. His only hope now rest in the plan he would set in motion. "I pray that one day you will have the chance to tell stories I never could."

She sighed, hands folded in her lap. "Will you tell the others? Hawthorne, Highland?"

Othniel swallowed, fixating on carving the block of wood in his hands. A cut here, a curve there. The image was clear in his mind. But he had such little time to execute it. "I don't trust Hawthorne. He has done things… There is blood on his hands… And Highland, well, I'm not certain."

Katherine settled a hand on her father's shoulder, leaned toward him. "You must trust someone, Father," she said.

Othniel's eyes flicked to hers, softening. "I trust you, my love. You and only you."

Kathrine's lips pursed. She straightened.

"Promise me, Katherine," Othniel said. He set the knife and the block of wood down on the desk, reaching out to take her hands in his. "Promise me that, should the worst come to pass, you will finish what I have started. That you will keep safe what we have worked hard to build."

With a nod, she replied, "I promise. Of course I promise."

June 14th, 1888

The Nile River glittered like diamonds beneath the morning sun. Brilliant colors brushed across the horizon, casting an auburn glow over homes and other structures formed from the mud. Bright pink flamingos waded on the riverbank, their crooked beaks dipping below the surface of the water in search of food while others preened in the morning glow. Elsewhere in the water, crocodiles watched and waited. Katherine Rhodes spotted them every now and then, their eyes breaking the surface of the river, hovering in place to give the appearance of a piece of wood set adrift.

Katherine's gloved hands tightened around the railing at the bow of the river boat. The weight of her dress and the density of the fabric felt oppressive in this heat. She'd already rid herself of the corset that would have molded her body to something befitting a society that had proven unwilling to accept her. Throwing off all propriety, she removed the gloves and tossed them to the deck of the boat, rolled up her sleeves and savored the feeling of the breeze across her skin, which had grown a shade darker since arriving to port in Alexandria a month ago. They'd spent some time in Alexandria – after the transatlantic journey, she'd needed a moment to breathe, to gather her wits about her as she prepared to do what needed doing. After two weeks in Alexandria, she was ready to embark on what would be the final stretch of their journey – back to where it had all begun.

Legacies were terrible burdens to bear. Katherine Rhodes wished on nobody the quest passed down to her by her father, the great Othniel Cuvier. The task of keeping safe all that her father had worked for had fallen to her and her alone – not even her husband could possibly understand the weight she bore. Her father had died for this, for discoveries that should have put his name in headlines across the globe. Othniel Cuvier should have become as indelible upon the pages of history as the likes of Washington or Franklin. Instead, his discoveries had made him a target and his meekness had made him vulnerable to lesser men – men who would use and deceive and betray and… If only

Katherine had discerned Hawthorne's motives sooner.

Hawthorne.

The man had been so quick to take credit for the discovery of the pair of woolly mammoths: a mother and her infant. Along with the mineral deposits in the Washington mountains, it had drawn the attention of captains of industry across the world. They had flocked to the newly established mining settlement, since named Mammoth. It didn't matter that the gold they plucked from the ground was soaked in the blood of the natives Hawthorne had slaughtered and buried beside her father, whose body she'd never recovered.

Would she ever truly be able to lay her father to rest? Would the world ever know of the man he was? Would anyone ever learn of the horrors hidden behind the eyes of men like Obadiah Hawthorne?

As the river boat approached the port in Asyut, Katherine's eyes trailed to the green riverbeds where the tops of palm trees rose above the shorter, stouter foliage. Very little had changed since her father had brought her here as a little girl. Katherine had all but grown up beneath the Egyptian sun. She closed her eyes and smiled as the wind whipped at her curly brown hair, tugging it free of her updo. She could practically feel the sand between her toes, the water lapping at her ankles. Part of her wished to be that little girl again, carefree and immodest in her childlike innocence. There was no illusion or mask of propriety – not in Egypt, not as a child. Her father marveling over some discovery while she played with the tools of his trade, stealing in bits and pieces the conversations he held with scholars and explorers from all over the world. Now as both a woman and a Black individual, her world was set firmly within barriers she'd only ever known to cross when she was younger. When had it happened? When had she traded the innocence of her youth for the rigidity of civilized society?

It didn't matter. Since her father's death a year ago, she could feel cracks forming in masks she'd spent years fitting herself into – and she wasn't certain that she cared. Let them break. Let the world see what would become of the aggrieved Katherine Rhodes.

Strong arms slipped around Katherine's waist, fingers tracing her stomach and coming to rest on either side of her. A bearded chin nestled into her shoulder, and Katherine leaned back, reaching up to touch a hand to her husband's face, running her nails through the short curls on top of his head. He sighed, burying his face deeper in her neck as they rocked back and forth to the sway of the boat beneath their feet.

"What's on your mind, my love?" he asked. A good, kind man who had followed both her father and her on their expeditions, never questioning, never second-guessing. He'd remained by her side even when he'd had good reason to leave. He saw her for who she truly was and not for what the world had made her out to be. It was his compassion and more that had stolen Katherine's heart.

"I'm thinking…" she began, then smirked. "That I am quite hot. I should like to go for a swim."

Timothy laughed. "Those weeks in Alexandria were pleasant. Perhaps, when we are finished here, we take a month – maybe two – and spend some time in Cairo. Just the two of us. No dusty bones to sit on shelves and watch our every move."

Katherine laughed. "They're not alive, you know."

Timothy pulled away and came to rest against the rail beside her, arms crossed over his broad chest, eyebrow raised as he looked down at her. His dark skin had become even darker beneath the Egyptian sun. "I'm not the one giving them names."

Pursing her lips, Katherine said, "It is to help me stay sorted."

"Yes, of course," said Timothy, slapping himself on the forehead in mock forgetfulness. "You named the bones Astrid in case you forgot where you placed them, so that you could call for them and expect them to come."

"Oh, stop," said Katherine, shoving her husband in the arm. He took the opportunity to grab her by the wrist and pull her to himself, and in one move he held his lips to hers, kissing her slow and deep.

His kisses come more frequently as of late, thought Katherine. Perhaps her father's death had taught him something about life and the shortness of it.

The port city of Asyut rose in the distance, along the western bank of the Nile.

"I will be glad when this is over," she said, her voice barely audible over the shouts of the boat's crew as they prepared to dock.

Timothy's arms tightened around her. He rested his chin on her shoulder as he stared out across the water. "Will it ever truly be over?"

No, she thought. *It won't.*

What had happened to her father was something she would carry with her always, and there would always be those who knew the truth about Othniel Cuvier and were determined to keep it buried. Those who would hunt Katherine, her husband, her life's work. That's why they were here, after all. Katherine couldn't give her father the credit he was due, but she could preserve his legacy and ensure its survival until the right moment in history.

Will it ever come?

She had been despised for the color of her skin all her life.

Her father himself had been a slave before, upon being liberated, becoming an explorer. Would history ever be prepared to honor them not for the color of their skin but for the good they brought into the world?

The boat floated into place alongside the old dock, and the workers climbed out to secure the mooring lines. With a loud crash, a ramp settled against the hull of the boat. Timothy guided Katherine across the deck, holding her hand as she stepped down the swaying ramp. The different sounds of port filled the air. Water lapping along the shore. Dockworkers shouting at one another. Birds calling to each other as they danced and dove their way across the sky. Boat engines sputtering and churning. The sound of a hundred different lives all being lived at once.

From the end of the dock where wood met dirt and rock, beneath the shade of a fig tree, Katherine oversaw the transport of the goods from boat to land, shouting orders for Baahir, the translator she'd hired from Alexandria to accompany her on the trip, to dictate to the workers. Her father's fortune – what was left of it – had been a great help in this whole ordeal. Baahir was a lean man, but he did not lack for muscle. He wore a red vest that hung open to reveal the sinewy muscles in his abdomen and the veins that bulged in his arms under this heat. Even the constant wind off the water wasn't sufficient to ward off the heat of the desert.

Overheating in her dress despite her rolled-up sleeves and gloveless hands, Katherine envied her husband, who had already removed his shirt due to the heat and now helped the workers carry crates down the docks and onto the shore. She admired the muscles that strained in his back, but the admiration quickly faded at the sight of the scars that marred the skin of his back. Like her father, he had been a slave as a child. Slavery had long been abolished, but men still lived who bore its scars.

The workers loaded the crates and the tools onto wagons to be pulled by camels. Katherine and Timothy opted to ride at the back of the caravan as they set out through the city, quickly trading the brown, mud and stone buildings of Asyut for the rolling dunes of the Egyptian desert. The shimmering blue of the Nile and the rustling green of the palm trees that grew along its riverbank soon disappeared behind them.

As the hours passed slowly, Katherine made herself comfortable on the wagon bench, the map unfurled in her lap. A wide-brimmed hat blocked out the sun as she studied it, penned by her father himself. She remembered sitting beside him at his desk as a child while he made this very map. She'd already plotted their course with Baahir, who led the caravan from the front.

Timothy's hand came to rest on Katherine's knee. She looked up to meet him in the eyes and smiled, leaning over to rest her head on his shoulder.

"You are certain Hawthorne never saw this map?" he asked.

Katherine nodded. "My father left it with his other things before ever embarking with Obadiah." She said the man's first name as though he were still the family friend he'd once been and not the murderer who'd betrayed her father.

"And the trail we left behind, do you think he will ever figure it out?"

"No, but someone will. Someday." Katherine could only hope the clues would fall into the hands of the right people.

A horn resounded from the front of the caravan, interrupting their conversation. Katherine stood up at the front of the wagon to peer over the top of the caravan ahead. "What is it, Baahir?" she shouted as he steered his camel toward her wagon. "Why have we stopped?"

His accent thick, he nodded toward the hill up ahead and replied, "We are here. Would you like to see it first?"

Katherine's heart thrummed inside her chest. She nodded, accepting Timothy's help as she dismounted the wagon. She hurried across the sand, her feet sinking slightly with every step. The climb up the side of the dune stole her breath and left her brow dripping with sweat in the heat, but the moment she crested the hill, she sucked in a sharp gasp.

The oasis sprawled out in a valley formed by the dunes, the brilliant green of palm trees and lush foliage a welcome sight amid an infinite canvas of browns and yellows. Even the blue sky seemed to brighten by several shades when contrasted by the glittering oasis. The lush paradise sprawled as far as her eye could see in the distance, but she knew it had an end. She had been here before. With her father, when she was only a little girl. This was where he had made his first discovery, and this was where his legacy would be laid to rest once and for all, for Katherine's own descendants to one day claim. When history was ready to remember Othniel Cuvier.

A hand fell over Katherine's shoulder, and she turned to meet the gaze of Timothy, her husband. He offered a smile, and she set her own hand upon his.

"You are sure that this is what you want to do?" he asked. In the year since her father's death, they had both changed so much. Gone was the dutiful little girl Katherine had once been, and gone was the lean, bright-eyed suitor Timothy had once been. He had grown a beard and had put on muscle until he no longer looked like the man she had married.

Katherine nodded. "My father died because the world wasn't

ready to admit what a Black man – a former slave – could accomplish. I pray that, one day, that will change. One day, they will see we are more than what they made of us."

Timothy brushed a lock of her hair behind her ear and bent to kiss her. She smiled against his lips and turned back to watch the dig. It was not the usual archaeological expedition. Rarely, if ever, did explorers and scientists such as herself put the things they discovered back under the earth. But since her father's death, her mission had changed, as had Timothy's. They would become protectors, and those who came after them would bear the same burden for as long as the world needed to prepare for something like this. Here in the heart of this oasis, they would build not a tomb but a vault. And whatever winding path their line would follow, never again would they be slaves.

ONE

TOMMY

A cold fog seeped from the shadows of Hollow Hill. Tommy Rhodes and his fugitive friends ran as far from the siren sounds and flashing lights as their legs would carry them. Evergreen pines and spruces rose like giants around them, overshadowing the earth and blocking out the pale moonlight that would have lit their path.

Tommy's arm hooked under Immy's, wrapping around her back and crossing Jude's who helped to carry her from the other side. She grunted with every step, her usually dark skin now pale from the blood loss. The hilt of the dagger protruded from the wound in her side, blood staining her shirt and pants red.

"Stop," said Tommy, lifting her arm up and over his head. "You need to rest."

She shook her head emphatically. "No. We need to keep moving."

"Immy…"

"The sooner we get somewhere safe, the sooner we can deal with the dagger currently cutting up my insides, so don't argue with me."

An owl hooted somewhere in the darkness. Branches rustled in the wind. Tommy studied her, then glanced over at Jude. His best friend's face told him he didn't like the thought of pushing Immy any harder either, but none of the Jailbirds could afford the time they'd lose if they wasted it arguing.

The pale fog masked the forest floor, which angled slightly to Tommy's right. The downward slope would lead eventually back to Mammoth, Washington – Tommy's hometown and currently the site of a citywide manhunt. Somewhere out there, Lydia was waiting for Tommy to come rescue her. Somewhere out there, Reid had given himself up to give them a chance at escape, and in the process he'd turned the key to the treasure over to Tommy.

Tommy could feel them in the pocket of his jeans – the three keys left behind by Othniel Cuvier, the explorer whose hidden vault of lost fossils and discoveries Tommy's father had died trying to find.

The Jailbirds continued, Mars up ahead, using a flashlight to light the way forward with Lucy at his side. Huffing, Tommy replaced his arm around Immy's back and forced himself onward.

"Any ideas where we should shack up?" asked Jude, his eyes dead ahead.

"Yeah," Maya interjected, coming up from behind to meet them. "I think I know a place."

TWO

REID

Handcuffs bit the flesh of Reid Clark's wrists as he sat in the Mammoth Police Department interrogation room. Sheriff Patterson leveled an unflinching gaze at Reid, sizing him up, doing his best to see past the cold, distant look in Reid's eyes. The span of silence made Reid's skin crawl, so he passed the time by fixating on the stains on the wall.

Patterson sighed and leaned over, palms pressed against the surface of the cold, metal table. "Listen, Clark. You're looking at spending the best years of your life behind bars if you don't open that pretty boy mouth of yours and get to talking."

Reid set his jaw, shifting in his seat at the discomfort of his hands being pressed up against the back of the metal chair. "Got nothing to say."

Scoffing, Patterson crossed his arms, backing away from the table to lean against the mirror. Reid stared past the sheriff, meeting his own reflection. For a second, he didn't see himself. Another face stared back at him, the face of someone long dead. Reid swallowed, blinking back the image of his father. This was always where Reid was supposed to end up, wasn't it?

"We're charging you with arson and murder, kid. You get that?"

Reid said nothing.

His mind flashed to that moment in the old mines, his heart pulsing faster in his chest. He fixated on the wall across the room, just on the other side of the mirror. Reid hadn't slept at all that night. Every time he closed his eyes, he relived it.

"I can't leave yet," Tommy said, eyes wide and fixed on Reid. "Not without the artifact. It's the only way I'll get her back."

"We'll come back when things calm down," Reid promised. "You're no good to Lydia in jail. Now, go!"

Reid could have left it at that, but just as he was seconds away from safety, he'd noticed it there, hidden at the base of the tunnel wall — a glint of metal. A false wall. The last key. He'd found what they were looking for — the thing that would have thwarted Orion's plans — but it had been too late.

"Go," he said when Tommy hesitated. "Now!"

Maybe he'd made a mistake; maybe he should have taken his own advice and come back later when the police weren't hunting them down. But Reid had made his choice, and it had brought him here. There was a time he thought he could trust Patterson, but once again that trust had been misplaced. Every time he trusted, every time he let people in, he got nothing but grief for it.

Reid winced, shifting in his chair.

"You gotta talk sometime, Clark," said Patterson.

Reid swallowed. Everything in his body screamed at him to

bolt, to fight his way out of the police department, but where would he go? He was trapped, his entire life – such as it was – completely unraveled in the span of a few months.

And all because he'd believed his uncle's lies. All because he'd believed that someone saw something worthwhile in him.

Patterson came around the side of the table and sat against the edge, staring down at Reid with his hands folded in his lap in front of him. His tan button-down was wrinkled. Something told Reid the man hadn't gotten much sleep that night either.

"Here's the thing, kid," said Patterson. "I don't believe any of it." He frowned and shook his head. "Ask me, it's a little convenient that we find your watch at the scene of the arson. And the attack on Quincy? It all feels a little too… orchestrated."

Reid looked up at the man, searching the sheriff's expression for any sign that he was being honest. Would Patterson play him like that? Reid wasn't certain he could trust his perception of people anymore.

"See, I think someone else is pulling the strings here," continued Patterson, lowering his voice. He leaned closer to Reid, looking him in the eye. "A name. That's all I need to start looking in the right direction. You trusted me once before. Trust me now."

Orion. He's the murderer, not me. He set the fire. He planted the watch. He killed my father. Not me.

That's what Reid should've said. It was right there, on the tip of his tongue. But who stood on the other side of the mirror?

The door burst open before Patterson got his answer, and Lorelai stormed in, a mixture of anger, grief, and fatigue barely hidden behind the light makeup on her face. She slapped her briefcase down on the table and turned to face the sheriff, folding her arms across her chest as she stared the taller man down.

"Interviewing my client without his lawyer present, Patterson? That's playing dirty and you know it. Even for you."

The sheriff looked like he'd been bitten as he backed away, his face flushing red with annoyance. "Now, Lorelai, your stepson-"

"Don't 'Lorelai' me, Patterson. This isn't high school debate club, and I'm not here to argue with you about whether video games promote violence or kids should be allowed to have their cell phones in school. My client has every right to have his attorney present, and if you want to deny him that, then I'm more than happy to rain down *hell* on this police department."

Sheriff Patterson's jaw tensed, his nostrils flaring as he stared the woman down. "Your *client* is looking at a couple decades in prison if he doesn't start talking."

Lorelai took a step forward, and Reid marveled as he watched her intimidate a man twice her size with arms that could snap hers in two. He was sorry he'd never gone to see her in court for himself – the woman was a force.

"My client is *innocent*, and last I checked, you haven't even concluded your investigation of The Boathouse fire or the death of my husband." She inched closer, until she was in his face." I don't know what kind of case you're building here, Sheriff, but right now it's looking to me like a house of cards, and I am just *seconds* away from blowing it down."

"Be that as it may, Reid Clark's going to stay right where he is. Bail's been denied."

"We'll see about that. Now, if you'll excuse us, I'd like to have a word with my client."

Patterson glanced from Lorelai to Reid, who offered a shrug. The man opened his mouth to speak, then turned and stormed through the door, slamming it behind him.

When Lorelai turned to face Reid, the tough exterior she'd erected melted away and she rushed to his side. He rose to meet her as she wrapped her arms around him.

"We're going to get you out of here," Lorelai said. "Orion won't get away with this."

Reid wanted to believe her, but he'd seen what Orion had done to those who stood in his way. He was living it.

THREE
MAYA

Maya Morales froze when she set foot on her parents' property – one of many rental properties they owned in Mammoth. This place, one of Maya's personal favorites, had been in the middle of a garage renovation for the better part of the past year, so it was in between tenants. It sat high up on the Wall – the range of mountains that encircled most of the city, where only wealthier citizens like Maya's family could afford to live. She'd never really connected with her family's wealth and certainly had no interest in benefiting from it or letting it dictate her life, but there were times – like now – where she couldn't help but be grateful.

The house sat at the back of a wooded property. A long driveway circled a large, stone fountain. The house had a midcentury flair, with a flat and angled roofline and lots of windows facing westward, toward the sunset. A path led from the porch to a nearby pond, where a gazebo stood in the hazy light of the moon.

Maya searched the property for any sign of movement or life, but there was nothing, construction likely on pause due to the winter weather. But her parents' houses never stayed empty for long. This house would provide shelter for a little while, but they'd need to come up with a long-term plan – preferably one that included rescuing her friends first.

Motioning for the others to follow, she led them across the lawn, the wet ground like a sponge beneath her feet, muddying her shoes and the hem of her jeans. Maya stepped onto the porch and punched in the code on the door. Fortunately, they always used the same code for everything and hadn't thought to change it. Yet. Maya wasn't sure if the fact they still used her birthday was supposed to make her forget about everything that had happened, about how her parents had never even wanted her in the first place and had considered terminating the pregnancy, or how they hadn't fought very hard to keep her after deciding to go through with it.

As far as Maya was concerned, her family – all but two – was right here. She was a Jailbird, through and through. Even if that meant being framed for someone else's crimes and being chased across town by the police.

"Quick. Inside," said Maya as she swung open the door, the alarm effectively disarmed. Jude and Tommy were the first through the door, practically carrying Immy between them, a trail of blood staining the driveway and the porch in the direction they'd come. Maya waited while the others filed in after them, glancing around the property to make sure they were well and truly alone. She quickly shut the door behind her, resetting the alarm.

The large foyer with white granite floors opened to the rest of the house. To the right lay a sprawling kitchen. To the left, the family room boasted dark-stained bookcases empty and waiting for new tenants. A grand piano sat in the bay window. Ahead, stairs led to the second floor and a hallway led to a set of double doors that opened into the backyard. Lucy climbed halfway up the stairs, her eyes darting around the house and taking it in while Tommy and Jude deposited Immy on the couch. Mars took up position at her side while the other boys backed away.

Maya watched them from the shadows of the foyer, the flicker of pain in Tommy's eyes as he gaped down at the blood on his hands, his hair falling down in front of his face. Jude ignored the blood that stained his own arms as he reached for Tommy's face, forcing his attention on him.

"Let's go get cleaned up," said Jude, grabbing Tommy by the arm.

Tommy gave a short nod, then followed Jude's lead as Maya guided him down the hall to the powder room beneath the stairs.

She waited outside while Jude left Tommy in the bathroom, closing the door behind him. Their eyes met in the shadows of the hallway, the faint bathroom light slipping beneath the door and washing over their feet. She wanted to fold herself into his arms, to take comfort in his strength, to tell him how much she admired him for the man he was. But the words wouldn't form, and Maya couldn't move.

Jude's hands still covered in Immy's blood, he reached up to tuck a loose curl behind Maya's ear, offering a half smile. Voices carried in from the living room – Lucy and Mars as he did his best to check Immy's wound.

"I wish…" Maya started.

Jude didn't interject, waited for her to finish.

She glanced away, chewing on her lip. "I wish we'd never discovered that cellar beneath the lighthouse. None of this would've happened."

Jude's thumb brushed her ear, then he pulled away, sucking in a breath. "There's a lot of other things that might not have happened either."

Her eyes flicked to his, but the bathroom door opened again before she could say anything further.

Jude traded places with Tommy, shutting the bathroom door behind him. Tommy leaned over to give Maya a brotherly kiss on the top of her head, squeezing her arm, then headed down the hallway toward the living room.

Maya inhaled, then followed him.

She found Mars sitting on the coffee table beside the couch, pulling back the torn hem of Immy's shirt to examine the wound on her stomach. Maya stood in the archway between the foyer and the living room, watching in silence until the bathroom door opened and Jude came to join her. He started to turn a light switch, but Maya grabbed his hand. "Don't," she said.

He raised an eyebrow.

"My parents know this place is vacant right now, and the police likely know all of our family's properties. Any sign of activity would be automatically suspicious."

"She's right," said Tommy as he crossed the room to join them. "We keep the lights off. Avoid the windows and stay down."

From the living room, Mars asked, "Maya, do your parents keep any first aid supplies at any of their properties?"

"Beyond Band-Aids and antibiotic cream? No."

He frowned, and Maya turned back to Tommy. "We need to figure out how to help Immy."

"I know I'm new here and all, but… she needs a hospital," whispered Lucy, her brow dipped in concern as she leaned against the archway, arms crossed over her chest.

"I'm fine," said Immy, but the coughing fit that ensued did little to inspire confidence.

Maya's eyes burned, heavy from exhaustion as she studied her friend, pale and bleeding.

"Liar," Mars muttered.

Tommy nodded, his arms crossed over his chest, bloodshot eyes staring at the floor in front of him. He'd scrubbed his arms clean, but his clothes were still covered in Immy's blood. Bags had formed under his eyes – probably under all of theirs. His flannel was torn in several places, snagged by tree branches or cut by the guys who'd tried to capture them, wounding Immy in the process. His shoes were caked with mud, and the holes in his jeans frayed and torn wider than normal. He wore his father's jacket and clutched the senior Rhodes' fedora in his hand.

"Don't," said Maya, her eyes locked on Tommy. He looked at her as she read the thoughts behind his eyes. The guilt and remorse. Jude wasn't the only one close enough to Tommy to discern the things he never said.

Tommy gave a slight, almost imperceptible nod and dropped his arms, sucking in a breath. "We can't take Immy to the hospital. But maybe we can bring what she needs back to her." Looking past Maya into the living room, he said, "Mars, can you get me a list of anything you think she'll need?"

He nodded. "Doesn't look like the knife cut anything serious. I can't stitch, but…"

"I know what you're thinking, Martian," said Immy, her lips pale as she looked up at him from her reclined position on the couch.

Lucy held up a hand. "I don't. I don't seem to have the telepathic skills you guys have."

Mars sighed and glanced over his shoulder at Tommy. "You bring me antibiotics and gauze and anything else you can find, and I'll… cauterize the wound."

"Cauterize?" Jude said. "As in… *burn*? Fire? *Del fuego*?"

"Give me an alternative," said Mars.

Jude's mouth hung open, but he snapped it shut when he failed to come up with anything. Maya watched him run his hands through his blond hair, combing it out of his face, puffing his cheeks up as he let out a slow breath.

"Alright then," said Tommy. "I'll be back as soon as I can."

He started for the door. Jude gave Maya a worried look, then said, "I'm coming too."

Maya watched them leave, then turned to Lucy. "Wanna help me see if there's anything to eat or drink around here?"

Lucy held out a hand. "Lead the way."

FOUR

LYDIA

Warm light kissed the side of Lydia Clark's face as she stirred. Something soft beneath her. A bed.

She struggled to remember what happened, how she got here. It came to her in bits and pieces as she struggled to open her eyes. The police surrounding Hollow Hill Lighthouse, her friends fleeing all while she sat helpless behind the tinted window of Orion's car, bound. And then... Lydia grunted, struggling to remember. Orion had climbed back into the car with her, a smug look on his face.

"You look tired," he said.

She was. Her throat and tongue were dry, her voice hoarse — partly from lack of water, partly from crying. She'd taken the bottled water when he'd offered it, and she'd drank. Then...

Lydia's heart sank. Her uncle had *drugged her*.

How long had it been since all that had happened? A day? A week, or more?

Clutching the blanket beneath her between her fingers, Lydia tried to force herself to wake up, but her body refused to obey. Finally, her eyes fluttered open, blinding light flooding her vision. The sky above her was bright. No, it wasn't sky. It was a ceiling. As her vision focused, Lydia forced her eyes downward, past the tropical-themed wallpaper and the Georgian wainscoting to the grand fireplace at the end of her bed. A fire roared in its heart, filling the room with warmth as everything came into focus.

Grunting, Lydia pushed herself upright. Her brown hair fell loose around her face. She still wore the clothes Orion had kidnapped her in, which came as some relief. No one had touched her – not like that, at least.

The bed was surrounded by thin, linen curtains that swayed in the breeze from a nearby open window. Beneath Lydia was an old quilt with patterned florals. To the right of the room, between the fireplace and a door, was a freestanding wardrobe. To the left, a pair of open windows, their linen curtains flapping in the breeze. Beyond the windows, another door led into what appeared to be a bathroom. Sconces lined two of the four walls of the bedroom, emitting a faint orange glow in the daylight.

Where had Orion brought her? And what did he plan to do with her?

Lydia turned and let her feet fall off the side of the bed. She stepped down onto the oriental rug that covered the center of the floor, partially under the bed. Beneath the rug, stained wood floors.

Her body felt heavy as she forced herself onto her feet. With one hand, she rubbed the sleep from her eyes while using the other hand to steady herself against the bedpost. For a moment, she thought she might pass out, but the dizziness went as quickly as it had come. She made her way across the room toward the twin windows, leaning against the trim as she stared out the glass.

She was two stories up, and beyond the house was a sprawling field with woods and mountains she did not recognize. She could see that the house was large — a mansion, really — for its two opposite wings were visible through the window, framing one end of the field in a U shape. Below her window sprawled an expansive patio lined by hedges with a fountain in the middle. Was this one of Orion's estates? How long had he owned this place? Even before all this had happened, Lydia had never known he had other homes elsewhere. For as long as she'd known him, he had always lived in Mammoth with their family.

Just as she turned away from the windows, movement caught her eye. Down at the edge of the patio, beside French doors into the east wing of the mansion, stood two men, rifles in their hands as they spoke to one another, one of them dropping a cigarette to the ground and grinding it into the stone with the heel of his boot.

She was trapped, a captive at the mercy of the man who had murdered her father. The memory of her father that night on the pier, blood gushing from the wound in his head, flashed across her mind. And with it, a wave of nausea crashed into her with tidal force. She tried to swallow it but her stomach continued to churn. She shoved away from the window as a sick feeling swirled within her, stumbling across the floor to the bathroom. She collapsed at the edge of the toilet and threw its lid open, leaning over it just in time as she vomited into the water. She hovered there for a moment, the taste of bile strong on her tongue as she panted and waited for her stomach to settle. She thought she might puke again, but it passed this time.

Running her hands through her hair, sweat beading on her forehead, she sat back, sliding across the bathroom floor against the far wall. She'd not bothered to turn on the light on her way into the bathroom, so she sat in darkness a moment longer before working her way to her feet. Her throat burned and her now empty stomach rebelled at the thought of food. The shoes of her sneakers squeaked on the tile floor. She lingered in the bathroom doorway a moment longer before turning to the only other exit in the room: the door beside the wardrobe.

Even before she turned the brass knob, she knew she'd find it locked. That didn't save her any frustration. She slammed her fists into the door, shouting for anyone to hear.

"Let me out! You can't keep me here, Orion!" she cried, nearly choking on the bile that lingered in her mouth. "Let me *out*, you sick, *sick man*!"

The door rattled but didn't budge. After a while, she stopped, her voice hoarse. She realized for the first time just how thirsty and hungry she really was. Especially now that she'd emptied her stomach completely. When was the last time she had eaten? Lydia turned from the door, her eyes combing the room for any other way of escape.

Footsteps on the other side of the door caught her attention, and she jumped away from the door as a key rattled in the lock. Glancing at the fireplace, Lydia retrieved the iron poker and wielded it in front of her, a glare fixed firmly on her face as she waited for her captor to step inside. Beyond that, she had no plan. But she would not be held prisoner.

The door swung open, and Lydia's breath hitched as Orion stepped inside. When he spotted the poker in her hand, he smirked, closing the door behind him.

"If you were going to kill me, you would have done it last time," he said, his voice laced with deadly humor.

"Maybe I'll just knock you unconscious, then," she bit back, ignoring the flashbacks in her mind to that moment in a dark room with Orion when she'd held his own gun to his head. She couldn't pull the trigger. She *should have* pulled the trigger – then she wouldn't be here right now, and the Jailbirds wouldn't be in jeopardy.

Orion took a step forward, and Lydia matched his step by going backwards, but she quickly ran out of room, her back pressed against one of the windows. He came closer, then struck out like a snake, wrenching the poker from Lydia's hand and closing the gap between them. Lydia pressed herself against the window, lifting her chin as she glared defiantly into his eyes, his breath hot on her face. She'd once loved her uncle as any little girl might, but now… she didn't recognize the man in front of her.

"Let me *go*," she hissed through her teeth, tears welling in her eyes. She kept her gaze locked on his. She would not yield, would not break.

Orion lifted a hand to pinch her chin like he'd done when she was a little girl, only this time it wasn't love. It was control. Fear.

"You've put me in a difficult position, Lydia," said Orion.

"What are you talking about?" Out of the corner of her eyes, she noticed the butt of his gun tucked into the waistband of his pants, exposed as his blazer hung open. She could grab it, do what she couldn't before. No, there were men outside with guns. She'd be shot on sight.

"You're the sole witness to your father's death. I can't have you out there spreading all kinds of nasty lies about me. So… what do I do with you, hmm?"

"How about the right thing for a change?" Lydia retorted.

Orion released her chin and straightened, and Lydia used the distance to shove away from him, backing toward the bed. Orion stayed where he was. He'd cornered her either way.

"People don't get to be as successful as I am by doing the right thing," said Orion.

"Depends on how you define success." Lydia straightened, crossing her arms as she leveled her gaze at him. "From where I'm standing, you may have all the money in the world. You may even have a whole lotta power. But you don't have a single person to share it with. No one to love, and no one who loves *you*." Lydia dared a step forward, her lips curving in a sneer. "Even for all your wealth and all your power, you are empty, Orion. You sold your soul to the highest bidder, and you wonder-"

Orion struck out, the back of his hand swiping across the side of Lydia's face. Blinding pain splintered through her head. She gasped and doubled over, covering the side of her face with her hand as tears stung her eyes.

"Thank you, Lydia," he whispered, towering over her, "for reminding me of the importance of what I must do."

Without another word, he left. Lydia listened as the lock rattled back into place. When his footsteps receded, she let herself fall to the floor, scooting into the narrow space between the wall and the nightstand. Grief washed over her as she made herself small, and a single soundless prayer escaped her lips between sobs.

God, please…

FIVE

LORELAI

A torrential rain fell over Mammoth, washing the entire city in hues of gray and blue. The winter snow had long since melted, leaving the rivers and creeks overflowing with the runoff from the mountains. There would be more snow to come in the colder days of late January, but for now the streets were clear.

Lorelai Clark's heeled boots struck the asphalt of the street in rhythmic pattern as she crossed to the courthouse on the other side, holding her umbrella over her head. At this hour, the courthouse was already closed to the public for the night, but as a defense attorney, Lorelai had special access to the building. A handful of cars were parked along the curb, some belonging to Lorelai's colleagues, others belonging to people working at the stores and restaurants on the city square. Behind Lorelai, a small courtyard sat at the center of the square, a stone fountain overflowing in the rain and pooling in the grass around it. Streetlights illuminated the darkness, highlighting the silvery rainclouds above.

Climbing the wide, stone steps, she came to the large, glass doors of the courthouse and slipped her key into the lock. The door pushed open, and she stepped out of the rain, greeted inside by a burst of warmth as the old furnace worked hard to pump heat throughout the hundred-year-old structure.

Closing her umbrella, she dropped it in the stand beside the door and adjusted her black trench coat. Since her husband, Oliver Clark's death a few months ago, Lorelai hadn't stepped foot in the building. She'd taken a sabbatical, both from work and from life in general. But things were different now. Lydia was missing and Reid was in jail – her children needed her.

Lorelai stopped halfway down the hall, a sliver of fear knifing its way through her heart as she remembered the meeting at The Boathouse the night it burnt to the ground. Even now, weeks later, the former restaurant – a beloved eatery for residents and tourists alike – sat in ruins at the end of the old pier. With Lorelai's stepson's watch at the scene of the crime, Reid Clark was the Fire Marshall's chief suspect. The reality was the police had no reason to look anywhere else, not with half the department – half the city, even – in Orion Clark's pocket. That would soon change if Lorelai had anything to say about it.

She'd been kept out of the loop for years, relegated to the sidelines while her husband and his friends harbored earth-shattering secrets that had since affected everyone they loved. While she couldn't travel back in time to convince Oliver or the others to let her in, she could do her best to make things right in the here and now.

Rounding the corner, Lorelai's footsteps echoed across the surface of the white-and-green checkerboard tile floors. Tan plaster walls lined either side of the courthouse with doors marked for the offices and courtrooms ordered by number.

Lorelai arrived at Judge Hanover's door just as it swung open, and she nearly collided with whoever was leaving.

"Oh, pardon me," she said, staggering backward, lifting her gaze from the man's woolen waistcoat and meeting him in the eye. Her breath hitched in her throat when she registered the smirk on Orion Clark's neatly trimmed face. Her jaw tensed, and she took another step backward, fingers tightening around the leather strap of her briefcase.

"Lorelai," he said, feigning surprise as he shut the judge's door behind him. The brass knob reflected the dim hallway light as his hand dropped to his side. "What brings you down to the courthouse? I thought you'd decided to put a little pause on your *meteoric* career? Isn't that what the Gazette called it last year?"

Lorelai allowed herself to remain flustered for only a moment. She would not be so easily intimidated. Not anymore. She'd let Orion get the better of her for far too long. Drawing on every skill she'd ever learned as a lawyer, Lorelai straightened her back, lifted her chin, and met Orion's gaze straight on. "The fate of my career is no concern of yours, thank you."

Orion laughed. "Now, now. I can't imagine what I could possibly have done to earn such… *hostility*."

Smiling, Lorelai crossed her arms as she took a step forward. "I am all too happy to draft the growing list of charges against you and recite them before the judge. Now's as good a time as any, don't you think?"

His smile faltering for only a moment, he visibly relaxed and buttoned his blazer as his eyes glanced up and down the hall. "Judge Hanover's a busy man, Lorelai. I think it would be best if you paid him a visit some other time – perhaps when you're not so emotional. I would hate for the judge presiding over my dear nephew's case to get the idea that, with everything that's happened to you, you've become weak. A weak defense attorney makes for an even weaker case."

Lorelai bristled, but she refused to allow it to show as she shoved past him and reached for the door. "What you see as mere weakness, Orion, is true strength. But I wouldn't expect *you* to know anything about that. Now, if you'll excuse me."

Orion stared at her a moment longer before stepping out of the way. Lorelai forced herself not to look back at him as she opened the door and stepped into the judge's office. He lingered on the other side of the door until she closed it in his face.

The man behind the desk looked up, the green shade of his desk lamp casting a warm glow across the otherwise dim room. The window behind him offered a view of the storm over Mammoth. Judge Hanover closed the file in front of him, leaning back in his seat as he turned his attention to Lorelai.

"Can I help you, Ms. Clark?"

Lorelai inhaled. "Yes, Your Honor. I'm here regarding my stepson, Reid Clark, if I may have just a moment of your time."

The judge hesitated, then gestured toward one of the two chairs on the other side of his desk. Lorelai sat in one and set her leather briefcase down in the other. She crossed one leg over the other and leaned back in the chair, hands clasped over her lower stomach. Posture mattered. The way a person carried themselves in a deposition or courtroom had the ability to influence a judge or jury's perception of them, of their aptitude and skill. Lorelai had always been able to connect with people in a way that other attornies struggled to do, and she hoped that in her absence she hadn't lost that skill – not in this moment when it counted the most.

"Go ahead," the judge said, gesturing with a bony hand for her to proceed.

"As you know, Reid Clark is being tried for arson and attempted murder, but you and I both know the evidence is circumstantial. I was with Reid the night the watch was stolen. It would be obvious to any jury that the watch was stolen, then deliberately planted at the scene of the crime in order for the *real* arson to effectively incriminate Reid. I've already spoken with Theodore and Claire Highland, the owners of the restaurant that burnt down, and they have agreed not to press charges-"

"Ms. Clark, let me stop you right there." The judge leaned forward, removing his wire-rimmed glasses and setting them on the desk in front of him. The loose skin on his neck rippled as he spoke. The lightning accentuated his bushy eyebrows. "This is not a civil court. Reid is facing *criminal* charges, so whether the victims wish to charge him or not is irrelevant. The district attorney has already filed those charges with the court, and your stepson is up against arson, murder, attempted murder, and grand theft – to name a few."

"Yes, and as I said before, the evidence for each one of these charges is circumstantial. I am Reid's alibi for the night his watch was stolen. Furthermore, without the testimony of the victims, the DA's case is weak and a waste of taxpayer money and time."

"But were you Reid's alibi for the night the restaurant was set on fire?"

"No, but-"

"Then who's to say that he did not stage the whole theft as a way to get you on his side? Lorelai, you know as well as I do that even if he is innocent, there is due process. If your stepson is somehow being framed, it will come out in court. If not… are you prepared to face the fact that Reid Clark might not be the man you think he is?"

Lorelai laughed. "You talk about him like he's some sort of criminal mastermind. He's a twenty-year-old kid – one who has been nothing but an upstanding member of this community his entire life. He's a Clark for heaven's sake!"

"Yes, and I have been granted keen insight into some of the… *troubles* that young Reid Clark has had in recent months. Substance abuse, vandalism, public displays of violence… The death of a parent is bound to take its toll on even the best of us."

Narrowing her eyes, Lorelai asked, "And who has granted you that insight?" She paused, then closed her eyes in frustration. "You've been listening to Orion Clark. Since when, Judge Hanover, do you take legal advice from businessmen?"

The judge's face grew taut. "Mind yourself, Ms. Clark." He sat back and returned his glasses to their perch on his large nose – one Lorelai wouldn't mind breaking right about now. "If you have evidence to prove your stepson's innocence, I expect you to bring it before the jury. It is for them to determine whether Reid goes free or not. Now, if you'll excuse me, I have a trial to prepare for."

Lorelai rose from her seat and grabbed her briefcase. She crossed the room to the door and turned the knob, glancing over her shoulder one last time to say, "Your Honor, when the truth gets out – and it will get out – make sure you find yourself on the right side of things. Kingdoms like Orion's are built to burn."

The judge's eyes darkened. "Goodnight, Ms. Clark."

Lorelai left his office, doing her best not to slam the door behind her. In the coming weeks, the Clark family — what was left of them — would be in the fight of their lives. And Lorelai wasn't so certain the law she'd sworn to uphold was on their side.

SIX

TOMMY

Sirens wailed in the distance, the manhunt still in full force. A January rain washed over the city as Tommy Rhodes crept through the shadows at the edge of town with Jude at his back. Anxiety pooled in his stomach as he hovered behind the wide trunk of a fir tree, the sheets of rain nearly blinding his vision. The bark scraped the palm of his hand, leaving behind the residue of sap. Sweat beaded on his brow, mingling with the rain and seeping into his eyes. He blinked, wiping his eyes with the sleeve of his flannel and running his hands through his drenched hair to pull it away from his face. The collar of his shirt hung wide open, letting in a gust of cold wind. He shivered.

Clouds of fog hovered in the air, penetrated by the rain, providing a veil of covering as Tommy crept forward, careful not to make a sound. Mammoth General Hospital sat just fifty yards ahead, but between the woods and the ambulance port was nothing but sprawling parking lot. A wide-open place where anyone could recognize him or Jude. But Tommy doubted anyone would think to search the town. All efforts had been focused on the mountains where the Jailbirds had fled.

Sucking in a shuddering breath, Tommy lingered beside the tree. A hand fell over his shoulder, and he turned to meet Jude's eyes. His blond hair glued to his forehead, the muscles in his jaw tense, his blue eyes pale in the shadows of night, he said, "In and out, that's it. We'll be back safe and sound before you know it."

Tommy gave a sharp nod, then turned back to the hospital.

"If it helps," whispered Jude, his voice a low hiss, "I'll pray the whole time."

Half-laughing, Tommy said, "Yeah, that helps."

With no more time to waste, he gave one last glance at the parking lot. Satisfied it was empty, he lunged from the shadows and out into the open, skirting along the sides of vehicles and keeping low to the ground. Jude's footsteps followed behind him as they moved in closer to the ambulance drop off zone where, Tommy hoped, the paramedic hadn't thought to lock all the ambulance doors.

When they made it across the parking lot, Tommy ducked behind the car nearest the drop-off zone. He held up a fist, telling Jude to stop. Leaning forward, he peered over the hood of the gray sedan, spotting a trio of paramedics talking beneath the concrete cover of the drop-off zone. Two looked like nurses on a smoking break while the other was no doubt the driver of the ambulance just ten feet from where Tommy and Jude hid.

Taking three long, deep breaths to steady the racing of his heart, Tommy waited for his moment. It came when the automatic hospital doors opened and the three men turned their attention toward the doors. Tommy closed the gap between the sedan and the ambulance, skirting the beam of orange coming from a nearby parking light.

Tugging the doors at the back of the ambulance only to find them locked, Tommy moved to the driver's door. The handle clicked open, and he let out a sigh of relief. Now he just needed the driver to keep his conversation going with the nurses.

Inside the cab, Tommy slipped over the seat and into the back. A gurney lay folded and covered in a white sheet with a clipboard on top, taking up most of the space in the back of the ambulance while on either side stacked along the walls were devices and boxes of medical equipment and paraphernalia. Tommy rifled through each box, gathering whatever gauze and antibiotics he could find. Mars had told him what to look for, and Tommy could only hope he hadn't forgotten anything.

Three taps on the exterior of the ambulance to signal Jude's warning told Tommy he was running out of time. The driver was coming back, but just as he was about to turn to leave, something caught his eye. A name at the top of the clipboard.

Tommy's breath caught in his throat as he read the name. *Evelyn Rhodes.*

His mother. He grabbed the clipboard, squinting to read in the dark, but all he could make out was three letters: *DOA.*

Tommy dropped the clipboard like it had caught fire, heart racing as his shock turned to horror, then grief. But he didn't have time to process. Jude tapped the side of the ambulance again, and Tommy looked up in time to see the paramedic circling the front of the ambulance toward the driver's door.

Tommy turned to the back of the ambulance, grabbed and released the latch, then slipped out the back door, closing it quietly behind him. He looked to his left, relieved to see that the two nurses had gone back inside. When the driver's door closed and the engine roared to life, Tommy ran back to the cover of the gray sedan. He watched the ambulance pull away, his heart beating out an erratic rhythm. He was suffocating, drowning, strangled by the fog and the shifting shadows and the rain. Someone moved beside him, and Tommy nearly jumped but settled when he saw Jude's familiar face.

"Did you get it?" he whispered, crouched behind the car.

Tommy nodded, swallowing the cry that threatened to tear from his throat. "Let's go."

They darted back across the parking lot in the direction they'd come from, keeping themselves low and hidden. When they made it back to the woods, Jude straightened, running his hands through his soaking wet hair as he let out an exasperated sigh.

"I'm getting real tired of all this sneaking around," said Jude, his humor doing its best to disguise the tremor of adrenaline in his voice.

Tommy stood, turning back toward the hospital, leaning against the tree as his eyes scanned every window and door.

"Dude, you alright?" Jude asked, the crunch of brush beneath his feet as he came to Tommy's back.

"No," said Tommy through his teeth. He turned away from the hospital, his mother's name on that clipboard burned across his eyes as he started up the hillside deeper into the woods. Jude hesitated, then followed.

Those three letters had changed everything. Every hope that Tommy had ever had for the future. Every dream he'd ever held onto. Because his mother had been found, dead on arrival.

SEVEN
MARS

The marble countertop felt cold under Marshall Highland's palms as he leaned over the bathroom sink, watching the water run from the faucet down the drain.

He closed his eyes, the sounds of their escape from the mines replaying in his head – feet pounding the dirt, the snapping of branches, the shouts of their pursuers, the sound of Immy being stabbed. All of it too much.

With a sharp inhale, his eyes snapped open. He met his reflection in the mirror. A candle flickered on the countertop, illuminating every line in his face. For the first time, he noticed the lines of exhaustion under his eyes. A few months ago, if Jude had told him that he – a kid with dreams of working in law enforcement – would become a fugitive, he would have laughed.

Now, everything had fallen apart. They'd walked through a door that their parents had tried years ago to close, lock, and throw away the key – and they'd paid the price for it.

He lifted his hands from the sink to find them trembling, anxiety and adrenaline like opposing currents coursing through his body, battling for dominance. His thoughts spiraled like a whirlpool, threatening to drag him under. He couldn't lose control – not now, not when his friends *needed* him.

A knock at the bathroom door pulled Mars from the trap of his own thoughts. "Just a minute," he said.

Lucy's voice came through the door. "They're back," she said.

Mars turned off the faucet and unlocked the door, swinging it open to find Lucy on the other side, waiting in the shadows of the dark hallway with a flashlight in hand. He followed her out into the hall and down the stairs. For now, so long as the Jailbirds laid low, kept the lights off, and didn't go outside, the police had no reason to suspect they were hiding in plain sight on the Wall – among the rich folks of Mammoth who had, since The Boathouse's fire, decided to issue a campaign against all of Mammoth's poor and lower class.

A radio on the kitchen counter narrated the police's efforts to track them down. Mars' ears rang as he tuned in for a moment to what the reporter was saying, how she called them dangerous, criminals, warning the people Mars had grown up with to stay away and report him and his friends on sight.

Mars turned the opposite direction, across the foyer toward the living room, his back to the kitchen. The sounds of the radio faded into the background. He swallowed the lump in his throat and tightened his fist.

Take control.

Tommy and Jude were in the living room, Immy laid out on the couch as they spilled their supplies onto the floor in front of them on the coffee table.

"Here," said Mars, "let me."

He knelt by Immy's side. Tommy and Jude both scooted out of the way. Lucy held her flashlight up and fixed the beam on the couch. He briefly surveyed the supplies they'd brought, making sure everything was clean, and went through his own mental checklist: sterilize the wound, give her some antibiotics, then seal it. Piece of cake.

Mars' gaze roved across Immy's body, landing on her face. She lay with her head on a pair of pillows, her eyes closed. Her chest rose and fell with every labored breath. Mars reached for the hem of her shirt, lifting it to reveal the makeshift bandage of old T-shirt cloth and Jude's belt that they'd used to stop the bleeding. As he undid the old bandage and set the soiled cloth aside, Mars was relieved to see there were no signs of infection, and it didn't seem that Immy's attacker had punctured any vital organs – if so, he was certain she'd be dead already. No, this was a flesh wound. A painful flesh wound that had cut through core muscle and, if left alone, would slowly bleed out.

Mars got to work cleaning the wound. As if on cue, Maya appeared with a knife from the kitchen. He glanced at it, then at the grim expression on her face. She extended a wooden spoon to Immy.

"Here. Bite down on this." said Maya.

Immy took it and placed it in her mouth. As Maya squeezed her hand reassuringly, Immy mumbled over the spoon, "Do it."

Mars inhaled, then took the knife. He turned around to set it on top of the candle that burned on the coffee table and wait until the metal turned red. He grabbed it by the handle and turned back to Immy. She clamped her eyes shut. He waited only a second before pressing the flat of the knife to the wound. Blood and skin sizzled under the heat. Immy grunted, gritting her teeth, bucking against the pain. But Mars didn't let up.

He pulled the knife away and gave the wound some air before rebinding it.

Somehow, despite the intense pain, Immy had remained conscious. When he sat back on his heels, she said, "That hurt."

Mars' eyes lingered on the scars on her neck. "Something tells me you've had worse."

She smirked, then turned her head and closed her eyes. She was asleep in seconds, her breath slowing down as her body relaxed.

A hand settled on his shoulder. "I'm sorry you had to do that," said Lucy. As if she could read his mind, understand the strange mix of guilt and grief that swirled in his brain at inflicting pain on someone he cared about.

"You do what needs to be done for the people you love." He glanced up at her and smiled, his fingers lighting on her hand before she pulled it from his shoulder.

Standing to his feet, Mars joined the others where they waited against the wall of the living room. They made a sad picture – Tommy's eyes heavy with grief and the loss of Lydia, every muscle in his body wound tight with anxiety and anger; Jude distracting himself by picking at the hole in his jeans, making it larger around his knee with every thread until Maya put a hand on his to get him to stop; Lucy fiddling with the fossilized Spinosaurus tooth that hung around her neck while staring off in to space. Mars wanted to ask what was on her mind, but at the moment that felt like a fairly ridiculous question.

"Tommy, can I talk to you for a minute?" Mars asked, his voice low so as not to wake Immy. Rest would be the best medicine for her body right now.

Wordlessly dragging himself to his feet, Tommy followed Mars into the massive foyer. Mars was barefoot – his shoes and socks both in the dryer after being caked in mud – and the marble floor was ice cold beneath his feet. What he wouldn't give for a roaring fire in the fireplace right now.

"What is it?" Tommy whispered.

Mars crossed his arms and leaned against the banister. "I think I should go into town, find my parents. They can help us."

"No," said Tommy.

"Well, we can't just stay here forever. The pantry's empty. This place is a fantastic fortress of solitude, but a very *cold and dark* fortress of solitude. Besides…" Mars paused, his eyes pleading with Tommy. "My dad could help us. He knows people. He could find a lawyer to defend us. We don't have to do it this way."

"No," Tommy repeated, his voice shuddering. His eyes wide, like the thought terrified him. "No one leaves. We're *safe* here."

"Tommy…"

"I can't lose you, Mars, or any of you. It's not safe out there, and if you walk out that door, I can't… I can't *protect* you."

Mars furrowed his brow, reading the near-panicked expression on Tommy's face. "You won't lose us," said Mars. "But we can't hide here forever."

"What's going on?" Jude and Maya appeared in the archway to the living room, their expressions tight with concern.

"Mars wants to go back into town where half the city's hunting us down," Tommy replied. "We almost got caught just getting these supplies."

"I'm just saying, we need a plan, and my parents have the resources to help us."

"It's not a bad idea," said Maya. "I'd ask my parents, but, you know, they kind of already disowned me *before* I was a fugitive, so…"

Jude winced, casting a sad glance toward Maya. She pretended not to notice his eyes on her.

"It's a bad idea," Tommy argued. "No, what we need to do is figure out where Orion took Lydia."

"And how are we going to do that if we're stuck here?" Mars asked. "We're lucky Immy's wound wasn't worse. If it was, we'd *definitely* need a hospital. As it is, we can only pray that she doesn't get worse. The police don't know who she is; we could drop her off and let the doctors take care of her."

"And you don't think the police would be suspicious of a *stab wound*?" Tommy said, his voice getting louder. "Come on, Mars."

Heat flushed in Mars' face. "Well, I'd rather deal with the police than lose a friend."

"Don't-"

"Hey," Immy called from the living room. "You guys keeping secrets over there?"

Mars leaned through the archway to see that Lucy had joined Immy, sitting on the floor beside the sofa. Immy stared down her nose at them.

"We're just trying to figure out what to do," said Maya with a forced smile.

"Well, don't argue on my account," said Immy.

Tommy turned back to Mars. "If someone were to follow us back here… Immy's not ready to move. We wouldn't be able to escape in time carrying her. She needs time, and so do we."

"Time for what?" asked Jude.

"To regroup, to figure out a plan. Lydia's out there somewhere."

"And Reid," Maya added.

Tommy met her eyes. "And Reid."

"Reid's in jail, guys," reminded Mars.

"He's innocent," said Maya.

"And what are we supposed to do about that?" said Mars. "We're going to need our own lawyers when all of this is over. We'll be lucky if we don't all get prison time. In fact, I'm fairly certain we won't get out of this without at least a *little* jail time, and I don't know about you but I'm not a fan of bunk beds."

"You could break him out," said Lucy.

They turned to her in unison.

Jude narrowed his eyes, scratching under his chin with his thumb. In the days since returning from Mariner's Cove, Maine, Jude had grown a thin layer of scruff that had managed to age him by several years older than his nineteen. "Why do I feel like you've contemplated jailbreaks before now?" said Jude, raising an eyebrow.

Lucy smirked.

"So, that's it, then," said Maya, glancing at Tommy, then Mars. "We break Reid out of jail, then find where Orion's keeping Lydia."

"Don't forget the treasure," added Immy from the living room.

"You say it like it's just another day in the life," said Mars, rolling his eyes.

"Isn't it?" Jude retorted.

Tommy ran both hands through his hair, turning from the others and walking to one of the windows that framed the front door. He stared through the windows into the dark outside. "I don't even care about the treasure or the fossils or any of it anymore. I need Lydia back, and I need to keep the rest of you safe."

Jude settled a hand on Tommy's shoulder, squeezing. Mars swallowed the lump in his throat and glanced away.

"The only way we accomplish any of that is if we kill Orion," said Immy from the couch. "Cut him off at the head."

"Why? So two more can grow in its place?" Mars retorted. "Also, I'm not interested in killing anyone, thank you very much."

Maya set a warning hand on his arm, and Mars shut his mouth before saying anything more. When he realized why Maya was giving him that look, he wanted to kick himself. Orion had murdered not just Immy's parents, but her uncle too. He was the reason Immy had no family left in the world, and he'd just dismissed her grief and desire for vengeance.

"I'm sorry," said Mars. So much for not waking her up.

Immy just nodded and looked away, her eyes glistening in the moonlight that filtered through the bay windows on the other side of the room where a black grand piano sat untouched.

Behind Mars, the door slammed shut. He spun around to see Tommy storming down the path in the darkness. Jude glanced back at Maya, who gave a subtle nod. Mars watched him go after Tommy, then turned back to Maya. "You and me," he said. "Let's figure out how to break Reid out of prison."

EIGHT
JUDE

Nine-year-old Jude Mayfield swiped at the tears in his eyes as he looked out across the ocean. It was midnight, and it had taken Jude a long time to get here from Silver Springs Trailer Park.

But his father was too drunk to notice his absence. That happened a lot lately. Jack Mayfield drank himself to oblivion, then spent the night a sobbing mess until he fell asleep. All Jude had to do was stay away and he'd make it through the night unscathed.

Pale moonlight shone across the surface of the Pacific. A gentle mist lighted on Jude's skin. Jude sat in the sand, knees to his chest. It was cold tonight, so he wore his father's jacket and wondered why other boys seemed to have such normal relationships with their fathers while he was trapped in a tin box with the monster under his bed.

His father had kept him home from school that week — it was the only way to make sure the teachers didn't notice the fresh bruises on Jude's arms. They were starting to heal, so Jude would be back to school on Monday.

He could tell someone the truth. But then they'd take Jack away, and Jude wouldn't have anyone. Kids his age weren't supposed to be making those kinds of choices. Jude just wanted his father — the version of him he was when he wasn't drinking. The one who'd taken him for drives on Sunday afternoons when he was younger. The one who'd camped with him in the woods last summer. The one who barbecued the best burgers in the world and sat on their tiny trailer porch with Jude while they ate.

Jude had learned early on not to ask about his mother. "It's just me and you, kid," his father would say, and then he'd pull out a beer and Jude would spend the night staying out of his way as the man became the monster.

And he swore he would never, ever touch a drop of alcohol when he grew up. Nothing should have that kind of power over a man, and that wasn't the kind of man Jude wanted to be. If he was lucky enough to grow up, he'd be better than his father. Stronger.

"Hey!"

Jude turned to see a boy riding a bike along the sidewalk. He'd come to a stop and now stood straddling the bike now, staring down the beach at Jude. Tommy Rhodes.

"You okay down there?" Tommy asked.

Jude nodded, sniffed. "Fine."

Tommy dropped his bike and stepped onto the sand, walking up to Jude. "You weren't at school today."

"Been sick."

"You don't look sick."

"And what does sick look like?"

Tommy shrugged. "Not like you look right now."

Jude frowned, then glanced over at Tommy as he sat in the sand beside him. "Shouldn't you be in bed?"

"Shouldn't you?"

Jude's turn to shrug. "Not like my dad would notice."

"My dad works late sometimes," Tommy explained. "Just down the road at the museum, so he lets me ride my bike while I wait on him."

"And he lets you stay up this late?"

"Not always and not always intentionally." Tommy laughed. "He gets lost in his work, I guess."

And Jude's father got lost in a bottle. Jude felt Tommy's stare and turned to see him looking over at the bruise on Jude's neck. He pulled up the collar of his father's jacket and crossed his arms.

Tommy's gaze lingered on Jude's neck, then his eyes flicked to Jude's. He almost seemed to nod, like he understood. He turned his head to look out across the ocean, folding his hands in his lap.

"I used to have friends, but I don't have any now," said Tommy.

"What happened to them?" asked Jude.

"I…" He squinted as if searching his mind. "I can't remember."

Jude had the same sense — like he'd once been surrounded by friends, but they'd been taken from him somehow. Maybe that was the cause of the loneliness he felt most days.

"We could be friends," said Tommy. "We could be best *friends, and then we could protect each other."*

"From what?" asked Jude.

Tommy glanced at him, a breeze tugging at the ends of his wild brown hair, and smiled. "From the monsters."

The boards creaked under Jude's feet as he stepped out onto the porch, closing the door behind him. The moon hung in the sky behind the Morales' rental property, shining down on the well-kept pond that made up the bulk of the front of the property. The porch stairs descended onto a carefully laid brick path that followed the perimeter of the pond toward the woods where a gazebo sat nestled between the trees. The house behind him had the appearance of a midcentury modern cabin – the kind no Mayfield man would have ever been able to afford on a fisherman's wages.

Jude followed Tommy all the way down the path to the gazebo. Tommy leaned against the railing, staring down at the silky surface of the pond and the round, silver moon reflected in the water. Jude stood beside him, leaning on the railing next to him so that their arms touched ever so slightly. He and Tommy had been best friends for as long as he could remember – sometimes all they required was the knowledge that the other person was there with them and that they weren't going anywhere. They'd done that since they were kids, just sitting with each other and drawing strength from one another. When one of them was weak, the other would be strong for the both of them.

As the silence stretched on, Jude turned to Tommy and asked, "What's going on?"

When Tommy looked up, Jude saw the tears in his eyes. Before he could answer, Jude straightened and threw his arms around Tommy, who buried his head in his shoulder in response. Tommy sobbed while Jude held him, his grip tightening with every second that passed. Tears stung his own eyes as he held his best friend there in the shadows of the mountainside estate. A cool fog rose from the surface of the pond. They stood in silence, holding each other. Tommy, the strongest one of them all, the one who usually had it all figured out, the one with the drive and determination to get them where they needed to go, was now falling apart in Jude's own arms. His fingers dug into Jude's back, gripping his white T-shirt as if he were terrified to let go, as if any separation between the two of them would create an irreparable rift.

Jude didn't have to say anything. There weren't words sufficient to express the love Jude had in his heart for his brother, but Tommy knew. He knew Jude wasn't going anywhere.

When he managed to compose himself, Tommy straightened, his arms falling to his sides as he looked away, leaning against the railing of the gazebo. He ran both hands across his face even as quieted tears rolled down his cheeks and disappeared in the cracks between the old floorboards.

"My mom's dead," whispered Tommy, his voice hoarse.

Jude's heart sank.

Evelyn Rhodes. He'd known her as long as he'd known Tommy – and Christopher.

"How do you know?" Jude asked.

"The ambulance where we found the supplies for Immy… they'd just dropped off a patient." He turned to Jude and looked him in the eye. "I saw her name on the clipboard. It said *DOA* – dead on arrival."

Jude swallowed the lump in his throat, clenching his jaw. He inhaled sharply and glanced away, his eyes staring past the fog into the forest beyond the pond.

"I have to go," said Tommy, the pain in his tone evident. "I need… I need to see her for myself. To somehow say goodbye."

"I know," replied Jude.

"My mom and I…" he started, casting his gaze to the gazebo floor. "In the end there was only heartache and grief between us, but I guess I always imagined that one day she'd find her way back to herself." He paused. "To *me*. But… I guess that door's closed for good now, huh?"

"Your mom loved you," Jude said. "Even if she forgot how."

Tommy wiped his nose with the sleeve of his flannel, and Jude crossed his arms as he stared off in the distance, thinking of his father. Like Tommy, what Jude shared with Jack Mayfield was little more than mutual trauma, but Jack was still his father. He'd done terrible, awful things. To Jude. To Henry. But Jude had always known it wasn't really his father – it was the monster that had burrowed its way inside of him, feeding on his worst fears and darkest impulses.

Evelyn's monster had won.

But Jack… how much longer did Jude have before his father, too, was lost?

"Go," said Jude as he stood up straight. "I'll take care of things here. He sighed.

"But I bit Mars' head off about staying put. I can't just go."

"You can," said Jude. "You *will*. Mars will understand."

Tommy nodded, sniffed. He walked past Jude and out into the shadows of the trees beside the pond. With a glance toward the house, he turned the other direction. Back into the woods, back toward Mammoth. Toward his mother.

Jude waited until Tommy was out of sight to head back inside. Maya met him at the door, her eyes big as she peered up at him, her fingers reaching gently for Jude's hand at his side, only to brush them before she withdrew. Without asking, Jude read the question in her worried gaze. Maya followed him into the family room.

Clearing his throat and swallowing the lump in his throat, Jude sat on the edge of a nearby chair and clasped his hands in front of him. In his heart, he offered a quick prayer for Tommy, that he'd make it to the hospital and back safely. Being unable to protect him, to throw himself between Tommy and danger, Jude felt helpless. But more than once he'd seen what prayer could do. He'd seen how situations just like this were best left in stronger hands than his own.

"What's going on?" Mars asked, leaning forward in his seat.

"Tommy's mom died," said Jude, meeting Mars' gaze. "He saw her name marked as DOA on a clipboard in the ambulance when we went to pick up the supplies for Immy."

The others remained quiet for a moment, absorbing the news, the tragedy of it all. The compilation of loss on top of loss on top of loss was taking its toll.

"So he gets to leave, but I have to stay put?" asked Mars. "I need to get to my parents. They can *help*."

Jude's jaw tightened. "No one leaves. Not now. I *told* Tommy to go. He wasn't going to, but he's more than earned the right to say goodbye to his mom. He's lost *both* his parents, Mars, and you still have both of yours."

"Jude…" warned Maya.

The tension in the room was wound like a coil. Jude could feel it, the pressure building in and around them. What would happen when it got to be too much? He thought of their parents, of the secrets and bitterness that had damaged their friendship beyond repair. They'd been best friends once – just like the Jailbirds – but now the only words they exchanged were filled with hatred and anger. Would the Jailbirds share their fate in the end?

"No," said Jude as he shot to his feet. "I'm sorry, but I'm not about to tell Tommy – who's lost his father and his wife – that he can't say goodbye to his mother. And I wouldn't expect that of any of you either. We're still people! Despite what the world says about us right now. Despite what's happened…"

Mars glanced away, wounded by Jude's outburst.

Running his fingers through his hair, Jude sat back down.

Maya's hand settled onto his shoulder, squeezing gently as she inched closer to him.

"We've lost so much," said Jude. "We can't afford to lose ourselves, too."

"That's not what I meant," said Mars, apologetic. He blinked. "I know you guys have all lost your parents. I just… I don't want to lose mine, too."

Jude inhaled sharply, then slowly released the breath. "I know. I'm sorry. I wish… I wish things were different. I wish I could fix this, but I can't."

"We should go with him, then," said Immy.

She tried to sit up, but Lucy caught her by the arm and forced her back down. "Um, I hate to be the bearer of bad news, but you're in no condition to ride to anyone's rescue right now."

"I owe him," Immy replied, a fierce look in her eyes.

"He can put it on your tab," Lucy argued.

The girls exchanged a glance before Immy finally relaxed and settled back against the couch cushions.

"No," said Jude, doing his best to shrug off the weight of emotion he felt pressing down on him right now. "We stay here and we wait, give Immy a chance to recover. Even if it takes days. We can only afford to have one Jailbird off the premises right now."

The others silently agreed, and Jude settled back in his seat. He glanced down at his hand resting on the arm of the chair, his fingers trembling. He tightened them into fists, could feel the heat of Maya's eyes on him, and turned his eyes toward the moon that hung in the window like a picture frame.

NINE
MAYA

There were five bedrooms and three bathrooms in the Morales family's rental property, and the Jailbirds chose instead to stay together in the family room, none of them willing to separate for longer than it took to use the restroom. Other than a couple of candles in the middle of the room, the only light they had to live by was that of the moon and stars outside. Maya Morales marveled at their beauty, her back against the wall beside the fireplace, a blanket wrapped around her shoulders as she stared through the bay window and watched the trees sway in the wind outside.

Immy lay under a blanket on the couch, her chest rising and falling with every breath. She'd already been asleep for a couple of hours. Lucy curled up under a blanket in one of the chairs, her head lolled to the side as she stared off into the distance, eyelids closing for a second before popping back open. Fighting sleep.

Maya wondered why.

Mars lay in the middle of the floor on a pallet made of old quilts Maya found in the garage, hands folded over his chest as he stared up at the ceiling. Maya knew when he finally fell asleep because Mars was a snorer. Lucy was the last to fall asleep, leaving Maya and Jude awake by themselves in her parents' living room.

Jude sat against the wall beside Maya, flicking open the lid of a brass Zippo and shutting it again. Over and over. The *clink* of metal was the only sound aside from Mars' snoring.

Maya wanted sleep, but it didn't seem to want her. Not yet. She slid to the side, her shoulder leaning into Jude's, her head falling onto his shoulder. He brushed her curls away from his face before turning and planting a gentle kiss on the crown of her head. An involuntary smile formed on her lips even as her eyes began to water. The tears came silently and without warning as she thought of Lydia, of Tommy and his parents, of Reid sitting in jail because of his uncle, of her own parents.

Jude stirred when the tears dripped from the side of her face onto his arm. He dropped his head a little so he could see her face.

"What's wrong?" he asked, concern written in the lines on his face, at the corners of his eyes and in the middle of his brow.

"Nothing," she whispered, the crack in her voice a dead giveaway that she was lying.

"Liar," said Jude. He shifted so that her head fell onto his chest as he reached his arm around her, pulling her close.

"Okay," she admitted. "Everything."

Jude's fingers massaged her upper arm as he rested his head on top of hers. The scruff on his chin scratched her forehead, but she didn't mind. These past weeks, she'd watched him change. It wasn't just the scruff; it was the way he carried himself. She thought of that day on the train just nearly two weeks ago. She had been hurt when she'd found out that Jude was planning to join the US Navy, to leave her. They'd fought, but it had become something more. Years of heartache and tension spilled out into the space between them.

"You want to talk about it?" asked Jude, his voice low.

"Hmm?"

"What happened on the train…"

"Yes."

Silence.

"But not right now."

"No."

She felt him smirk against her head.

"What's on your mind?" asked Maya.

"Henry," said Jude. "It's only been a few months, but…"

"You miss him."

Jude nodded.

They sat in silence for a while, and Maya started to wonder if Jude had fallen asleep. She thought of Lydia and prayed that she was okay. When she thought of Tommy, worry pricked her heart. She'd never seen so much anger in his eyes. Anger like that was dangerous, volatile. Maybe Mars had been right. Maybe it was stupid to let Tommy go.

No, she decided. *It would have been cruel to make him stay.*

A flick of the lighter told Maya that Jude hadn't fallen asleep. She turned to see a flame shot into the dark. He held it in front of his face for a few moments, watching it burn. Maya noticed, illuminated by the flame, that Jude had taken a Sharpie to his wrist and written just two letters: *J + M.*

Maya smiled but said nothing.

"We're going to burn it all down," said Jude. "Orion's kingdom. He'll answer for his crimes."

"How can you be so sure?"

"Because for as smart as he is, he's continually made the same mistake."

"What's that?"

"He's underestimated us at every turn. So, yeah, let him think he's got it in the bag for a second. Let him relax now that he's got us on the run. Let him grow complacent. Because he won't see us coming."

Maya paused, burrowing her head against Jude's chest, feeling it expand and deflate with every breath. "And when this is all over? Where will we be?" Maya asked.

"Right where we've always been, May," said Jude as he flicked the lighter closed, dousing them in darkness. "Beside each other."

TEN

TOMMY

Christopher Rhodes was the greatest man who ever lived. Eight-year-old Tommy surveyed his father's office at the Mammoth Museum of Natural History — the fossils on display in pockets of the dark-stained bookshelves that lined most of the four walls. Lights shone down on the skulls and claws of smaller species, each collected on one of his father's many expeditions to different parts of the world.

Tommy gaped at the shelves. Strong arms wrapped around his middle and lifted him from the ground. He squealed as his father lifted him up and over his head, planting Tommy square on his broad shoulders, muscled from years spent chipping away at dirt and rock.

Giggling, Tommy took his father's mop of brown hair in his hands as the man carried him around the room, offering Tommy a better view of the fossils and relics that sat on the tallest shelves.

Christopher pretended to almost drop Tommy, and Tommy laughed even as he wrapped his small arms around his father's head. "Daddy!" he squealed.

The man laughed and tightened his grip around Tommy's ankles, stranding up straight. "You okay staying all day, Bridger?" his father asked. "Your old man's got some work to do, so I don't think I'll be able to run you back home. Of course, I could always have your mom come pick you up." He stared up at Tommy as the boy shook his head emphatically.

Laughing, his father set Tommy back down on the ground. "Okay, then. I'm sure I can find some work for you to do around the museum. Dust some shelves. Maybe clean some toilets."

"Ew!" Tommy said, scrunching up his face in disgust.

His father mussed his hair and laughed. "Okay, then. No toilets." He tapped a finger on his chin, crossing his other arm over his chest as he pretended to be deep in thought. Morning light shone in through the window in his office, centered behind his desk, making his father a towering silhouette, sunlight framing him.

"How about you shadow me for today, huh? You can see what your old man does every day, but I'm afraid it's not all adventures and fossils."

Tommy didn't mind. He would have followed his father anywhere, no matter how dull or boring. He'd learn to file paperwork if it meant more time with the man.

Squeezing his son's shoulders, Tommy's father said, "Come on. Let's go see how the team is doing in the preservation room."

Tommy nodded and took his father's hand as the man led him out of the office and down the hall to another room. His father punched a series of numbers into the keypad, and the door clicked open to reveal paleontologists, archaeologists, and archivists hard at work.

Tommy followed his father's lead as he spoke, "We just got a new shipment in from a friend of mine in Africa. Lions, giraffes, zebras, and other native species, of course, but I think you'll like this."

Tommy stopped alongside his father beside a large white table with a bright white light coming from beneath. A collection of bones sat along the smooth surface, each bone tagged and numbered.

"Have you learned about Afrovenators yet?" his father asked, referring to the book of dinosaurs he'd given Tommy several months ago.

Tommy shook his head.

His father smiled. "That's okay. Here." He pointed to a short trail of fossils that were flat on two sides and circular on the other sides, with small protrusions here and there. "These are the vertebrae of an Afrovenator, a bipedal carnivore native to Northern Africa. He's just a loaner — my friend will want him back — but how cool will this guy by on display here, huh?"

Tommy frowned.

His father raised an eyebrow. "What is it, son?"

He shrugged. "It just… doesn't look like much." He was used to seeing the fossils put together and on display, postured and posed to look magnificent and terrifying. But laid out on a table like this? They didn't seem like much.

Smiling, his father scooped Tommy up and lifted him onto his shoulders again. From this height, Tommy could see that what looked like a table full of rocks had been meticulously laid out on the surface of the table so that, at this angle, it looked exactly like a dinosaur, squished down and laid flat.

"How about that, huh?" said his father, giving Tommy's legs a squeeze. Tommy grinned. "Sometimes you just need to see the whole picture, Bridger."

In little Tommy's eyes, Christopher Rhodes was Superman. A hero faster than sound and stronger than stone. Invincible.

Until he wasn't.

Rainwater spilled into Tommy's eyes. He blinked, fists tightening in the pockets of his father's brown bomber jacket. The rain slicked off the leather and onto the asphalt at the edge of the hospital parking lot below. A puddle formed around his boots. His jeans were soaked, and the holes in them did little to ward off the cold. The strange mix of moonlight and rain caused an eerie fog to slip down the mountainside, slithering between the trees that rose like shadowed silhouettes around the hospital.

The building sat like a beacon in the dark, bright white lights a stark contrast to the dead of night. Either a sanctuary or a tomb, depending on the person.

Tommy spent a long time working up the courage to sneak inside. The last time he'd been inside, he'd been a patient after the showdown in Apocalypse Island had gone sideways. He'd vowed from his hospital bed that he would come for Orion. The words seemed so empty now, when Tommy had lost so much more than he ever thought possible.

It was in the belly of this very hospital that he'd last seen his father, laid out on the cold steel of the coroner's table in the morgue. He'd been trying to find a way to say goodbye ever since. Now his mother? Tommy couldn't…

With a sharp inhale, Tommy set out across the parking lot. He wore one of Jude's trucker hats – the logo of The Boathouse emblazoned on the front – and hoped that it would be disguise enough to get him in the door. As he approached, he saw a car pull up to the curb. A large group filed out, toting stuffed animals and balloons sheltered beneath umbrellas. Pink "Congratulations" cards and "It's a Girl" banners passed between them as they made their way excitedly to the door. Seizing the opportunity, Tommy snuck through behind them, hoping nobody would pay any attention to him as the large group moved down the corridor.

When they arrived at the nurse's station, he ducked away and followed the signs toward the morgue downstairs. Up ahead, a nurse scanned her badge and the door swung open. He waited until she was out of earshot and slipped his fingers through the opening, catching the door before it latched. His heart pounded as he stepped into the elevator that led to the bowels of the hospital, where the dead would be exhumed and embalmed.

The elevator doors opened to a dimly lit room. Fluorescent lights hung over metal slabs in the middle of the room. There was nobody here, but he knew well enough to know coroners rarely left for long. The elevator doors slid closed behind Tommy as he stepped into the room, the smell of chemicals wafting through the air.

A bright, white light shone down on a still body laid out on a table and covered in white cloth. The vent overhead hummed, making the morgue feel strangely alive.

Tommy hovered by the elevator, terrified to come any closer. The last time he'd seen his mother, it had been just before The Boathouse burnt to the ground. Now, here she was, laid out on a table like one of his father's fossils, reduced to memories and moments they would never have. If Christopher Rhodes knew what had become of his wife and son, and the distance that had formed between them, he would have been so grieved.

But he was gone, and Evelyn was gone, and Tommy was all that was left. He would never again feel his father's strong arms around him. Never again know his mother's kiss on the crown of his head. All of that had been taken from him. *Stolen.*

Taking in a shaky breath, he inched forward, fingernails biting into the flesh of his palms as he clenched his fists. He came to stand beside her, his eyes fixed on the white cloth. Her feet stuck out at the end, a white tag tied around her big toe.

Hesitantly, he reached for the cloth and pulled it away from her face. His fingers brushed the skin of her cheeks, cold to the touch. "Hey, Ma," he said, his voice quiet, hoarse.

He waited a second, as if expecting a response. But she just lay there, still and unmoving.

A jolt of pain pierced Tommy's heart. He blinked back tears, inhaled. "It's Tommy. I… I'm sorry… that I wasn't there."

How could he blame himself? He'd *tried*. It hadn't been his plan to leave his mom, but she'd left *him* long before he moved into the lighthouse. After his father's death, she'd drowned herself in alcohol. She'd disappear all night and stumble home, drunk after a wild night of partying. And she couldn't even *look* at him. Not even when he took off her shoes for her and helped her to bed. Or when he made sure she ate something the morning after to dull the hangover. To her, he didn't exist. He may as well have died with his father.

Tears rolled down Tommy's cheeks as he stared down at his mother's face, both hands gripping the side of the metal table, knuckles just inches away from the pale skin of her arms. And it was horrible, but all Tommy could think was that this was the best she'd looked in a year – she wasn't drunk, her face wasn't twisted in grief or anger, her words weren't stumbling over one another, her eyes weren't bloodshot. No, as he looked down at his mother's dead body, all Tommy could think was that she looked at peace. And he hoped it was true.

"I loved you, Ma," he said. "I wish I could've told you that just… one last time. I wish you would've believed it."

Tears stung his eyes as he looked at her, desperate for any flicker of movement, but she was gone. There were no miracles here, not in a place like this. Not for someone like him.

Tommy choked on a sob as he stumbled away. He held the back of his hand to his mouth, struggling to keep himself quiet even as he stared through tears at the lifeless frame of his mother on that metal table under a probing light.

Outside the morgue, the sound of conversation drifted toward Tommy. "Excuse me!" a woman shouted. "You can't go in there!"

Tommy stumbled toward the elevator. A man walked in through the doors on the other side of the room, his eyes fixed on the body, not seeing Tommy. Silver glinted on his hip, half hidden by a black blazer. A cop.

Tommy didn't wait for the officer to notice him. He slammed the elevator button and darted inside before the doors had fully opened, jamming the button repeatedly to close the door.

"Stop!" the officer called as he ran after Tommy.

Tommy didn't wait around as the elevator opened on the main floor, but there were cops at the hospital entrance, so he ran the other way. Toward the emergency exit. He kicked it open and ran out into the rain, the fire alarm filling the night air behind him as he ran.

ELEVEN

THEO

A sea of people crowded the sidewalks and roads in front of the Mammoth Police Department. Signs bobbed above their heads, calling for action to be taken against "Jailbirds" – those the city had decided were born on the wrong side of the tracks.

Despite the fact that Theodore Highland was every bit the Jailbird his son was, he saw friends among the protesting Bluecoats, and they parted for him and his wife as they crossed the street to the stairs that led up to the police station doors. The Boathouse had become a landmark in Mammoth. With it gone – the one thing that tied Theo to the other side of this decades-old bitter rivalry – it was only a matter of time before they began protesting *his* presence, too.

Claire's arm tightened around Theo's. She sidled closer to him. Theo glanced down at his wife, her curly brown hair pulled up in a bun, dusted with the gray she'd collected over the years. A gust of wind carried down the street, tugging at the signs the protestors carried.

CATCH THE JAILBIRD FIVE.

TAKE OUR CITY BACK.

LIFE IN PRISON FOR EVERY LIFE TAKEN.

Theo cringed away, avoiding the stares of those around him. When someone recognized him, they seemed to aim their chanting right at him.

"They hate us," Claire whispered, her tone horrified.

Theo patted her hand around his arm. "They've always hated us, love."

"Not like this," said Claire. "This is Orion's doing."

Theo's jaw tightened at the name of his former friend. Years ago, he'd been fooled into taking part in the Clarks' foolish hunt for lost treasure. Orion and Oliver had wanted to make a name for themselves, but they needed what the Highlands had to offer, along with the Mayfields and the Moraleses. Years later, Theo was given the chance to make up for what had happened to Danny Dawson when Christopher Rhodes came to him for help. Twice Theo had failed his friends. Twice he'd turned his back on them.

Jack Mayfield met them at the top of the steps, his face wound up in a perpetual glare, arms folded over his chest. He looked less disheveled than usual – the stained wife-beater exchanged for a blue long-sleeved shirt with *Mammoth Surf Co.* printed in orange over the heart. A red trucker hat covered his tangled mop of graying blond hair. Theo's optimistic side thought maybe some sense had been knocked into Jack, but optimism rarely went anywhere with this man.

"They call you in, too?" Jack asked with a grunt.

Theo nodded, setting his arm around Claire's shoulders as he guided her through the open door and away from the jeers of the crowd outside. Inside the police station was warm, so Theo shed his coat and hung it over his arm.

He turned to the right to see Oscar and Alicia already standing at the clerk's station. Theo couldn't make out the conversation, but Alicia's voice rose above all the rest. She'd always been like that. Loud. Pushy. Before Alicia, Oscar had more of a personality. All these years later, he'd traded his independence and his sense of humor for his wife's favor — though Theo was certain he still hadn't managed to earn that. Oscar was the only reason Theo and the others had befriended Alicia in the first place. She'd always planned to make a Bluecoat of herself, and by all appearances she'd done just that.

That didn't change where she'd come from, and Theo hoped it hadn't changed her willingness to fight for what was right in the eyes of the law.

Jack, Theo, and Claire dared to approach the clerk's desk where the Moraleses stood.

"You mean to tell me it's been sixteen hours, and you haven't found a single trace of our daughter?" Alicia said, her eyes wide, the vein in her neck bulging under the collar of a fur coat. "You should be out there right now looking for her. *All* of you!"

"Ma'am," the clerk said, holding out his hands to calm her. The man didn't stand a chance against the walking pillar of fire that towered in front of him. His face and neck were already mottled red from the stress — or perhaps the exertion of trying to tame what essentially amounted to a wildebeest trapped inside the body of an adult female lawyer. "If you'll please calm down... We've been doing everything we can to bring your daughter in safely. Believe me, we've got the entire city on alert."

"And by everything, you mean chasing them into mines that have been deemed a *hazard?*" Oscar said, his eyes nearly as angry as his wife's. "Our daughter is not some… some *criminal.*"

The clerk stammered. "Sir, your *daughter* is a fugitive. We can't well control the danger she puts *herself* in. When she's in our custody, you can–"

"How *dare you!*" Alicia seethed. She yanked the gloves off her hands and stepped forward, but Oscar wrapped an arm around her, holding her back. For the moment, the woman seemed to have forgotten that she herself was a lawyer. Purportedly, she could win just about any case, her argumentative skills unrivaled. She'd certainly dominated the debate club back when they were in school.

"Mr. and Mrs Morales," came a voice from down the hall. Sheriff Patterson stood with his hands shoved in the pockets of his khaki pants. The radio clipped to his belt chirped, the speaker's voice riddled with static. "Please try not to make a scene in my station."

Alicia started to say something else, but Claire stepped forward, casting a sideways glance at the fuming woman. Theo noted the tears that seemed to well in Alicia's eyes, whether from grief or frustration he couldn't be sure. "Sheriff, please. We just want to know what's going to happen to our children."

"That's exactly why I called you here. Please, this way." He gestured down the hall, and Claire was the first to follow with Theo on her heel.

Sheriff Patterson led them into his office, where a blackboard hovered along the wall to Theo's left. Theo's eyes lingered on the board – pictures of Marshall and his son's friends at the center with notes around each photo. Pictures of Oliver and Christopher hung to the right of the board.

"What's this?" asked Theo.

"This is everything I know," the sheriff replied. "Now, I'm hoping that perhaps you can fill in some of the blanks for me."

"Why's Chris on the board?" asked Jack as he scratched at his graying beard, his frown deepening, brow furrowing. "What's he got to do with this?"

The sheriff sighed, leaning against the edge of his desk, arms crossed as he stared at each of them in turn. "Folks, whatever's going on between your families is starting to affect the way I run my city, and I don't much like that." He paused, perhaps waiting for one of them to say something, but they met him with silence. Straightening, he said, "Thing is, I got three dead bodies now, and I got a whole mountain of evidence that says your kids are the ones responsible. Now, my gut's telling me otherwise, but I can't well tell the District Attorney not to prosecute a case based on gut instinct."

"Three?" asked Oscar, his arm still cinched around Alicia, perhaps an attempt to keep her under control.

The sheriff moved toward the board, pulling another large print photo from a folder stacked on top of his desk. He taped it to the board and stepped away. A lump formed in Theo's throat as he stared at the newer photo.

"The hospital just called thirty minutes ago," said Patterson. "Quincy Hodge is dead, and this city's about to have a riot on its hands."

Episode Two

NO WAY OUT

"These were his friends, his family. He'd laid it all on the line for their quest – they all had – and he was going to see it through."

TWELVE
CHRIS

March 21, 2006

Thunder rumbled, shaking the house. Lightning cut across the dark sky outside the window of Christopher Rhodes' home office. He massaged his temples, a migraine splitting down the middle of his forehead, threatening to tear him apart. His vision blurred as he studied the journal splayed out in front of him for what felt like the hundredth time since he'd returned from Peru. The others had agreed to go their separate ways. Some things were better left unsaid, some secrets better off buried. Their children would never know what their parents had once been to each other. They would never know what it had cost them.

But Chris couldn't shake the feeling that there was something else here, something he was missing. Orion had told them what had happened — Danny Dawson had slipped in the rain and fallen off the side of the mountain. It was an accident. A horrible freak accident.

As three-year-old Tommy slept soundly two doors down the hall, Chris felt relief. He'd never have to explain to his son that he'd led his best friend to his death. Tommy would never know his father's greatest failure.

They'd returned home defeated, terrified, grief-stricken. And they'd each taken a piece of the key that would have led to the greatest paleontological discovery in the last hundred years. Chris had followed the journal to the letter, practically memorizing every stroke of Othniel Cuvier's pen. But it had only ruined everything.

Anger and grief bubbling up inside him, Chris leapt to his feet and threw the old leather journal across the room as a strangled cry escaped his lips. The journal hit the far wall with a thud and slid to the floor. Chris clamped a hand over his mouth as tears welled behind his eyes.

He had failed.

It was better this way.

Clamping his eyes shut, he ran his fingers through his hair. Forced himself to breathe, to still his racing heart. With a resigned sigh, he crossed the office floor and picked up the journal and its contents now strewn across the floor. Wrapping the cord around the journal, he tossed it in the box on his desk and placed the lid over it. It was time to move on. When the journal had been passed down to him, he'd seen it as his destiny. He'd been wrong. There was only one future that mattered now, and it lay sleeping under the gentle glow of a stegosaurus night light.

Tomorrow, Chris would go to Orion and take the offer to work with him at the museum. The pay was decent and the position was worthy of his education. The idea of working for the man wasn't attractive, but for Tommy and Evelyn, any job was worth it. But more than that, the man was hiding something — and Chris intended to find out what.

Flicking the light off in his office, Chris closed the door and slipped down the hall to the room where his wife slept. As the thunder slowed to a low rumble, he fell asleep to dreams of arrows carved into the bark of palm trees.

LYDIA

Lydia tore through her room, scrambling for a way of escape. Quickly and quietly, she examined every surface. The windows were screwed in from the outside. The room's only door was locked. The bathroom had no windows, and the vent was barely bigger than her head. After hours of searching, she had no choice but to give up.

She was a *prisoner*. Caged like an *animal*.

Tears stung her eyes as frustration bubbled up inside of her. Powerlessness coiled like a rope around her neck, threatening to strangle her. She wanted out, away from him and whatever he planned to do with her. Anger bubbled up inside of her, a rage like nothing she'd felt. Her teeth ground into each other, her breaths quickening.

How *dare* he? How *dare* he take her father from her? How *dare* he manipulate her brother? How *dare* he come after Tommy and her friends? So much evil had lived in her midst, and she'd been so *blind* to it. So *stupid* to have wasted years of her life loving her uncle, admiring him.

With a cry of anger and frustration and desperation, Lydia tore the quilt off the bed and threw it to the floor. She lifted the mattress and flipped it. The bed frame scraped against the floor. She grabbed the lamp, the cord yanking from the wall as she threw it across the room. It struck the far wall, shattered, and fell to the floor. She ripped the nightstand drawer from its track. Pulled the window curtains from the rod and tore them in half as hot tears spilled down her face. And when there was no more damage to do, she fell back against the wall, gasping for breath, swiping at her eyes.

She slid against the wall, trembling fingers combing her hair away from her face. She clamped her eyes shut. She thought of Tommy, and for a moment it was like he was in the room with her. She could almost see the exact shade of brown in his eyes, hear the tone of his laugh, feel the grooves in the palm of his hand. She wished so desperately she were with him, but she wasn't. She was here. Alone.

When she finally caught her breath, Lydia let her head roll back against the wall. Her eyes surveyed the room around her. The damage she'd done to the furniture, the walls.

Lydia's eyes stopped on the wallpaper. Her brow furrowed.

Slowly pushing herself to her feet, Lydia tiptoed across the floor to the wall. She ran her palms over the surface of the wallpaper, then stopped. The surface of the wallpaper here was raised. She continued her search until she found two more ridges in the paper, above and below the first in a straight line.

Something hid behind the wallpaper.

Lydia found the seams of the paper and tugged until it began to peel away, but the dresser mirror was in the way. Grabbing it by the sides, she shoved. Wood scraping against wood, it slid out of her way, and Lydia returned to continue peeling the wallpaper. It came off in a single sheet, the glue all but dissolved, and hung at an odd angle without the dresser to keep it upright. Lydia's eyes widened as she saw what the ridges had been.

Hinges.

A knock on the door startled Lydia from her search. Her eyes darted to the door, shadows shifting through the gap between the bottom of the door and the floor. A panicked hitch in her breath, she slid the dresser back in place, moving it just a little further to the right so that the mirror held the wallpaper almost fully back in position along the wall. She backed away and pressed her back against the window, praying whoever entered wouldn't notice the dog-eared corner near the ceiling. The knob turned, and the door swung open.

Lydia's breath caught in her throat as Graham Robinson smiled at her from the dim light of the hallway. He took a step forward, then stopped, folding his arms as he leaned his shoulder against the door frame.

"Lydia Clark," he said. "The girl who broke my heart."

Lydia wanted to break more than that. She swallowed her disgust. "You're with Orion now," she said, more of a statement than a question. *Of course* he'd weaseled his way into Orion's good graces. *Of course* Orion had set out to replace Reid as soon as his nephew had forsaken him. The man was a predator.

Graham straightened and moved forward until he stood at the corner of the bed, his fingers brushing the wrinkled surface of the blanket. "Your brother didn't understand what Orion has to offer.

I do."

"You've never been one for ambition, Graham." Lydia did her best to hide the tremor in her voice as she stared him down. Her mind flashed to the last time they'd been alone together. The Founder's Day Gala, in a closet at the Mammoth Museum. The pit in her stomach grew heavier.

Smirking, Graham rested his hand on the bedpost. "You know," he said, "I'd rethink your attitude if I were you. Your little boyfriend's not here to protect you anymore. Who's to stop me if I wanted to… finish what we started?"

Lydia's fist tightened, her fingers going to the keyring around her ring finger. Her chest rose and fell as she inhaled, eyes locked on Graham's — prey cornered by predator. "Tommy's a better man than you could ever hope to be," she hissed.

Graham's nose twitched. Another step forward. Lydia's lips trembled as she held his gaze.

"He manipulated you, Lydia," Graham said, the smile on his face gone — replaced by a fiery intensity Lydia hadn't seen since that moment at the museum. Then, she'd had an escape. A way out. Here, she was trapped. She was tired of being trapped, her life held in the grip of someone else.

"Before him, we were happy." He moved closer. Close enough now that Lydia could feel his breath on her face. His hand came up to pinch the ends of her hair between his fingers. "You and me against the world, Lydia. That's the way things were supposed to be. The way they could *still be*."

She shuddered against the cold glass of the window, desperately wishing she could melt through it and into the open air beyond. But what if…

Lydia looked into Graham's eyes, searching for a glimmer of

the boy she'd once loved. Was there a way to dig past this new, horrible version of Graham and reconnect with the version she'd fallen in love with? The boy who had been her date to countless movies, who had bought her popcorn and listened to her rant and rave about how terrible movie adaptations of books were, who'd sat through more family dinners that Lydia could count, taking the time to get to know the intimidating, imposing force that was her father when most other boys would have run the other way. Lydia didn't love Graham Robinson anymore, but could she forgive him long enough to get through to him?

With a sharp inhale, Lydia blinked, whispered, "We were happy, Graham. Things changed, but… that doesn't mean we can't move past it and become better. Better than we were. And maybe, one day, we could be friends."

Graham stared down his nose at her, the moonlight reflecting off his close-cropped dark blond hair. "Friends," he repeated.

Lydia's heart thrummed with hope, and she straightened, latching onto that sliver of connection, that glimmer of recognition between them. "We broke up, but that doesn't mean I don't care what happens to you. And my uncle, he's a monster. He steals and he bullies and he kills anyone who gets in his way. Don't let the next body to fall be yours, Graham. Please… Let's just… get out of here."

Graham's eyes darted between Lydia's. "Stop," he hissed, his voice barely audible.

But Lydia couldn't stop. The only thing they had left between them was the memories they'd shared, and those memories had become a lifeline. Lydia couldn't let go. Not now. She was so close; she could see it in his eyes. He wasn't a monster like Orion. Not yet. There was still time. "Graham, listen – remember how much you loved me. Don't let go of that, because that's what made us special, and that's what's going to get us through this."

She didn't see it coming. The punch landed in the center of her stomach and buried itself in her gut. She doubled over, coughing as she struggled to catch her breath. Tears stung her eyes.

"You were right about one thing," he said as he crouched down in front of her, his face a blur. He reached out to cup her chin between his fingers. Lydia clutched her stomach, glaring at him through the tears. "I did love you. But you've moved on. I see that now. But the thing is, Lydia? So have I."

FOURTEEN
REID

Thunder rumbled outside the jailhouse. On his back on the thin bed, his feet dangling off the end, Reid stared up at the ceiling. Rainwater leaked through a crack in the plaster. Behind him, the jailhouse was in uproar. Reid tried to drown out the noise, the shouting and jeering, the clanging of cell doors. He closed his eyes and pretended he was somewhere else. In the cold, it was almost possible to imagine he was on the lake in the dead of winter, skating and launching puck after puck into the net. As a kid, he'd practically lived on the ice. It was the only place he could go where his father couldn't reach him – Oliver Clark never did have any interest in Reid's athletic pursuits. Reid could count on two fingers the number of games his father had attended.

Reid still hadn't figured out what he had done to make his father hate him so much, and now he would never know.

Ironic, then, that Reid was being tried for the murder of Oliver Clark. Granted, much longer and he might have eventually killed the man anyway.

No, Reid didn't have that in him. So, where did that leave him?

Words flashed across Reid's mind. *Abused. Manipulated. Forgotten. Lost.*

He'd spent most of his life running from those words and what they meant, donning a false identity, a false front to try to cover up the kind of man he'd become. Admitting, even to himself, that he was all these things and more made him less of a man, didn't it? That's what his father would have said, at least.

A memory flared briefly back to life, and for a moment Reid was ten years old again, standing in his father's study, clutching the red welt on the side of his face as he sobbed.

"Man up," his father had said. *"You're a Clark, and Clarks don't cry."*

His father had spent a good deal of time making sure Reid knew all the ways he'd failed at being a Clark. He'd never stopped tearing down long enough to build anything in its place. Reid knew what a Clark wasn't — emotional, weak, kind, gentle — but he'd never been able to figure out what a Clark *was.* Until now, sitting in a jail cell. Completely alone. Completely abandoned.

What a man did was more important than what he didn't do, and Reid was here because of what he had done for his sister and her friends. He would find a way to accept that — no matter what it looked like. Funny thing was, Reid wasn't sure he'd ever felt so at peace as he did behind these bars.

This is where I belong.

Metal slid into a lock, and the door to Reid's cell opened. "You're getting a roommate, Clark," said the guard as he shoved the prisoner inside the cell. The door closed quickly behind him. Reid sized the newcomer up – easily six feet tall and at least three hundred pounds. Earrings in both ears. His head had gone bald, but he wore a patchy beard. Tattoos lined either side of his thick neck, vanishing behind the collar of his leather vest. He grinned at Reid, revealing three gold teeth.

Reid swallowed, ignoring the man. He went to the edge of the cell and called for the guard. "Hey, what's going on out there?"

The man turned around, his eyes darting between the cells, now overflowing with the day's arrests. With a sigh, the guard shrugged. "Guess you probably haven't heard, huh? Seems the whole town's in uproar. We've got protests going on downtown calling for the capture of your friends and riots breaking out all over the city. I guess the Jailbirds aren't keen on the fact your uncle's running for office."

Reid blinked. Riots?

The Jailbirds don't want a Bluecoat mayor.

"What about my hearing?" Reid asked.

The guard shrugged. "You'll have to ask your lawyer about that one, pal."

He turned to leave, and Reid didn't call him back. He slouched against the bars, ignoring the overshadowing presence of his cellmate behind him.

"You Clark's kid?" the man asked, his voice deep and gruff.

Reid turned, hesitant to meet the man in the eye. "Nephew," he said.

Nodding, the man smiled. "Good. I've got a message for you."

The punch landed before Reid saw it coming, the impact to his temple sending him immediately to the concrete floor. Reid's ears rang. He tried to stand, but the man's boot kicked him in the stomach and sent him flying into the wall, the back of his head shattering the plaster and sending dust into the air around him. He gasped for breath, unable to inhale, unable to do anything but shield his face as another kick came. The neighboring cells burst into chaos, cheering his attackers.

Reid's body screamed, bones cracking and breaking.

An alarm. The screech of metal.

The kicking stopped, but not before Reid lost consciousness.

FIFTEEN
IMMY

"Immy, stop it. You're not moving."

Immy shoved Mars' hands aside and sat upright – too quickly. The room spun around her, and the cauterized wound in her side screamed in pain. She ground her teeth through it and forced herself into a seated position.

"It's been a week. I'm fine," Immy said, though the sharp inhale at the end didn't help her case. But she was tired of being forced to lie on the couch all day. And she knew they'd only stayed here as long as they had because of her – she was putting them in danger. If she could just get her strength back, they could move before the cops caught up to them.

Or they could go on without me.

Last time she'd suggested that they'd all but laughed at her.

Mars frowned at her, his brow furrowed, his arms folded over his chest. He'd spent the last seven days coddling her – which had gotten old after day one. Immy had grown up sleeping on jungle floors amid underbrush and beneath falling coconuts. She didn't need coddling.

"You were *stabbed*," Mars said.

"I'm aware, thank you." With her hands, she pushed herself off the couch and onto her feet. If she didn't make any sudden movements, she'd be fine. The pain in her side would linger for a while to come, but that was to be expected. She'd lived through much worse.

Immy turned her attention to the other Jailbirds in the room, ignoring Mars' piercing glare. Tommy and Jude sat at the dining room table, playing a game of chess they'd pulled out of the attic. Lucy dangled upside down in the chair, her head dangling over the cushion as she flipped through the pages of an old book, her legs kicking back and forth in the air. Maya was off somewhere in the kitchen, pulling together whatever boxed and canned goods remained in the house, left behind by the previous renters.

They'd managed to go the entire week without power, operating solely by candlelight. During the day, it was easier to pretend they weren't in hiding. But they were running out of food, and as far as Immy could tell from her place on the couch, they hadn't come any closer to deciding how to move forward than when they'd left Hollow Hill.

Lydia, still missing.

Reid, still in jail.

Orion, still running for mayor.

And I thought things were bad in Peru.

"We're out of food," Maya announced as she walked into the room holding up a can. "Unless someone feels like okra with a side of okra tonight."

Jude wrinkled his nose. "Why does okra even exist?"

"We could hunt," Immy suggested, leaning against the arm of the couch for support. She managed to catch her breath, and the pain began to subside.

"You plan to take down a deer with what? A fork and spoon?" Tommy said. The weary expression on his face in the red in his eyes didn't match the sarcasm in his tone. Jude had told them what happened the night Tommy left. His mom had died. When Tommy returned, he'd disappeared into one of the bedrooms without a word.

Grief was something Immy understand intimately. Orion had taken everything and everyone she'd ever loved from her. He needed to pay for what he'd done. He needed to *suffer*.

"Actually, you could probably rig a pretty nice trap with—" Mars started before Tommy waved him off.

Lucy held up a finger. "I have an idea, actually. Thing is, nobody here actually knows who I am, so what's stopping me from going into town?"

Tommy raised an eyebrow, sharing a look with Jude who shrugged.

Maya pointed the can of okra at Lucy. "She's got a point."

"Perfect," said Lucy. "I'll head into town now. Any requests?"

"Yeah," Jude said, "I'd kill for a nice, juicy cheeseburger."

"A pepperoni pizza with jalapeños," Maya added wistfully.

"Fish and chips," said Mars.

Tommy smirked and said, "Just get what you can carry."

Lucy saluted with two fingers to her temple and headed for the door.

"Wait," Immy called, pushing away from the couch, ignoring the throbbing in her side. "I'm going with you."

"What?" Mars said. "No, you're definitely not."

"Hmm? This little thing? I just need to walk it off."

"Seems foolish," said Tommy.

"Because we just happen to be pillars of wisdom over here," Jude retorted with a snort.

Maya flicked him in the ear, and he winced, clutching his ear as he looked up at her smirk.

"I'm *going*, because if I have to lie on that couch another day, *that* is going to kill me. Trust me, Mars," she said. "I'll be fine."

Mars' frown deepened. He turned to Lucy. "Keep an eye on her, Lu. If the wound starts bleeding through her shirt, drag her back here unconscious if that's what it takes."

Lucy smiled and nodded. She turned and led the way out the door.

The cold morning air swept over Immy, and she savored it as she shut the door behind her. She'd never spent so much time inside in her life. She'd been raised among the trees and rivers, born barefoot in the dirt and grass. A house was for sleeping, but the world outside? That was for living.

It took a two-hour walk to get from the Morales place on the hill down to the city, and then another forty-five minutes to find a convenience store. It took just as long for Immy to form her own plan in between scattered conversation with Lucy.

The store certainly wasn't prime pickings, but it would do in a pinch. They browsed the aisles, gathering as much canned and boxed food as they thought they could carry on the walk back to the house.

"So, Lucy," said Immy as she filled her basket with cans of chili and ravioli, "why *did* you decide to come with us?"

Lucy Adler had jumped into things with them without even a pause – why? Immy hadn't left her home because she'd wanted to, though she was glad to have a place here with her newfound friends; but she'd been forced into it. Lucy had a choice, and she'd chosen to leave Mariner's Cove – everything and everyone she'd ever known. A life she'd built for herself. She'd traded it all for a life on the run with a group of fugitives.

Lucy reached for a box of mac and cheese, revealing a tattoo on the inside of her wrist. A devilfish. Did it mean something, or did the girl just like eight-legged sea creatures?

"You believe in fate, Immy?" she asked without looking Immy's way. "God, a higher power, something like that?"

Immy's parents had instilled in her a strong sense of belief in God, but she realized suddenly that it had been a long time since she'd given her faith much consideration. "Yeah," she said after a few seconds. "I believe in God."

Lucy nodded, a slight smile playing at the corner of her lips. She seemed to be deep in thought, judging by the way she studied the nutritional facts on the side of the Rice-A-Roni box. "I don't really know what I believe – never had someone to help me figure things like that out – but I know what it's like when you meet someone and you feel connected in a way you've never felt before, or you go someplace and it feels like home even though you've never been there before."

"You're saying that's what you felt when you met us?"

Lucy shoved the box into her basket and shrugged. "Maybe," she said. "Maybe that's what I'm trying to figure out."

Immy followed her down the aisle to the next one over, lined with chips and dip. She looked up over the tops of the shelves to see the cashier watching them as he ran a rag over the countertop.

Immy's heart skipped a beat, then calmed when she remembered nobody knew who they were. Only that they weren't from around here.

"I didn't have anyone left back in Mariner's Cove," Lucy continued. "I guess I was… alone."

Immy could certainly understand the feeling, so she decided not to press anymore. The Black Flag had taken her in after she'd lost her parents, but Emilio had been her family. Until Orion had killed him.

"Well," said Lucy, "I think this is all I can carry. What about you?"

Immy held up a basket full of cans, straining under the weight. "Probably a little *too* much, but we'll manage."

At checkout, the cashier took his time ringing them up. Immy stood to the side of the counter, browsing a stack of newspapers with Orion Clark's face on the front page.

CLARK RUNS FOR OFFICE, the headline read, but below that in smaller print, JAILBIRD RIOTS LEAVE CITY IN CHAOS.

"This too," Immy said, tossing the paper on top of the cans.

The cashier grunted as he scanned a can of ravioli. It didn't beep, so he tried again, but it didn't go through. "I'll be right back," he said, then slipped out from behind the counter.

Immy's eyes fell to the back of the counter where he'd been standing a second ago. The handle of a pistol stuck out from a shelf, half-buried by magazines. The cashier was worried they were Jailbird looters – that's why he was eying them.

And suddenly Immy's plan began to come together. She elbowed Lucy. "Hey, would you keep an eye out for a second?"

"Why?" she asked, brow furrowed.

Immy didn't stop to answer. She slipped behind the counter and pulled the gun out from under the stack of magazines. She reached behind her back, the movement causing a jolt of pain to course through the healing wound in her side and tucked the barrel of the handgun in the waistband of her jeans. She slithered back out from behind the checkstand and pulled her shirt over the gun's handle just as the cashier reappeared. He typed the can of ravioli into the computer manually, then finished ringing the rest of their items up. They paid and split the goods as evenly across four plastic bags as they could, then left the convenience store.

"What was that?" Lucy hissed.

"Don't turn around," Immy said. "Keep walking."

Lucy did as she said, and soon they were out of sight of the convenience store. They spent the three-hour walk back to the house in silence, but Immy was rehashing her plan in her mind. Orion Clark – the man who had murdered her parents like dogs, who had years later murdered Christopher Rhodes, then her uncle Emilio in the same manner – wanted to run for mayor, destroying half the city to get what he wanted. But he wouldn't get far – not if Immy put a stop to it herself.

SIXTEEN
TOMMY

Hot water ran down Tommy's back as he stood in the upstairs shower, his head leaning against the shower wall and his eyes closed. Every bruise, every scar inflamed by the heat. Soap ran from his hair down his face. The bathroom light – like every other light in the vacant house – was off as he showered in pitch darkness.

More than a week since his mother had died. More than a week since Lydia had been taken from him.

Tommy's fingers found the keyring, tracing the metal wire that encircled his finger. Every time he closed his eyes, he saw her face. The curve of her lips, the way her chin dimpled slightly, her full cheeks, her wavy brown hair that fell to her shoulders in waves, her skin soft beneath his rough hands. The look in her eyes every time he managed to make her laugh. Like a sailor bound for the world's edge, he'd told himself that he'd spend the rest of his life searching for ways to make her laugh – just to capture a glimpse of the way her eyes lit up like the sky over the sea in the earliest part of morning. A wonder of the world reserved solely for him.

Tears mingled with the shower water, running down his face and pooling at his feet. Tommy was the last to shower, and so he waited until the hot water ran out and began to turn cold before turning it off and climbing out. In the silence of the bathroom, Tommy prayed, lifted his heart's petition to a God who'd never left his side before – so why would He now? And as he dried, his felt an assurance in his soul. Orion would face justice for what he'd done to Tommy's father and to Lydia's father and to so many others over the years.

Tommy would finish what his father had started.

"We need a plan," Tommy said. He stood at the head of the dining room table, arms crossed. His flannel was still hot out of the dryer. His hair still wet and cold on his head. He ran his fingers through his hair, combing it away from his eyes. He hadn't had a trim in months, and his hair was growing longer than he'd ever kept it and wilder as a result.

Immy and Lucy had returned while Tommy was in the shower, bearing boxes of mac and cheese and cans of chili, which now simmered on the stovetop while the Jailbirds sat around the table. Tommy's stomach growled as the smell of food wafted through the house.

Lydia should be here… and so should Reid.

"We can't squat here much longer," Tommy continued. "Sooner or later, Maya, your parents will either notice the water and electric bill has suddenly gone up, or they'll lease a new tenant. I don't plan to be here when that happens."

"Where do we go, then?" asked Mars.

Tommy grabbed his backpack and set it on the table. One by one, he removed the three keys: the Mammoth Key, the Titan Key, and the Leviathan Key. He laid them out on the dining room table in a row. While similar in their hexagonal shape, each of them had a distinct look to them. Their surfaces were carved to reflect the fossils they'd been hidden with: Wooly Mammoth, Titanosaur, and Spinosaurus.

"When the time comes, we leave and head east," Tommy said. "Away from Mammoth and back to Mariner's Cove."

Jude raised a hand. "Wait, by leave, you mean… for good?"

"I don't know. Maybe not forever, but at least… for a long time."

Silence fell over the room as the Jailbirds exchanged a glance.

"Listen." Tommy grabbed the back of the chair in front of him, his fingers tightening around the wood as he searched for a way to say what was on his heart. "You guys have gone with me further than I had any right to ask, and… it wouldn't be fair for me to ask you to leave your families and come with me."

"*You* are our family," Maya said, her voice soft. Tommy looked up to meet her gaze. She gave a smile, looking around the room at the others in turn. "*This* is the only family we have left."

Tommy nodded. Maya's parents had all but abandoned her. Tommy's parents had both died, and Jude's dad was a deadbeat. The only one with any roots left in Mammoth was Mars. Tommy met his eyes, and Mars shrugged, though uncertainty played across his features.

Jude leaned forward, folding his hands in front of him. "If this is it – if we're leaving for good, then… there's something I need to do first. I've got to go see Henry. Make sure he's okay, and that he knows I'm okay."

"You're right, you should go see him," Tommy agreed. "And while you're in Seattle, the rest of us have a few things to take care of."

Lucy held up a finger, chipped blue nail polish catching a ray of daylight. "And by 'a few things,' you mean…"

"We find where Orion's hiding Lydia and break Reid out of jail."

"Okay, but why Mariner's Cove?" Lucy asked. "You already found the key."

"We missed something. I'm sure of it. Lucy, you said Katherine Rhodes was your ancestor. She's mine, too. If her legacy left a mark on Mammoth, it's bound to mean something to Mariner's Cove too. We just weren't there long enough to figure it out. Somewhere in Mariner's Cove is the answer where Othniel Cuvier hid his vault before he died."

Lucy nodded, chewing on her lip. She looked out the window as a trio of crows flew down to land in the grass, their shiny black beaks poking at the earth.

"Okay, start with Lydia," Maya said, leaning forward. She held a cup of coffee between her hands, the steam rising in front of her face. "How do you plan to find where Orion's keeping her?"

Tommy smiled.

Jude groaned. "Oh, I don't like that look."

"Yep, that's the look of a man with a *terrible* idea," Mars added.

"Whatever it is," Maya said, "I'm in."

"At least let the man lay it out first," Jude said beside her.

Immy smirked from across the table. "You chicken?"

Jude jutted out his chin. "Never."

"Okay, then," Mars said, "let's hear it."

Tommy leaned on the table in front of him, his eyes meeting each one of theirs. "I'm going to break into Orion's house."

Mars sighed. "The dragon's den. Nice."

"Bro," Jude said, folding his hands behind his head as he stared up at Tommy – half amused, half concerned.

"Well, I like it already," said Immy.

"I'm never going to be able to get a job in law enforcement now," Mars groaned.

"Like that ship hasn't already sailed," Jude retorted.

"Okay," Maya said, shoving Jude to silence him. "What about Reid?"

Tommy paused, pacing the floor. "We need an opening of some kind. If we could find out when his hearing is, we might be able to intercept the car taking him to the courthouse."

"Maybe Lorelai Clark can help us," Maya offered. "I assume she's representing him, so she'd have his court date."

"Yeah, but Lucy doesn't know Lorelai," Jude said.

"We could call her," said Tommy.

"With what phone?" Mars asked.

"How about I go to the police station and ask to see Reid?" Lucy said. "I could just tell them I'm an old girlfriend of his, let them think I'm a Bluecoat like him so they don't think I'm a threat or anything."

"The cops wouldn't know any better," Jude agreed.

Tommy gave a sharp nod. "Which is exactly why she's the best person to go. If we're going to do this, we're not going to land anyone else in hot water. Not our parents, not our friends. Nobody else needs to get hurt."

Jude nodded while the Jailbirds considered the plan. "When?" he asked.

"Tonight," said Tommy. "Jude, you catch a bus to Seattle. Mars, you and I head to Orion's place. Maya, you give Lucy the address to the police station. We need that court date. The minute Reid leaves the jail to head to his hearing, we move."

SEVENTEEN

MAYA

Maya found Jude in one of the upstairs bedrooms. They'd waited until nightfall for him to leave, hoping there'd be less eyes on the bus stop. But Maya still felt nervous. The cops were everywhere. Before Jude could safely make it to Seattle, where hopefully the Seattle police weren't up to date with what was going on in Mammoth, he had to first make it safely to the bus stop. There were a million things that could go wrong, and a million things Maya wanted to say.

She stopped in the doorway, watching Jude as he pulled a clean T-shirt over his head, mussing his wild, blond hair in the process. He hadn't noticed her yet. She blushed, realizing her eyes had lingered a little too long on the cords of muscle shifting on his back. The pair of dimples above his waist.

Things had changed between them, and she was still figuring it out. Maybe he was too. All she knew was that after that moment on the train – after the kiss – she couldn't stop thinking about him. For so long, Maya had felt adrift. A boat at sea, tossed by the wind and the waves, desperately trying to stay afloat. And the Jailbirds had been her anchor. In the moments when things with her parents became too overwhelming, when life felt too scary, their friendship had kept her head above the water. And then they thought they'd lost Tommy and Lydia after they'd gone over the cliff in Peru, and Jude was planning to leave too. Join the military, disappear into a world of violence and chaos. The wind blew stronger and the wives grew wilder, and Maya could barely keep her head above water.

Until that kiss.

The taste of his lips, the heat of his breath, the racing of his heart beneath her fingertips – like a radiant light bursting through the tempest, all the sudden the seas had calmed, the clouds had parted, and the world had stopped. Frozen for a moment as if it could possibly revolve around them for just one split second in time. And life had moved on, tumbling forward as it always did, but in Maya's heart she was still there. Alone in that boat with the boy she loved. The boy she was *scared* to love. Because no one had ever taught her that love was anything but loss.

There was a world waiting for her on the other side of that kiss, and Maya had caught just a momentary glimpse, but she was terrified to open that door again. What if loving him meant losing him? Losing herself?

Jude turned just then, pulling a trucker's hat forward on his head. His eyebrows arched. "Oh, hey, May. Didn't see you there." He shoved his hands in his jeans pockets.

Maya smiled, memorizing the way he said her name. Like there was nothing in the world he enjoyed more. She watched his eyes dance as he walked toward her, his jaw flex as he seemed to consider his own words. Did his heart race when he thought of that kiss? Did he lose his breath when he remembered the warmth of her skin?

Maya wanted to know every thought on his mind, but the answers terrified her. So, for a moment, she pretended that nothing had changed. That the world was the same as it had been before the train. That they were best friends and nothing more. That his eyes didn't dance and his heart didn't race and they hadn't kissed. Because it was easier than admitting to herself that something inside of her, apparently, had been broken. That there was some small part of her heart that didn't think she was worth loving. That the lies she'd spent her entire life pretending to ignore because of her parents' actions hadn't become true in her own mind. That she didn't look at this boy in front of her and think that he was better off finding someone else to love, because she wasn't worth the effort.

"I just…" she started, her lips parting, her breath hitching in her throat as she met his inquisitive stare. And then he started toward her, sending both a bolt of thrill and panic darting through her. Because what if he kissed her again, and Maya had to acknowledge all the terrible things she had come to believe? No, it was easier to keep things the way they'd always been. It was easier to be adrift in that boat alone, to weather the storm alone, because then the only person she had to worry about drowning was herself.

"I wanted to tell you to be careful," Maya finished before Jude made it across the room to her. He stopped, smiled.

"Who? Me? When have I ever *not* been careful?" He chuckled.

Maya smiled, then turned away from the door and left him

alone to finish getting dressed.

Because, for as often as she tried and as much practice as she had, lying to herself was getting harder and harder.

EIGHTEEN
GRAHAM

Searing pain emanated from the fresh brand on Graham Robinson's chest. A *W* to symbolize his newfound role as a member of the Wild Hunt.

Smiling to his own reflection in the bathroom mirror, Graham buttoned his shirt, the fabric sending a sliver of pain through the tender patch of skin. He'd done everything Orion Clark had asked and more. Mammoth was in chaos, Bluecoats and Jailbirds practically at each other's throats. Orion would win the election, and then Mammoth would be theirs.

Graham left the bathroom and joined the others in the headquarters of Orion's campaign office. The sounds of a dozen different conversations filled the building as volunteers worked overtime to put up posters, book ads, and schedule press conferences. Signs lined the walls and sat along desktops, boasting Orion's many promises to the people of Mammoth.

VOTE CLARK FOR A SAFER MAMMOTH.

Graham didn't particularly care for politics, but whatever game Orion played wasn't strictly political. There were shadowed layers to the man, and Graham could appreciate that.

The door to the campaign office opened. A bell rung, and Graham's eyes widened to see Alicia Morales waltz inside, briefcase in tow. He moved closer to hear her ask someone where to find Orion. The volunteer pointed a thumb over her shoulder, and Alicia followed it to the back of the building, brushing past Graham as if he wasn't even there.

Graham bristled but set his annoyance aside to follow her as she stormed into Orion's office and shut the door behind her.

He turned the knob quietly and cracked it open just enough to hear the conversation.

"This isn't part of our agreement," Alicia said, her voice muffled as she tried to keep it down.

"Neither was your daughter's involvement," Orion replied, his tone calm and collected. "You're not getting cold feet, are you, Alicia? After all these years, you're suddenly going to pretend you don't have the stomach for what *we've* done?"

"You lied to me," Alicia snapped. "*You* were the one who killed Danny. You said he'd died in an accident. You showed me his death certificate!"

"A simple forgery," said Orion, hands clasped in his lap in front of him. "I had to make sure the police didn't suspect anything."

"And what other secrets have you kept, huh? I'm your *lawyer*, Orion. I can't help you if you keep things from me! And I *won't* help you if you keep villainizing my daughter!"

A chair scraped across the floor. Orion have stood up.

Graham leaned in closer.

"You know exactly what you need to know. The goal remains the same, Alicia. But if you don't keep your daughter in check, I can't guarantee her safety."

"Then I can't guarantee my loyalty," said Alicia. "I'm done."

The door swung open, and Graham startled backward. Alicia's eyes widened when she saw him, then turned to a scowl. She stormed off. Graham watched her leave the building and stalk down the sidewalk.

A hand fell on his shoulder, and he turned to see Orion at his back, staring past him at Alicia as she climbed into her car.

"Follow her," he said.

"And then?"

Orion drew his lips in a thin line. "I suppose now's the time for you to prove yourself, Robinson." A pause. "No loose ends."

Graham nodded, then jogged through the campaign office and out the door to his car, grinning all the way.

NINETEEN
REID

A voice called to him in his dreams — a whisper in the dark, gentle and familiar. Like a memory from his childhood. A friend he hadn't spoken to in years.

Reid's eyes opened slowly, blinded by white light. After a moment, they adjusted. He tried to move, but his body felt frozen. Weighted down by an invisible pressure, and at the same time he felt outside of himself. The only time he'd ever felt this way was when he'd been popping pills. There was something in his system now, numbing him, freeing him.

Groaning, Reid let his head roll to the side. It took him a moment, but he finally registered his surroundings. Machines with black screens and green, blinking lights surrounded him. He was in a bed. The walls around him were white. The hospital?

Reid tried to sit up, but they'd drugged him, sapped all the strength from his body. He panicked, clawing at the IV line injected into his arm, yelping as he fingers tugged at the tube. The door swung open, and a nurse rushed in.

"Mr. Clark!" she shouted. "You need to stop.

"Get it out!" Reid shouted, pulling at the IV line, heart racing, mind still fuzzy. The edges of his vision blurred, but he focused on the needle in his elbow. The drug trying to pull him back under.

Strong arms grabbed hold of Reid's shoulders and pulled him back against the bed.

"Please!" Reid begged. "You can't drug me. I'm an addict!"

He'd never said it out loud before, but after finally getting clean – however inadvertently – he was terrified of going back to who he'd been.

Reid's body trembled as he stared up at the ceiling, pleading with the nurse to pull the IV out while an officer pinned him to the hospital bed. "Please. I can't have painkillers. I'm an addict."

"I'm sorry, Mr. Clark," said the nurse as she checked the machines to his left. "Doctor's orders."

Something cold cinched around his wrist. He glanced down to see the officer snapping a pair of silver cuffs around his wrist and the rail of the hospital bed. Tying him down.

Ignoring his pleas, they left him alone in the white, sterile room. He blinked, struggling to find himself in the haze of drugs coursing through his veins.

Beeping. The hum of the ventilation system.

Someone had changed Reid's clothes. He wore nothing but the thin hospital gown and the blanket over his lap. His arms were littered with bruises and cuts now bandaged. Memories of the attack came flooding back as he realized what had happened.

The door opened, and a different nurse walked in, her eyes glued to a clipboard in her hands. She glanced up, eyebrows arching as she saw Reid.

"I hear you put up quiet the fight when you woke up."

"What-" Dry. Reid's mouth was dry. The nurse registered his need and came to his side, lifting a big, plastic cup with a straw to his lips. He drank greedily before ejecting the straw. "What happened?"

"You got lucky," the nurse said. The badge hanging from her hip read *Nancy*. "If the guards hadn't gotten to you in time, you might not be awake right now."

"I was attacked," said Reid, his eyes still roaming around the room. Was he at Mammoth Memorial?

"Afraid so." Nancy patted his leg and offered a smile. "I'm going to go let the doctor know you're awake, okay?"

Reid nodded. She turned, her brown ponytail bouncing off her shoulders. She reminded Reid of his stepmother. "Wait," he said.

She paused, turned.

"How long have I been here?"

"Two days," said Nancy. "Why?"

My hearing's tomorrow.

"Please. I can't be on painkillers. Ask the doctor to take me off," he said. "Please."

Nancy gave him a sympathetic look. "I'll see what I can do."

Then she left and Reid was alone again. The longer he sat there, remembering the attack, remembering his uncle's threats, the angrier he got. His heart rate increased, the beeping in the monitor increasing in turn. The pain in Reid's chest inflamed, and with his free hand he rubbed at the throbbing muscle just below his throat. After a few moments, the pain subsided.

The door opened again, and Reid noticed for the first time the deputies stationed outside his hospital room. Their presence reminded him that he wasn't free and maybe never would be again.

But they are.

Tommy, Jude, the others… they were free because of what Reid had done. Maybe the only good thing his life had ever amounted to.

The doctor walked in, her hands in the pockets of her white coat. Like the nurse, her black hair was pulled back in a ponytail. Her badge hung from the breast pocket. Red-framed glasses perched on the bridge of her nose. Her expression was firmer than the nurse's, and Reid wondered what her opinion of him might be. Had she already written him off as a murderer, a thief?

"Mr. Clark, my name is Dr. Angela Novak, and you've been under my care for the past forty-eight hours. Are you able to recall what happened?"

Reid nodded. "I was attacked by my cellmate."

"Good." The doctor nodded, her expression softening some. Perhaps what Reid thought was annoyance had only been concern. "When it comes to blunt force trauma like this, where the patient falls into a coma, one of the biggest concerns we have is whether they have experienced brain damage, which can manifest as amnesia or other gaps in cognitive function. The fact that you remember what happened is a good sign that you should make a full recovery."

"Okay, thanks," Reid said. When the doctor didn't leave, he asked, "Is there something else?"

Dr. Novak pursed her lips. She removed her hands from her pockets and clasped them in front of her. "I'm afraid there is." She paused. The pain in Reid's chest returned as anxiety flooded his body. "While you were you out, we were able to run a few tests, and we discovered something else. Something… unrelated to the attack."

The possibilities flashed across Reid's mind in an instant. A pit formed in Reid's stomach.

"Mr. Clark, you have what's called coronary artery disease."

"What?" Reid asked, his mouth suddenly dry again. His eyes stung, but he kept them fixed on the doctor. His lungs seemed to stop working. It got harder to breathe, and in seconds he felt like hyperventilating.

The doctor understood immediately and came quickly to his side, resting one hand on his shoulder and the other on his arm as she coached him through his breathing. "Slowly," she said, "In… out. In… out."

When he managed to catch his breath and the room stopped spinning, he settled back in his bed. "Sorry, doc," he said. "I get these… panic attacks sometimes."

Coronary Artery Disease… he repeated to himself as he stared past her at the door out into the hospital hallway.

"That's just it, Mr. Clark. I don't believe that what you're experiencing are panic attacks – at least, not on their own – rather, they're a symptom of a disease that your body has harbored for some time now."

"Am I… dying?"

As soon as the words left his mouth, he wanted to reel them back in and swallow them. Pretend it wasn't happening. Go back to those seconds before the doctor had walked into the room and all he'd felt was desperation to be free of the drugs being funneled into his veins. This fear of dying, of what came next, and the resulting sense of loss seemed it would swallow him whole.

"Long-term stress can cause higher levels of inflammation in the body that contribute to increases in plaque buildup in the arteries—and that can lead to things like CAD. Without knowing how long you've gone untreated, there is no way to know the full extent of the damage. At best, your condition will shorten your lifespan by ten – maybe fifteen – years. At worst… CAD can lead to heart attack, abnormal heart rhythm, and even catastrophic heart failure."

Reid swallowed, his head swimming. "Can it be treated?"

"There are a number of treatments available. We will want to put you on blood thinners to start, but we will need to run some tests to discern the full extent of the damage your heart has endured over the years. It is likely that your condition is entirely treatable, but we won't know for sure until we take a closer look." She paused. "Mr. Clark, while you were comatose, we discovered heavy scarring on your body."

Reid blinked. "Well, I was attacked, Doctor."

Novak shook her head. "No, this scarring predates your attack – some of it seems almost as old as you are." She paused, inching closer, lowering her voice. "Mr. Clark, we have several trauma therapists on staff. Perhaps you should speak with someone."

"I don't need a shrink."

Her eyes lingered on him for an uncomfortable moment. She patted his arm, then turned to leave.

"You think I killed him because he hurt me, don't you," Reid said, not so much a question as a painful observation. Where once people looked at Reid Clark and saw his father's legacy of success and power walking around, now they saw a failure, a prodigal, a criminal.

The doctor stopped and turned around, returning her hands

to her coat pockets. "It's not my job to assess my patients' guilt – or innocence."

"I didn't, though," said Reid. "My whole life, he hurt me. There were times where I even wished I was dead. He would've deserved it – if I'd done it, that is. Problem is, even if I'd had the chance to hurt him like he hurt me, I couldn't have. My father convinced me I was weak, that I was nothing. Small and insignificant." Reid paused, inhaling as he blinked away the tears that had welled in his eyes. He sniffed, wiped his eyes with the back of his finger. "*God*, I believed him."

Novak offered a tender smile that contrasted the matter-of-fact expression she'd worn when she'd first walked into his room. "Like I said, we have therapists available if you–"

Reid shook his head. "No." He paused. "But maybe there's something else…"

TWENTY

JUDE

Jude stepped down from the Greyhound bus and onto the sidewalk. A gust of wind traveled up the busy highway, whistling between rows of buildings as it went. The city of Seattle framed the horizon in every direction, and in the distance, Jude made out the Space Needle half obscured by gray clouds in an otherwise pale blue sky. Telephone lines draped across the street. Streetlights blinked between red, yellow, and green. Pigeons perched on the awnings of nearby businesses as Jude shoved his hands in the pockets of his sherpa-lined corduroy jacket. He reached up to pull the trucker's hat – the one with the logo of the now-incinerated Boathouse – lower on his face, the only disguise he had against any prying eyes. Not that he expected anyone in Seattle to be too concerned with the goings-on in a smaller town like Mammoth.

Jude's breath formed a cloud in front of him as he followed the upward angle of the street, heading for Henry's grandparents' place. His heart skipped a beat as thought of his little brother, of the chance to see him again. It had been nearly two months. Too long. And in that time, Jude hadn't even been able to call Henry.

A horn honked as an impatient driver tried to pass an older man in a sedan. Jude glared at the car as it swerved into the opposite lane, narrowly missing oncoming traffic, then shot out ahead of the sedan. An impatient driver like that was bound to get someone injured – or worse – one of these days.

Jude arrived at the Monroe place. Henry's grandparents had owned the house for nearly twenty-five years, and Jude still remembered when the street was mostly homes and the Seattle skyline seemed further away. Now the city seemed to creep up behind them, swallowing up suburban neighborhoods one at a time. Most of the homes had been bought by businesses and converted to retail outlets, but there were a few who remained, puffing up their chests against the gentrification of their homes. The Monroes were one such family.

Jude turned onto the sidewalk that led to the porch and stopped short. His heart leapt to his throat as he gaped at the door open wide and leaning on its hinges, the trim around the latch splintered inward. Someone had broken in.

Breaking into a jog, he ran for the door and threw himself inside. "Henry!" he called, anger and panic bubbling up inside his chest. "Henry! Where are you?"

No answer.

Jude stopped in the entryway, gaping at the chaos inside the house. Furniture had been turned over. Couch cushions cut open and destroyed. Pictures lay shattered on the floor, glass littering the wood and tile. Holes had been punched into the walls. The French doors leading into the backyard stood wide open. In the kitchen, cabinet doors had been ripped open, some hanging at odd angles by a single remaining hinge. Food from the pantry and fridge had spilled out onto the kitchen floor.

Hands through his hair, Jude spun as he searched the house for any sign of life. Anything at all. Had they been robbed? Had Orion found Henry? Had he taken him just like he'd taken Lydia?

Rage swelled in Jude's stomach as he reeled.

A noise echoed down the hall from one of the back bedrooms. The shuffle of shoes on carpet.

Jude clenched his jaw and burst forward, grabbing the trim of the archway into the hall, letting his momentum carry him around the corner. In the shadows of the hallway beneath the flickering light of a sconce that had been knocked free of its screws, stood Jack Mayfield.

"*You!*" Jude growled.

The man's eyes went wide. He opened his mouth to speak, but Jude surged forward and threw his entire weight against his father.

Jack fell backward against the wall, the impact from his head causing the plaster behind him to cave in.

He grunted and stumbled forward, still trying to speak. But Jude didn't wait to hear what the man had to say. He swung his fist through the air with a cry, his knuckles connecting with the older man's chin. Jack flung backward, anger flashing in his eyes. Jude tried to swing again, but Jack ducked low and wrapped his arms around Jude's middle, pushing him backward. Jude brought his elbows down on the man's upper back, and Jack buckled under the impact, tripping and falling to the floor.

He quickly scrambled up, and Jude swung again. Missed. Jack lunged out, trying to grab Jude's arms. Jude fell back, his fists raised in front of his face as he glared wild-eyed at his father.

"Where is my brother!" he shouted.

Jack spat to the side, blood from his lip staining the entryway rug.

With a shout, Jude lunged for his father again, but Jack sidestepped. Jude stumbled past him. He whirled around to face the man. "Where is he!"

"I *don't know*," Jack yelled back in his face.

"You're *lying*," Jude hissed through his teeth, his fists clenching at his side as he stared the man down. The man who'd beaten and bruised him in a drunken rage more times than Jude could count. The man who would've done the same to Henry had Jude not stood in his way. And now Henry was gone, and Jack was here standing in the middle of it. "You just couldn't leave him alone, could you? You couldn't stand the fact that one of your sons might grow up happy – *safe*!"

"I had nothing to do with this!" Jack shouted, his eyes wide, but it wasn't anger that flickered in the man's eyes.

Jude's anger faltered as he met his father's gaze, and in a second he realized what he'd missed in his anger. For the first time in Jude's entire life, the man's breath didn't reek of alcohol. And though his lip was bleeding, his eyes weren't bloodshot.

His chest heaving with every breath, Jude struggled to calm himself, to quiet his anger. He dropped his fists, but his shoulders tensed as he maintained the distance between himself and his father. Distance caused by too many nights spent terrified, hiding in closets and beneath beds. Too many holes in walls caused by hands that were supposed to protect, to defend. Too many shattered bottles littering floors with glass instead of toys. Too many broken chairs and fractured windows. Jude's memories of his childhood were dark, and what little light there was had come at too great a cost.

"What are you doing here?" Jude said, his voice shaky, adrenaline still coursing through his veins. He wanted to hurt the man, to make Jack suffer like he had. But his own words to Maya just days ago came back to rebuke him.

We can't afford to lose ourselves, too.

Jude sucked in a breath, allowing the oxygen to flood his lungs, slow his heart.

"Looking for you," Jack replied. "And your brother."

"Leave Henry alone."

A flicker of something — sadness, or maybe fear — flashed across Jack's eyes. He wiped the blood from his lip with the back of his hand. "I can't do that, son."

Jude winced. "Don't call me that."

Holding out his hands, Jack took a step forward. "I know I ain't done right by you — not by a long shot — but that doesn't change the fact that I'm your father, and you're my boy."

A lump formed in Jude's throat. His eyes stung. He blinked, sniffing as he shuffled on his feet and turned away from his father, his eyes surveying the damage that had carried into the hallway. "Christopher Rhodes was more of a father to me than you *ever* were."

Jack winced.

But Jude's confession brought with it memories, a handful of bright moments amid the bleak backdrop of his childhood. Of one of the first times meeting Tommy on the beach when they were kids. Tommy appearing as if by chance when Jude had ridden his bike down to the coast on his own after one of his father's rampages. Tommy had noticed the bruises on Jude's arms and decided then and there that they would be best friends so that they could protect each other. Until that moment, Jude was little more than a ghost. Floating through life, drifting from place to place, moment to moment, never really seen, never really understood. But his best friend Tommy Rhodes changed all that. Tommy saw in Jude what Jude didn't have the strength to see in himself: courage, fortitude, and the willingness to go where others wouldn't.

Jude wasn't a ghost. Not anymore. Jude Mayfield was the man his father should have been.

"There was a time when Chris and I were friends," said Jack. He gave a wry laugh. "'Course, I suppose you know that by now."

Jack paused, settling against the hallway wall. He slid to the ground, propping his arms up on his knees. Jude crossed to the opposite wall, keeping his distance, but he sat down, one leg out in front of him and the other bent, his elbow resting on his knee.

"I went to him once," said Jack. "Years ago now, but I… I knew the man I was becoming. Knew what it was doing to you boys, and I asked Chris. I said, 'You gotta watch out for 'em. Make sure I don't do something I'll regret. And if it ever comes down to it, Chris, you do what needs doing. You make sure I never break them. Not like I was broken.'"

Jude stared at his father in the dim, waning light of the hallway.

"Chris did his best. He watched out for you like I asked him to. Took you in when things got… bad."

Jude allowed his mind to wander back to those early years when he was young. The nights he slept over at the Rhodes house. The times Christopher Rhodes seemed to show up out of nowhere to take him and Tommy for a ride or on a camping trip. All those times, and he'd never known that his father had been fighting a war. Desperately trying to hold onto the kind of man he could've been. And, in his strange way, protecting them by asking another man to do for the boys what he couldn't.

Maybe, in some way, his efforts had worked out. He'd bruised and hit Jude more times than he could remember, but there was always something holding him back, preventing him from making things worse. And he'd *never* laid a hand on Henry. Jude had always thought that was because he'd protected Henry, stood between his father and his brother – and maybe that was part of it – but what if it was more than that? Maybe that's what Jude saw in his father's eyes now, in the way they shone in the pale light with emotion Jude hadn't seen in years. They weren't empty, hollow. They were the eyes of a man with two opposing forces living on the inside of him, dueling to see which one would win. Good and evil, light and dark, saint and sinner.

Jude stared down at his fist, at his bruised and cracked knuckles and the blood seeping from the wounds – some of it his father's. There were two forces inside of him, too. The part that wanted to see his father suffer the same kind of pain he'd inflicted. And the part that wanted to do whatever it took to provide a remedy.

Clamping his eyes shut, Jude let his head roll back against the wall. His eyes burned, and he cleared his throat against the lump that threatened to choke him. Memories of pain and trauma, of fear and grief, of hope and defeat washed over him in waves, relentless and consuming.

"I know that I failed you. A long time ago, but… I'm trying, kid. All that's happened these last few months, and there's only one thing left in this world that I know for sure: I *can't* lose you, and I can't lose Henry."

Silence hovered in the hallway.

"But it's too late," said Jack. "Isn't it?"

Jude sniffed. "Why'd you do it?" he asked. "Why'd you drink yourself away? We *needed* you."

"Because the man you needed died with Lena. At least that's what I believed."

"But she's still alive. She came *back*."

"What does that change? She could've asked me for help, could've come to me. I would've been happy to knock Orion on his backside."

Jude sighed, forcing himself to his feet. "That's the problem," he said. "You and the others – the Highlands and the Moraleses – you've been so trapped in the past, in what happened *then*, that you've let it destroy what's happening now. Look at what it's cost you. What Orion did to you was *wrong*, but it happened. Nothing's going to change that. But what you've done? That's on you."

"Then tell me what to do, kid," said Jack, staring up at Jude from the floor. "Tell me what I gotta do to make it right. To *prove* to you that I can be the kind of father you boys deserve."

Jude's chest tightened. He studied his father, considering whether the man had really changed or whether it was just another empty promise.

"You can start by telling me what happened here."

Jack blinked, then nodded. He stood, dusting his hands off on his pants. "Some guys busted the place up," he said. "I got here while it was happening. I ran them off, chased them down the street, but they got into some car and peeled away."

"And Henry? The Monroes?"

"They weren't home," Jack said.

Relief flooded Jude's chest. He leaned back against the hallway wall and stared up at the ceiling, whispering a silent thank you.

"They showed up after I got back to the house," Jack continued. "I figured this had to be Orion's doing, so I told them to leave town for a little while."

Jude's heart sank. He wouldn't get the chance to say goodbye to Henry after all. "Where'd they go?"

"Family cabin down in California. Lake Tahoe, I think."

"Good," said Jude. "That's good."

"What would Orion want with Henry?" Jack mused.

Jude turned around, fighting tears as he thought of his little brother, of the last time he'd seen him. He ran his hands over his face, patting his cheeks to shake himself out of it. "To use him against me and my friends," he said, hands shoved into the pockets of his jacket. "He already has Lydia. God only knows what he plans to do with her, but we're going to get to her before he has the chance to carry out whatever plan he's got in that twisted mind of his."

"What then? You kids can't possibly hope to take on Orion by yourself."

Jude didn't answer. The choice had been made for them years ago. Even if unknowingly.

A hand fell over his shoulder, and Jude turned to meet his father's eyes.

"You're leaving," the man asked. "Aren't you?"

Jude nodded.

Jack sucked in a breath, his lip twitching as he stared at Jude.

"I'm sorry, kid," Jack whispered. "I'm sorry for what we did, what we put on you. I'm sorry I couldn't protect you from this, from *him*."

It wasn't much, but it was a start.

TWENTY-ONE
MARS

Thunder rumbled through the January sky. A light rain fell over Mammoth, the clouds veiling the moon and casting a shadow over the city. With Tommy at his side, Mars crept through the woods toward the fence that surrounded the perimeter of Orion's estate in the mountains to the southeast. The property offered a spectacular view of the city, though Mars could only make out the pinprick lights that dotted the distant darkness.

Tommy came to the fence first, crouching low to the ground as he peered between the wrought iron poles.

"Doesn't look like anyone's home," he said. "Driveway's empty. Lights are off."

Mars frowned. Why wouldn't Orion at least leave some of his lights on? Mars' parents did that whenever they left their house – that is, before it burned down. Criminals were less likely to bother with a house if its lights were on and they thought someone might be inside. Would Orion leave his place vulnerable like this?

"There could be an alarm system," Mars said.

"Probably is," Tommy agreed. "Which is why I brought these."

Tommy reached into his backpack and produced a giant pair of shears, the pale moonlight glinting off the curved teeth.

"What are those for?" Mars asked.

"We'll cut power to the whole place."

"And if someone's inside?"

"Why would they notice? All the lights are off anyway."

Mars sighed. "Okay, fine."

Tommy clapped a hand down on Mars' shoulder. "Hey, you okay?"

Mars blinked. *Was* he okay? Tommy had gone off to see his mom. Jude had gone off to see his brother. But Mars still hadn't had the chance to see his parents, to at least make sure they knew he was okay. There were times he felt like he was just a background character in someone else's story. For a moment, when Tommy and Lydia had been missing in Peru and Mars had taken it on himself to finish what they started while Jude and Maya languished in the grief, he'd felt like maybe he could take charge. Take control of his own life, forge his own destiny.

But here he was again, just along for the ride. How was he supposed to feel? The frustration was foreign and unwelcome, but it lingered in the back of his mind. How did he tell his friends – the people who meant more to him than anything in the world – that he was tired, that he wanted to go home, that he couldn't find it in himself to care about taking Orion down when they'd lost so much already and he was terrified of losing anything more? Lydia and Reid were gone, but Jude and Maya, Lucy and Immy – they were *right here*. How many more would they have to lose before they defeated Orion?

But Mars couldn't give up on Lydia either, and guilt pricked his conscience at even the thought of it. So he just shrugged and said, "About as well as can be expected, I guess."

Furrowing his brow, Tommy gave Mars' shoulder a gentle squeeze, then released. "You stay here. I'll go in alone. You can be my lookout."

"No way."

"Mars, it's risky. I know that. I'm not about to ask you to put yourself in danger for me when you don't have to."

Mars stood and crept toward the fence. He jammed his foot between two of the horizontal rails and hoisted himself up and over, careful of the pointed posts. He dropped to the ground on the other side, staring at Tommy through the fence. "You never had to ask."

That was the problem. Mars would do anything for the Jailbirds and he knew it. So, there was no point in arguing with himself. They were his friends, his family. He'd laid it all on the line for their quest – they all had – and he was going to see it through.

Tommy gave a nod, then hoisted himself up and over the fence to join Mars on the other side.

Keeping themselves low to the ground, they hurried across the lawn to the back of the house where the power box was mounted to the exterior wall. Tommy pulled out the shears again, set the teeth to the thick, gray tube that connected to the power box, and, with a deep breath, snapped the shears closed.

Mars held his breath as the line severed, waiting for alarms to start ringing and sirens to start flashing.

Nothing.

With an exhale, Mars' shoulders relaxed. "Front door or back?"

"Neither." Tommy pointed to a lattice that scaled the back of the house, leading to the first floor's roof line, which led to a balcony over the back patio.

Mars nodded and went first because this was his fight, too. And as much as he wished things had been different, that they'd never discovered that cellar beneath the lighthouse, he wasn't going to give up. So he scaled the lattice, avoiding the thorny creeping rose bush that tried to cut through his gloves. He shimmied to the right and dropped off the lattice onto the balcony.

Tommy came up behind him as Mars got a good look of the place from the new angle. At the far end of the balcony was a Jacuzzi, an arbor over it with curtains tied to the corner posts. Three French doors sat in a row. Mars moved to them one at a time, peering through the glass inside the house. The first led to a bedroom, the second to an open space that seemed to connect with the hall, and the third – the one nearest the Jacuzzi – seemed to lead to an indoor spa. But none of that was what caught Mars' attention.

"Tommy, look," he said, waving Tommy over. He peered through the glass, then pulled away, frowning.

"Why is everything in boxes?" Tommy asked the question at the front of Mars' mind.

"The guy's running for mayor, but he's packing like he's leaving Mammoth altogether," said Mars.

"Stand back," Tommy said. "Moment of truth – hopefully the alarm system isn't battery-operated."

"He'll know it was us either way," Mars replied.

"We'll be gone before he can do anything about it."

Mars thought to object, but he kept his mouth shut. More and more, Tommy was becoming reckless. And that was enough to set a fire in Mars' own heart. Reckless or not, Tommy's drive was the one thing that had kept them from languishing in their losses, propelling them forward, toward a win they all so desperately needed. There was a fire raging in Tommy Rhodes' eyes – one that would burn the world down to save the people he loved.

Tommy turned his back to the door, then in a single quick movement, he launched his elbow into the pane of glass nearest the handle. The glass shattered. Still no alarms. Using the handle of the shears, Tommy brushed the remaining fragments of glass loose from the frame and reached inside, twisting the lock. The door swung open with a creak and Tommy stepped inside. Mars hesitated, then followed.

The house was bathed in darkness. Mars stumbled his way through the room, the mud on his boots leaving tracks on the hardwood floors. He followed Tommy through the bedroom and out into the hall. They checked each room one by one – all empty.

"Any idea what we're looking for?" Mars whispered.

"Orion's office," Tommy replied.

They found Orion's office at the end of the hall, in a large room toward the front of the house on the second floor. A wall of windows opened onto another balcony, which overlooked Mammoth. If not for the rain, the view might have been spectacular.

Mars marveled at the size of Orion's place, which only reminded him of the house the Highlands had lost. He'd lived on the second floor of The Boathouse his entire life, there at the end of the pier. As a child, he'd fallen asleep countless nights to the sound of waves buffeting the shore. He'd sat at his desk by the window watching pelicans dive into the water and come up with a mouth full of cod while seabirds called out to one another in the pale Washington sky. He'd felt the way the pier rocked back and forth during windstorms. That restaurant – that house – had been home to him and his family. Now they were left with nothing but whatever insurance was willing to pay out. Until then, where would they live?

Mars winced as he realized he wouldn't be around to find out. His parents would be left behind to find a new place where they'd start a new life. Without him. All because of the decisions they'd made over a decade ago.

Gone were the summer sleepover nights spent sneaking downstairs into the restaurant pantry for snacks. Gone were the hours spent waiting tables when the restaurant was understaffed. Gone were the years spent doing homework in the dining room while his parents cleaned the restaurant at the end of the night. All these things he'd lost, and more.

Mars stopped at the door to Orion's office, closing his eyes as he called to mind memories of the restaurant, of the way it looked, the way it felt beneath his feet, the way it smelled at the start of the day – like pastries and coffee.

Everything was gone – and what remained, Mars was supposed to leave behind? Was there nothing else that could be done except to run away?

Mars shook himself out of his thoughts and stepped forward. It didn't matter now. The Jailbirds had been set on this course months ago. In a way, it was inevitable. They knew things now that they were never meant to know, and that made them dangerous. Until Orion fell, he would expend every resource to hunt them down, to silence them. And when the chance came, what would it take to make a giant like Orion Clark fall?

Tommy rifled through the boxes stacked around the perimeter of the office. Half the room had been packed away, but the desk remained. Mars slunk toward the desk and began searching the drawers. He pulled out file after file until one caught his attention.

"Tommy," said Mars.

Tommy straightened, his hands holding the flaps of the box he'd been searching. "What is it?"

"I don't know," Mars said. "It seems like flight plans, maybe? Shipping receipts?"

Mars looked up, glancing at the boxes, then at Tommy, then back at the file on the desk in front of him. "Tommy, do any of these boxes happen to have shipping labels?"

Tommy searched the outside of the boxes until he found one with a label. "Got one."

"Where's it being sent to?"

"Spokane."

"Tommy, these flight plans show that Orion's booked several flights in the last few weeks to Spokane, and these shipping receipts? For what looks like the past week, Orion's had trucks shipping things off to Spokane. Orion's uprooting his entire life and moving it east, away from Mammoth. So what if..."

"What if Lydia's in Spokane too," Tommy finished, his eyes widening at the realization. "Here, give me a pen and a piece of paper."

Mars found them in one of the drawers and tossed them to Tommy, who caught them.

"What are you doing?"

"Writing down the address. That's where she is, Mars. It has to be."

Mars nodded, but something didn't sit right with him. "Tommy, Orion's running for mayor."

"Yeah?" Tommy asked as he scribbled the address down.

"So why is he planning to move to Spokane?"

Tommy shoved the note in his pocket, then straightened. Mars waited for an answer as his friend stared off into the shadowed corner of the office.

"To protect himself," Tommy muttered. He turned toward Mars. "Whatever he's planning on doing next – whatever he intends to do to Lydia – he doesn't want anything that might incriminate him anywhere near Mammoth. This is ground zero, Mars. Something goes down, and everyone's going to be searching Mammoth; nobody's going to even think about any sort of connection between Orion and Spokane."

"Tommy, if he succeeds – if he moves his operation out of Mammoth – he'll take any evidence with him. All of *this*," Mars held up the file he'd found, "will be gone, and our chances of exonerating ourselves and exposing him go with it."

Tommy furrowed his brow, an uneasy expression passing over his face, but he didn't say anything.

"Tommy, if we leave…" Mars paused. "I don't know that there will ever be any coming back for us."

TWENTY-TWO
LYDIA

There was no one like Tommy Rhodes, the boy who owned the museum.

Eleven-year-old Lydia Clark laughed as she followed Tommy through the shadowed halls of the Mammoth Museum of Natural History. Somewhere in the museum, Tommy's father was hard at work. A scientist. A paleontologist. An explorer, like Tommy wanted to be.

As Tommy guided her from exhibit to exhibit, Lydia marveled at the boy she'd come to know so well over the years. Their families' work had brought them together, but it was something else that had forged their friendship. More than shared interest or forced proximity. It was late nights alone in museum exhibits and ice cream under the light of the moon through the glass ceiling. It was naming fossils together and laughing at each other. It was her hand in his as they ran through the museum, smiles on their faces.

There was nobody like Tommy Rhodes.

No one in the world.

Tommy stopped short, overshadowed by the triceratops mounted on a massive pedestal. He turned to Lydia, holding a finger to his lips. "Shhh," he said. "Don't wake the dinosaurs."

Lydia giggled.

"Here," said Tommy. "I want to show you something."

He led her to the far end of the museum where a mobile maintenance staircase sat in the corner, left behind by the night's janitorial staff. Tommy unclipped the chain, ignoring the sign that read "Museum Staff Only" and took the first step. He turned back to Lydia and extended his hand to her. "Careful, Princess," he said.

Lydia feigned annoyance and crossed her arms, but when Tommy cocked his eyebrow in the way that he did, causing his cheeks to dimple with the turn of his lips, her smile gave her away.

She took his hand, and he led her up the staircase. Lydia glanced down, a pit forming in her stomach as they drew higher — to the height of the second floor.

Tommy led her to the top of the staircase, where it reached the glass ceiling.

"What are you doing?" Lydia asked, a little nervous at how high up they were. In the distance, she saw Christopher Rhodes step out of his office. He glanced up at them, and she half expected the man to reprimand them. Instead he smiled and winked, then went on his way.

"You'll see," Tommy replied. He reached for a latch at the edge of the pane of glass above his head, unhooked it, then pushed the glass open. He found a bar somewhere and propped the windowpane open with it, then pulled himself out onto the roof. He turned around, crouched, and reached his hands through the opening toward Lydia.

"I don't know…" she said, acutely aware of how high up they were. A fall from this height… would hurt. At the very least.

"Come on," he urged. "Don'tcha trust me?"

Lydia bit her lip, then relented. She reached for Tommy, and he locked his hands around her arms, hoisting her off the staircase and through the window, out onto the roof of the museum.

She stood, moving away from the window as she took in her surroundings. From this perspective atop the Mammoth Museum of Natural History she could see the whole town. Not like she could from her house on the mountains, where the entire city was small in the distance and where the city's lights were like stars. No, from here the city was up close and personal. Every light through every window provided a painter's view of life inside. She could see into nearby homes where families gathered around the dinner table and coffee shops as the baristas shut down for the night. The clock tower across the green was silhouetted by the moon at its back, but its face was aglow with yellow light, illuminating the hands as they marked the hour.

"I've never been up here," Lydia said, her voice a whisper.

Tommy nudged her arm with his, smiling down at her. At only twelve, he was already nearly his father's height, and his face boasted a thin layer of adolescent stubble. He was growing up fast, becoming every bit the man his father was. Good and strong and so very kind.

"Thank you," she said. "For showing me things I've never noticed before."

Tommy smiled.

"Why does your father call you by your middle nam?" Lydia asked, turning her eyes from the city lights to study his face.

Tommy shrugged. "Dad always says that people are rarely their beginnings or their ends. In the middle's where you really get to know who they are." He paused and winked at her. "But I think he probably just likes the way it sounds."

Tommy broke away from her suddenly, backing up toward the glass ceiling that angled up before flattening out at the top. He climbed onto the glass, and Lydia nearly shouted for him to get down.

Laughing, Tommy walked out onto the middle of the glass ceiling. There was no fear in the eyes that fixed on her.

"What are you doing?" she asked, her heart leaping as she watched him turn in circles on the glass, a hundred-foot drop just beneath the glass.

"Walking on air, Princess," Tommy said as he held his arms out to his sides. Then he stretched out his hand out to her.

"What? Me? You're crazy."

"Come on. You've spent your entire life behind walls and fences. What's it hurt to get a look at life on the wild side, huh?"

Lydia sighed. She stepped toward him, took the hand he offered, and let him pull her up onto the glass. Her stomach lurched as she glanced down and saw the shadowed ground floor a hundred feet below. And then her eyes focused, and she saw only the reflection of the moon and the night sky in the glass. Images of Tommy and herself beneath her followed their movements.

"See that?" Tommy asked, leading her across the glass. "It's just like walking on air."

"What if the glass breaks?" Lydia asked.

Tommy tightened his hold on her hand. "It won't break."

"But what if it does?"

"Tell you what, Princess," Tommy said, inching closer to her, her hand still in his. He'd never come this close. His face hovered inches from hers. "If we fall, we'll fall together."

Lydia smiled, his breath hot on her face. She turned away, pulled her hand from his, and stared up at the moon.

"I like it up here," she said as she looked up.

"Me too," he said, and she felt his eyes on her.

Little by little, over the course of hours and days while she was alone, Lydia chipped away at the wall that housed the hidden door, pulling pieces of plaster away and dumping them in the toilet. And when the toilet was full, she flushed and prayed the mansion's old pipes would hold out long enough for her to get this door free.

Every time she heard footsteps out the door, she rushed to put the wallpaper back in place and shove the dresser in front of it. Each time she barely made it before the door opened.

This time, she sat on the end of the bed and tried to control her breathing as one of Orion's guards walked in with a tray of food. There was a rotation, and she'd seen this guard a few times before already. He was younger – her age maybe. Dark, curly hair. Dark skin. A rifle strapped over his shoulder and keys hooked to his belt.

Lydia eyed the keys as he set the food on the dresser. He glanced her way, and she flicked her eyes to him, smiled.

"What's your name?" she asked.

He gave her a look, said nothing, and turned toward the door.

"Wait," Lydia called.

The man stopped short, his hand on the knob.

"Please, just… wait."

He sighed and turned to face her, hand still on the doorknob.

Lydia seized the opportunity. "Why are you doing this?"

"I have my orders," said the guard.

"You realize my *uncle* is holding me here against my will, don't you?"

The man's eyes seemed to consider her. He didn't seem cold and callous like Graham or calculating like Orion. What could possibly have drawn this man to join up with a group like the Wild Hunt?

"Please, let me go," Lydia said, her desperation getting the better of her as she stood to face the man, willing him to see her as more than some object, some tool in Orion's arsenal, some pawn in whatever grand plan he was forming.

"I can't do that," said the man.

"Why not?"

"I have my orders."

"*What* orders?" Lydia wanted to scream, to kick some sense into this guard. "To keep me here until you put a bullet in my brain? And, what? Will you be the one to pull the trigger? Some twisted little initiation into your cult?"

The guard flinched. Lydia dared a step closer.

"Maybe you don't know who these people are, but I do. They're thieves and raiders, hunters and murderers – and Orion's the worst of them. Don't let them manipulate you into becoming something you're not."

The guard's lips thinned. He straightened. "Eat your food. I'll be back for the dishes in an hour."

He turned to leave.

"At least tell me your name," Lydia called after him, not sure what good his name would do in the end.

Glancing over his shoulder as the door closed, he said, "Cam."

The lock clicked into place, and Lydia was alone again. She turned her back to the door, eyes drifting to the silver platter of food on her dresser. Mashed potatoes, turkey, and a bread roll slathered in gravy. Her body floated toward the food, stomach growling despite the nausea.

A cry bubbled up inside of her as she lifted the tray, food and all, and threw it against the dresser mirror. The glass splintered and shattered and fell to the floor with the glass.

Tears blurred Lydia's vision. Her chest heaved. Frustration and hopelessness giving way to anger – pure anger.

Stepping over the food on the floor, she came to a stop in front of the panel of peeled wallpaper. With a grunt, she ground her teeth and dragged the dresser out of the way, leveling her glare at the secret door sealed by decades of plasterwork.

She got to work.

TWENTY-THREE
MAYA

"When do you think they'll be back?" Lucy asked.

Maya hovered over the kitchen sink, staring out the window into the yard. Shadows crept across the property, turning crooked branches into bony fingers and wisps of fog into formless specters. A shiver chased down Maya's spine as she shrugged off the feeling that something terrible was going to happen.

She set her mind to sorting through the supplies laid out on the kitchen counter, lit only by a single pillar candle out of view from any windows. She'd found a couple spare backpacks in the garage, so along with Tommy's they had three backpacks total waiting to be filled with food, medicine, water, and anything else they could scavenge. She'd retrieved the first aid kit from under the kitchen sink, and Immy was sorting through the bathrooms for any medicine that may have been left behind by the previous tenants. Lucy carried in an armful of toiletries and laid them out on the counter next to some fleece blankets Maya had found upstairs.

It was just the kind of project Maya needed to keep her mind off the fact that her boys were gone, off somewhere she couldn't look out for them. She'd spent nearly their entire lives getting in the middle of their arguments and making sure they didn't get into trouble; letting them go off without her went against the feeling in her gut that something terrible would happen because she wasn't there to stop it.

They were hers. They were the Jailbirds. If something happened to Tommy or Mars or Jude... Maya wasn't sure she would want to hang around to see what life without them was like.

"I don't know," she said finally, zipping up the first full backpack and sliding it onto the floor next to the island. "But as soon as they get back, we're out of here. Hopefully Tommy and Mars were able to find something useful in Orion's house."

Lucy shoved her hands into the pockets of her jeans and leaned her back against the side of the island. "You really love them," she said.

Maya sucked in a breath to hide the tremble in her throat and looked up at her. "They're all I've got left."

"And Reid? From what little I know of him, he's not exactly been a model friend."

"We all have our moments." Maya paused. "Reid is family. Lydia, too."

"And Immy?" asked Lucy. "Me?"

Maya met Lucy's stare, searching it. Immy was a Jailbird. She'd put her life on the line for them more than once. She'd earned her place in their lives. But Lucy? Maya wasn't sure what to make of the girl who'd decided almost on a whim to throw in her lot with them. Could Lucy Adler really be trusted?

But Maya wasn't sure she was willing to pay the price of suspicion and mistrust.

"Fourth rule of being a Jailbird," said Maya. "There's always room for one more."

Lucy nodded.

"Hey, can you see if there's any matches or lighters around here?" Maya asked, changing the subject.

"Sure thing." Lucy walked off to check the bathrooms while Maya took a minute to herself.

The dryer buzzed from the mudroom, so Maya set aside the supplies to go grab the clean clothes. She folded, sorting things into piles as best she could, then took everyone's clothes to their corners of the living room, where it had been turned into a squatter's paradise. Chairs had been pushed together, mattresses had been carried down from upstairs, the sofa had been shoved to the side of the room, and the blinds were turned up so nobody could see inside.

Maya put Tommy's clothes with his things, then carried Immy's over to her corner of the room. She crouched to set the clothes by Immy's small pile of belongings. Something caught her eye. A glint of metal under her backpack. Maya glanced over her shoulder, then reached for the object. Her breath caught in her throat as her fingers wrapped around the grip of a gun.

"What are you doing?"

Maya stood and spun to see Immy standing behind her, hands full of bottles of Tylenol and other over-the-counter meds she'd found.

"What is this?" Maya asked. "You have a gun?"

Immy set the medicine on her cot and took the gun from Maya. "I found it," she said.

"You *found* it? And what were you planning on doing with it?"

"What do you think?" said Immy. "People are hunting us down. We need to have something to defend ourselves with."

Maya's stomach turned. The Jailbirds were innocent of what they'd been accused of, but so were the people who'd fallen for Orion's deception. The idea of shooting one of the police officers to save themselves didn't sit right with her.

Then again, neither did letting an overzealous reward seeker stab Immy.

"Fine. Just… be careful," Maya said.

Immy nodded, and Maya grabbed the medicine off her cot and carried it into the kitchen. Truth was, Immy was probably the best person to have that gun, given she had the most experience thanks to her role with the Black Flag.

Her hands flat against the surface of the marble countertop, Maya hung her head and let out a slow breath. Eyes closed, she let her hair hang around her face. Movement out of the corner of her eye caught her attention, and she thought Lucy had already returned, but when she glanced up, there was no one there.

Frowning, Maya straightened, reaching behind her head to pull her hair back in a ponytail as she crossed the kitchen to the foyer. A shadow moved past the window outside, and Maya nearly yelped.

Someone was outside the house.

Run.

Maya steeled her nerves and waited there in the middle of the foyer, but the shadow didn't return. She approached the front door, peering through the peephole, but there was something blocking the glass. With a deep breath, Maya unlocked the door and pulled it open just enough to peek her head through the crack. Her eyes scanned the yard for any sign of the intruder, but whoever it was, they were long gone now. She started to close the door, but something to her left caught her eye. A piece of paper, taped to the door just over the peephole.

Yanking it free, Maya quickly locked the door behind her. She read the note in the shadow of the foyer.

I know you're here. I can help. Meet me at The Boathouse. — Mom

Maya's breath caught in her throat. She glanced up to see if either Lucy or Immy had seen, but they were still off gathering what they could. Maya crumpled the note into a ball and threw it in the kitchen trash.

Alicia Morales had figured out where the Jailbirds were staying. Somehow their presence at the rental property had alerted her parents.

So why weren't the cops already flooding the property?

Why was her mother offering to help?

Or was it someone pretending to be her mother just to draw them out?

There was only one way to find out. Only one way to make sure that the Jailbirds were safe.

Maya grabbed her coat and slipped out the front door into the night. She'd be back before the boys.

TWENTY-FOUR
PATTERSON

Sheriff Luke Patterson massaged his temples, doing his best to soothe the headache that plagued him as he sat in his office at the police station in the dark. Photographs and files stared back at him, mysteries begging to be solved, crimes pleading for resolution, victims demanding justice. He'd been at it for hours, unable to pull himself away except for another cup of coffee or a restroom break.

Luke's stomach growled, reminding him that he also hadn't eaten since… A glance at the wall clock that read 10PM told him it had been more than ten hours since he'd had a bite to eat.

Three bodies. Christopher Rhodes. Oliver Clark. Quincy Hodge. What did they have in common? Luke turned over the list of common denominators in his mind. The fugitives – the Rhodes boy, Jack Mayfield's son, Maya Morales, the Highland kid, and Bluecoat princess Lydia Clark herself. Victims or perpetrators?

Thomas Rhodes had no reason to hurt his father, but if Orion's claims were true – that Tommy had manipulated Lydia and taken advantage of her – he had motive to harm Oliver Clark. And the others – along for the ride? A twisted sense of familial loyalty despite the lack of blood bonds between the five of them?

That wasn't to mention the veritable smoking gun he'd been handed weeks ago – he was still waiting for forensics to come back on that one.

No, there was more in common than just the "Jailbirds" that half the city had already all but written off as would-be criminals since birth. Graham Robinson and Orion Clark were no less persons of interest as far as Luke was concerned.

But that wasn't what he was looking into tonight. No, the file in front of him was much older than all of that, and the tab on the manila folder bore a different name than those on Luke's current list.

Helena Clark.

A cold case nearly a decade old. A car explosion that had burned so hot there were no remains left but residual DNA recovered by the forensics team. The report said she had died, but as Luke mulled over the names and files that piled high on his desk, he wasn't so certain her death – or disappearance – wasn't connected to everything happening today.

Luke's stomach growled again. With a sigh, he closed the file and shoved away from his desk. He started to stand when a knock at his door interrupted him. Without looking, he waved the newcomer off, shrugging his jacket over his arms. "Come back tomorrow," he said. "I'm going home for the night."

"And here I thought justice never slept."

Luke stilled and looked to where Orion stood in the doorway, his long coat and the shadows at his back giving him a larger-than-life appearance. How was it that a man could control the way even the light hit him in order to afford himself the power of intimidation?

Shoving his arms through his jacket, Luke shook his head. "Justice may not sleep, but I do. You can come back tomorrow morning, Clark."

Orion held up a hand. "I'm only here for a friendly drink." He held out a bottle of whiskey. Unopened. Aged. Patterson considered himself something of a hobbyist when it came to liquor, which led him to wonder how Orion could possibly know the temptation of a bottle of Macallan 1926 would work on him. "Sit with me for a moment, Sheriff?"

Luke relented, gesturing toward one of the empty chairs. Orion sat, reaching into his briefcase to produce a pair of whiskey glasses. He set them on Luke's desk and began to pour while Luke returned to his own seat, watching the man with careful eyes.

Orion passed him a glass, and Luke took it, savoring the aroma of the whiskey as it wafted toward him. He swished it around, then took a sip and sat back in his chair. Taking the seat across from him, Orion held his own glass as he glanced around the room, eyes lingering noticeably on the chalkboard littered with pictures of suspects and victims. "Have you made a break in your case?" Orion asked.

"Getting there," Luke replied. If only the forensics results had come in. "What's a man like you doing out so late, Clark?"

Orion smiled, taking a whiff of his whiskey before drinking. "All the best conversations are had after dark, Sheriff." He nodded toward the board. "I can't help but notice that you've marked the Rhodes boy as both a suspect and a victim. I'd love to hear how you came to that conclusion, given he's currently responsible for the disappearance of my niece."

"It's my job to consider all possibilities, Clark."

Orion smirked. "Be careful with that open mind of yours, Sheriff. You never know what sort of dangerous ideas might slip inside."

Luke took another drink. "That sounds an awful lot like a threat."

"Consider it a friendly warning." Orion paused. "Sheriff, are you familiar with Greek mythology?" One of Orion's hands hung lazily over the arm of the chair while the other held the whiskey glass aloft. The way he sat in the chair across from Luke's desk – like a man who believed he owned both the chair and the room in which it had been placed – left an uneasy feeling in the pit of Luke's stomach.

Luke leaned back in his own chair, one hand turning the whiskey glass in circles on the surface of his desk. He leveled his gaze at Orion, the man around whom every dark and evil thing in this town seemed to orbit. "Should I be?"

"You might be surprised to know how much modern society owes to Greek mythology, at the influence they had upon the history of civilization." Orion lifted his glass to his lips and took a slow drink, his gaze never wavering. "I've always found one myth particularly fascinating. The ancient Greek poet Hesiod wrote of the origins and genealogies of the Greek gods – Ares the god of war, Poseidon, the god of the sea; Apollo, the god of truth and prophecy… they all have their root. Their genesis. In Hesiod's Theogony, Chaos is the very first being to exist, and is described as an empty, infinite, and formless abyss. The spirit that hovered over the face of the deep, if you will."

Luke bit his tongue at the comparison between Greek paganism and Christianity.

"On the one hand, Chaos is associated with the darker, deadlier aspects of the universe because it is parent to Nyx, who gives birth to War and Famine. On the other hand, however, Chaos is also the creator of the Island of Creation, where all of life began and where he birthed the gods themselves."

"Cute story," Luke said, leaning forward in his chair, elbows on the desk in front of him. A wave of nausea churned in his stomach, then passed. "What's it got to do with me, Clark?"

"It's the answer to the question you're not asking," said Orion.

"Oh?" Luke's throat caught, and he coughed. "What question's that?"

Orion stood as he downed the last of his whiskey. He reached into his pocket and removed a white handkerchief, reaching for the bottle of whiskey and returning its cork stopper.

Luke covered his mouth as he coughed again and struggled to catch his breath through the fit. His chest burned, and he watched Orion through the tears that gathered in his eyes. The man gathered both glasses of whiskey and returned them with the bottle to his briefcase. With the handkerchief, he wiped down the wooden arms of the chair, then the handle of the office door. Luke tried to speak, to call out for help as realization crashed in around him along with the shadows at the edges of his vision.

"You want to know why I did it, why in my ambition I have killed and stolen and incited this city to tear itself apart even while I promise peace and prosperity." Orion paused, and through the shadows that swallowed Luke's vision and stilled his body, he saw the man offer a parting smile. "Chaos," he said, "brings the formless abyss upon which I will build my kingdom, and I will rule it like a god."

TWENTY-FIVE
MAYA

A cold wind whistled across the water. Moonlight filtered through the clouds. At the end of the pier, the charred remains of The Boathouse rose like a funeral pyre. Maya ducked under the crime scene tape and followed the pier down to the old restaurant. She glanced over her shoulder to see if she'd been followed, but the city was fast asleep.

Maya came to the door of the restaurant – at least, where the door had been. The glass had shattered and the door had turned to ash. All that remained were the hinges twisted at odd angles on what was left of the door's frame. She crossed the threshold, careful to avoid anything that looked hazardous. It would be a long time before the pier was opened back up to the public. The city would have to make sure the fire hadn't damaged the structure of the pier itself.

Her gaze swept over the restaurant, memories superimposing

themselves over the ruins. The Jailbirds crowded into the corner booth to do homework after school. Summers spent working for Mars' parents – anything to avoid home for as long as possible. Learning the truth about their parents, about their secret history. Just before the building went up in flames.

The Boathouse was gone – maybe for good.

Maya inhaled, wincing at the acrid scent of burnt wood, a reminder of things lost.

"Hello?" she called into the shadows. A second later, someone emerged from where the kitchen used to be.

"Mom," Maya said past the panic in her throat.

She should run, should never have come here in the first place. Alicia Morales was a sought-after lawyer who'd never wanted Maya in the first place. What would stop her from turning in her own daughter?

Alicia studied her daughter, her hands shoved into the pockets of her long, fleece coat. The woman's big, curly hair was pulled back in a ponytail just like Maya's was now. Her face was drawn tight – worry? Fear? Anger? Regret? Maya tried to discern her mother's temperament, but she was unpredictable. A wild horse that refused to be broken.

The woman stepped forward, and Maya took a step back. Her mother held up her hands. "Don't go," she said. "I'm glad you came."

"I'm not really sure why I did," said Maya.

Alicia blinked, lowering her hands. "I'm your mother, Maya."

"You never wanted to be," replied Maya, her voice trembling. "You never wanted me, so congratulations. You don't get to have me anymore. You don't *get* to play mother-daughter anymore."

Alicia's eyes glistened in the moonlight. "Then why'd you

come?"

Clenching her jaw, Maya shook her head and shrugged. "I don't know."

All Maya had ever wanted was to look at her mother and see love in her eyes, to know that she was wanted, cared for. Maya had wasted so many years vying for the affection of a woman who had no love to give. So why had she come?

"Maybe there's a part of me that's still desperate for you to love me," Maya said, blinking back tears. "But that's not going to happen, so maybe… maybe it's time for me to let go of you."

Alicia straightened. Maya thought she might have seen a quiver of her lip, but whatever emotion had tried to come forward, the woman was quick to hide it. "You're right, Maya," she said. "You weren't planned, and I probably wasn't meant to be a mother. But – maternal instinct or no – I'm not going to sit by and watch you throw your life away."

"Why do you care?"

"Because I won't let you become *me*!"

Maya winced. "What are you talking about?"

"Maya, I *was* you. Before Orion, before Peru, I was just like you. A *Jailbird* in over her head, and it cost me *everything*."

"You're wrong," Maya said, forcing anger to overtake her sorrow. "I'm nothing like you."

"Why do you think I pushed you so hard?" her mother continued. "Why do you think I hated that you'd become so involved with the Jailbirds? All I wanted was to make sure you had the kind of life that I worked so hard to build, so that you wouldn't have to pay the prices that I've paid to get here, but you fought me at *every turn*."

"So that's it?" A tear rolled down Maya's cheek. She swiped it away with the back of her hand. "All I am to you is a reminder of the consequences of your actions."

"You were never the price I paid, Maya," her mother said. "You were the prize I didn't deserve."

"Don't do that," Maya snapped. "You don't get to *do that*. You don't get to stand there and pretend I mean something to you when you've spent my *entire life* making sure I felt like *nothing*."

Alicia pursed her lips, inhaled. "You're right. I haven't earned a relationship with you. I'm sorry for that." A pause, then she lifted her chin. "There are still things you don't know about me, about my involvement with Orion. But this…"

She held out a hand. There was something there.

"This is the rest of the story. And the only thing that can stop Orion Clark from finishing what he started all those years ago."

Maya stepped over the rubble, reaching for the object in her mother's hand. She stared at it in the moonlight – a flash drive.

"I *do* love you, Maya," Alicia said. "In my own, awful way. And I'm sorry I couldn't love you in the way that you needed."

Maya blinked back tears, and she saw tears in her mother's eyes too. She wanted to run to her mother, to let this moment erase the years of cruelty and animosity, but histories like theirs couldn't be rewritten in a moment. It would take time – time they didn't have.

"What's on it?" Maya asked, holding up the flash drive.

An explosion pierced the night air, and Maya jumped. She spun around, searching the darkness for a fire. She saw movement at the end of the pier.

"We need to go," Maya said. She spun back to face her mother. The woman's face had gone pale. She raised a hand to her stomach, and Maya's eyes fell. A ring of red expanded in the middle of her mother's stomach.

"Mom?" Maya choked.

The woman collapsed.

Maya screamed and dove for her mother. She pressed her hand to the bullet hole in her stomach. So much blood. Everywhere. Pooling down her pants and onto the ground beneath her mother's body.

"Mom! Wake up, Mom," Maya said, shaking her mother. Alicia's eyes stared straight up at the sky, unblinking.

Maya sobbed. "No no no. Don't die. *Don't die!*"

Something grabbed Maya from behind. Hands hooked under her arms. She tried to wrench free and started to scream for help, but someone clamped a cloth over her face.

Her world darkened as her body fell limp.

TWENTY-SIX
JACK

Jack Mayfield couldn't escape his guilt, no matter how many years he'd spent drowning it at the bottom of a bottle, or scaring it off at the end of his fists.

Sitting at the bar, Jack turned the full glass of beer in circles in front of him. The TV over the bar played some news station, but the only voices Jack heard came from someplace deep inside. They'd followed him for years, taunting, accusing, tempting, shaming. Every time, Jack tried to set things right. Every time, he failed. Again and again, and right back to the bottle he went.

He wasn't stupid. He knew the booze wasn't going to fix anything, but it worked wonders to keep the voices quiet and the pain at bay. At least, it used to. The more he drank, the less it seemed to do the job. And now he was left with the consequences of his decisions; the losses he'd suffered, deservedly.

Henry was better off without him.

Jude was better off without him.

Lena was right to run away without him.

Without him…

There was nothing that could set Jack Mayfield's world right again. Nothing temporary anyway. No bandage to staunch his bleeding heart. No drug to numb the ache in his soul. No prayer to wash the guilt away.

He'd been a good father. Once. But that had been a long time ago.

Look at me now…

Jack lifted the glass, his eyes watching the bubbles rise to the surface of the gold liquid. The smell as familiar to him as a lover's perfume. He craved the warmth it would bring, the memories it would bury.

But his stomach turned at the thought of taking even one more drink.

As a kid, he'd hated alcohol. If seventeen-year-old Jack could see the man he'd become, he'd be disgusted. He'd been a lot like Jude in that way. Jack could see the judgment in his son's eyes when he'd found him at the Monroe place. There was a time in Jack's life where he never would've imagined taking a drink, but the more he did it the easier it became. And there was a time in his life where he never would've imagined he'd lay a hand on his own son, but then it happened once, then twice, and then again.

His vice had cost him everything that had ever mattered, and now Jude was going to leave for good. All because Jack, Theo, and the others couldn't cast out their own demons.

Jack had vowed he'd never drink again, but here he was.

As a dog returns to its vomit…

Licking his lips, Jack brought the glass up a little higher. He could smell it, practically taste it. In seconds, everything he hated about himself would fade into the background. White noise. Nothing would matter and nothing would hurt.

But he stopped.

And instead of drinking, he sat the glass down on the bar and stood, the stool scraping across the wooden floor as he backed away from the bar.

"You okay, Mayfield?" Stan, the bartender, asked.

No, Jack thought, *but I want to be. More than I want anything right now.*

Jack started to turn, but his ears finally tuned into the TV above the bar, and he stopped in his tracks.

"Breaking news," said the newscaster. "We've just heard that Sheriff Luke Patterson has been found dead in his office at Mammoth Police Department."

A chill coursed down Jack's spine as silence fell over the bar, every head turning toward the TV.

"Deputy Sheriff Frank Boone, has reported that while an investigation is still underway, the late sheriff seems to have died of apparent poisoning. Officials have not named any suspects at this time, though an anonymous source on the inside has informed us here at the station that investigators have reason to believe the Jailbird fugitives – also responsible for the recent murders of one Oliver Clark and Quincy Hodge – are allegedly involved in the slaying of Luke Patterson due to his involvement in the ongoing investigation."

"No," Jack breathed.

An explosion rocked the bar, and Jack ducked, spinning on his heel toward the windows. A fire billowed into the night sky as a group of people in black ski masks raced away from the scene. Jack bolted for the door just as one of them hurled a burning bottle through the bar window. The glass shattered, and the bar erupted into flames as patrons scrambled for the door.

Sirens wailed in the distance as Jack skidded out onto the sidewalk, shielding his face from the fire.

He glanced around to see dozens of individual fires burning along the street.

The sheriff had been murdered.

They thought his boy was to blame.

Mammoth was going to eat itself alive.

Episode Three

THOSE WE LEAVE BEHIND

"She wanted only to lay down on the bed behind her, close her eyes and wake up in the heart of Hollow Hill Lighthouse with Tommy by her side, to unwind time to when they were kids running wild inside the museum."

TWENTY-SEVEN

JUDE

Jude walked into the house and nearly tripped over the baggage piled by the front door. "Hello?" he called, leaning against the wall as he found his footing. Early morning light filtered through the living room windows, brilliant rays of light cutting through the shadows of the foyer at an angle.

"In here," Tommy said, his voice carrying from the living room.

Jude turned left to find the Jailbirds huddled in the middle of the room around the coffee table.

"Find any leads?" asked Jude as he slipped his jacket off and tossed it over the back of a chair before falling into it and kicking his feet up on the coffee table. He glanced around the room, frowned. "Where's Maya?"

Tommy and Immy exchanged a glance across the coffee table.

"We were hoping you knew," he said.

"Knew what? I just got back."

"So did we," said Mars.

Jude shook his head, leaning forward on his knees. "Okay, *where's Maya?*"

"We don't know," Lucy said, her brow furrowed. "The three of us girls were here pulling stuff together, then she just disappeared."

"Disappeared?" Jude bolted upright. "What do you mean?"

"She pulled a Houdini," Mars said. "Poof. Vanished."

Lucy elbowed him in the ribs. He yelped, rubbing his side.

Jude stood, scanning the room, but it wasn't like she was hiding behind the couch, waiting to pop up and say, "Gotcha!"

He went through the house room by room, checking the upstairs bedrooms, the bathrooms, the closets.

"We've looked everywhere," Tommy said as he followed Jude back down the stairs.

"Maybe she went to go say goodbye to her parents," Lucy offered.

Jude shook his head. "No, her parents have practically disowned her. Besides, she wouldn't leave without telling someone where she was going."

Without telling me.

Jude leaned against the counter, hanging his head between his arms as he forced himself to breathe slowly through his nose. His blond hair fell in his face, and he noticed something on the floor near the trash can. Jude shoved away from the counter and crouched to retrieve the piece of crumpled paper that had just barely missed the can.

He squinted as he read.

His heart sank. "Read this."

Tommy took the note, frowning. "It's from her parents," he said.

"They know we're here," Mars whispered. He ran his fingers through his short, curly hair, backing away as he forced air through his lips. "We need to go. They've probably already called the cops on us."

"But the note's asking Maya to meet at the restaurant," Tommy said.

"Yeah, so they can get their *daughter* out of the way while the cops descend on this place. I'm telling you guys – this isn't good."

Tommy turned to Jude. "He's right. It could be a trap. It's not safe to stay here any longer."

"So we move now," Jude said. "We don't wait. I'll go find Maya, you guys go get Reid, then we leave to find Lydia."

Tommy nodded. "I'll go with you." He turned to Mars. "You three go get Reid. We'll meet back here, then get outta Dodge."

Jude was already heading for the door even before Tommy had finished talking.

TWENTY-EIGHT
MARS

"This is a terrible idea," fifteen-year-old Mars hissed. The whir of the garage door as it opened out into the cold drowned out his voice, but it wouldn't have mattered anyway. The Jailbirds weren't likely to break their risk-taking streak just because Mars was a little nervous about taking the Morales' Lamborghini out for a spin.

"The Lambo will be tucked back into the garage safe and sound before my parents ever find out," said Maya as she popped the driver's side door open. "Besides, I'm getting my license in, like, a month anyway."

Mars narrowed his eyes at Jude on the other side of the vehicle. "You're starting to sound an awful lot like Jude."

"Well, Jude's right."

Jude smirked and offered Mars a two-fingered salute before sliding into the passenger seat beside Maya. "It happens a lot," he said. "Don't act so surprised, Mars."

Tommy patted the hood of the car. "Get in, Mars. It'll be fine."

With a sigh, Mars yanked the door open and slid into the back seat beside Tommy. "You know, I expect better from you."

He shrugged. "Maya's got her permit, and Jude and I are both licensed."

"Yeah, but you think that'd stop her parents from freaking out?"

The Lamborghini roared to life. Maya glanced at Mars in the rearview mirror as she adjusted it. "If they'd ever make the time to help me practice driving, I wouldn't have to teach myself. Every time I ask, they're 'too busy.'"

Mars frowned, swallowing any further argument for Maya's sake. His father had started teaching him how to drive as soon as he turned fifteen, but Maya wasn't blessed with a father like Theodore Highland. There were things in her life that she'd had to figure out on her own or with the Jailbirds' help.

"Although…" said Tommy. "Maybe we should've had you practice on my dad's Jeep."

"No, it's fine. I can do this."

Maya shifted the car into gear and barely pressed the gas before it shot out of the garage and into the driveway. She slammed on the brakes, narrowly avoiding the mailbox at the end of the driveway while Mars' stomach did somersaults, his fingers clutching the car door.

Tightening her grip on the steering wheel, she grinned over at Jude. "See? Fine."

Jude swallowed, nodded. "Alright, May. Nice and slowly."

Letting out a breath, Maya slowly released the brake and the car began to inch forward. She let out a nervous laugh.

Something darted out in front of the car, and Maya slammed on the brakes again. Her father stared back at her, anger written all over his features.

"Maya Morales, get out of the car!" he shouted.

Sheepishly, she shifted the car into park and turned off the engine. All four doors opened as the Jailbirds hesitantly slid from the vehicle.

Oscar Morales surged forward, seizing Maya by the shoulders. "Are you insane, Maya? What on Earth was going through your mind?"

"I– I–" Maya stuttered, gaping at her father.

Mars took a step forward, glancing at Maya, then back at her father. "It was my idea, sir," he said. "She wanted to practice for her driver's test, and so I suggested she use your car."

"Mars, don't," said Maya.

"It's okay, Maya." He smiled at her. To her father, "I take full responsibility."

Oscar glowered down at Mars, then looked back to his daughter. "Get inside."

"But Dad—"

"Maya!"

Her face beet red, Maya turned around and offered Mars a look of apology before heading toward the house. When she was out of earshot, Oscar turned to the three remaining Jailbirds. "Get off my property. You're not welcome here anymore."

"Sir, we were just trying to help," said Jude.

Oscar opened the passenger door, glancing at the boys, a scowl permanently fixed on his face. "You want to help my daughter? Stay away from her."

He slid into the car and turned the key. The Jailbirds watched as he reversed it back into the garage, closing the door behind him.

Mars' shoulders sagged as he stared up at the house and found Maya peering through the living room window at them. He smiled, waved, but it didn't seem to cheer her up any.

"We should go," said Tommy as he retrieved his bike from where he'd dropped it in the front yard. Mars grabbed his, straddling the seat as he turned his back on the house.

"Why'd you do that?" Jude asked. "Why'd you take the hit?"

Mars shrugged, feet on the pedals as the boys rolled forward onto the road. 'Maya's taken enough hits already. Figured I'd spare her at least one. We're Jailbirds — it's what we do."

Mars waited with Immy in the woods outside the police station while Lucy headed inside. Immy paced back and forth, her feet shuffling through the grass wet from morning rain.

"Careful," Mars warned. "You're gonna dig yourself a hole to China."

Immy glanced his way but didn't say anything.

Mars watched her from where he sat at the base of a tree, his back to the police station. He let his head fall back against the bark, hands resting on his knees.

Sirens wailed in the distance. Something was happening in the city. On their way down from the Wall, Mars had seen the smoke in at least three different locations. Fires. Whatever was going on, it was keeping law enforcement busy enough that they didn't notice them loitering right outside the police station. But the distraction only came as some small relief; his parents were out there. Were they okay? And if they were, how was Mars supposed to say goodbye to them?

He understood his friends. Neither Tommy nor Jude had anyone left to hold onto. Maya's parents had made their decision a long time ago, pushing her away their entire lives. But Mars' parents? They'd lied, yes, but they weren't evil. Mars was angry with them, but he didn't hate them, and he wasn't sure he wanted to leave them.

The way things were happening… did he have any choice in the matter? He tried to shove it out of his mind. They'd all made sacrifices to get here; maybe this was his. He'd see his parents again someday, but for now, he needed to give his whole heart to the Jailbirds, to making sure they were safe and taking down Orion.

Of all people, his parents had to understand that. They knew firsthand the damage it did for them not to be there for their friends. And they knew firsthand the danger in letting Orion succeed.

"How's the wound?" Mars asked.

"It hurts."

"No kidding."

Immy cocked an eyebrow at him.

Mars shrugged. "You should've stayed in bed longer. It may have been a flesh wound, but that doesn't mean you don't have core muscles that need to heal themselves."

"When things calm down enough, I'll rest."

"*If.*"

Immy frowned. She glanced at Mars, then away through the woods toward the city. "I'll be back," she said and started off toward the city.

Mars scrambled to his feet. "What? Where are you going?"

"I have something to take care of," she said. "I'll meet you guys back at the house."

"What could you possibly have to take care of?"

But she was already halfway across the parking lot.

Mars glared at her back, then picked up a piece of bark and chucked it across the forest floor in frustration. Everyone was off doing something else. He couldn't remember the last time they'd all been together, where things had felt normal. Certainly not now, with Lydia missing and Reid in jail, Tommy going off to see his mom and Jude visiting his brother.

And me being left behind alone to wait and hope and wonder.

Mars slid against a different tree, positioned now so that he could see the police station through the branches. Several minutes later, Lucy stepped through the door and bounded across the parking lot toward where he waited.

"He's not here," she said, worry dancing in her eyes.

Mars bolted upright. "What? Where is he?"

"They wouldn't tell me anything except that he'd been injured, so I'm assuming they took him to the hospital."

Mars held his hands behind his head, closing his eyes as he struggled to assess the situation. How bad were Reid's injuries? If they could get to him at the hospital, would he even be able to move? His hospital room was probably guarded, and he was likely cuffed to the bed, but a guard was easier to bypass than a jail cell.

"Okay," said Mars as he dropped his hands to his sides. "We can work with this. Come on."

"Where are we going?" Lucy asked as she followed him.

"Hopefully to rescue Reid."

TWENTY-NINE
LYDIA

Days had passed.

Maybe weeks.

Lydia stared straight ahead at the secret door, the wallpaper hanging limp to the side, plaster dust littering the floor where the dresser belonged. Lydia's fingers were rubbed raw from prying at the plaster and scraping it from the seam around the door. She'd eventually switched to using a shard of glass from the mirror she'd shattered, which she'd hidden from the guards when they'd come to clean the rest of the glass up, and now the door was finally open to a dark passageway in the walls.

She hesitated. If she left now, how would Tommy find her? Did he even know where to look? Lydia certainly had no idea where Orion had brought her. What if the worst had already happened? What if he *couldn't* look for her, because he'd been arrested? Or…

No…

No.

Lydia forced a step forward, bracing against the door's frame, feeling the warmth of the morning light through the window along the skin of her left arm. It had been hours since anyone had come to check on her. Cam had brought breakfast, and then hours later he'd taken the untouched tray away. He'd pretended not to notice the mess she'd made of the room – the broken glass and the holes in the wall and the lamp strewn on the floor. Why did they bother feeding her? He had to know Orion's plan for her was not long-term.

Tears gathered under Lydia's eyes. Tears for the father she had lost and for the uncle who had betrayed her. Tears for her brother who had suffered so long in silence. Tears for her husband who would be going crazy trying to find her. Tears for her friends whose lives had been turned upside down. She cried until it seemed she had nothing left to shed. She wanted only to lie down on the bed behind her, close her eyes and wake up in the heart of Hollow Hill Lighthouse with Tommy by her side, to unwind time to when they were kids running wild inside the museum.

But that wouldn't change the truth; it wouldn't undo the lives their parents had led in secret.

The Clark family would still have taken countless lives.

The Rhodes family would have continued to strive for justice.

The Morales family would have carried on as if none of it had happened.

The Highland family would still have ignored their friends' cries for help.

Nothing Lydia or the others did could change what their parents had already done. So much of their stories had already been written. The choices their parents had made all those years ago had paved the path their children would one day walk. Lydia, Tommy, Jude, Maya, Mars – there was no escaping the legacies that had been thrust upon them. They couldn't alter their pasts, but maybe they could influence their futures.

But first, Lydia had to step through the door and follow wherever it led, and hoping that it would lead to an escape.

Lydia sucked in a deep breath and did just that.

Shadows swallowed her. She tried not to think about the spiders on the walls or the cobwebs in the corners or the rats that surely scurried around her feet as she slunk through the shadows. The passageway seemed to go on forever. Did Orion know these were here, or did they precede him?

Lydia prayed he was oblivious to them, but they'd find out sooner or later that she'd escaped. The next time they brought a meal, they'd see she'd found the hidden door.

She had to move quickly.

The sound of voices carried to Lydia, muffled by the walls around her. She kept walking as the voices grew louder until she stopped behind a section of wall that she was sure led to whatever room the voices had come from.

Pressing her ear to the musty slats, Lydia struggled to listen.

"As soon as I give the order, I expect you to carry it out without delay," said one man.

Orion.

"Of course, sir."

Lydia couldn't make out the voice. One of Orion's Hunters maybe?

"Are you certain this is what you want, Orion?" came a woman's voice. "She is your niece after all."

"And Oliver was my brother," said Orion. "I will do what I must to see this treasure found. Nothing – *no one* – will be allowed to stand in my way."

"And you're not at all worried that the bodies piling up around you will draw suspicion on you? Patterson was beginning to catch on. You've made too much noise, Orion."

"The *sheriff* has been dealt with." Orion paused. "As soon as I'm elected mayor, we'll install those loyal to us to ensure that suspicion does not fall on me."

The sound of rhythmic tapping slipped through the slats in the walls. Someone paced inside that room. The woman maybe? Why was her voice so familiar?

"And if you lose the election?" asked the woman.

"There are contingencies in place. I've already moved the bulk of my operation here, and if the worst should happen, I have a private jet on standby to carry me wherever I need to go."

"You're risking an awful lot for this quest, Orion," she said. "All of the Hunt's resources have gone into making sure you succeed, but they will only follow you so far. How many Hunters have been lost?"

"Enough!" A shadow moved on the other side of the wall. Orion had stood up. "I will not allow you to call into question everything that I have worked to accomplish."

"There's a reason you asked that I join you, Orion." The woman again. "You *needed* someone to question you, to make sure that you weren't taking too big a risk, that you weren't putting yourself or the rest of us in jeopardy. You know I have already paid a steep price for our success." She paused. "I only question you now because what you are about to do… there will be no going back."

Orion's shadow stilled. "There was never any going back for me. You know that."

"If you are certain…"

"I am."

"Alright. Then you give the order, and we will take care of the girl."

Lydia's heart lurched. Her hands trembled.

"Good. Make it public. I want the whole *city* to see what Jailbirds do to Bluecoats when they get too close." Orion paused. "The people of Mammoth will be desperate to make me mayor once Lydia Clark is made a martyr."

THIRTY

GRAHAM

Graham's eyes lingered over Maya Morales' unconscious body, folded into the trunk of the sedan. Behind him, the burned remains of the restaurant contained her mother's body. He'd have to deal with that later.

When he'd followed the woman, Graham hadn't expected to find Alicia Morales betraying Orion to the Jailbirds. There had been no time to think, to call Orion for the green light. He had to act, to make sure that the work they were doing succeeded.

That's why he'd pulled the trigger on the woman.

And that's why he would do this.

Graham closed the trunk and moved to the front of the car. He opened the driver's side door and slid into the seat, shifting the car into neutral. Climbing out, he slammed the door behind him and moved to the back of the car. Hands on the trunk, he pushed.

It lurched forward slightly and began to move across the pier until the momentum was enough to carry it without Graham's help.

Backing away, Graham watched it for a moment as it headed for the end of the pier, toward the open ocean. Behind him, nearby fires cast the morning sky in an orange glow. Mammoth was at war with itself. So what was one more Jailbird to die in the crossfire?

THIRTY-ONE
JUDE

The sun rose over Mammoth. An orange haze veiled the normally pale gray clouds. The scent of smoke permeated the air, carried on the wind. As Jude and Tommy made their way down the Wall, toward the city, they quickly realized why — fires had popped up all over Mammoth. The wail of fire engine sirens echoed through the chill air in all directions.

Tommy stopped in his tracks, squinting out over the city. "Riots," he whispered. "Doubt anyone will be paying any attention to us right now, but still…"

In silence, they continued toward the pier, using alleys and back roads to make their way through Mammoth while avoiding the crowds of both peaceful protestors and rioters that had amassed seemingly on every other city block.

Jude glanced over at his best friend. How had things gotten to this point? Just months ago they'd discovered the cellar beneath the lighthouse and the clues left behind by Tommy's father. Now they were fugitives. The city they loved had turned against them, and now it was falling apart at the seams. They'd lost everything.

And gained so much more.

Jude's heart weighed heavy, beating erratically as he thought of Maya. Since that day on the train, the moment they'd shared, he hadn't slowed down enough to really consider what they were. What they were becoming. And now the doubts began to creep in. What if Maya regretted the kiss? What if she wanted things to go back to the way they were? What if she was still angry at him for almost leaving to join the Navy? What if Jude wasn't good enough for her?

What if I end up like my father?

"She's probably fine," Tommy reassured him, his voice gently piercing through the cyclone of thoughts swirling around in Jude's mind. He'd said the same thing repeatedly since they left the house. Maybe more for himself than for Jude.

"I think I love her," Jude said before he could stop himself.

Tommy stopped in the middle of the alleyway they'd found themselves in. The building to their right cast them in a long shadow. A police car roared past the alley, sirens blaring.

"You love her?" Tommy repeated.

Jude nodded.

"Did you tell her that?"

"Yes. Kind of… but…"

Tommy angled his head toward Jude, cocking an eyebrow. "But you're not sure how you feel about it."

"I know how I feel," Jude said.

"Do you remember when it was just me and you, before Mars and Maya came along?"

"Yeah," said Jude, thinking back to their childhood.

"Maya's always been, well, Maya." Tommy chuckled. "Fierce, independent, *bossy*. But no one – not Mars, not me – was ever able to get you to come out of your shell like Maya did. There's something about her that's always made you… *you*. I guess what I'm trying to say is you don't have to worry about how you feel or how she feels because whatever it is between the two of you, it's real. And it has been for a long time."

"We haven't even had the time to really talk about it. And I'm just… I don't know how to do this, I guess. I don't know how to be the kind of person she deserves."

Tommy stopped in his tracks, turning to face Jude. "Don't go there. You're the best of us, Jude. Everything you've ever gained in life, you've had to fight for. You've never backed down before, so why start now?" Tommy's eyes grew distant as he stared past Jude. "I don't know much, but I know this. If you love her, you fight for her and you don't give an inch." The words caught on his tongue, maybe as much for him as they were for Jude.

"I can't lose her, man."

"You're *not* going to lose her," Tommy said. "Just like I'm not going to lose Lydia. We're going to find Maya and Lydia, and we're going to get Reid back. We'll be a family again. *All* of us."

Nodding, Jude sniffed and blinked back the tears that threatened to spill from his eyes.

They left the alley behind as the street turned toward the coast. The eyes of the city seemed to be focused squarely on the fires burning in the distance. Jude prayed no one was seriously hurt. He hated Orion for what he'd turned Mammoth into, for what he'd turned the Jailbirds into.

They moved quickly along the street, hurrying toward the pier. Jude could make out the wreckage of The Boathouse in the distance, no more than a black dot on the orange-gray horizon. They came to the entrance of the pier, ducking under the police tape. Jude glanced over his shoulder – not a car in sight. Whatever was happening elsewhere in the city, no one had any reason to keep an eye on the month-old crime scene.

Moving quickly down the pier, they came to The Boathouse.

"May!" Jude called. He started toward the door – where the door used to be – and stopped short when he saw a head pop up from the ruins.

He almost called Maya's name again until he realized it was someone else.

"Graham," Jude growled. He started to bolt toward the door, but Tommy's arm flung across Jude's chest, stopping him.

He glanced over to see Tommy's eyes go wide. Jude turned back to Graham to see him hovering over a body. Caramel skin. Chocolate hair.

Something snapped inside Jude's mind, and he burst forward in a flash of adrenaline and rage.

Graham bolted as soon as Jude crossed the threshold. He clambered out a shattered side window, turning back only to fire off a shot. Jude ducked behind a wall while Tommy took cover across the room behind a blackened dining table.

"Forget him!" Tommy shouted.

Jude was already scrambling for Maya's body in the middle of the charred floor.

Eyes burning, heart pounding, chest tightening, he fell to his knees beside her. Grabbed her shoulders and pulled her onto her back.

It wasn't Maya.

It wasn't Maya.

Jude fell back, his hands soaked in blood, his jeans stained red. His entire body trembled as he stared down at the body of Alicia Morales. A strangled gasp escaped his lips like a groan as Tommy checked Maya's mother's pulse.

He glanced at Jude. Shook his head.

Dead.

Jude stood, nearly fell, straightened.

Where was Maya?

Movement to his right caught his eye. At the end of the pier, a beige sedan made its way slowly toward the water.

"Oh, *God...*" Jude cried.

He broke into a run, Tommy shouting after him.

Jude's feet pounded the wood of the pier as he raced toward the car. Tears stung his eyes. His mind raced. Bloodied hands pulled his jacket free and threw it to the ground. The wind tugged at his hair as he pumped his legs as fast as they would go.

The front of the car broke through the railing at the end of the pier with a sickening splinter, and seconds later the car pitched forward and fell into the water.

Jude cried out, propelling himself forward, faster than he thought possible. Sweat trickled into his eyes. His heart banged like a drum inside his chest. He came to the end of the pier and launched himself over the edge, throwing himself like a stone toward the water as he sucked in an impossibly deep breath.

He broke the surface, the water crashing in around him. The world fell silent. His eyes searched the dark, grey-green water until he found a white license plate reflecting up at him. The car was angled straight toward the ocean bed.

Swimming downward, Jude prayed with everything he had that his lungs would hold just long enough to get to her.

The car sank further, deeper, and Jude swam after it. He came to the trunk, grabbing onto the wheel well to pull himself forward to the driver's side. Pressing his face against the glass of the windows, he could see the seats were empty. Moving to the back, they were empty too.

Had he been mistaken?

The trunk.

Jude turned around and swam back toward the trunk just as the car settled on the silty bottom of the ocean, the impact jarring Jude's bones. He swam back just enough for the car to come to a rest along the stone and sand. Lurching forward, he tried to open the trunk, but it was jammed. The pressure too much.

There's still air inside.

But time was running out.

Jude planted his feet on the bumper, latched his fingers onto the trunk's handle and pushed with his legs as he pulled with his arms. His muscles protested as he struggled to lift against hundreds of pounds of pressure. He screamed into the water, air escaping in waves of bubbles.

Finally, the trunk opened just enough for the pressure to break, and it flew open the rest of the way. Inside, Maya lay still. Eyes closed. Unmoving.

Jude reached his arms under hers and pulled her from the trunk, launching himself upward. He swam toward the surface, toward the light that shimmered through the water overhead. His legs didn't seem strong enough. His arms couldn't push him fast enough.

His lungs burned.

The frigid water fought against him with every kick.

His mind focused on how still Maya was.

She couldn't be dead.

Not like this.

Jude broke the surface, gasping for air. He tugged Maya's body, holding her head above the water.

Tommy was already there, reaching for them from the ladder at the end of the pier. Jude lifted Maya as high as he could, and Tommy looped his arm around her chest and helped to pull her up. Jude climbed after them.

Tommy laid Maya out on the pier, and Jude shoved between them. An ear to her lips. No sound. Her chest completely still.

Jude pressed his palms to her chest just below her ribs and pressed. Once, twice, three times.

Nothing.

He tried again, his eyes fixed on her face as he *willed* the air into her lungs, lips moving inaudibly as he uttered desperate, rapid-fire prayers.

A flicker of movement, a hiss of air.

"She's breathing!" Jude shouted as he stopped compressions.

Maya coughed, water bubbling out of her mouth, and he helped her roll onto her side as she vomited.

She gasped for air, eyes opening wide, panicked. She reached for Jude as soon as she saw him. "Jude?" she sobbed, clawing at his shirt. He wrapped his arms around her, gasping for breath as he held her to him, and she sobbed into his neck.

"I got you. I got you," Jude said, over and over, his hands clawing at the back of her soaking wet shirt. His eyes burning. "I got you, May."

Her body shook as she sobbed, clinging to him as if he were a lifeline.

Jude glanced up at Tommy who stood nearby, hands behind his head, eyes red as he stared up at the sky. His lips moved inaudibly.

"I'm here," Jude repeated.

THIRTY-TWO
IMMY

The man who killed Immy's parents stood within her sights. The barrel of her gun pointed at his head. She hid behind the crowds, in an alley between a grocery store and a yoga studio. They had gathered for some sort of press event. Cameras rose above their heads. Signs bobbed in the air, protesting the Jailbirds and the rise in crime, calling for justice.

Justice.

Immy's finger tightened on the pistol grip as she fixed her gaze on Orion. He said something into the microphone at the podium, but she couldn't make it out from this distance.

She could end it all now. No one else had to die. No one else had to suffer. And the Jailbirds – the only family she had left – would be safe. She'd probably be arrested, but it would be over. *Over.*

With her free hand, Immy clutched the pendant Christopher Rhodes had left with her in Peru all those years ago. Another man Orion had taken from her. Just like he'd taken her uncle who had tried and failed to infiltrate Orion's group, to bring him down from the inside. This city called for justice on behalf of a man who'd spent years running from it.

If they wouldn't deal with him, Immy would. She'd pay the price so no one else had to.

Closing her left eye, Immy aimed her gun and slowed her breathing. In seconds, it would be over.

Someone screamed. "Gun!"

Immy dropped her arm as the crowd exploded into chaos. She'd been spotted.

With a growl of frustration, Immy shoved the gun back into the waistband of her pants, and broke into a run down the alleyway, away from the scattering crowds.

THIRTY-THREE

TOMMY

ommy stared at Alicia Morales' lifeless body through the burned-away door of The Boathouse. The woman had died trying to get something to Maya. He never would've thought she'd go to such lengths for her daughter.

"Let *go*. I need to see her."

Tommy turned around to see Maya shoving away from Jude, her clothes soaked, her eyes red. As she stumbled toward the restaurant, Tommy grabbed her by the shoulders and held her there. She tried to look past him, but he moved his head until she was forced to meet his eyes.

"You don't need to see this," he said, his voice a whisper.

"She's my *mother*," Maya insisted.

"I'm sorry. I am, but she's already gone, Maya. Seeing her like this isn't going to help you."

"But it's *my fault!*" Maya said as tears streamed down her face.

"It is *not* your fault!" Tommy said, squeezing her shoulders. "Your mother died making things right with you. Let that be your last memory of her – not this."

Maya studied his eyes for a second, then nodded. She turned away, holding the back of her hand to her mouth as she held in another sob. Jude wrapped his arms around her and pulled her against his chest as a wave of fresh tears came. He met Tommy's gaze, his own eyes red. Tired. Grieved.

Tommy's head rolled back as he gaped up at the gray morning sky. So many had died for this secret. The names echoed in his mind. *Cuvier, Danny, Christopher, Oliver, Emilio, Quincy, Alicia.*

Sirens in the distance pulled Tommy from the spiral, and he stepped back through the charred doorway onto the pier, looking toward the road. A group of police cruisers flew past, headed downtown. But one of them skidded to a stop. The sound of brakes squealed as the car flew into reverse, parking at the end of the pier.

Through the windshield, Tommy spotted the driver saying something into his radio. The officer's gaze connected directly with Tommy's.

"Time to go!" Tommy shouted.

Jude grabbed Maya's hand and they broke into a run down the pier as the officer left his car and ran toward them, shouting.

Tommy veered left as they neared the shore. He vaulted over the railing without thinking, launching himself into the air. He landed and tumbled onto the rocky beach. Jude and Maya landed behind him, and they started down the beach, pumping their legs as fast as they could go.

A glance over his shoulder, he saw the cop taking the stairs down onto the beach, running after them, service weapon drawn.

"Where to?" Jude said as he panted for breath, arms pumping, legs pounding the earth, Maya's hand in his.

"The lighthouse," Tommy said, then sucked in a breath of cold air. "I need to get my car."

THIRTY-FOUR
REID

Light filtered through the stained-glass window. The hospital's chapel had been built to face east so that the rising sun shone through the glass, illuminating the colors and sending fractals of light dancing across the small room. Save for Reid and the guard stationed outside, the chapel was empty. Reid had come here every day since his diagnosis. Not sure what he was looking for. Not sure if he'd find it.

Reid looked down at his hands, cuffed, folded in his lap. His fingers picked at one another as he sat in silence, unsure of himself, unable to find the words. Prayer was foreign to him. He'd gone to church here and there as a kid, but as soon as he could get away with it, he'd bailed. Church was for people like Lydia – people who were kind, who reflected the best of humanity's traits. Reid had never belonged; his father had made certain of that.

Emotion welled in Reid's heart, and he found himself looking at the window. He was facing death and yet somehow it wasn't the most terrifying moment of his life.

The doctor's diagnosis echoed in his mind like a judgment passed. An indictment. Reid hadn't even gone to trial, and already he'd been sentenced.

But what had really changed? Reid had been dealing with the pain in his chest for years. The doctor implied the disease could've been triggered by trauma and manifesting as anxiety, but Reid had never really thought of himself as traumatized before. Never seen himself as a victim. And now that he did, he wasn't sure how to feel. Victimhood implied a level of weakness that had been beaten and burned out of Reid first by his father and then by his uncle.

He wasn't weak.

He *couldn't be* weak.

And yet here he was...

Reid sniffed, blinked his eyes. It wouldn't be long before the guard opened the door to take him back to his room. He tried to pray, but every time he opened his mouth, the prayers seemed to die on his tongue. Like standing before a father knowing you'd messed up, Reid wasn't sure how he was supposed to pick up the pieces of a faith he'd never really had in the first place. But the questions Reid asked weren't *Is God real?* Or *Is God good?* Or even *Where will I go when I die?*

No, different questions swirled together in Reid's mind. *What if I'm unforgivable? What if I'm too broken to mend? What if He doesn't want me?*

Reid lifted his head and stared again at the stained-glass window, watching the way the colors and lights danced in the morning hours. Weak – it was time to admit it, at least to himself.

Maybe that was a start. Grabbing the back of the seat in front of him, Reid stood, turning into the aisle. He shuffled toward the door and stopped when he lifted his eyes and noticed for the first time the Scripture painted on the back wall of the chapel.

"My grace is sufficient for you, for My power is made perfect in weakness." – 2 Corinthians 12:9

Reid blinked as a wave of emotion crashed in around him. Too much all at once. He yanked one of the hymnals from the seat back beside him and let out a cry as he hurled it across the room. It slammed into the wall, denting the drywall.

He was not weak.

He couldn't be weak.

Weakness had cost him everything. If he was weak, then his father, Orion – they'd already won.

Tears blurring his sight, heart pounding and aching and throbbing in his chest, he picked up one of the chairs and threw it into the wall. Chipping away at the plaster and the paint until the Scripture was unreadable. Because Reid didn't need God to fix his mess. Reid didn't *deserve* a God like that.

Man up, His father's voice echoed in his mind as he tore through the chapel, wreaking havoc on a space that until now had brought him a small measure of peace.

The doors flung open as the guard rushed inside to subdue Reid. He didn't resist as the man grabbed Reid's arms, pulled them behind his back, and dragged him from the chapel.

For a moment, Reid had come face to face with the kind of God who could love a man like him – and he was terrified of what that meant.

The guard pushed the door open to Reid's room and he shuffled inside, his heart still racing as he struggled to swallow his emotions.

"That was a bad move, Clark," said the guard as he grabbed the door to close it. "They're going to push to have you released from the hospital now. Hope you enjoyed your little vacation."

The door slammed, leaving Reid alone in his room. At least the guard had forgotten to cuff him to the bed. He couldn't leave the room, but at least he wasn't bound to one spot inside it.

A hiss came over the guard's radio on the other side of the door. Reid stepped closer, leaning his ear against the door to make out the voice. Through the window into the hallway, Reid watched the guard's expression shift from confused to alarmed. He glanced through the window at Reid, then switched the lock on the door, trapping Reid inside.

The guard ran down the hallway as Reid slammed on the door.

"Hey! What's going on?" he shouted, but the guard was long gone. Seconds later, doctors and nurses hurried down the hallway in the same direction as the guard. Then a fire alarm went off, blaring through the building.

The entire hospital descended into chaos, and here Reid was trapped inside a locked room.

Pounding his fists on the door, he called for help, but everyone who ran past ignored him.

Was there a fire? What about the patients?

Reid crossed the room to the exterior window, throwing open the blinds. He'd expected to see smoke billowing toward the sky, but it was something else. The hospital parking lot had become a war zone. Reid watched in disbelief as two groups of people seemed to push against one another. On one side, the police decked out in riot gear. On the other side, protestors bearing signs – some of which had Reid's own name on it.

He'd heard about the riots but never would've imagined they'd come anywhere near the hospital. The concept of Bluecoats against Jailbirds had taken on a whole new meaning in the past week. What had once been a high school rivalry between the betters and the lessers had become a full-blown class *war*.

Reid's heart pounded as a wave of anxiety washed over him. He clutched his chest through his hospital robe and tried the breathing exercises the doctor had showed him – just like Emilio had done in the jungles of Peru all those months ago.

What if the rioters made it inside? Would they come for Reid? With the guard gone, anyone could get into this room. If it came down to it, Reid would need to be able to protect himself.

Turning his back on the window, Reid did a visual search of the room for something he could use as a weapon. The cuffs on his wrists limited his options, but he doubted the doctors had left behind any bolt cutters. The IV pole would have to do.

Reid unhooked the empty bag and rolled the pole across the floor, taking up position in front of the door. He watched through the window to the side as doctors, nurses, and security guards streamed toward the chaos. His heart pounded in his chest. Silence, save for the distant sound of shouting outside. The hospital suddenly felt empty. Hollow.

Fingers tightening around the cold, metal pole, Reid took in a breath. Mouth dry, he tried to swallow.

Suddenly the doorknob began to rattle.

Reid braced, eyes on the doorknob.

The click of the lock. It turned, and the door swung open.

Wielding the IV pole over his head, Reid angled it toward the opening. He prepared to thrust it toward the intruder when someone shouted, "Stop!"

Mars stood in the doorway, hands out in front of him, eyes wide, Lucy at his back.

"What are you *doing* here?" Reid hissed, dropping the IV pole.

"Not trying to die," Mars retorted as he and Lucy shuffled into the room, shutting the door behind them. "Who'd you think I was?"

"Don't know if you noticed, but there's a war going on outside and I seem to be the target."

"Oh, don't flatter yourself," Mars said.

Reid ignored the sarcasm. "What are you doing here?"

"Saving your skin," Lucy replied as she peeked through the window, the hallway empty outside.

"You can't do this," Reid said. "You're already in enough trouble. You don't need to add a jailbreak to the list."

"Well, this isn't a jail, to be fair," said Lucy. She leaned against the wall, adjusting her red beanie.

Mars smirked, glancing at her. "Didn't take you for a martyr," he said. "Thing is, we're getting outta Dodge. The others didn't want to leave without you, but I'll go ahead and let 'em know you're loving your new life as a *jailbird*."

Mars turned toward the door.

"Wait!"

He stopped, smirking over his shoulder at Reid. "Attaboy."

Rolling his eyes, Reid held up his cuffed hands. "I won't get very far with these."

"Don't worry," said Mars, jutting a thumb at Lucy. "Lucy over here's apparently an expert lock picker."

THIRTY-FIVE

TOMMY

Hollow Hill Lighthouse rose into view, and a pang of sadness struck Tommy's heart. His home – the Jailbirds' home – had been turned into a crime scene.

Black and yellow tape surrounded the perimeter, the door to the lighthouse had been blocked off. But what Tommy needed right now wasn't inside. It was parked outside under the shade of a pine tree.

Glancing up and down the hillside for any sign of the cops, Tommy rose from his hiding place behind the rocks. Jude and Maya followed him across the road toward the lighthouse. Tommy fished the key out of his pocket, unlocked the car, and slid behind the wheel. Jude helped Maya into the backseat, then climbed into the passenger seat next to Tommy.

The familiar smell of his car brought back a wave of memories and emotions.

"You okay?" Jude asked, shifting in his seat and staring over the console at Tommy.

Tommy tightened his grip around the steering wheel as he fixed his eyes through the windshield at the lighthouse.

"This car will be the only thing I have left of my father," Tommy whispered.

Jude reached over and squeezed Tommy's shoulder.

"No, it won't be," Jude said. "Everything important, you carry inside your heart."

He glanced back at Maya. Tommy glanced in the rearview mirror to see her tear-streaked face. He'd lost his parents, and now she'd lost her mother.

"We remember those we leave behind," said Jude, glancing between the two of them. "*That* is how we win."

Tommy gave a sharp nod, then turned the key in the ignition. Shifting into drive, he tore through the crime scene tape and steered the car further up the hill, as far as possible from the lighthouse and the cops no doubt in pursuit.

The hospital parking lot was chaos. Tommy parked at the far end, grateful the Wrangler's windows were tinted as he watched the madness unfold.

"Do you see them?" he asked.

Jude shook his head. "Not yet."

"What if they got caught?" asked Maya.

"They didn't," Tommy replied. He'd already considered the possibility, but there was no way he'd leave them behind. He'd sooner turn himself in than let Mars take the fall.

"Wait!" Jude shouted. "I think I see them."

Tommy leaned forward, fixing his eyes on the back of the hospital where an emergency exit door flung open. Three people stumbled out, around the corner from the riot. Nobody saw them in the chaos.

Tapping his fingers erratically on the steering wheel, Tommy muttered to himself, "Come on, come on, come on."

Mars spotted them, waving the others on.

"They've got Reid," Jude said, glancing back at Maya.

A look of relief flashed across her eyes, and she settled back in her seat.

"There should be four of them," Tommy said, knitting his brow together as he squinted through the windshield.

They moved quickly past the crowds, giving them a wide berth as cops and rioters pushed against one another. Rocks hurtled through the air, striking riot shields.

Gunfire went off, and the crowd burst into a frenzy.

Mars, Reid, and Lucy bolted toward the car. Jude jumped out, making room for them to pile inside. Screams echoed across the parking lot as bodies dropped. Tommy didn't look to see if they were dead or just unconscious.

My fault… all my fault.

"Where's Immy?" Jude shouted over the chaos at Mars.

Mars glanced at Lucy. "We were hoping she was with you."

Jude slammed the door behind him and climbed back into the passenger seat.

"Drive," he said, and Tommy didn't hesitate. He slammed on the gas, flying through the parking lot.

Something flashed toward them, darting in front of the car. Tommy slammed on his brakes, narrowly avoiding a collision with

Immy. She slapped the hood of the Wrangler, then rounded to the side as Maya threw open the door for her.

Immy climbed into the back seat with Reid, her eyes wide as she caught her breath, and Tommy stepped on the gas. The hospital shrank into his rearview mirror as he made a beeline for the house.

Once there, they wasted no time and quickly loaded their supplies into the trunk. No time for conversation, no time to catch up, no time to say goodbye to their families.

In silence, Tommy followed the mountain back roads where they couldn't even see the city through the trees. He couldn't think about what they were leaving behind. Couldn't think about what his choices had cost them. The only thing on his mind was Lydia, waiting for him to come rescue her.

Mammoth behind them – maybe for good – Tommy turned onto Interstate 90.

Episode Four

THE SMOKING GUN

"Smoke wafted through the night air. In the distance, the sky glowed orange as the fire raged. A voice echoed through the woods."

THIRTY-SIX

CHRIS

Thirteen months ago...

The hind wheels of the Jeep Wrangler skidded across the asphalt as Christopher Rhodes barreled down the highway. The twilight shadow of snow-kissed Mt. Rainier loomed in his rearview mirror.

A heavy fog slithered from the forest to envelop the highway on all sides. Chris flicked on his high beams as he dared to lift his foot of the gas ever so slightly.

Blood pooled on his tongue. He rolled down the window and spat onto the highway, wincing at the jolt of pain emanating from the cut on his lip.

His mind raced, the truth becoming clearer with every second that passed. All those years ago, Orion had used him. He wasn't his friend — he was a villain, willing to use people up and throw them away when he got what he wanted. And Chris had fallen for it. Swept up in the dream of it all — the possibility that he might actually recover Othniel Cuvier's great discoveries, *that he might make the Rhodes family name famous again. He'd been a fool!*

Orion had murdered Danny to keep his secret. And Oliver – how involved was he in what Orion was doing? Did he know? Did he help him cover it up?

White spots dotted Chris' vision as he pushed the Wrangler through the fog, his heart beating out the seconds as he willed himself toward Mammoth. The fog finally broke just as he came to the city limits sign. Relief settled over him as he turned north, toward Hollow Hill.

He hadn't meant to confront Orion, but he wasn't expecting the man to show up at the dig. The excavation of Mt. Rainier was supposed to be Christopher's job, but Orion had arrived anyway. He'd always been ambitious, quick to step in when he felt the prize worthy of his attention. This time it had been the discovery of sabretooth tiger remains. Last time it had been a treasure in the hold of a sunken merchant ship off the coast of Oregon. Each time, Chris' name had been little more than a footnote at the bottom of the scientific journals that chomped at the bit to publicize another "Clark discovery."

All these years, Chris had managed to hold his tongue, to put his pride aside, his sights set on the only discovery that truly mattered – the missing tusk that would prove the Rhodes family name belonged in the history books. Making his family proud was all that had mattered until today. Until the moment Chris had overheard Orion on the phone with someone else. He had intended it as little more than a passing comment, but it stuck to Chris' mind like a cattle brand: Obadiah Hawthorne was not the true founder of Mammoth. Othniel Cuvier had been the first. And just as Hawthorne had killed Cuvier to cover it up, Orion had murdered Danny.

The Wrangler ground to a halt, tires slipping in the gravel outside Hollow Hill Lighthouse. He threw it into park and snatched the journal from the passenger seat. Jumping from the car, he made a beeline for the cellar door outside the lighthouse. Hollow Hill Lighthouse had long been a refuge for him.

Though they hadn't spoken much in years, Theo had allowed Chris to use the lighthouse from time to time. Often, when he wasn't at the museum, he brought Tommy and his friends here to work on their sailboat.

Chris mentally kicked himself for being caught. Orion *had seen* him, *listening in on that phone call. There was no way he hadn't. Now, Chris would do whatever it took to keep the tusk and Cuvier's legacy out of Orion's reach.*

Taking the steps two at a time, Chris descended into the cellar. He found the ammo box where he'd left it in the false bottom of the barrel. At the time, he just didn't want Orion taking over his own personal project. Now, the need for secrecy was so much more important.

What if something happens to me?

Chris swallowed. He knew Orion had already determined what he would do. Chris was a loose end to be tied up. When he was finished here, he would pull Tommy from school, grab Evelyn, and they'd leave Mammoth. Only when they were safe, Chris would call the police. Yes, that would work.

But if not...

Chris stared at the ammo box, his vision blurring. He reached into his pocket for his knife and carved three letters into the face of the metal box: JRH. There were only two people who would know what that meant.

Pocketing the knife, he placed inside the ammo box the key to the Boston Whaler, currently docked at the marina in Mammoth; a photograph of Hawthorne and Cuvier together; and a page from Cuvier's journal. The page. The one that had changed everything.

Chris returned the box to its hiding place, then set to work. Carving small arrows around the room. A contingency he hoped would work. When he was finished, he grabbed the journal, gave the room one last look, then climbed the stairs out into the cold.

Locking the cellar doors behind him, he turned toward the car. A pair of headlights pierced the fog, coming up the road behind the Wrangler. Chris' heart lurched. He glanced down at the docks where his son's boat swayed in the water. With a split second, he made his decision. He took the rocky trail down to the dock as quickly as he dared so as not to send himself tumbling headlong down the cliffside. He winced at every creak of the dock boards under his weight.

He stepped from the dock onto the boat, turning the key in the ignition until the engine rumbled to life. He'd coast out into the open water before he opened the sails.

"I wouldn't do that if I were you."

Chris froze, his hands on the wheel. Cold sweat beaded on his forehead. Swallowing his fear, he turned to meet the silhouette of a man materializing from the fog that swallowed the dock.

"Orion," Chris said, trying his best to sound nonchalant. "What brings you here?"

Orion smirked. "You left the dig in such a hurry, I worried something was wrong. I thought I'd come check in on you."

"Nope. Nothing's wrong. Just, uh, remembered there was something I needed to do."

Orion's eyes narrowed. The wind caught the hem of his blazer. A sliver of sunlight pierced the fog and struck his black hair, turning it molten gold. "Care to explain why you were eavesdropping on a private conversation, Rhodes?"

Chris swallowed. "I don't know what you're talking a—"

"Enough!"

The flash of anger from the normally composed Orion was enough to make Chris flinch. He didn't even notice when Orion reached behind his back and pulled a gun. Chris knew that gun — the antique pistol from Orion's private collection. Chris had gone to the auction on Orion's dime, handpicked which among the collection of antiques to spend Orion's money on. The irony that its barrel was now pointed at Chris didn't escape him.

"Give me the journal, Rhodes," said Orion.

Chris felt the journal's weight in his waistband and thought of Tommy. For the better part of two decades, Chris had wanted to show him that his father could do great things. He'd told Tommy stories of explorers and adventurers his entire life. For once, Chris wanted to be the reason for that spark of adventure in Tommy's eyes. For once, he wanted to be the hero. But he could feel the sands of time slipping through his fingers, and the future he'd longed for faded just as quickly as he leveled his gaze at Orion and remembered the evils the man had committed in the name of greed.

Orion shifted, sighing. "I'm not going to ask again. Give me the journal, and we can pretend none of this happened."

"You killed Danny," Chris spat. "I can't pretend that didn't happen."

Something flashed across Orion's eyes. Regret? Anger? "Don't play games with me, Rhodes."

Chris said nothing, mind racing for a way out. He could jump in the water. Shove the Perdition*'s throttle forward and hope the engine would drive him out of Orion's sights before he could shoot. But every plan that came to mind had a flaw, and suddenly the grim realization that Chris would never see his family again settled over him like a fog.*

"Fine." A dangerous smile spread across Orion's face as he returned the pistol to its place and stepped onto the boat. "I'll take it myself."

Chris dove for Orion, taking the man by surprise. They fell against the deck of the Perdition*, a tangle of limbs.*

He urged himself to fight, grasping for purchase. An elbow struck his side, and he gasped for breath. He managed to bring his knee up to shove Orion back, but the man was scrappier than Chris thought. He latched onto Chris's legs as he stood. Chris tripped, his head colliding with the side of the boat. Stars whirled overhead. A ringing pierced his ears. He gasped for breath, reaching for his head. His fingers came away red, hot, sticky.

Hands clasped around the collar of his shirt. Chris clawed at them, fingers dragging at the meat of Orion's arms. Orion lifted him, and Chris tried to find his footing but his feet were useless. He tried to yell, to beg Orion to stop, but the words came out a garbled mess.

Orion shoved Chris against the side of the boat, wrapping his hands around Chris' throat, cutting off the oxygen. Chris choked, his eyes finding Orion's. Deranged, bloodthirsty. He'd never seen evil until this moment, and it terrified him.

Chris thought of Evelyn, his wife. He remembered the moment they met twenty years ago. He'd bumped into her on the marina and nearly cost her the ice cream cone she'd just bought from a street vendor. He'd caught it before it hit the boards and he looked up to see the prettiest smile in the Pacific Northwest. He'd fallen in love with her then and there.

And he thought of his son, the pride of his life. He remembered the way his heart swelled upon holding a newborn Tommy in the hospital for the first time. Tiny fingers and tiny toes, so delicate, so completely dependent upon the love of his mother and father. And he'd realized in that moment that he'd been born to be a father.

As the last trace of oxygen deflated from Chris' lungs, he felt himself slipping. Chris clamped his eyes shut. He would not spend the last second of his life staring into the eyes of evil. He would spend it remembering only that which was pure and good — his family.

THIRTY-SEVEN
LYDIA

Lydia let out a shaky breath as she shoved away from the wall.

A martyr.

Her uncle didn't just want her out of the way. He wanted to *kill her.*

Lydia struggled to control her breathing. In, out. In, out. She couldn't panic – not now.

When the room on the other side of the wall fell silent, Lydia continued her search down the hidden passageways. The estate was massive, but surely these tunnels led to an exit somewhere.

As she pressed onward, the shadows swallowing her, the cobwebs sticking to her skin, she forced her mind to focus on other things – on Tommy and the scent of a butterscotch lollipop on his breath, on Jude and the brother she'd found in him, on Maya's constant friendship, on Mars' laugh and the way it always reached his eyes, on Reid and the strength he'd had to endure what their father had done to him, and on Immy and the sacrifices she'd made for the Jailbirds. Oliver Clark was dead, and maybe he deserved it. Orion Clark was a thief and a killer. But Lydia was not alone. She was not without a family.

And whatever Orion intended for the Jailbirds, Lydia was not about to let him get away with it.

New resolve filled Lydia's lungs. She stopped in her tracks, glancing at the dim passageway around her. A plan began to form.

Lydia retraced the passageway in her mind. She'd started toward the outside of the building and would have followed the tunnels deeper inside. She'd gone straight, then taken a left before stopping to listen in on Orion. She was heading toward the mansion's west wing. If this passage continued straight, she'd eventually hit a wall on the exterior of the mansion.

Following the passage, careful to step over debris and steer clear of spiders, it ended where Lydia imagined the wall might be before banking left, deeper into the west wing. Further down, the passage descended underground, trading the dry, wooden walls for wet, dank stone. And in the distance, a pale blue light pierced the blackness.

An underground railroad.

Lydia ran. Ignoring the fact that the tunnel might be littered with rubble, that she could trip and hurt herself, or that the ground could fall out beneath her. Cold wind blew against her face, the scent of fresh air mingling with the smell of mud and moss.

She stopped short at the end of the tunnel as she came to a gate. Beyond, dark blue sky hung over a stream that carved its path through a forest. Freedom lay just on the other side of these metal bars.

Searching the gate, she found it chained. With a frustrated growl, Lydia slammed her hands against the gate. It rattled, then stopped.

Letting out a shuddering breath, Lydia's head fell against the metal bars. Tears threatened to fall. She'd come so close to escape only for it to be wrenched from her grasp. It wouldn't be long before a guard came to check on her and found her room empty, the wallpaper peeled back.

Lydia tried to pray, but the only sound that escaped her lips was a desperate, strangled gasp. Words failed to express her heart's deepest needs. She clamped her eyes shut, refusing to cry. Refusing to let herself fall apart. Not here. Not now.

Think, she urged herself, banging her head against the bars. *Think. There's a way out of this. There must be.*

Eyes snapping open, Lydia searched the gate. A rusted hinge. A fractured bar. A key under the doormat. Anything at all that could get this gate open.

And then she found it.

The ground was muddy, trails of water carving paths under the gate that led to the river. Rising water levels during the winter had eroded the once rocky earth. She could dig.

Dropping to her knees, Lydia grabbed a nearby stone and began to claw at the ground, pulling mud and patches of grass up and away from the gate until she formed a hole big enough beneath the bars to slip through. She laughed, relief flooding her lungs along with a gust of fresh air as it swept through the tunnel. But she didn't wriggle through. Not yet. There was one more thing she had to do before she freed herself.

Orion wanted a martyr, but he couldn't have her. He couldn't have the Jailbirds, their legacy, their families. She'd had her chance to take him out, but she'd failed. She couldn't bring herself to do it. But something had changed inside of Lydia since that moment. She hadn't pulled the trigger because she'd been thinking about herself, about what it would do to her. She couldn't afford to think that way now. This wasn't about her anymore.

Lydia stood as resolve strengthened her, steeling her bones. She stared down at the hole she'd dug beneath the gate – her path to freedom. She turned her back and disappeared back into the shadows of the tunnel.

She would free herself, but before she did, Lydia Clark would burn his kingdom to the ground.

THIRTY-EIGHT
TOMMY

ommy's heartbeat didn't slow until they'd driven an hour east of Mammoth. The city now lay far behind them and with it, the cops, the riots… *home.*

"We need to stop," he announced to the quiet car. "Fuel up, get some food. Reid needs a change of clothes."

Even as the words came out, Tommy wasn't certain he was the one saying them. A pounding headache pierced his skull, and a fog had settled over him. He was moving by memory alone at this point.

He pulled into a shopping center in Ellensburg and found a gas station. One by one, all the Jailbirds but Reid slipped out of the car and stretched their limbs. Tommy sat in the driver's seat for a second longer, his hands clenched around the steering wheel.

Mars said something about getting food, and Lucy went with him. Jude and the others offered to check out a nearby outlet store for clothes.

When they left, Tommy let his head fall forward against the steering wheel. It had been forty-eight hours since any of them had any sleep, but he couldn't crash now. Not when they were just hours away from finding Lydia.

He sucked in a breath, forcing the tears that welled in his eyes to retreat. His heart swelled, a lump forming in his throat. He swallowed.

Without Lydia, Tommy wasn't himself. A stranger lived inside of him. Someone he didn't recognize, foreign and unfamiliar. Like an animal moving on instinct. He just wanted her back. Nothing else mattered. Not their quest, not his anger toward Orion, not the things they'd left behind. The things that Tommy felt, the impulses that played over and over in his mind, the things he would do to get her back… terrified him. Losing Lydia had changed something inside of him, but he wasn't sure he cared. The truth was, they'd all changed since stumbling into that cellar beneath the lighthouse. Not one of them was the same person they'd been four months ago – and maybe that was a good thing. Because Lydia didn't need the Tommy he'd been before; she needed the Tommy he was becoming *now*.

He sucked in a breath, pushing away from the steering wheel as he sat up straight. Nothing would stop him from getting her back.

"Why'd you come for me?"

Tommy startled. He'd forgotten for a moment that he wasn't alone. Glancing over his shoulder at Reid in the back seat, he relaxed. "The same reason you turned yourself in so we could get away."

"And why's that?"

"We're not who we used to be," Tommy replied. "None of us."

"And that's a good thing?"

Tommy shrugged as he shoved open his door. "Good or bad, I don't know. But it is what it is."

Reid leaned forward against the seat to talk to Tommy through the window while Tommy fueled up the Wrangler. "You know where Lydia is?"

Nodding, Tommy inserted the gas nozzle and watched as the numbers on the digital display climbed. No doubt the police were monitoring his bank account activity, but by the time they tracked the Jailbirds to Ellensburg, they would be long gone. "Broke into Orion's place. Everything was being shipped to an address in Spokane. I assume his new HQ or something like that."

"He never mentioned Spokane to me," Reid said. He ran his fingers over the hospital bracelet around his wrist, then snapped it off and tossed it out the window. Tommy scooped it up and dropped it in the nearby trash.

"Seems like there's a lot your uncle never shared with you. I guess just be glad you're not in his inner circle anymore."

Reid's gaze dropped. Tommy watched him through the window, his jaw set. He wasn't sure what he felt toward Reid. A mix of gratitude and anger, of empathy and regret. When Tommy looked in Reid's eyes and saw the guilt, the sorrow, the anguish, he saw himself. He and Reid weren't so different – not in the ways that mattered. Both were men reduced to something they never imagined they'd become. Instinct and desperation rolled into one.

"I didn't think it'd be like this," Reid said, his voice breaking. Looking at him, he was unrecognizable from the man he'd been just a few short months ago. His normal crew cut was grown out and unkempt. His normally clean-shaven face was scruffy. His bright eyes had dimmed. And had he lost weight?

"Like what?" Tommy asked.

Reid opened his mouth to answer, but he closed it again. Whatever he wanted to say, the words seemed to die on his tongue.

"You don't have to say anything if you don't want," said Tommy. "I'm no priest, and this isn't confession."

Pursing his lips, Reid rubbed his eyes with the heels of his hands. He let out a forced groan. "Sorry. It's just… there's things I've got to say – need to say. Just don't know how."

When the tank was full, Tommy replaced the gas nozzle and twisted the gas tank cap closed. He leaned through the open window, waiting until Reid met his eyes. "Whatever it is will wait until you're ready. We're not going to abandon you somewhere just because you didn't talk. When you're ready, we'll be here. All of us."

Reid nodded. He smirked. "A Bluecoat saved by a Jailbird. Who would've thought."

Chuckling, Tommy slipped into the driver's seat. "I'm not sure that means much anymore."

"Probably a good thing."

Tommy nodded. "Probably."

THIRTY-NINE
MARS

As the day drew to an end, the shopping center was mostly dead, the parking lot nearly empty save for a few cars. Mars pushed the cart down the sidewalk in front of him, a few bags of groceries inside. Lucy hung onto the front of the cart, laughing when he broke into a run and stopped just short of crashing into one of the concrete pillars that supported the roof.

It felt good to laugh, and wrong at the same time. But Lucy made things easier, more bearable. He loved the way she laughed, the way her eyes lit up and seemed to dance in the light. The way her cheeks dimpled when she smiled. He'd never felt this way about anyone before, and he wasn't sure what to do or say or how to approach it. But for now, he was glad to be with her. To find in her something he hadn't found in anyone else. He could only hope that, just maybe, she was feeling the same things.

Still, Mars couldn't seem to quell the guilt that his parents wouldn't know what had happened to him. They may never know, and here he was, pretending he was okay with moving on? They deserved to know the truth – at the very least that he was okay.

Mars glanced at the computer shop a little further down the sidewalk and remembered the flash drive Maya had practically shoved into his hands when they'd left Mammoth. Whatever was on it, she didn't have the emotional bandwidth to deal with it. That was okay – he'd take care of it so she wouldn't have to. He just hoped that whatever was on it was worth the price Alicia Morales had paid.

"What gives?" asked Lucy when he parked the cart up against the wall.

"Watch the cart," said Mars. "Just need to take care of something really quick."

"Sure thing."

He felt her eyes follow him as he opened the door.

Inside the computer shop, Mars made a beeline for the display models and found a laptop with some battery. He logged into his email first, then froze.

What could he say? Goodbye? That hardly seemed adequate.

Running his hands through his hair, he stared at the blank screen for a moment, then sighed. He typed out a quick message and hit send.

Closing out of his email, he reached into his pocket for the flash drive. Plugging it into the computer, he waited for the contents to download.

Mars' breath caught in his throat as the screen came to life. He covered his mouth with his hand, struggling to process what he was seeing.

The smoking gun.

There was one more thing Mars needed to do.

FORTY
IMMY

Well, it was slim pickings in there, but hopefully this'll make do," said Jude as he dropped a bag of clothes on the hood of the Wrangler. Immy's side throbbing, she leaned against the side of the car and exhaled while Jude pulled Reid's clothes out of the bag.

Tommy had moved the Wrangler to the far end of the parking lot, in the shade of some trees where nobody would notice them – not that anyone this far from Mammoth would give a group like them a second glance.

Immy pressed her hand to her healing wound and breathed through her teeth as she willed the throbbing to fade. A steady breeze carried dried pine needles across the asphalt. Dusk fell over the town, the sunset slipping behind the distant horizon and casting the streets in streaks of yellow and orange.

Beside Immy, the door opened, and Reid climbed out in his

hospital gown. Jude tossed the wad of clothes over the hood at Reid. He caught it midair, then passed in front of Immy. He glanced at her out of the corner of his eye as he rounded to the back of the Wrangler.

"No peeking," he said.

"Ain't nothing nobody wants to see anyway," Jude retorted.

Clothes rustled as Reid changed. Immy didn't mean to, but she glanced his way just as he pulled the gown up and over his back. He stood beside the trunk in a pair of boxers, his bare back angled toward Immy. For a split second, she couldn't look away from the scars that marred his skin, the bruises and burn marks.

She'd been able to catch on to some of what had happened with Reid, what his father and uncle had done, but suddenly it was real. He wasn't a monster anymore, the man who'd been with Emilio when he'd died. He was something entirely… different now.

"We got the goods," Mars announced as he and Lucy returned to join the others, tossing a bag of chips toward Jude.

"Took you long enough," said Jude as he caught it in mid-air. "I'm starving."

"There are kids in Africa," Mars retorted. "*They're* starving. *You're* a pig."

Mouth full of chips, Jude said, "Takes one to know one."

Catching herself staring at Reid a little longer than was comfortable, Immy quickly looked away to find Lucy looking right at her. The girl smirked, and Immy blushed. She pushed away from the side of the car and headed toward the front where the others waited. Maya was still quiet, her eyes red and Jude quietly fussing over her. Tommy was staring off in the distance, arms in the pocket of his bomber jacket. Lucy and Mars were chattering about something Immy didn't understand. She felt out of place, but looking at the rest of them, she wondered if they felt the same.

Everything was… *off.*

They'd managed to escape Mammoth, to free Reid, and were on their way to rescue Lydia. But the victory paled in comparison to its price.

A few minutes later, Reid rejoined them. Immy met his eye as he rounded the car, wearing the clothes Jude had found for him. A pair of blue denim jeans and white sneakers, a white T-shirt and gray pullover, and a baseball cap.

Balling up the hospital gown, he tossed it through the open window into the back seat. "How do I look?" he asked, his eyes landing on Immy again.

Immy cleared her throat, shifting on her feet. "Like someone who just broke out of jail," she said, opening the car door and climbing inside.

"Wonderful," Reid said.

The Jailbirds piled into the car, and Tommy quickly pulled out onto the street. Only one thing on his mind – on all of their minds. If only she'd managed to do it. Orion could be dead now. Instead, he continued to loom over them.

In the back seat, Immy let her head rest against the window. Before long, the moving car and the hum of the engine lulled her to sleep.

FORTY-ONE
LYDIA

Lydia peeked through the hidden door back into the room. Empty. They hadn't discovered her disappearance yet, but they would soon.

She slipped inside and turned toward the vanity, searching the drawers. Nothing. The nightstands, too, were empty. She slipped into the bathroom, tucking her hair behind her ears as she crouched to search the drawers.

There, at the back of the bottom drawer. It wasn't what she was looking for, but it would work. A single matchbook. She snatched it and left the bathroom, heading back for the secret passageway.

The doorknob rattled.

Lydia froze.

It swung open, and Cam, the guard, stepped inside. Rifle hanging over his shoulder. A tray of steaming soup in front of him.

He looked up, saw her, saw the hidden door standing ajar. His mouth fell open in surprise.

Lydia leapt forward before he could say anything, deliberately knocking the tray of soup so that the hot liquid spilled all over his neck and chest. He hollered in pain, and Lydia took advantage of the distraction, bolting into the hidden passage.

She ran all the way down to the first left and stopped, glancing over her shoulder. Voices echoed down the tunnel. She didn't have much time.

Plucking a match from the matchbook, she struggled to light it as her hands trembled. It sparked, then finally ignited. Lydia tucked the match between the dry, wooden slats of the interior mansion walls. It quickly caught fire. She ran down another twenty feet and lit another match, tucking this one in a pile of debris on the ground.

Lydia followed the passageway to the end, lighting matches and setting the walls on fire as she went. Smoke began to billow through the passageway.

As she lit the next match, something slammed into her. She fell to the ground beneath the weight and turned to find Cam on top of her. He snarled as he grabbed at her wrists, but she snatched them away and kicked at him. The heel of her shoe caught him in the chin, and he yelped, falling back into the wall. Lydia scrambled backwards, struggling to get her feet under her.

"Cam, please, let me go," she begged.

Cam stood upright, glaring down at her, ignoring her plea. Lydia felt along the ground for a weapon as he slipped the rifle down his arm. Her hands latched onto something long and cold. Metal. A pipe or a tool. She didn't have time to think about what it was or how to use it, but she jumped to her feet and thrust the object in front of her. The orange light of raging fires behind Cam illuminated the copper pipe in her hand as it impaled his side. He cried out, his weapon clattering to the ground. She pulled the pipe free, blood spurting from the wound. Cam clutched his side as he fell to the ground, letting out a choked and panicked cry.

Eyes wide, Lydia gaped at him for a second. She only wanted to hurt him – not kill him. But there was *so much blood.*

No time for that.

Lydia stepped forward to grab his rifle, but Cam let go of his wound and clutched at the barrel with bloodied hands.

Frustrated, Lydia tried to wrestle it free. With her other hand, she brought the pipe down against his wound, smacking it. He cried out and released the barrel of the rifle, sending Lydia reeling backwards. She caught herself before she fell. In the distance, the fires she'd set began to swell to a roar.

She coughed, breathing into the crook of her arm as she backed away from Cam. "You need to get out of here!" she told him. He didn't act like he'd heard her.

Glancing behind her, toward freedom, she froze. She turned back to Cam, now sprawled out on the ground. Unconscious. The fires spreading toward him.

A growl of frustration, Lydia moved toward Cam, toward the fire. She slung the rifle over her shoulder and scooped her hands under his arms, dragging his dead weight away from the fire and down the tunnel. Old wood crackled and popped as it caught fire above her head.

Descending into the underground tunnel, Lydia thought she might leave him here. She stopped for a second to consider her options. There was nothing to catch fire, and this tunnel was wet, likely flooded by the rising water of the creek outside. But the smoke would need somewhere to go. Cam wouldn't burn, but he could die of smoke inhalation. Lydia couldn't bring herself to leave him here with that possibility.

She glanced down at him, taking several deep breaths before continuing to drag him down the tunnel. What had Orion done to earn such loyalty that this boy was willing to die for him?

Ignoring the question, Lydia grabbed the unconscious Cam's arms and dragged him down the tunnel to the gate. She crawled out first through the hole she'd dug, then she reached back under the bars and dragged him through after her.

Pulling him away from the tunnel's mouth, she set him upright against the hillside, away from the entrance. His head rolled to the side. Still, she couldn't leave him like this.

Glancing down the tunnel to make sure they hadn't been followed, she patted Cam down, searching his pockets. Shouts echoed in the distant night. The fire had become a full-blown disaster now. Nobody would be paying attention to her disappearance. But the distraction wouldn't last long.

Lydia undid Cam's belt and tore a piece of his shirt off, balling it up and pressing it against his wound. She cinched the belt around his torso and tightened it.

She left him there and prayed it would be enough to stop the bleeding. And maybe when he woke up, he'd realize who the real villains were.

Wielding the rifle in front of her, Lydia found the creek and followed it into the shadows of the forest.

FORTY-TWO
MAYA

Maya's eyes fixed on the world outside the car window in the back seat of the Wrangler. A blur of colors. The sky's deep blue hues mixed with fading oranges and purples. The distant snow-capped mountains glittering like diamonds. The deep green forest, vast and dark. The yellow and white lines on the highway. The blinking reds, greens, and yellows of traffic lights. So much color in the world, and it all seemed suddenly so dull.

Mom's dead.

Until now, she hadn't been able to admit it to herself. It felt like a terrible dream. All of it. The murders, the kidnappings, the riots — now this. In the back of her mind, she wondered about the flash drive, but she'd handed it over to Mars. Whatever it was, she wasn't certain she'd know what to do with it.

"Dad doesn't know," she whispered.

Beside her, his hand on her knee, Jude leaned in. "What?"

A tear fell from Maya's eye and dripped onto her jeans. She wiped at her eyes, keeping them fixed on the passing scenery outside the window. She couldn't look at Jude, at anyone. She didn't want their pity, their sympathy, the reminder that she had lost something. The only thing she wanted was to rewind the clock to a time when things felt normal. There were no fossils to find, no bad guys to outrun, no killers to take down.

Jude squeezed her knee, his thumb tracing circles on her jeans.

"He doesn't know she died," Maya said again, her voice quivering. "Or why…"

She sniffed, inhaled. Forcing down the wave of emotion that tried to bubble to the surface. She turned to Jude, who waited patiently.

"Everyone's going to think we did it, Jude. *He's* going to think we did it."

His eyes shone with sympathy. His touch gentle, his nearness offering a comfort Maya didn't deserve.

"We'll set things right, May," Jude said.

She wanted to believe him, to believe that there was any way at all to erase the disaster that their lives had become, but maybe it was better this way. Maya had already been so disconnected from her parents. They'd rejected her at every turn, treated her like she was a nuisance, a disappointment, an inconvenience. Alicia Morales was her mother, but she was a terrible mom. They'd never had mother-daughter slumber parties, never talked about boys together, never went anywhere just the two of them. When Maya was a baby, it had been the nanny that stayed up with her night after night. And when Maya was a teenager, it was her teachers who taught her about her biology, about life and love. And what her school didn't teach, her friends filled in the gaps. She'd learned more about being a woman from Tommy, Jude, and Mars than she'd ever learned from her parents.

But none of that seemed to matter when the only thing Maya saw when she closed her eyes was her mother's lifeless body crumpled and bleeding on the floor. Nobody deserved that, no matter how terrible. And all because Alicia Morales had tried to do the most unexpected, unpredictable thing she'd ever done in her entire life – help her daughter.

It didn't erase the painful memories, the absence or the emptiness, the fear or the mistrust. It didn't undo the damage done by years of avoidance and distance. But it did something Maya never thought possible – it redeemed her mother in her own eyes.

Maya could grieve for her mother, for the woman she might have become if she hadn't been killed. For the relationship they might have had. And maybe, one day, she could make things right with her father.

Resting her hand on Jude's, Maya slipped her fingers through his. He leaned over, gently pressing his lips to the top of her head. He lingered there, and Maya closed her eyes, cherishing his nearness, the smell of him.

"It's okay to let your heart break," he whispered. "It doesn't mean you're weak or you're broken or whatever it is that's going through your head right now. And it doesn't matter if they deserve it or not, because it's who you are. You love people, May, and you fight for them, and you see the best in them. Stop trying to hold it all together and let someone else hold *you* for once. Let *me*."

Nodding, Maya leaned over and rested her head on his shoulder as the tears broke the surface again. They dripped down her face and onto the front of Jude's shirt, but he didn't even seem to mind.

FORTY-THREE
TOMMY

Tommy's hands tightened around the steering wheel as they neared their destination. The route led them through Spokane toward a property outside of the city in the forested hills. Tommy had driven into the night while the others had fallen asleep. All but Reid.

He glanced in the rearview mirror, saw Reid staring out the window from the back seat. Mars slept against the door and Lucy slept on his shoulder. Jude and Maya piled into the very back of the Wrangler, their heads rolled to the side as they slept. Immy sat in the passenger seat next to Tommy, her arms folded on the console to support her head as she slept. Tommy almost didn't want to wake them.

"Guys," he said after giving them another minute, "we're almost there."

The Jailbirds began to stir, stretching and yawning as they

woke.

"Sleep well?" Tommy asked.

"Not a bit," Jude muttered in reply.

"Can't remember the last time I had a good night's sleep," Mars said.

"Would've been before we found that secret cellar in the lighthouse," said Maya.

Not for Tommy. He hadn't had a good night's sleep since his father's body washed up on shore over a year ago now.

"Man, remember when the only thing we had to worry about was how we were going to beat the Bluecoats in the sailing competition?" Jude asked, reaching over the seat to give Reid's shoulder a shove. Tommy had to applaud Jude's efforts to include Reid, to make him feel like less of an outsider. The Jailbirds would have to prove themselves to Reid as much as he would to them — prove that they could be trusted, that they were honest and genuine, that they actually cared. With what Reid had been through, it could take time for him to heal enough to believe something like that. But it was different for Jude now that they'd discovered they shared the same mother — they were half-brothers, and it would take time to figure out what that meant for them.

"I miss taking the *Perdition* out," Mars agreed.

"That's because you let us do most of the work," Maya said with a laugh. Somehow, after all that she'd endured, she could still laugh and smile with her friends.

"Hey, can I help it if my expertise lies elsewhere?" said Mars. "I'm happy to let you guys sail me around the world."

"We find this treasure hoard of Cuvier's, and we could buy a bigger boat," said Jude. "Maybe a yacht."

Immy laughed. "With that kind of money, you could buy

yourselves a fleet."

Tommy tapped her arm. "It'll be your money, too," he said, then glanced back at Reid. "And yours. We all get our cut."

It had been a long time since Tommy had really thought about the treasure, the fossils, or the money they were bound to make from it. But with Lydia so close now, he got to thinking about their future. He could give her the kind of life she deserved. A big house for their kids to grow up in with a big yard. Tommy would build a playground in the backyard. They'd spend summers pushing their children on the swings, rolling out blankets for makeshift picnics. They'd get a dog. A Golden Retriever, maybe, or a German Shepherd. Their kids would grow up knowing they had both a mom *and* a dad who loved them. They'd go to church every Sunday and have the Jailbirds over for family dinners after service. They'd host holidays in that house – Christmas trees and garlands, Thanksgiving pumpkins and the smell of pecan pie, Fourth of July barbecues and firework displays. A life built for a girl with a heart as big as hers.

Tommy realized now that he'd always imagined all of this in Mammoth, but what if there was no Mammoth to go back to?

The dream would have to change, but not in the ways that mattered. Wherever they went, wherever they built their life, it would be him and Lydia together – them against the world.

Tommy slammed on the breaks, the Wrangler skidding to a stop at the end of the long, gravel road. He gaped at the scene before him – a mansion engulfed in flames.

"No," he breathed. "*No*."

Tommy swung the door open and broke into a run as soon as his feet hit the ground. A gate at the end of the road barred entry, but nobody was paying attention to the newcomers. Orion's men ran for their lives, scattering in the lawns. Some threw themselves from windows to escape the inferno, landing on the ground outside with sickening thuds. The entire estate was in flames.

Thump thump thump.

At the other end of the field, a helicopter's blades spun in the air as it slowly lifted off the ground.

Tommy collided with the gate, his hands wrapping around the wrought iron rungs. Wind whipped through the air, tearing at his clothes, fanning the flames that consumed the mansion.

Spotting Orion inside the helicopter as it circled in the air, Tommy noticed he wasn't alone. There was a woman beside him, but it wasn't Lydia. That meant…

"No!"

Tommy scaled the gate just as Jude and the others caught up to meet him. The metal rattled. He nearly slipped but caught himself and threw his body over the top of the gate. He landed in the grass on the other side and bolted toward the mansion, his eyes wide with panic, his heart hammering in his chest.

"Lydia!" he screamed, running toward the inferno. Heat whipped against his face as he neared the mansion, threatening to engulf him.

An arm wrapped around his midsection, and his feet fell out from under him. He rolled over to find Jude kneeling beside him, holding him back.

Tommy wrenched away from Jude's grip, scrambling backward on the grass before finding his footing. "I need to get to her!" Tommy shouted over the roar of the fire.

Jude gaped at the fire, then back at him. "Tommy…"

"No," Tommy said, shaking his head wildly as he backed away. "No, she's not gone. She *can't be gone!"*

Tommy spun on his heel, his head spinning. His stomach turned. Bile rose in the back of his throat as horror gripped him. He glanced over his shoulder at Jude as the others ran up behind him. Maya's hands went to her mouth as she watched the fire rage. Mars gripped the back of his neck. Immy's face streamed with tears while Lucy looked like she might throw up. And Reid… he stood there, his eyes red as he watched the fire consume the house where they were certain they would find Lydia.

Horrific images crossed Tommy's minds of his wife trapped inside somewhere, calling his name as flames licked at her skin. Skin that was so soft against Tommy's calloused hands. Skin that radiated warmth and life every time they touched.

"No," Tommy said again. "She's around here somewhere. She has to be. She escaped, or… or…"

Jude threw his arms around Tommy and held him as he rambled, his mind racing. Tears streamed down his face. Because even if she wasn't here, even if she was alive somewhere else — where? This was their only lead, their only hope of rescuing her. And if she was inside…

Tommy's eyes burned with smoke and tears as he clawed at the back of Jude's jacket, grasping for any sliver of hope he could find. She couldn't be gone. The girl he'd spent a lifetime loving — the girl who'd given up her family, her home, everything to follow Tommy on his endless quest to prove his father right — this couldn't be how her life ended.

"Hey! You!"

Tommy broke from Jude's embrace and turned toward the voice. One of Orion's men — a guard — ran toward them, wielding a rifle as he slowed, considering the group that stood in the flickering shadows of the blazing inferno. Without even thinking about it, Tommy ran toward the Hunter, throwing his full weight at the man as he tackled him. The guard didn't have time to raise his weapon. They collided and fell to the ground.

In a blind rage, Tommy wrenched the rifle from the Hunter's grasp and when the man reached for the gun in his holster, Tommy kicked it away and stooped to retrieve it. With the guard flat on his back and Tommy straddling him as he stood, he slung the rifle over his shoulder and aimed the handgun at the guard. A knife appeared, slicing across Tommy's side. He grabbed the guard's wrist, twisting until the knife fell to the ground.

"Where is she?" Tommy roared, his scream barely audible over the cacophony of the fire and the fading sound of the helicopter as it disappeared into the night.

"Who?" the guard asked, holding his hands up in surrender as he stared wide-eyed up at Tommy.

"My *wife!*"

"I-I don't know who you're talking about."

Tommy bent down and grabbed the man by the collar of his shirt, lifting his torso off the guard as he got in his face. "Don't play stupid. Lydia Clark, the girl your boss kidnapped and has held hostage for the better part of a month. Tell me where she is or I'll blow your brains out."

"Woah!" Jude appeared at Tommy's side, holding out his hands as though standing face to face with a wild animal. "Tommy, take a breath, man. You don't want to do this."

Tommy ignored Jude, jamming the barrel of the gun into the guard's chest.

Jude shouted for the others. "Can I get some help here?"

"You people think you can just take whatever you want, that you have a right to *hurt* whoever you want," Tommy hissed through his teeth, his eyes locked on the horrified guard's. "How's it feel to be on the other end of the gun, huh?"

"Please," the man pleaded. "I don't know. I don't—"

"Tell me where she is!" Tommy demanded, shouting over his friends clamoring for his attention.

The guard clammed up, and before Tommy could register what he was doing, he pressed the barrel of the gun against the guard's thigh and pulled the trigger.

FORTY-FOUR
LYDIA

The crack of a gunshot pierced the night, and Lydia stopped in her tracks. Covered in mud and freezing in the cold, she spun toward the sound. Smoke wafted through the night air. In the distance, the sky glowed orange as the fire raged. A voice echoed through the woods.

"*Tommy*," Lydia breathed.

She broke into a run back toward the estate, slipping in the dirt and mud, tripping over roots and underbrush. Her heart raced. Her thoughts tumbled over one another. Was it really him? Had he found her?

A scream rippled through the air.

Lydia's legs couldn't move fast enough. She could hardly see through the tears that blurred her vision. She prayed she was right, but fear told her she was hearing what she wanted to hear.

She ran anyway.

FORTY-FIVE

TOMMY

A scream exploded from the guard's mouth as he clawed at the wound in his leg, his body writhing beneath Tommy.

Tommy's ears rang, the gunshot echoing in the air. He tightened his grip around the collar of the guard's shirt, lifting the guard's face to meet his. Tears poured from the man's eyes as he unraveled into a sobbing mess, blood spilling from the wound in his leg. Tommy didn't care. These were the monsters who'd taken both his father and Lydia from him, who'd pillaged and murdered and terrorized. Why should he care? Wasn't this justice?

His hands trembling as he exhaled a shaky breath, Tommy pressed the gun to the guard's temple. He whimpered as Tommy asked again, "Where is she?"

Tommy dismissed the pang of guilt that formed a lump in his

throat in favor of the rage tearing through his chest.

Reid appeared in his peripheral vision, crouching beside Tommy, resting a hand on Tommy's shoulder and locking his eyes on him. Sweat dripped down Tommy's face, mingling with tears. His hair hung wildly in front of his eyes. He didn't look toward Reid or Jude or the others. His eyes were fixated on the one person who could help him find his wife, who could confirm that she wasn't inside the mansion when it went up in flames, that she was somewhere else. Safe. Alive. Waiting for him to come find her.

"Tommy, I get what you're feeling right now, man," said Reid, his voice low so only Tommy could hear. "I really do, but this isn't you. This anger, this *hate*. What? You going to kill him? And when you find Lydia, what will you to tell her? You think she'll be happy you killed someone – probably someone who had nothing to do with her disappearance – to find her? Think this through, man."

"Reid!" Maya snapped.

"What?" asked Reid, glancing back at her. "This is what he needs to hear." He turned back to Tommy, who pressed the gun harder into the Hunter's temple. "You do this and there's no going back, Tommy. Once you take a life, once you pull that trigger, it marks you forever. Believe me," he said. "You pull that trigger, and he's not the only person who'll die here."

Tommy eyed Reid out of the corner of his vision, his body trembling with rage. Past Reid, the others stood still, their eyes wide and bright as the fire cast its monstrous glow across the group. In the distance, shouting. The rumble of thunder as the clouds in the night sky above began to open and pour forth rain, but even the sudden torrent wasn't enough to extinguish the pillar of fire the mansion had become.

Agony tore through Tommy's chest as he met Reid's eyes. "What if she's *inside?*"

Reid squeezed Tommy's shoulder, then moved his hand to grab the side of Tommy's face. And in his eyes, Tommy saw a side of Reid he'd only ever seen once before – that day in the tunnel when Reid had traded his life for theirs. It was remorse and sorrow and guilt and shame. The same emotions that suddenly came crashing down around Tommy now.

"I don't know if she's inside," Reid said, "but killing this man is not the way we get the answer."

Tommy looked back down at the sobbing Hunter, lingering for a moment before finally releasing the collar of his shirt. He stood up straight, let Reid take the gun from his hands as he staggered backward, away from the wounded guard as he clutched his bleeding leg.

"Help me bind his wound," said Reid to someone, his voice an echo in the back of Tommy's mind. "And get him to the edge of the property before anyone else spots us."

Jude moved to help while Tommy stayed where he was, watching the mansion burn. A terrible groan arose from the place, and moments later the second floor ceiling began to cave in on itself. A hand slipped into Tommy's as he stood, watching with a mix of shock and horror. He glanced down at the person who'd come up beside him and expected Lydia to appear as if by some miracle, but it was Maya. Tears in her eyes, she squeezed his hand. One of his closest friends, she'd been by his side through everything that had ever mattered in life, and now here they were. Grieving together over their shared losses.

"I don't know how to do this," Tommy said, but the words came out a sob.

Maya moved in front of him and threw her arms around his neck. He buckled, bowing his back as he let go, sobbing into her neck, his body weak and his head spinning. He fell to his knees, and she fell with him, holding him while he sobbed.

In the distance, through the sound of howling wind and pouring rain and the crackling of wildfire, a voice called out.

Tommy froze, glancing up through blurred vision at Maya. Confusion wrinkled across her face as they looked at each other, then turned toward the woods where the sound had come from. Tommy stood, releasing Maya's hand.

"Tommy!"

The cry came again. Tommy took a step toward it, his eyes scanning the shadows in the tree line, along the fence and down the road past the gate, searching for movement. Then he spotted her.

"Lydia?"

She appeared alongside the fence from the other side of the field, behind where the mansion stood. She was only a shadow, but Tommy would have recognized the shape of her anywhere.

He surged forward, his feet carrying him across the field toward where she stood, a rifle in one hand while her other hand rose to her mouth.

"Tommy!" she cried, her voice a choked sob.

His body collided with hers, his arms finding their place around her middle as he pulled her body against his. They fell together, clinging to one another. She asked how he'd found her, and he asked if she was okay — the answers spilled out of them in a tumbled, weepy mess. He grabbed the side of her face, his eyes inches from hers, and he kissed every exposed, muddy, tear-stained surface, inhaling the scent of her, remembering the feel of her.

"You're… alive." The words hitched in his throat.

"You found me," she whispered.

Thunder rumbled, the smell of rain and smoke and earth thick in the space between them as he clung to her as tightly as he dared. "I will *always* find you."

The others came running, falling in around them, clinging to Lydia and to Tommy while a kingdom burned behind them.

FORTY-SIX
MARS

A wave of heat washed over Mars as he huddled with his friends around Lydia, relief welling inside his heart to see that she was okay, to have his family back together. But their reunion was short-lived when gunfire pierced the night. They'd been spotted. Glancing down the field, Mars saw the injured guard limping toward his buddies, clutching the wound in his leg where Tommy had shot him.

Scrambling to their feet, the Jailbirds made for the gate tripping in the mud as they ran. Plumes of smoke billowed from the mansion. Rain fell in sheets around them. Mars hung back with Jude while the others scaled the gate, helping the girls up and over. Dragging Lydia behind him, Tommy darted for the Wrangler to get the engine started. Lucy planted her boot in Mars' interlocked fingers and he prepared to hoist her up, but another shot rang out.

She slipped and fell. He caught her as the two of them crouched with Jude beside the gate.

Jude pointed further down the fence line where trees swallowed the border of the property. "Hurry! This way!"

Mars grabbed Lucy's hand, and they followed Jude into the shadows.

Behind them, shouts arose in the night air as the Hunters organized themselves. Mars glanced over his shoulder to see them jogging across the field toward the gate while others hung back to tend to the wounded. Orion had left them to burn – why couldn't they see him for the monster he was? Why were they so willing to fight for him?

Ignoring his indignation, Mars skidded to a stop behind Jude. The fence line trailed into the forest that surrounded the estate property. Here the ground was slick with mud where grass was replaced with pine needles and twigs.

"Up the tree," said Jude, watching past Mars for the Hunters trailing toward them.

Mars whipped his head toward Lucy. "You first. Come on." He boosted her up to reach the lowest branch, and she pulled herself the rest of the way, twisting flat onto her belly on the branch and reaching down to lend Mars her hand. He grabbed it and pulled himself up behind her.

Lucy scooched forward across the branch, which hung over the other side of the fence. She came to the end, twisted around and dropped so that she was holding herself up by her arms, then let go. She tumbled to the ground, slipping a few inches in the mud before catching herself. Mars turned to help Jude up on the branch.

"Stop where you are!"

Mars snapped his head up to see the Hunters spilling into the forest, their guns trained on the two stragglers stuck in the tree. The slick ground kept them from moving any faster.

"*Hurry!*" Mars hissed.

Jude gripped Mars by the wrist and pulled him up onto the branch. They scurried across. A gunshot rang out, and Jude yelped, then slipped from the branch.

"Jude!" Mars turned onto his stomach and started to lower himself. A bullet struck the branch beside his hand, and the branch snapped under his weight. He fell to the ground, the collision knocking the wind out of him.

Groaning, Mars rolled onto his side, crawling toward Jude even as his vision spun. Lucy was already at his side, her hand on a wound on his arm. He hissed as he pawed at the wound, blood spilling down the sleeve of his jacket.

"We gotta go," Lucy said, doing her best to pull Jude onto his feet.

Mars shook his head, forcing himself onto his feet despite the vertigo. Lucy managed to get Jude upright just as the Hunters came to the fence. Too tall to climb, they settled for aiming their guns through the gaps between the iron bars.

Mars, Jude, and Lucy ran, sliding in the mud as they raced for the Wrangler.

Up ahead, the Wrangler's headlights shone into the night, a haze of smoke floating in the air around the driveway. The fire's glow cast an ominous, flickering shadow over the forest as the three stragglers broke through the forest and onto the gravel driveway.

The Wrangler flew into reverse just as Mars and the others arrived. It spun in the gravel as the passenger door flung open.

Gunshots pinged against the side of the car as the three Jailbirds piled in, Maya, Reid, and Immy grabbing at them while Tommy slammed on the gas. They shot forward before the door was even closed behind Mars. He settled into his seat, glancing over his shoulder to see distant muzzle flashes in the dark.

His heart racing, he struggled to catch his breath, running his hands over his head. Eyes wide, he glanced around at his friends, their chests heaving with every breath, their hearts racing so loud he thought he could hear them beating out of their chests.

Mars' eyes landed on Lydia in the front seat beside Tommy, her eyes red, her hand clutching Tommy's free hand while he drove them away from the wildfire and toward freedom.

A grin forced its way onto Mars' lips as he hung his arm out the open window, the cold air rushing into the cab of the car. Adrenaline coursing through his veins, he pumped his fist and let out a whoop. Despite the panic, despite the near loss, the others joined in.

The Wrangler wound through the mountain roads, their whoops and hollers of celebration echoing through the vast, empty forest and fading into the night air.

They were together again. Battered and bleeding, but together.

Nothing else mattered.

Rain and thunder swept over Spokane, dousing the city. The Jailbirds, still reeling from their close call and Lydia's rescue, pulled into a motel at the edge of town. Cheap little place that was severely lacking in amenities, but Mars couldn't find a single thing worth complaining about in light of their small but sure victory.

They piled into the room, exhausted, filthy, and starving. Jude and Maya disappeared into the bathroom. Mars figured out how to tend to the wound left behind by the bullet that had grazed him. Immy and Lucy sought out a vending machine and returned several minutes later with armfuls of potato chips, candy bars, and sodas.

Laughter gave way to conversation as they ate, though Reid sat in a chair in the corner of the room, away from the others. A little while later, Jude and Maya reappeared. Jude's bandana — usually around his wrist — was now wrapped around the wound on his upper arm. Tommy sat on the floor between the two creaky beds, Lydia sitting in front of him and leaning back against his stomach with his arms wrapped around her. Every few seconds, it seemed, Tommy leaned over to kiss the top of her head or whisper something into her ear. And Mars noticed how Lydia clung to him, unable to let go of him even for a second since her rescue.

At Mars' side, Lucy elbowed him. "You're staring," she whispered so only he could hear. "Penny for your thoughts?"

Mars smirked, his arms propped up on his knees as he sat against the wall opposite the beds, where a TV hung mounted above his head. He angled his head toward Lucy. "I used to be jealous of them," he admitted. "They have something I've always wanted. The kind of love you write books about."

Lucy glanced at Tommy and Lydia, then back at Mars. "You're not jealous anymore?"

Mars shrugged. "Maybe a little. But mostly I'm happy, and I'm thankful. Not many people have friends who love each other like they do." He paused. "Tommy would've killed that guy for her."

"But he didn't."

"But he *wanted to*. I could see it in his eyes. And even if he didn't, well, I guess I just want that kind of love."

"The dangerous kind?"

"The kind that lays it all on the line for the ones we love."
Mars bit his lip. "I don't think I've ever seen Tommy as blatantly honest as he was when he was holding that gun to that guy's head. He's always been the kind to hold it all together, to bottle it all up for everyone else's sake, but in that moment... none of that mattered. Every part of him – his anger and his fear and his love – he laid it all out there on that field." Mars paused, sniffing. "It may have been messy and it may have been dangerous, but it was pure, it was honest. God help your enemies when a good man like Tommy Rhodes decides to wage a war."

Lucy rested her chin on her arms as she rolled her head to the side to look up at Mars. "There's something—"

Jude's voice rose above the rest, cutting her off. "We need a plan," he said.

"Goodness, give us a chance to breathe why don'tcha," said Mars.

"Or at least catch up on our beauty sleep," said Immy.

"No rest for the wicked," Jude retorted. "Anyway, I figure we can't stay here, right? With the Hunters so close to the city, they'll spot us if we stay too long. Orion's not going to let us go that easily. With Lydia gone, with Reid out of jail, and with the fact that we have all three keys, he's going to hunt us down. So, now that we're all together again, we need to be thinking about where we go from here."

"Back to Mariner's Cove," said Tommy. "That's where we'll find the next clue."

"That could take days," Maya added. "Weeks. We don't have the money to hop from motel to motel for that long."

Beside Mars, Lucy raised a hand. "I think I can help with that."

All eyes turned to her. Tinges of pink brushed her cheeks as she looked over at Mars. "I haven't been... entirely honest with you guys."

Mars arched an eyebrow.

Lucy sighed. "I'm kind of... filthy rich."

Episode Five

ONE IN THE CHAMBER

"In a single moment, with a single shared look and hands almost touching but not, what she found when she peered into his blue eyes was enough to fill that vacant space in her heart."

FORTY-SEVEN
MARS

A bitter chill swept in from across the Atlantic Ocean, bringing fresh snow with it. Naked maple trees bent and bowed beneath the weight of the snow. The ocean tumbled along the rocky coastline.

"This the place?" Tommy asked as the Wrangler rolled to a stop in the morning hours of early February – a week after they'd left Spokane behind.

"Yep," said Lucy from the seat beside Mars.

Mars leaned out the open window, gawking at Lucy's house, though "house" was the understatement of the century. She wasn't kidding when she said she was "filthy rich."

The Jailbirds climbed out of the car one by one, marveling at the place. Perched on a hillside overlooking the Atlantic Ocean to the east and the rest of Mariner's Cove to the south, the three-story mansion boasted a curved front porch that led to a large set of double doors made of solid wood. The roofline was broken up by a series of dormer windows. Ivy crept up the old, brick-and-mortar walls of the mansion, enshrining the place in a sense of mystery and old-world comfort. A soft glow from the interior lights spilled through the windows. The morning fog surrounded the property, but Mars could see through the haze and the hedges that the estate's property extended even further beyond the walls of the mansion. In the distance, he saw stables and horses roaming the dewdropped fields.

"You're not just rich," Jude said with a grin as he glanced at Lucy. "You're *old money* rich."

Lucy blushed, and Mars tried not to gape at her. The more he learned about this girl, the more he wanted to know. What secrets did she harbor? What dreams did she hold in her heart? He found Lucy Adler utterly fascinating – like a starry constellation that burst to life just to dazzle and amaze.

"Come on in," Lucy said as she led the way. "Conrad'll be starting breakfast soon."

Mars stopped, exchanging a glance with Tommy and Jude in turn. He grinned. "She has a *butler*?"

Tommy whistled, then followed after Lucy, leaving Mars to fall behind. He gave the exterior of the mansion one last once-over, then followed the group inside.

The mansion's interior was even more spectacular. Marble floors and mahogany doors, tall ceilings and glittering chandeliers, sprawling built-in bookcases and carved pillars, wallpapers that boasted old-world artistry and molding that put modern architecture to shame. Stepping inside Lucy's mansion was like stepping into the past – in the kind of way that watching a romantic, historical film felt like traveling back through time. Mars had never given much thought to money – except when his parents didn't have any, scraping whatever they could together to pay the restaurant's bills. But now he could almost picture himself in a place like this.

"They don't build 'em like they used to," Jude said, running his hands along the curled banister at the base of the stairs. A round table occupied the middle space of the massive circular foyer. To the right, a sitting room with old paisley-printed chairs and tea tables. To the left, a larger family room with a polished grand piano set against the windows.

Lucy walked into the living room, turning to face the others. "*Mi casa es su casa*," she said, waving them in.

"Girl, you've been holding out on us," said Immy, turning in circles as she stared up at the ceilings.

"This place feels like it should be in a museum," added Maya.

Her hand slipped into Jude's as he moved forward to explore, climbing the stairs and leading her along room by room. He half expected Lucy to tell him to stop, but he found her smiling.

"So, who else lives here?" asked Reid.

She crossed her arms and leaned against the arch. Her short black hair fell into her eyes, and she brushed it back behind her ear, her cherry red lips curved in a smile. "Just me and Conrad – he's the butler – and then there's Sylvie, the maid, and Bruno, the stableboy. Oh, and Jesse sometimes stops by for a few days at a time to take care of the cars. He's kind of a hobbyist mechanic, so I offered to let him work on mine."

"*Just?*" Lydia said with a laugh, her arms around Tommy's middle.

"*Cars?*" asked Tommy. "*Plural?*"

"Hold on," said Mars. "It's just you, then?"

Lucy gave him a puzzled look.

"I mean, other than the staff? No family?"

She frowned. "What I told you weeks ago was true, Mars. My family's dead. This is just… what I'm left with."

"I'm sorry. I didn't-"

She held up a hand. "It's okay. I get it. I lied to you guys, but how was I to know how you'd react? Besides, it's not like we had a ton of time to exchange net worths."

"Well, mine's *zero*, so…" muttered Tommy.

Mars smiled. "No, I get it. It's just pretty amazing, is all."

Lucy smiled back, her eyes dancing in the light, then straightened. "Anyway, let me give you guys the tour."

"Do we get our own rooms?" Jude hollered from the second-floor balcony. Maya laughed as she followed him.

"For sure! There's plenty of space," Lucy replied. "Mine's the biggest room at the end of the hall, but all the others are up for grabs. The staff live in a separate house on the west end of the property."

Reid started up the stairs while Jude and Maya disappeared to choose their respective rooms, leaving Tommy, Lydia, Mars, and Immy to follow Lucy as she gave them the official tour. Not only did this place have a massive kitchen and formal dining area, but it also had a *second* kitchen behind the first. A "prep kitchen," Lucy called it. That and a butler's pantry bigger than Mars' old room. On the main level, there were three bathrooms, a ballroom, a study, a conservatory, a private museum, and a mud room in addition to the rooms they'd already seen. Lucy led them upstairs where Jude, Maya, and Reid had already claimed rooms for themselves, Reid disappearing into his and closing the door behind him.

Lydia whispered something to Tommy, then slipped inside Reid's room after him.

The second and third floors were mostly bedrooms, bathrooms, and closets, but the balcony overlooking the main floor had a small sitting area.

"You ever host any parties here?" asked Tommy.

"A few," Lucy replied, crossing her arms as she leaned against the railing that overlooked the foyer. "Not in a long time, but when we did… they were a sight to behold."

Immy shook her head. "This place is too rich for my blood."

"Don't worry," said Lucy. "It isn't contagious."

Mars chuckled, his eyes drawn to the series of oil paintings that lined the second floor hallway. One painting in particular caught his eye, depicting a Black woman dressed in clothes that, he guessed, must have been from the early nineteen hundreds. Her hair was piled on top of her head. She wore a white dress, the collar halfway up her neck, the shoulders poofed out, and lace at the end of the sleeves around her wrists. She was married, judging by the modest wedding ring on her finger. Her hands were folded in her lap as she stared off to the right, but something was off about the painting. Something Mars couldn't put his finger on.

He crossed the floor toward the painting, and as he neared it, the light from the sconces along the wall shifted and fell over the painting in just the right way to reveal what was bugging Mars. In her hand was an envelope, but it was the envelope's seal that caught Mars' attention.

"This is Katherine Rhodes, isn't it?" he asked Lucy. "Your great-great-great-grandmother?"

Lucy nodded.

"That symbol," Mars said, pointing. Tommy and Immy

inched closer to them, squinting at the painting. "On the envelope's wax seal. I've… seen it before."

"You have. Here." Lucy rolled up the sleeve of her sweater, revealing the devilfish tattoo on her forearm.

Puzzled, Mars frowned and looked up at her.

"That's the other thing I guess I haven't gotten around to telling you guys," Lucy said with a sigh. "The *Devilfish*. It's the name of the pirate ship that Katherine Rhodes and her father, Othniel Cuvier, chartered for their overseas expeditions. But… it's also the name of the organization that Katherine Rhodes founded to protect her father's life work." She paused. "My family, *me*… we're part of that organization, and that's the real reason I was so quick to throw in with you guys – my family's entire mission, for as long as I can remember, has been to make sure that the wrong people don't discover Cuvier's treasure."

FORTY-EIGHT
LYDIA

Shutting the door behind her, Lydia found Reid leaning against the windowsill in his room, staring out at a property saturated in a layer of heavy fog. Orbs of light twinkled in the distance. Trees waved bare branches in the cold February air.

"You're here," Lydia said, and as soon as she said it her eyes began to brim with tears. She'd wanted to save Reid, to rescue him from the spell Orion had him under, and he'd saved her instead — him and all the others. Seeing him with the Jailbirds had taken her by surprise, but she hadn't had a chance to be alone with her brother since they'd found her in Spokane. To understand where his head was at.

Sitting at the end of the bed, she waited for him to turn, to notice her. "Reid…"

"I shouldn't be here," he said without looking her way.

"Doesn't really matter now, does it?"

There was something he wanted to say, but whatever it was, he swallowed it. Lydia tried to remember the last time they'd spoken. Orion's men had captured her at the Mariner's Cove Museum – before Reid had intervened to save the Jailbirds' lives. She wasn't sure they knew how to be brother and sister. Their childhood hadn't exactly been… normal. They'd always had a strained relationship, but Lydia wanted more, and she knew – at least, she was certain she could see – that Reid wanted more, too.

"Mom's alive," Lydia said, desperate for a conversation between the two of them that felt like it meant something.

"I know," said Reid.

"You do?"

Reid nodded, turning away from the window. He leaned against the sill and crossed his arms, smirking down at her. "I found out in Peru."

"Apparently, she faked her death to get away from Orion."

"And left us to pick up the pieces."

"Where do you think she is now?"

Reid shrugged. "She's never been one to stick around."

"Yeah, I guess. But… that's not all," said Lydia.

"Oh? This family has more secrets? Color me surprised."

Lydia chuckled. "Um, Mom had an affair before I was born with, uh… Jack Mayfield, and…"

"You're kidding…"

"Nope. Jude's our brother. Well, *half*-brother."

What seemed like genuine shock registered on Reid's face. He ran his hands over his hair, sucked in a breath, then exhaled sharply.

"Thank you," said Lydia. "For helping us."

Reid's jaw tightened.

"I don't know what's going through your mind right now, but I know what I'd be thinking about myself if I were in your shoes, and I'm telling you – *stop*. Stop beating yourself up, stop blaming yourself, because none of us blame you. You and I didn't have the same father – not really."

"But what kind of excuse is that, Lydia? And how am I supposed to feel about the fact that I did what I did because I wanted Dad, Orion, *someone* to…"

He stopped short, inhaling.

Lydia pursed her lips. "To see you?"

As soon as she said the words, his lip quivered. He bit it to stop it, but his eyes began to water, and he looked away, tightening his arms around his chest.

"We all want the people we love and admire to see us," she said. "It doesn't make us weak to admit that. I don't know why Dad failed you, or why Orion turned out the way he did. I can't undo the damage they've done, but I can tell you that *I* see you, Reid."

Tears welled in her eyes, but she didn't look away from him. Grief at the death of her father – a brutal murder that she herself had witnessed – washed over her, emphasized only by the revelation that her own uncle had been the one to kill him.

"You're my brother, Reid, and I see you for the man that you are. Brave enough to change your course when you realize you're heading in the wrong direction. Strong enough to join with people you once believed were enemies and admit that you were wrong. Selfless enough to risk your own life to save theirs. You would've gone to prison for them. What kind of man does that? Certainly not Orion, or Dad…"

Lydia stood, inching toward Reid. He remained unmoving.

"I see you, Reid, and maybe that scares you. Maybe there's things you don't want other people to see, and I get that. And I know my approval doesn't mean much because I'm just your sister, but I love you and I'm *glad* you're here with us. *This* is where you belong. Bluecoat, Jailbird – it doesn't matter."

Reid stiffened, running a hand over his chest.

"There's wounds in your heart that'll take time to heal," she said, "but that won't start until you admit that they're there. Maybe not to me or anyone else, but to yourself, to God, to a stranger – I don't know. But don't let them fester, and don't think that we'll think any less of you for them. If you think you're broken, you're not alone. Just ask any of us. But there's more to you than what's broken. See the whole picture – see the *good*."

His eyes snapping to hers, he straightened. "The *good*? How can you say that when *everything good* has been taken from me?"

Lydia took a step backward, her eyes widening. A flash of hurt, of frustration, pricked her heart. "Really," she said. "Seems to me like the only things that have been *taken* from you are the things that were *destroying* you in the first place. There's still some good that's left, but–" Lydia bit her tongue before her own hurt got the better of her. "What about me? I'm *right here*. Is that not *good enough*?"

Reid's jaw tensed as he exhaled through his nose. "That's the problem, Lydia. I look at you, and all I see is my failure."

"Then maybe it's time you started looking for something different."

Reid swallowed. "You should go. I need to take a shower anyway, so…"

Her hopes deflating, Lydia nodded. "Okay. I'll leave you to it then."

She left the room, closing the door behind her. Alone in the hall, she let out a breath and leaned against the bedroom door, staring up at the ceiling as tears lingered in her eyes. She kicked herself mentally for allowing herself to get so emotional. What if her hurt pushed him away? What if all she'd managed to do was inflict more guilt onto her brother?

Closing her eyes, Lydia took a moment to pray for her brother, then wandered down the hallway to find the others. Would the Jailbirds ever find peace, and if they did, who would they be when they found it?

FORTY-NINE

MAYA

Maya sat on the end of her bed, running her hands over the quilted blanket as Jude explored the connected bathroom. He had taken the room on the opposite side of the hall – the door directly across from hers.

Her family was all together again, and Maya should be thrilled. Over the moon, even. Instead she found herself unsure, and mostly because of the blond boy currently exploring her bathroom.

They'd hardly had a moment together since their kiss on the train. Things hadn't slowed down long enough for either of them to figure out what they were, where they were going. She'd always felt so sure of herself around Jude, but now suddenly she found herself worrying about whether or not he would even want a girl like her. And if he decided that he didn't, then what? With her mother dead and herself an outlaw in her own hometown, the

Jailbirds were all Maya had left. Was a chance at love worth the risk of losing who they were, who they'd always been?

"Hello? May? Anybody home?"

Maya shook herself from her thoughts and glanced at Jude standing in the bathroom doorway. "What?"

He chuckled. "Welcome back, Space Cadet."

"Sorry, what were you saying?"

Crossing his arms over his chest, he leaned against the door frame and stared down at her with eyes that seemed to see right through her. "Nothing nearly as important as whatever is on your mind."

"The train."

Jude's cheeks flushed red and he shifted on his feet, but he stayed where he was. "Oh."

Picking at the quilt beneath her, Maya avoided Jude's eyes. Embarrassment warmed her cheeks, which only made her angry. She'd never been bashful around him before. Why now?

"We haven't… really talked about it," she said. "What it might mean. For us."

"No, we haven't."

Jude moved from the doorway to the end of the bed, sitting down beside her, his hand landing on the bed next to hers, their fingers brushing each other but just barely. They stared down at their hands for a moment, silence passing between them.

"Do you regret it?" she asked, her voice a whisper. Desperate to know what was on his mind, in his heart. "Us?"

"Not for a minute," he said, blond hair falling in front of blue eyes as he looked over at her. "You're all I think about, if you know what I mean."

Maya lifted her eyes to meet his, and suddenly the embarrassment vanished. In its place was something she hadn't felt for a long time. Her entire life, growing up with borderline absentee parents and finding out that they'd wanted to abort her, Maya had been searching for a place to belong, to call home. She'd found it in the Jailbirds, but still there was something missing. A place in her heart that had been hollowed out by years of disappointment and rejection. In a moment, with a single shared look and hands almost touching but not, what she found when she peered into his blue eyes was enough to fill that vacant space in her heart.

She never would have imagined that the boy who used to tease her and give her endless grief would become the great love of her life, but that's what he was to her, and she wanted to tell him. Oh, how she wanted him to know what he meant to her, but words fell short. So, as she wrapped her hand around his and leaned across the gap between them, her lips found his.

She inhaled the scent of him, savored the taste of him, the cut on his lip, the feel of his hand as it found its way to the side of her face. His thumb brushed her cheekbone, and they shifted on the bed, turning toward one another, their hearts opened for the first time to the kind of love they'd only ever dreamed about.

When Jude pulled away, his eyes stayed on hers. His skin felt hot to the touch, and his nearness set Maya's nerves on fire.

"I should go," he said, glancing toward the open door that led out into the hall. Their friends' voices carried down the hallway.

Maya nodded, understanding. He stood, his hand slowly slipping from hers. She watched him go, and when he disappeared around the corner, she fell back on the bed. Running her fingers through her curly hair, a smile broke through her face even as tears slipped from her eyes.

She had lost so much, but, oh, the love that she had gained.

FIFTY

JUDE

Jude slipped out of Maya's room, his heart like a hummingbird inside his chest. He followed the hallway and found Tommy, Immy, Lucy, and Mars at the balcony.

When Tommy saw Jude, he cocked an eyebrow. "You run a marathon or something?" he asked as he sidled up to Jude. "You look flushed."

Jude grinned. "Something like that."

Tommy smirked, crossing his arms. "What do you think?"

"What do I think of what?"

"This," he said, gesturing around them.

"I think... we should've made friends with rich people a lot sooner."

Lydia appeared at the other end of the hall, her expression drawn tight. He and Lydia still hadn't even had time to process their newfound blood ties, much less his relationship – whatever it could be called – with Reid. Did Reid even know?

Jude watched Tommy's eyes find her from across the balcony, noticing the furrow in his brow as his jaw tensed. Jude's mind flashed to the scene in Spokane – the burning mansion and Tommy holding a gun to the guard's head. He could only imagine what was going through his best friend's head now, the guilt and remorse. If it had been Maya, he couldn't honestly say that he wouldn't have done the same.

As if by some secret signal, Tommy crossed over to Lydia. They whispered between themselves before disappearing into one of the bedrooms.

Maya left her room a second later, her gaze pointedly avoiding Jude's as she announced, "I have an idea. Where is everyone?" she asked.

"Tommy and Lydia just left," said Immy. "And I think I heard Reid say something about a shower earlier."

Lucy perked up. To Jude, she seemed almost… nervous? Excited? Who knew how long it had been since she'd had anyone other than an employee in this mansion with her. She offered, "If everyone wants to take a shower, I'll have Sylvie bring up a bunch of robes so she can launder our clothes."

"Yes, please," said Immy. "Shower via rest stop water fountain this past week just hasn't done the trick."

"You saying we smell?" Jude said, feigning offense.

"Some of us more than others," said Mars.

"You know what they say about finger-pointing, don't you?" said Immy with a smirk.

"Hey, I got plenty of fingers to spare."

Jude held out his hands. "Alright, alright. Let's hear Maya out."

"Thank you, Jude. At least *someone* can hear my voice," she said with a smirk. "Anyway, I'm actually glad Tommy and Lydia aren't here because I think this would be a nice surprise for them."

"Well, out with it, then," Immy urged.

"I know we're all itching to pick up the trail on this treasure, but we haven't all been together in I-don't-know-how-long. And since we *do* have a couple of newlyweds who never really got to celebrate their wedding, it'd be a shame to put an entire castle to waste."

"Oh!" Lucy exclaimed, clapping her hands together. "Yes! I love it already!"

Mars nodded. "I think we could all use the chance to decompress."

"Yeah," Jude agreed, "I didn't even think about it until now, but this is the first time in months that none of us have been on the run. I mean, technically we're still on the run, but nobody knows we're here."

"And your staff is trustworthy?" Immy asked Lucy, a glint of suspicion in her eyes.

She nodded. "They've been around since before I was born. For a family like mine, discretion is practically in the job description."

"Alright then," said Maya. "Today, we clean up and get some rest, then tonight, Lucy, maybe you could have your cook put together a sort of celebration feast?"

"Sure thing, and I'll have the maid pull out some clothes for us to wear."

"Great." Maya turned to Jude. "Can you have her drop them off in Tommy and Lydia's room with a note to meet us in the dining room?"

She nodded, then they quickly dispersed to their separate rooms while Lucy headed downstairs to put in the order with her staff.

Jude grabbed Maya by the elbow before she turned to leave, pulling her toward him. "You're amazing, you know that?" he said, his face inches from hers.

She grinned, then gave his hand a squeeze before heading back to her own room.

FIFTY-ONE

IMMY

Music drifted up the stairs, swirling around Immy as she descended. She wore a wine-red dress that Lucy had left on the bed for her while she was in the shower. Immy had been right to think the girl was keeping something from them, but she never would've imagined it would be her wealth. Lucy had left her a pair of high heels too, but Immy had never worn that kind of shoe before and now, as she took the last step onto the foyer floor, she regretted giving them a try.

Rubbing her hands along her arms, she followed the music to the formal dining room where she found Reid waiting alone, the others still in their rooms.

Seeing her, Reid stood, a look of surprise playing briefly on his face before he caught himself. His eyes looked her up and down for just a moment before meeting her gaze.

Immy blushed. Maybe it wasn't too late to throw the robe back on over this dress.

But Reid wasn't the only one taking in the sight of her. She'd noticed him, too. He wore a pair of gray twill paints and a matching blazer over a white button-down shirt. His hands were tucked in his pockets until he remembered his manners and moved to pull out a chair for Immy.

Immy almost asked why he picked the chair next to him until she noticed the place cards on the table. The staff's doing.

"Thank you," she said, taking a seat, all too happy to get off her feet. These heels were killing her.

"You're welcome." Reid sat down beside her, leaning back in his chair, his hands folded in his lap as he glanced around the dining room. Immy did the same, absorbing the scene around them. She didn't think she'd been in the shower *that* long, but the dining room looked like something that had taken hours to prepare. Oil paintings depicting shipwrecks and stormy seas hung on paneled walls painted red. The intricate molding from the rest of the house continued in the dining room, and three massive chandeliers hung in a row along the length of the solid wood dining table. One of the walls that ran the length of the table featured three French doors that looked out over the estate, burgundy curtains framing each set of doors as the moon shone through the glass. Candlesticks of varying heights trailed down the center of the table, evergreen branches and golden ribbon intertwining between them. The plates at each setting looked a hundred years old, printed with beautiful patterns. Sparkling glasses and silverware sat beside each setting, and the napkins were folded on the plates to look like flowers.

"Do rich people like you always eat dinner with such…?" Immy couldn't decide on a word.

"Flair?" Reid suggested.

"That's the word."

Chuckling, Reid said, "No, but my family didn't take many meals together. Holidays were the only time we all gathered around the table, and even then it was nothing like this. New money and old money are… very different."

"I'd take *any money* at this point."

"Fair enough."

More silence. A chill swept over Immy's arms, sending goosebumps prickling across her skin. She folded her arms over her chest – partly to warm them, partly to hide. This was the first time she'd ever been alone with Reid, and she wasn't sure what to do with the strange feelings that fluttered through her chest, like when she caught herself watching him change in Ellensburg.

"You cold?" Reid asked.

"No," she said, then changed her mind. "Yes."

Reid stood, slipping his blazer down his arms. Immy watched him out of the corner of her eye, leaning forward so he could drape his coat over her shoulders. "Thanks," she said.

"You're welcome."

After another moment of silence, Immy turned to look at Reid. A couple months ago, she'd hated him. He'd been part of the reason her uncle, Emilio, had died at Orion's hands. Yet Emilio's death seemed to have been the reason for Reid's sudden turnaround. What had happened between the two of them?

"What?" Reid asked, raising an eyebrow.

"I used to hate you," Immy said.

He scoffed. "Thanks. Take a number."

"*Used to.*" She paused, searching for the words. "Emilio was the only family I had left, and I blamed you. But you loved him too. Didn't you?"

Reid chewed on his lip, his jaw tensing. "He was a good man. A better man than any I've ever known."

Tears gathered in Immy's eyes, and she looked away. "He probably would have died whether you'd been there or not, but… I'm glad you were there. Emilio was always the kind of man who made people feel like they could be better. I'm glad you got to see that before he died." A pang of guilt struck her heart. She looked down at her hands, her fingers picking at her nail beds. "And I'm glad he isn't here now, because he'd be ashamed of me if he knew…"

Reid's chair shifted on the floor as he leaned forward. "What do you mean?"

"When we were in Mammoth, I… got my hands on a gun, and I was so… *angry*. And I figured if I could just find Orion and take care of him then and there, then things would be better. He'd be gone, and things could settle down. We could find Cuvier's treasure without being hunted down by him or his goons. But mostly…" An edge of anger in her tone, she looked Reid in the eyes. "I wanted revenge, Reid. I wanted to kill him for killing Emilio, and I almost ruined it for all of us."

Sighing, Reid said, "Believe it or not, I understand."

She did believe him.

A man in a black suit appeared with a carafe of water in one hand, a towel draped over his forearm as he wordlessly filled the glasses in front of Reid and Immy, then disappeared through the doorway into the kitchen. Immy sat back in her chair, folding her hands in her lap.

"I helped my uncle bury my father's body, and then I helped him bury Emilio's." Reid paused as Immy's eyes shot to his, the blue in his eyes catching in the candlelight. "Immy, I only grieved *one* of those men."

"I guess you and I aren't so different," Immy said.

They held each other's gaze a moment longer until the sound of approaching footsteps broke the silence.

Reid cleared his throat, leaning back in his chair. Immy turned to see Jude and Maya sauntering into the dining room. Maya's arm was hooked through Jude's and she wore a green, satin dress that hung to the floor. Jude's wild blond hair was brushed back and he wore a tan suit with a blue button-down underneath.

"I thought everyone else would've been down by now," Maya said, glancing between Immy and Reid.

"Nope, just us," Immy said.

Before long the others joined them, and conversation began to fill the dining room. Lydia and Tommy arrived hand in hand – Lydia's dress blue and Tommy's suit brown.

"So, *this* is the surprise," Tommy said, marveling at the dining room. "A mysterious note said to get dressed and come downstairs. What's the occasion?"

"You," said Maya. "Well, both of you. You never got to celebrate your wedding, and we want to celebrate with you."

Lydia smiled, blushing as she glanced up at Tommy. "You didn't have to do that."

Mars followed shortly behind with his black suit, then Lucy in a peach-colored dress. Immy and Maya exchanged a humored glance when Mars' eyes lingered on Lucy a little too long.

"I don't think we've ever been so well-dressed," Lydia said over their first course. She glanced down at her plate. "Or well-fed."

Immy leaned across the table to whisper, "Yeah, but these heels are *killing* me."

Laughter erupted across the table followed by thanks to Lucy for the borrowed clothes. Immy watched the way she interacted with the Jailbirds, and she thought she might have felt jealous, but she'd once been where Lucy was – the outsider this group of people had welcomed in with open arms. It had taken Immy a while to get used to the fact that she wasn't on her own anymore. The Black Flag had been like a family to her, but that was only because she had little to compare it to. Now this... *this* was family.

Her eyes wandered to the boy in the chair beside her. He joined in on the jokes and added the occasional comment, but for the most part he sat quiet. Immy wanted to know what was on his mind, but maybe belonging didn't always come easy. Maybe it took time, and maybe Immy was willing to wait with him.

Glass chimed, and Immy turned to see Jude standing as he tapped the blunt side of a butter knife against the side of his fluted glass. With everyone's eyes turned his way, he smiled, his gaze passing over the table. "I'd like to propose a toast."

Jude turned to Tommy and Lydia, raised his glass. "I've watched the two of you love each other for longer than you were willing to admit it, and now we get to celebrate the fact that you've found each other not just once... but *twice*." He glanced down at Maya seated beside him. "I think I speak for all of us when I say that we can only hope to share with someone the kind of love that burns like a torch against the night – in defiance of the dark – and we are thrilled at the chance to honor what the two of you have become now as husband and wife before God, and now before us. So, to Tommy and Lydia for showing us the way."

The others raised their glasses as Tommy leaned over to Lydia, grinning as he kissed her. "To Tommy and Lydia," they said in unison.

Conversations passed over the table, changing from one subject to another like water tumbling over stone. Immy had never had anything like this – friends and family gathered around the table. She drank it in. The laughter and the shared stories, the food and drink, the hours passing long into the night as they savored one another's company. They stood upon unfamiliar shores as an ocean of fear and loss raged around them; everything they knew and everything they had once believed lay behind them. She could almost imagine it – the light of what once was home piercing the dark of what lay ahead.

For now, in this moment, they found a glimmer of peace in the eye of a storm sure to soon come crashing down.

FIFTY-TWO
TOMMY

The bedroom door clicked shut behind Tommy. He leaned against it, watching Lydia as she moved across the room, her blue satin dress rippling like water. Her fingers found the silver locket that dangled around her neck as she met her reflection in the vanity mirror. Tommy's head rolled back against the door, exhaustion overtaking the emotions warring for dominance in his heart.

"That was nice of them," she said, her words soft. It was past midnight before the Jailbirds had decided to call it a night. They would gather for breakfast in the morning to decide their next course of action, but for tonight, they could just… *be*.

Tommy removed his blazer and draped it over the bedpost as he sat down on the end of the bed, the old frame creaking under his weight. He unbuttoned the cuffs of his shirt, then stopped. Lydia climbed up onto the bed behind him, resting the side of her face on his shoulder. He turned to kiss the top of her head, inhaling the smell of strawberry-scented shampoo in her hair mingled with perfume.

"I almost killed someone trying to find you," he whispered.

Lydia lifted her head to look at him, surprise playing in her eyes.

His jaw tensed. "And the thing is… I don't even regret it."

"You found me," she said, a hand climbing up his back, sending a chill dancing across his spine. "That's all that matters."

He inhaled, absorbing the feeling of her beside him again. "When you were gone, I became someone… I didn't recognize. I had all this anger, all this hate…"

"Was it anger?" she asked, pulling away. "Was it hate? Or was it a side of love you'd never felt until now?" She paused, glancing away before adding, "Love is not some… passive thing."

Maybe he did have a shallow, immature understanding of love. Love was more than goosebumps and a featherlight kiss. It was wild in coming to the defense of those you loved. Could Tommy live with what he'd done? He'd hurt someone, but that person was still alive. And they had hurt others. If a soldier could bear the cost of battle for the sake of their homeland, couldn't Tommy bear the cost of a bullet for the sake of Lydia's life?

"If you're wrong for hurting someone to save me, then I'm wrong, too," Lydia said. "Because I'm the one who started that fire, and who knows how many people…"

Tommy shifted on the bed, turning toward her. "Hey, hey. Don't do that to yourself. You were a *captive*. You had every right to protect yourself."

"But I could have escaped without setting that fire. I went *back in* to do it."

"And if you hadn't set that fire, you may not have had the distraction you needed to find us, and we may not have been able to get away."

She sniffed. "Maybe it's better that I don't know if everyone made it out or not."

His hand moved to the side of her face, his thumb wiping away the tear that fell from her eyelid. "Let's make a deal, you and me. The past stays right where it is. What we've done and what's been done to us, we leave it all behind from here on out. The only thing that matters is what we do next. Deal?"

She nodded.

Smiling, Tommy kissed her forehead, then stood to unbutton his shirt. He slipped it off, tossing it to the floor, wincing at the bandaged wound in his side where the guard had cut him. At the time, with adrenaline coursing through his veins, he hadn't even noticed.

Lydia's fingers reached out to touch the skin around the bandage. "How's it feel?"

"Better than it did a week ago," he replied, taking her hands in his. Her eyes trailed up to his eyes, and he leaned over to kiss her. That night, they shared themselves with one another in a way that they had craved since being separated. Together, they left their regrets behind on a castle floor.

FIFTY-THREE
MARS

"Now that we're finally all back together," Mars said over the clatter of silverware on porcelain plates as the Jailbirds reconvened in the dining room for breakfast, "we need to figure out a plan."

"Don't get caught," Jude said, mouth full of cinnamon roll.

"That's a goal, not a plan," Immy retorted from the other end of the table as she took a drink of orange juice.

"A worthy goal," Jude replied.

"A *lofty* goal," Maya added.

"Are you guys always like this?" interjected Reid.

Jude said *yes* at the same time that Mars answered *no*.

"Better get used to it, Reid," Tommy said with a smirk. "You're a Jailbird now. And once a bird…"

"Always a bird," the others finished automatically.

"Okay, okay." Mars shoved his half-finished breakfast away

and held up his hands. "Back to the subject at hand. Let's start with what we know."

Tommy wiped his mouth with a napkin. "Othniel Cuvier's greatest discoveries were stored away in a vault before he died. The Mammoth, Titan, and Leviathan led us to the three *keys*." Tommy reached into the backpack on the floor by his feet and pulled them out, setting all three on the edge of the table. Mars had studied them every way he knew how, but as far as he could tell, these *keys* were just octagonal blocks of carved wood about the size of his thumb.

"These keys don't seem to have any hidden hinges or secret slots, which means that they must themselves must *be* the key. Lucy…" He turned to her, still wrestling with whether to feel betrayed because she'd kept secrets from them — from *him* — or guilty for holding it against her. "You said your family was tasked with protecting the lost vault. Do you have any idea where it might be?"

Lucy shook her head, frowning. "Katherine Rhodes may have shared that info with the earlier generations of Devilfish members, but the exact details were lost along the way. After my grandparents died, I searched the family archives for any sign of a lead, but the only thing left behind is some cryptic message."

"What's it say?" Jude asked.

"'Follow the captain's eye.'"

Mars knit his brow together.

"Well, that's nonsense," Lydia said, stabbing her fork into a bowl of freshly sliced fruit.

"We'll circle back to that later." Mars reached into his own backpack for his journal, flipping through his pages of notes, acutely aware of Lucy's eyes on him as he spoke. "So we have the keys and a single clue to Cuvier's vault. What else do we know?"

Reid spoke up. "We know that Orion's not going to stop until he gets his hands on that treasure. He's probably already sent hundreds of Hunters after us." He paused, turning his glass of water in circles on the table, leaving a condensation ring on the white tablecloth. "He has resources. He's probably already identified Lucy, so I wouldn't bet on her being able to fly under the radar much longer. It's only a matter of time before they figure out where we are and come after us."

Silence fell over the table. Mars remembered the flash drive that Maya's mom had died to get to them. Its contents could mean life or death for the Jailbirds, but he didn't want to give them false hope. Not until he figured out if it would get them anywhere. Maya hadn't asked about it since shoving it into his hands, but then, she had other things on her mind. She'd entrusted it to Mars, and Mars could only hope that he was making the right call.

"There was a woman with him," said Lydia. "I heard her through the walls of the mansion in Spokane, but I didn't recognize her voice."

Reid ran a hand over his hair. "I'm not familiar with any woman. Was she just a lackey?"

"No, she seemed almost like a colleague, like Orion relied on her to help him keep things straight."

"So there's a new player," Maya said, taking a bite of buttered toast. Jude reached his arm around her shoulders, resting it on the back of her chair.

"A mystery woman," Immy added. "Emilio never mentioned anything to me before he…" She glanced at Reid, then looked away. He cleared his throat, shifting in his seat.

"I recognized her voice," said Lydia, "but it was muffled, so I couldn't place where I'd heard it before. It almost seemed like she was a voice of reason for Orion, like that's why he'd recruited her, for all the good it's done."

Mars half-listened to Lydia's assessment, struck by how much things had changed. It used to be just the four of them. Tommy, Jude, Maya, and himself. But now they'd added Lydia, Immy, Lucy, and Reid to their group. The dynamics were constantly changing, and it was making his head spin. He'd been jealous of Tommy, insecure in his own ability to connect with a girl in a way that truly mattered. And Jude and Maya seemed to fit so well together. Then, Lucy had come along, seeing things in Mars that he hadn't seen in himself. Back in Mammoth, she'd said he could be more. Until then, he'd let his voice fall to the wayside so much, let others lead while he went along for the ride. But with Lucy…

There was so much going on in Mars' heart and mind, he couldn't keep it all straight. Opinions and beliefs intermingled with feelings and desires in a way that wasn't always productive. Maybe it was his fault for spending so much of his life focusing on himself – *his* plans for *his* future, *his* dreams, *his* goals, *his* education. Because his life had suddenly become about everything and everyone but himself in such spectacular – even painful – ways.

But maybe it was okay to say goodbye to who he'd been last September, and to his dreams for his future. His life had become about something much bigger, so maybe he needed to just lean into that. Maybe his resistance to what was happening around him was only causing him to feel more unsure of himself. Unstable. Lost.

Mars didn't want to feel lost anymore, and he didn't want to spend his life second-guessing himself or where he fit. The

Jailbirds had proven time and again that Mars was a part of them, flaws and all. Maybe the first step to finding someone to connect with in the way he'd always dreamed about was to stop trying to warp himself to fit who he thought he should be and start accepting who he was becoming.

"Hold on," said Tommy. "*Follow the captain's eye.*" He turned to Lucy. "At the Mariner's Cove Museum, wasn't there a statue of some sea captain?"

"Yeah, so?"

"When was it built?"

"The early 1900s…" Lucy's eyes widened.

Tommy glanced at the others as his lips turned up in a smile. "That statue – there was an octopus, a *devilfish*, and one of its tentacles was wrapped around the sailor's arm and the spyglass in his hands. I'd bet anything that the spyglass is pointing us right to Cuvier's lost vault."

FIFTY-FOUR
TOMMY

ommy hunched his shoulders against the bitter chill of the wind that blew in across the harbor. A fog of snow settled over Mariner's Cove so that most of the city was veiled in white, while in the distance Tommy could make out the silhouette of the *Devilfish* rocking in its place beside the dock, its masts vanishing into the fog. A sign hung in the museum's door to the left, stating they had closed "due to inclement weather."

The Jailbirds gathered around the statue beside the water. A stone depiction of a nineteenth century boat captain. Over the years, weather had dulled some of the defining features, but the details could still be discerned despite its age. The man wore a hat, a coat, and trousers. In his right hand he held a long spyglass, his left eye squinted as he looked through the spyglass out across the Atlantic Ocean. The figure of an octopus was wrapped around his right leg, one of its eight tentacles reaching up to wrap around his right arm and the spyglass he held as though they held it together – man and creature working in tandem.

"Follow the captain's eye," Tommy whispered.

"'Pirate Captain Barnaby Taylor,'" Jude read from the bronze plaque at the statue's base. "'The transatlantic sailor was famed for his fearsome navigation skills through stormy seas and was trusted to carry many precious cargos back and forth across the Atlantic Ocean. Captain Barnaby and his crew were known to visit ports in South America, Europe, and Africa before retiring in New England in 1917. Captain Barnaby's seafaring expeditions are recorded in greater detail in his captain's logs, donated to the Mariner's Cove Museum in 1956 by his heirs.'"

"Sounds like the kind of man Cuvier or his daughter would hire," Mars said.

Lydia, hands shoved into the pockets of her parka, asked Lucy, "Do you think there's anything in the captain's logs that might help us?"

Lucy crossed her arms, tapping her chin with one finger. The fur of her parka's hood blew into her face, but she ignored it. "I've read Barnaby's logs before, but I don't remember anything of interest that stood out. He never mentioned Othniel Cuvier or Katherine Rhodes. But he did have a map of all the places he made port."

Reid wandered away from the others, his eyes scanning the road leading to the museum. Paranoid that they'd been followed, that Orion hid out there somewhere like a lion waiting to pounce. But Tommy had to admit that he was also having a hard time feeling completely safe. Reid was right – it was only a matter of time before Orion figured out Lucy's identity and tracked them here. They needed to be gone by the time he did.

Tommy rubbed his hands together, the friction warming them against the cold. He puffed out his cheeks and blew, a cloud forming in front of his face as he walked circles around the statue. "Mars, you have that GPS?"

He held up the device. "State of the art, thanks to Lucy."

She blushed, brushing a loose strand of hair behind her ear.

Tommy glanced at Jude, who smirked.

"See if you can figure out the trajectory of the spyglass. Where's it pointing to? Lucy, can you go get Barnaby's map? If we're lucky and I'm right, this telescope is going to point to a port our dear former captain visited once upon a time."

Lucy's eyes sparkled with excitement, and she jogged over to the museum. She used her keys to get inside, then disappeared.

The others waited for Mars as he punched the information into the GPS. But an idea had already formed in Tommy's mind. One that made sense. With luck, Mars would only confirm what Tommy had already believed.

"Got it," he said a couple minutes later. Maya leaned over his shoulder to read the screen with him.

"Hover much?" Mars glanced at her.

She scowled and flicked his shoulder, and he pretended it hurt.

"Just read the screen, Cyber Punk," Lydia said with a smirk.

Jude laughed. "I'm rubbing off on you."

"Must be genetic," Lydia replied with a smile. Her newfound sibling bond with Jude would take some getting used to – it still boggled Tommy's mind every time he thought of it.

"Okay, so we've got the statue's location – latitude and longitude – here," Mars said, pointing at a dot on the screen that

Tommy only half paid attention to. "I just needed to figure out the angle of the spyglass, which gives me this trajectory." His finger followed a line on the screen. "Which could lead to anywhere in Morocco, Algeria, Southern Tunisia, Libya, Egypt, and Saudi Arabia."

"That's… a lot of options," said Jude.

Lucy reappeared, carrying an old leather roll. She dropped to her knees beside Mars and laid it out on the sidewalk in front of them, the corners of Barnaby's map tucked into the leather roll at the edges. She glanced at Mars' screen to see the results. "Okay, so Barnaby frequently made port in Morocco, Libya, and Egypt."

"Narrows it down," Maya muttered.

Tommy crossed his arms, staring up at the image of Barnaby, the spyglass in his hands. "Egypt," he said.

The others looked to him.

"Barnaby's clue. It's leading us to Egypt."

"How do you know?" asked Mars.

"Because that's where the Spinosaurus was unearthed. Cuvier's first discovery." His eyes found Lucy's. "After her father died, Katherine Rhodes took his discoveries back to where it all began. The lost vault is in Egypt."

Jude grinned. "I've always wanted to ride a camel."

Lucy chuckled.

Tommy glanced over at Reid, whose mind seemed somewhere else entirely. "Reid, you with us?" he asked.

He grunted an affirmative. "You figure out where we're supposed to go, and I'll help you get there. The rest doesn't matter to me."

"I think he thinks he's our bodyguard now," said Lydia.

"Well, he *does* owe us for breaking him out of jail."

"I would've been fine," Reid called out without looking their way.

"You're welcome," Jude hollered back.

Rolling his eyes, Mars sat back on his heels and stared up at Tommy. "Okay, so it's Egypt. That still leaves us with hundreds of miles of ground to explore. Any way we can narrow down the search area?"

Pacing across the sidewalk, Tommy struggled to think of any other clue. If only Cuvier had given them the traditional treasure map with an X to mark the spot. Except he didn't do things that way. Instead...

Tommy spun on his heel, eyes on the statue. "For the mammoth tusk, Cuvier gave us the smoking pipe shaped like the mountain the tusk was hidden inside. For the titan, the crystal pendants each had a different etching, and we had to layer them to see the full picture. And for the leviathan, the engraving on the tooth led us back to Hollow Hill where we found the third key."

"So?" Jude asked.

"*So...* Cuvier's maps have never been direct. They've always been clues on top of clues, different pieces of a larger puzzle." Tommy stepped past Mars and came to the base of the statue, looking it up and down. "There's something we're missing here. Something else we're supposed to see." He glanced back at the others. "Look for anything like a hidden compartment or a trigger or a latch or something."

"Like in the mines," Jude said, joining Tommy at the statue.

"Exactly."

The Jailbirds gathered around the statue, running their hands over every surface, tugging at the different facets of the sculpture. But nothing moved, budged, or sprung suddenly open.

But Tommy was certain there was something here. They had Barnaby's map – his life's work. The just needed to know where to look.

Follow the captain's eye…

Tommy's gaze landed on the plaque at the front of the statue. The plaque was engraved with a small illustration of the statue. He dropped to his knees on the snow-covered grass. He pressed a finger to the smaller iteration of the spyglass and traced its trajectory across the surface, his finger landing on the top right screw. Only, this screw was round while the other three were hexagonal.

"Gotcha," Tommy breathed. He pushed the circular screw. At first, nothing. But as he pressed harder, it gave way beneath his finger.

A click.

The plaque popped open like a drawer, only coming out a couple inches.

"Tommy coming in with the Hail Mary," Jude muttered.

He reached into the slot, feeling around for something until his hands touched canvas. Grabbing it, Tommy removed a drawstring bag. He resealed the secret compartment and stood to his feet, turning to face the others. They gathered around, expectant. Tommy unfastened the drawstrings and slid its contents into the palm of his hand.

A single, circular piece of glass.

"What is it?" Lydia asked.

Tommy held it up to the daylight, turning it over in his fingers.

"I don't know, but it looks like it's scratched," said Lucy.

Smiling, Tommy glanced at her. "Not scratched. Give me the map."

She handed it over to him and rolled it out on the statue's square base. He pressed the glass flat against the map over Egypt. There were two lines, and one of them lined up perfectly with the contour of the Nile River in Barnaby's map. The other led to a destination in the middle of the Egyptian desert.

FIFTY-FIVE
REID

A strange sound startled Reid from his sleep. He sat up, his arm supporting his weight as his eyes roved around the unfamiliar room around him. Despite his attempts to stay awake, to keep watch, he'd fallen into a deep sleep. It took a second for his mind to register his surroundings. Adler Mansion.

Reid's feet slipped over the side of the bed. He sat there for a second, massaging the sudden ache in his chest as his eyes adjusted to the darkness. Knowing what he knew now, he felt like he was walking around with a stick of dynamite for a heart – one wrong move and it could blow. As the wave of pain subsided, he stood slowly, his bare feet padding across the oriental rug centered on the wooden floor. Window curtains pulled back, he glanced out into the midnight fog. Fresh snow blanketed the ground. The exterior lights shown like beacons into the night, but the late winter fog draped over their surroundings like a thick veil.

The doctor's pronouncement echoed in his mind as it had in his dream just moments ago. *If left untreated…*

Something flashed across the window, and Reid startled, then eased when he spotted the snowy owl settling to perch on the roof outside.

With a sigh, Reid grabbed his shirt from where he'd tossed it over the bedpost last night, slipped it on, then left his room. Now that he was up, he could use a drink of water.

Tiptoeing down the stairs, Reid tried to remember the way to the kitchen – across the foyer, through the dining room, and past the butler's pantry. The door swung shut behind him, and Reid stopped, surprised to see he wasn't the only insomniac awake at this hour.

Immy sat in the breakfast nook by the window, both hands wrapped around a steaming cup of coffee. The smell wafted through the kitchen toward Reid. When he walked in, Immy straightened and glanced his way. Either she'd never changed out of her clothes from last night – jeans and a T-shirt – or she'd already changed out of the nightgown Lucy had provided to all the girls.

"A little early for coffee, don't you think?" he asked.

"I gave up trying to go back to sleep an hour ago," she replied. "Might as well get a head start on waking up."

"That's the spirit." Reid shuffled across the kitchen floor toward the cabinets. It took him two tries to figure out which one held the glasses. He glanced at the stove clock. Four in the morning. Filling a glass of water from the fridge, Reid took a seat in the breakfast nook across from Immy. The wall of windows faced the back of the property. There was no telling how far the grounds stretched, but the white hills behind the mansion sprawled far into the fog. The wide, open space unsettled Reid. He wanted walls. Someplace small, easily monitored. One way in, one way out. Instead, this mansion was one giant variable, and they couldn't possibly keep watch over the whole thing.

It wasn't a question of *if* Orion would find them; it was a matter of *when*.

Swallowing his unease, Reid took a sip of the water, trading his view of the New England landscape for a long look at Immy. The moonlight that filtered through the windows seemed to set her skin aglow. Her hair woven together in a braid that trailed down her chest. Her fingers pulled idly at the end of the braid as she stared down at her coffee.

"Penny for your thoughts?" Reid asked.

Immy smirked. "You're about to become a very poor man, Reid Clark."

Smiling, he waited until she was ready to offer more. Finally, she sighed and sat back in her chair.

"I keep dreaming about my parents," she said, her eyes on the hills outside the window. "I see them in the jungles of Peru. Smiling, laughing. And every time the dream ends the same. Orion comes and snatches them away from me, and I'm left standing in the middle of a dark cave. Alone."

Reid pressed his lips together, listening. He could understand parental loss, even if his experience was different.

"I finally have a family again," she continued. "And I don't want to lose them. I don't want to end up alone because I've been alone before. The Black Flag took care of me, but they weren't a family. But this? Reid, I can't lose this."

Lydia came to mind. Tommy, his now brother-in-law. And Jude, the younger half-brother who'd been hidden from him. Reid had only begun to feel like he could find a place among the Jailbirds. He understood Immy's fear – it was the same thing that had been on his mind since recovering his sister in Spokane. Orion was coming, and when he caught up to them, what would he take? Reid couldn't promise Immy that everything would be okay. He couldn't even guarantee that they wouldn't end up alone when it was all said and done – he'd seen Orion's ruthlessness firsthand enough times to know that nothing short of death would stop the man.

"Then we fight," he said, his voice low. "We fight to keep what we have, and we don't let him take it from us. Not this time."

Here they sat, two people who'd been alone most of their lives. Immy in the treacherous jungles of Peru. Reid in the suffocating world of greed and power and abuse.

Reid leaned forward, locking his eyes with hers. "Immy, you and I, we're here because we fought tooth and nail to be here. We didn't always make the best decisions. People hurt us, and we hurt others. But it's because we were all that mattered – our survival was all that mattered. But somehow, despite all that, we've managed to find ourselves here. We have something *new* to fight for now," he said. "Something we've never had before – a *family*."

"It doesn't feel real."

"But it *is* real. We're real. *This* is real. Don't let him steal what doesn't belong to him."

She squinted, took a drink of her coffee, then crossed her arms as she stared across the table at him. "Why are you suddenly so optimistic? You've been withdrawn since we got here."

"I've been… figuring out my place, I guess. These guys saved my life when I didn't deserve it, and I've been trying to figure out what I'm supposed to do with that." He paused, his eyes tracing the veins of black and white on the surface of the marble table. "But I think I'm getting there. I don't know how much longer I have left, but with what time I do have, I'll spend it making sure they're safe."

Immy frowned. "What do you mean by 'how much longer you have left?'"

Reid opened his mouth, but a loud clattering sound startled him. He whirled toward the direction it came from.

"What was that?" Immy hissed.

Slipping out of his seat, he snuck toward the butler's pantry. His heart rate began to climb, his chest tightening with it. As he inched toward the butler's pantry, he practiced the breathing exercises the doctor had given him while Immy hovered at the edge of his vision.

Reid reached for the handle and slowly pulled the pantry door open. He froze when he saw a man standing over a body on the ground. The butler, lying on the floor, blood spilling from a wound in his head. The man over him, dressed in black tactical gear, froze when the door opened. They stared at each other for a split second, then the man raise his gun.

Reid slammed the door in his face and pivoted toward Immy.

"They're here," he hissed, grabbing her arm as they ran the opposite direction. The pantry door splintered as it flung open, the intruder sprinting after them. A silenced bullet whizzed past Reid's head as he dodged left through the doorway out of the kitchen and into the hallway behind the foyer. They had to get upstairs to warn the others.

But the first intruder wasn't alone. Another man stood in the foyer, surprise registering in the arch of his eyebrows as Reid and Immy slid to a stop. He raised his gun and fired. Reid wrapped his arms around Immy, throwing both of their weight out of the way. They landed on the floor behind the staircase, Reid on top of her. Breathless, he registered the fear in her eyes at the close call. They scrambled to their feet and dove through a door that led beyond the foyer into the south wing of the mansion as the hallway door leading back to the kitchen burst open.

Two intruders on their tails. The butler already dead. And the rest of their friends asleep upstairs with no clue that danger had found them. Reid couldn't let these guys get to them.

His eyes searched his surroundings for a weapon, and he spotted one down the hall. Antique armor stood on display against the wall, and in the mannequin's hand a sword.

"Hold this door," Reid told Immy.

She nodded, pressing her back to the door behind her. It would do little against gunfire once the intruders realized the door was blocked. But Reid only needed a second.

He jogged toward the armor, glancing at the ceiling above him. He needed to warn the Jailbirds.

As he yanked the sword free of the mannequin's wooden grip, his eyes found a vent in the ceiling across the hall from the armor. Perfect.

Reid slid the mannequin across the hall, then shoved it. The armor clattered to the ground, and Reid hoped the sound would be alarm enough as it echoed through the vents.

Something struck the door, and Reid spun toward Immy as she ducked beneath a hail of gunfire. The door splintered. Bullets whizzed past Reid's ear. He ran toward the door, his hands tightening around the sword's hilt, and positioned himself just inside of it against the wall.

On the other side of the hall, Immy reached for her boot and revealed a dagger. Smart girl.

They waited. One of the intruders kicked the door in, and as soon as Reid saw a flash of black, he swung the sword down. The blunt length of the blade struck the intruder's arm, and the gun clattered to the floor with the sound of breaking bone. The man cried out, gripping his wound, and Immy, still crouched on the floor, thrust her own smaller blade toward the intruder's leg. He hollered in pain, falling to the floor. The other man whirled his gun toward Immy, but Reid lunged his blade forward, the point driving itself through the man's vest and into his side.

He fell to his knees, and Immy sliced her blade across his gun-wielding arm, then followed it up with a punch to his masked face. His cry cut short, and he collapsed the ground alongside his now-unconscious partner.

As the intruders fell silent, Reid's ears tuned to the sound of movement. Boots shuffling along floors.

These two weren't alone.

"Quick," said Reid. "The guns."

Immy scooped both pistols up, tossing one to Reid. He traded his sword for the handgun and turned toward the door to the foyer.

"He's here," Immy whispered.

Reid's jaw tensed. "We fight," he said, meeting her eyes. "And we don't let him take anything else from us."

She gave a sharp nod.

FIFTY-SIX
JUDE

Jude bolted upright as a crashing sound reverberated through his skull. What was that noise? It came from the vent in the floor, somewhere downstairs. Maybe one of Lucy's staff had dropped something.

At this hour?

He threw off the covers and crossed the room to the door, pulling on his shirt and pants, then his shoes. Out in the hallway, Jude listened. Everything was still, and the sound seemed to have faded. He started for the stairs but stopped short when he heard voices from below. His hand on the banister, he leaned forward to peer down into the foyer. A flicker of movement, then a group of armed men in black moving through the foyer, into the family room and sitting room, deeper into the house. The man in charge gestured up the stairs, and Jude's heart jolted.

He turned and ran for Maya's room, slipping inside. She sat

on the edge of the bed, awakened by the same noise.

She started to speak, but Jude held a finger to his lips, his eyes wide. "They're here," he whispered.

Maya tensed.

"Get dressed. I'll get the others."

She nodded and flew into action, fishing her shoes out from under the edge of the bed. Jude slipped out into the hall and snuck across to his sister's room. He opened the door and found Tommy sitting upright in bed, Lydia still asleep beside him.

Confusion registered on Tommy's face, then understanding. He shook Lydia awake as he shoved his arms through the sleeves of his flannel and buttoned his jeans. He shoved the glass disc and Barnaby's map into one boot and the three keys into the other. In case they were captured, it would be the safest place on him to hide it.

Jude leaned out the door. Down the hall, on the other side of the staircase, Mars and Lucy stood outside their rooms. Mars started toward Jude, but he waved him off. Mars stopped, but before he could ask, the barrel of a rifle appeared from around the corner at the top of the stairs.

Maya's door opened, and she darted across the hall to join Jude in Tommy and Lydia's room. Jude watched Mars and Lucy as they disappeared inside Mars' room.

Quietly, Jude closed the bedroom door and turned the lock.

"Help me with the dresser," he whispered to Tommy.

They each grabbed one side of the nearby dresser and half-slid, half-carried it to block the door. Maya threw open the window, and one by one they slipped out into the cold and onto the rooftop. At the other end of the roof, Mars and Lucy appeared. They skirted the dormers and joined the others.

"Is there a fire escape?" Tommy asked Lucy.

"South end," she replied.

"Did anyone see Reid or Immy?" Lydia asked, glancing back at Jude.

He shook his head. "The bad guys showed up before I could get to either of their rooms."

"Let's hope they made it out some other way," said Mars.

They arrived at the fire escape, and Jude waited to go last while the others jumped the few feet to the second floor landing. The metal creaked and groaned beneath their sudden, shifting weight. Behind Jude, a window opened.

He glanced over his shoulder just in time to see one of the intruders aiming his rifle through the open window. The muzzle flashed and a hail of gunfire burst around Jude.

With a yelp, he fell over the side of the rooftop, barely catching the railing of the fire escape landing. His fingers started to slip, but Tommy grabbed his arms and helped him up and back onto the stairs. They descended two at a time.

All attempt at stealth vanished as the intruders barked orders at one another, chasing the Jailbirds down.

Jude's feet sank into the snow. The Jailbirds ran along the southern perimeter of the mansion, eyes surveying their foggy surroundings. Shadows moved in the distance.

Glancing over his shoulder to make sure they were still together, he nearly collided with someone as they exited one of the doors up ahead. Jude balled his fist and prepared to strike, stopping short when his eyes met Reid's.

"Oh, thank God," he breathed.

"They're all over the place," Reid said, glancing back at the others. Immy stood behind him, her eyes flicking back and forth over their surroundings.

"Can we get to the car?" asked Maya.

"We can try," said Tommy.

Hunkered down, they snuck along the edge of the mansion. Jude spotted the Wrangler parked in the circular driveway. He waited for any sign of movement, but they must have all been inside, searching the rooms. It would be seconds before the guys on the roof radioed to the others that the Jailbirds were outside.

Moving as a group, they made a beeline for the car. Jude reached for the door.

Bright light flooded the air around them, dispelling the shadows and illuminating the fog.

The Jailbirds froze.

Jude squinted, shielding his eyes with his hands.

Boots crunched through snow, then thumped on the concrete driveway. Shadows formed a wall around the Jailbirds.

Eyes adjusting to the sudden light, Jude spun in circles as he took in the small army that had completely surrounded them. His heart plummeted.

They were trapped.

"On your knees!" one of the soldiers barked. When they didn't respond, he shouted again. "Do it now!"

Reid and Immy dropped their guns on the ground as the Jailbirds, one by one, fell to their knees in the snow. A gust of wind howled around them. Jude aimed a murderous glare at the man who'd spoken. His hands itched for a knife, a gun, anything to save his friends.

For a moment, no one moved. The Jailbirds kneeling in the middle of the driveway. The soldiers dressed in black surrounding them like a wall – several dozen guns trained on the eight fugitives.

Jude's chest heaved with breath. Adrenaline coursed through his veins. He could lunge for the man in charge, make himself a distraction to give the others time to escape. He'd die, but he'd die knowing he'd done what he could to save his friends.

But Jude never got the chance to try.

The sea of soldiers parted to let someone through. A man in a gray peacoat sauntered across the snow. His gray eyes appeared even paler in the floodlights that shone around them as he stared down at the kneeling Jailbirds.

Orion Clark had found them.

He came to a stop just feet away from Tommy, whose glare burned with rage as he looked up at the man who'd murdered his father.

In a single, quick motion, Orion drew the antique pistol from its holster at his hip and pressed the tip of the gun to Tommy's temple as he pulled the hammer back and rested his finger on the trigger.

FIFTY-SEVEN
TOMMY

Snow tumbled in the sky around the Jailbirds, kneeling beside one another as before a tyrant king. Waves of rage rippled through the air around Tommy, eyes fixated on the man who had killed his father in cold blood. For greed, for power, for vain ambition. The voices of those who had died seemed to rise from the ground with the howling of the wind.

Orion sneered down at Tommy. The cold steel of his gun pressed against Tommy's temple. There was no doubting that, if he decided to, this man would pull the trigger and Tommy would die in a second.

A gust of wind pulled Tommy's hair across his face. He set his jaw and lifted his chin. Hands balled into fists at his side, body vibrating with adrenaline and emotion. He felt Lydia's presence beside him. She did not cower or tremble. None of them did. They had been bent beyond belief, but they would not shatter, they would not break.

Orion spoke, his words like a knife as they cut through the tension in the air. "I've underestimated you after all, Thomas," he said. "I could not have predicted how much of an obstacle you would become."

"I am my father's son," Tommy replied through clenched teeth.

"Hmm. It seems I have not done enough to impress upon you how deadly serious I am in my quest." He paused. "Mistakes will be made, I suppose. Now, tell me, where are the keys you stole?"

His eyes flicked to Reid. No one said a word.

"If your father's death was not enough to convince you, then perhaps I should take another life."

Panic tightened around Tommy's heart as Orion swiveled the gun toward Jude on his left. "Jack Mayfield, the perpetual thorn in my side. Should I rob him of his son?"

"Don't!" Tommy shouted.

He pivoted toward Lydia on Tommy's other side. "Or Lydia Clark, the prodigal princess. *You* burned down my house."

"And I'd do it again," she spat.

"I lost good men in that fire," Orion said, though the look in his eyes told Tommy he couldn't care less who he'd lost.

"*Good* men would never work for you," said Maya from the other side of Jude.

"Ah, Maya. I believe I have someone here who'd like to say hello. The two of you have… unfinished business."

Orion gestured with his free hand, and a man stepped forward from among the Hunters. He reached for the mask around his mouth and tugged it free. Tommy scowled at Graham Robinson, whose sneer was aimed at Maya.

"Graham?" Reid said. "What are you *doing*?"

Graham aimed the barrel of his rifle toward Reid. "What you didn't have the strength to do."

"You call this strength? Siding with Orion? The man's a monster!"

"Ah-ah!" Orion held up a finger. "The only one passing judgment here… will be me."

Orion paced in front of the Jailbirds as silence fell around them. A sense of utter helplessness threatened to strangle Tommy as Orion moved to the end of the row and pressed the gun against Mars' head. He hummed an eerie, familiar tune as he pulled back the hammer.

His finger tightened around the trigger.

"No!" Tommy screamed, and somewhere in the distance Lucy screamed with him.

A click.

No bullet.

Mars trembled, his eyes closed, tears staining his cheeks.

Tommy gasped, choking on the lump lodged in his throat.

As if to play some twisted version of Russian Roulette, Orion continued down the line.

"Eight little birds, and one in the chamber," he said in a singsong voice. "Who is going to die today?"

Everything inside of Tommy screamed at him to throw himself at Orion as he pulled the trigger for the second time. Lucy whimpered and flinched at the click.

No bullet.

Tears streamed from her eyes, though they were clamped shut. Mars reached over and tightened his hand around hers.

Tommy sucked in a breath as Orion came to Lydia. Terror

gripped him. He lunged for Orion, but Graham got to him first and forced him back down on his knees.

"I will kill you!" Tommy screamed, spit flying from his mouth. "*I will kill you!*"

Orion ignored him as he pointed the pistol at Lydia's head. Her body jerked with the snap of the hammer, but she did not die.

Rage and terror and helpless desperation churned with hurricane force inside Tommy's head.

"Four tries left," Orion said.

The cold steel of the gun pressed against Tommy's temple.

He prayed it would be him.

He closed his eyes as rivers of tears spilled down his face. His head pounded, ears rang, heart hammered. There was so much he wanted to say to Lydia, to his friends, but he could only trust and hope that they already knew what was in his heart.

Let it be me.

Orion pulled the trigger, and Tommy jerked. It took him a second to realize he had not died, and when he opened his eyes, Orion was already standing in front of Jude.

"No," Maya whimpered, shaking her head. "Please don't. Please..."

The world spun around Tommy. Bile rose in the back of his throat.

A click.

Another empty round.

Tommy's hand scrambled for Lydia's. His fingers hooked through hers, cold and stiff.

God, please...

There was no prayer to quell the torment that wreaked havoc on their souls as death crept closer. Who would it be? Maya?

Immy? Reid?

Don't let him take anyone else. God, please!

Sweat beaded down his face, stinging his eyes, gluing his hair to his forehead.

A click.

Maya would live.

He came to Immy, and with rage in her eyes she lifted her chin just a little higher and met his gaze. Orion had slaughtered her parents. He had stolen her uncle. Hadn't enough of her family's blood been spilled?

A dull *thunk*. Metal grinding against metal.

Orion stopped and held his gun up to the light. He grunted.

"The bullet jammed," he said matter-of-factly, passing the gun off to Graham.

Immy deflated, her body trembling.

"It seems fate has afforded you a little longer to live," said Orion.

Silence hovered over the Jailbirds like a harbinger of death.

"Bind them," Orion ordered his men. "We bring them with us. If any of them tries to escape… shoot on sight."

Episode Six

STORMWALL

"Everything he needed to survive the world they'd stumbled into had been inside him all along."

FIFTY-EIGHT
MAYA

Darkness.

The hum of an engine.

Maya's fists bound behind her back, her body had all but locked into position after hours spent like this. The hood over her head made it impossible to breathe, so she took slow, deep breaths and did her best not to let the claustrophobia kill her.

From the sound of it, they were on a plane. The upward trajectory of takeoff combined with the pop in her ears was enough to tell her that. But where was Orion taking them?

Judging by the solid, cold surface, the Jailbirds had been relegated to the belly of the plane. The luggage or cargo hold.

Jude sat next to her. His shoulder bumping hers. The others had all checked in, but now they were mostly quiet. Hushed whispers carried through the hold, but Maya couldn't make out any of the conversations. But Jude was here, by her side. It was enough to settle the anxiety that burned a hole through her chest.

"Maybe when we land, they'll take off these hoods and we can make a break for it," Jude muttered.

Maya didn't have the heart to argue, but she doubted Orion would be stupid enough to give them an opening for escape. It was hard to plan when they were blind. There was no knowing where they were going and how many Hunters would be around them at any given time. If they tried to escape, someone would end up hurt.

Or worse.

Bile rose in Maya's throat at the memory of the cold steel of Orion's gun pressed against her skin.

The snapping of the hammer.

That split second of terror, helplessness, and grief before she realized she hadn't died.

"Maya?"

Maya shook the memory loose. "Hmm?"

"I was asking you to see how tight your bindings are. Any way you could slip free?"

She pulled against the rope around her wrists, then gave up after a few seconds. "No dice."

Jude grunted.

"Jude, I think it might be best to wait to try something until we get on the ground. There's not much we can do up here, given the plane probably doesn't even have eight parachutes, and I don't really think I could jump anyway."

"Afraid of heights?" he asked, his tone laced with teasing.

Maya smirked. She wished her hands were free so she could flick his ear.

"Not… *afraid*," she said. "*Averse*."

Chuckling, Jude bumped her shoulder with his.

"Alright, then. We can wait."

They sat in silence for a moment, and Maya struggled to keep the worst-case-scenarios and what-ifs at bay. Her mind spiraled. She was sure it was a trauma response, but that fact didn't help her manage her thoughts any better. In five short months, Maya had come face to face with more bloodshed and death than she'd ever thought she would. All because their parents had let Orion get away with murder. What if they'd stopped him back when they were kids? The Jailbirds were forced to face the giant their parents were too afraid, too selfish, too absent to face for themselves. Who else would die for it?

Maya closed her eyes, not that there was any difference with this stupid hood over her head.

She wanted to live a long, happy life. She wanted to have kids that she could raise and love better than her parents had done with her. She wanted to build a life with someone she loved, and more and more Jude's face populated the lifelong dreams she'd held dear to her heart. She couldn't lose him. She couldn't lose any of them.

But once again, none of it was within her control. Whether they lived or died wasn't up to them. Somehow, she had to make her peace with that.

Psalm 23 came to mind, and Maya recited what she could remember of the passage in her mind until she found herself repeating just one line over and over, her mind caught on it.

Even though I walk through the valley of the shadow of death, I fear no evil, for You are with me.

There was no denying that the Jailbirds were walking through their own valley of the shadow. The only reason one of them hadn't died last night was because the gun had jammed, which struck Maya as providential. She'd never thought much of miracles, but now she found herself asking over and over for them.

A lone tear rolled down Maya's cheek, and she wished she could wipe it away. "Jude?"

"Yeah, May?"

"In case… something happens," she started, "Jude, I need you to know that I love you, okay?"

"Hey, hey, hey. We can't talk like that. Nothing's going to happen."

"You don't know that."

"Yes, I do," he said.

Maya sighed.

"May, don't give up. If you give up, and he's already won. We have to keep fighting."

Nodding, Maya leaned over and rested her head on his shoulder, and he rested his head on hers. The air in the plane shifted, and Maya got the sense that they had begun their descent. Fifteen minutes later, they touched down.

I fear no evil…

FIFTY-NINE

REID

Reid's body jolted as the plane touched down. Tommy bumped against him, then righted himself.

Having spent the entire flight tugging at his bindings, Reid's wrists were raw. He'd managed to cut himself too, and the blood trickled down his hand and off the ends of his fingers.

"Where do you think we are?" Tommy asked.

Reid had an idea, but the confirmation came when, just a few minutes after the plane lurched to a stop, the door of the cargo hold opened and a wave of warmth slammed into them. They'd spent the entire flight shivering, since they'd been taken in nothing but a light layer of clothes, but the climate outside instantly warmed them.

Reid swallowed, listening. Voices in the distance. A language he didn't recognize. Thick Arabic accents as men barked orders to one another.

"I think we're in Egypt," Reid whispered. The floor of the cargo hold shifted. Metal clanked as Hunters moved past them. Reid couldn't see, but by the sound of it, they were unloading the cargo. Saving the Jailbirds for last.

"How did he figure it out?" Tommy hissed back, frustration in his tone. "We just found out about Egypt *yesterday*."

"He's probably had eyes on us since we left Spokane."

Tommy grunted, a growl in his tone, but Reid couldn't make out what he'd muttered.

"Do you still have the disc and the map in your boot?" Reid asked.

"Yeah. They patted us down but didn't think to check our shoes."

"Good."

On the other side of Tommy, Lydia said something. A question. Tommy answered, his voice low. Then he said to Reid, "We need to figure out a way out of this."

"Yes, but we need to wait for the right time. There's too many people around right now. Too many things could go wrong. If we're at an airport, there's too much wide-open space. Orion's going to hold us somewhere. We wait for that, and we figure things out then."

"The longer we wait, the less likely it is that all of us will be able to escape."

Reid swallowed. The same thought had crossed his mind. The more time they spent at Orion's mercy, the more opportunity the man had to change his mind and take them out for good. Reid knew his uncle well enough to know that his keeping them alive wasn't an act of mercy. He planned to use them somehow, and

Reid didn't want any of them to be around when Orion put that plan into motion.

Darkness had descended over the Jailbirds like the wall of a storm they were desperate to outrun.

Gruff hands gripped Reid's shoulders. The Jailbirds grunted and threw insults as they were led roughly down the ramp and onto the tarmac. The asphalt radiated heat through Reid's shoes. His mind raced to form a plan, but it was impossible with their shifting surroundings. As much as he wanted to fly into action now, he needed to wait. They all did.

Shoved inside a car, the doors slammed shut behind them, Reid listened to their surroundings as best he could. The sounds of people. Children playing in streets. Vendors peddling their goods. They were in a larger city – probably Cairo, given the airport. But the sounds of the city were soon traded for the sounds of men at work. Metal on metal. Wood on wood.

Foghorns wailed in the distance. A nearby body of water.

The Nile River.

The car stopped, and the Jailbirds were yanked outside. Reid noted the swaying boards beneath his feet as the guard's hands cinched around his arms, leading him down a ramp. Docks.

Fresh air rolled in off the water, cooling the warmth that had caused Reid's brow to sweat beneath the canvas bag. He nearly tripped over something hard, metal, but the guard caught him. Dragged him across another wooden surface. Judging by the swaying and bobbing, the Jailbirds were being loaded onto a boat.

"Hey, watch it," Jude shouted somewhere behind him.

Reid stopped, his instincts demanding he make sure everyone was okay.

A thump.

"Keep moving," one of the guards barked.

Grunting with pain, Jude retorted, "You can't expect her to watch where she's going with a bag over her head, you *idiot*."

"You don't shut your mouth, I'll shut it for you. *Permanently*."

"Jude," Reid warned from the front of the group. He couldn't see what was happening, but he had a pretty good idea.

Silence. Though Reid was certain he could feel the wave of anger that emanated from Jude's glare all the way from over here.

Feet shuffled, then someone tugged Reid forward.

A few minutes later, they traded the cool, fresh air for someplace hot and stuffy. Another cargo hold?

The guard shoved Reid onto a chair, Reid's bound wrists catching against the back of the seat. He winced, his wrists suddenly remembering the cuts he'd caused in his attempt to get free.

Seconds later, the hood was yanked from his head. Lights blinded Reid. It took him a second to adjust to his surroundings. The red and yellow glow of the boat's interior lights cast a menacing glare over the guards who stood in the middle of the room, scowling down at the seated Jailbirds.

"Don't try anything," one of the men warned.

Reid didn't see Graham among them, which was probably a good thing. Reid wasn't sure he'd be able to restrain himself if he laid eyes on his former friend again.

Reid watched as the Hunters filed out of the room, slamming and latching the metal door behind them. One of them stayed behind, just barely visible through a round window in the door.

As he caught his breath, he glanced around the room, relieved to see everyone together. Exhausted and beat down, but together.

They still had a chance to outrun the coming storm.

SIXTY

IMMY

Immy should be dead.

If not for Orion's gun jamming, she would be.

Whether it was providence or coincidence, it didn't change the fact that Immy's entire life had flashed before her eyes. She'd stared down the barrel of that gun, watched him pull the trigger, and in an instant all of her grief and trauma and thirst for revenge seemed to fade into the background. Nothing else mattered except what her life had meant to the people kneeling beside her. To her friends, her family.

Immy had more than survived. She'd discovered her reason to live.

For them.

As the door slammed shut behind the last Hunter, her eyes snapped to Reid's.

"What's the plan?" she asked.

He smiled. "First, we need to get these ropes off. No telling how much time we have before one of those Hunters comes to check on us."

The boat lurched. They were underway.

"Does Orion even know where to look?" Mars asked, glancing around the boat's hold. There was only one door. No windows. And the Jailbirds were seated on crates of cargo in the rusted belly of the boat.

"My guess is that's why we're here," said Lucy.

Jude nodded. "Which is why we need to get out of here before Orion figures out that we have Barnaby's map."

"Tommy, put your back to mine." Reid angled his back toward Tommy's.

Immy winced inwardly when she saw the blood on Reid's wrists.

"Ah," Tommy grunted. "It's too tight. I can't get my fingers in there."

"Quick," said Lydia as she glanced around the hold. "Look for something sharp."

"No need." Jude held his booted foot in the air. "I grabbed my Swiss before things went down at the mansion."

"Nice!" Mars scooted forward, turning his back to Jude's foot while he dug inside the boot for the Swiss Army knife. Finding it, he popped open the blade and began cutting at his bindings. Once free, Mars set to work on the others.

Immy let out a sigh of relief when her hands were finally free. She stretched her arms and massaged the fresh bruises on her wrists. But no one looked as bad as Reid. Lydia moved to sit on the crate by her brother's side. He held out his hands, the pain evident on his face.

"Reid, what'd you do?" she said.

"I've always been bad at sitting still," he replied with a wry smile.

"Here," said Lucy. She tore the hem of her shirt and separated it into two pieces. Lydia helped wrap them around both of Reid's wrists.

"What I'd give for a drink," he said.

Lydia pursed her lips but didn't say anything.

Getting to her feet, Immy paced the room, searching for any other way out, but there wasn't even a vent worth slipping through. "Looks like there's only one way out."

"Here's what I'm thinking," said Jude. "Two of us stand on either side of that door while someone else gets the guard's attention. Then, when he walks in, we knock him out, take his guns, and shoot our way off this rig."

"Okay, calm down, Rambo," said Mars. "I'd rather minimize our exposure to any further gunfire."

The reminder of Orion's confrontation was enough to silence the group for a moment. They all felt it – they were lucky to be alive right now.

"It's not a bad idea," Tommy said, glancing around at the group. "I mean, we can't avoid a fight. But we can try. First things first… we gotta get out of this room. We can figure out the rest when we get there."

"Take it as it comes," said Maya.

Jude smiled. "Jailbird rule *numero cinco*."

"Alright," said Tommy. "Reid and I'll get by the door. Who wants to be the bait?"

"Feels like a Mars job." Jude pointed a finger at Mars, who rolled his eyes.

"I always get the raw end of the deal."

Jude clapped him on the back. "Suck it up, buttercup."

The rest of the Jailbirds returned to their seats and put their hands behind their backs to pretend they were still bound while Reid and Tommy positioned themselves on either side of the door. Mars waited for the nod from Tommy and called for the guard.

"Hey! You with the face! I need to take a leak!"

The guard turned to peer through the round window. He glanced around the room. Metal ground against metal and the door swung open. Gun first, the guard stepped over the threshold and into the room.

"Surprise," said Reid. He swung a fist at the guard's face while Tommy reached for his rifle.

It was over in seconds. The guard lay sprawled on the floor, unconscious.

"Quick," Tommy whispered, pulling the rifle's strap over his shoulder. "Get the rest of his weapons."

Immy scooped up a dagger while Reid took one handgun and passed the other from the guard's ankle holster to Jude.

They gathered at the doorway. Tommy glanced back at them. "Ready? Let's go."

SIXTY-ONE
JUDE

The corridor, dark and empty, led to stairs in either direction. Jude followed Tommy's lead, holding the smaller of the two pistols. Safety off.

Moving quietly toward the stairs, Jude kept his eyes on the doors, bracing for a Hunter to walk out any second and find the Jailbirds had broken free. Laughter came from the deck above. Footsteps on metal.

"Hide," Tommy hissed, ushering the eight of them into a side room.

The stairs rattled as Jude slipped inside the room, closing the door all but an inch behind him. He watched through the gap as two Hunters descended the stairs, arguing about football by the sound of it. He held his breath, waiting for them to pass. They disappeared down the other end of the corridor.

Jude let out a sigh and opened the door, stepping back out.

He glanced up the stairs. The deck above was open. Blue sky gaped down at him, nearly blinding him after so long without setting eyes on the sun. He held up a hand to block out the light.

Glancing back at Tommy, Jude swallowed. "They'll spot us as soon as we get up there."

Reid nodded. "We make a run for it."

"But a run for where?" asked Mars. "We don't know the layout of this boat."

"Boat like this'll likely have emergency dinghies hanging over the side," Jude said. "We find one, we drop it in the water and take off."

"Everybody keep your eyes peeled, and stay together," said Tommy.

They nodded, then one by one filed up the stairs.

Jude's heart pounded as they inched toward danger. Tommy was the first to slip out onto the deck, then Jude.

Daylight washed over him, warming him. He squinted against the light, taking in his surroundings. They were on some sort of transport ship. Not nearly the size of a freighter, but big enough that the Jailbirds managed to keep themselves hidden behind the cargo strapped to the middle of the ship's deck. The minute a Hunter rounded the corner, though, they'd be spotted, and they'd have to leave their temporary hiding place to get to any dinghy.

"There," Reid said, pointing starboard.

A giant mechanical arm with a pulley system held a black, rubber dinghy up and over the edge of the ship.

"Alright, on three, we run, okay?" said Tommy.

The others nodded, steeling themselves for the mad dash to the dinghy. Tommy counted to three, and all eight of them broke into a sprint across the ship's deck.

Shouts arose from the bridge behind them. Jude risked a glance over his shoulder as Reid slid to a stop beside the dinghy. He immediately began working the pulley.

Gunshots rang out, bullets whizzing past Jude's head.

"Get down!" Jude shouted.

He and Tommy whirled toward the Hunters now swarming the deck, guns drawn. Orion ran from the ship's bridge, leaning against one of the railings a couple stories above the ship's deck. He shouted, his face red and angry. Jude almost smiled.

Tommy pointed his rifle toward the oncoming Hunters and fired. A spray of bullets took out the Hunters at the front of the group. It only took them seconds to rally. There was no way the Jailbirds would be able to hold them off forever. With just three guns, their ammo was limited. Whether or not Reid could lower the dinghy in time would determine their freedom.

A splash behind Jude told him Reid had managed to work the pulley system.

Jude glanced back to see the girls climbing down the rope ladder onto the dinghy. He fired another round at a Hunter getting too close for comfort. The man let out a howl of pain, clutching his arm.

"Tommy, go," Reid shouted, patting Tommy on the arm.

Tommy unloaded his magazine on the Hunters, then dropped it when the clip emptied out. He swung onto the ladder and dropped the rest of the way.

"You next," Reid said.

Jude didn't argue. As he slid down the ladder, gunfire roared overhead.

"Reid!" he called from halfway down. "Hurry it up!"

A bullet flew, and Reid grunted, then fell backward over the side of the ship. He landed in the water.

"Reid!" Lydia screamed.

Jude jumped the remaining distance to the dinghy just as Immy dove into the water after Reid. Tommy worked the engine, and Jude clutched the side of the dinghy as it spun about, pulling away from the ship and toward their friends in the water. Immy had her arms under Reid's. He was conscious, but blood pooled around his shoulder. Jude leaned over the side of the dinghy, grasping Reid's hand when Immy lifted him over her head toward him.

Bullets zipped into the water around them, threatening to pierce the dinghy and deflate it before they had a chance to get more than fifteen feet away from the ship. Jude hooked his arms under Reid's and pulled him up while Maya and Lydia both helped Immy back into the boat.

"I'm okay," Reid reassured Lydia, clutching the bullet wound in his shoulder as he fell into the boat. That didn't stop Lydia from worrying over him, pressing her hand to the wound herself as Jude shouted at Tommy to go. Reid's feet still dangled over the water as Tommy forced the throttle forward. Water sprayed into the air behind them as bullets whizzed past their heads. The dinghy sped away, the larger ship shrinking into the distance behind them.

SIXTY-TWO
LYDIA

You okay?" Maya asked, pulling Lydia's hair back as she vomited into the Nile River over the side of the rubber dinghy. Her stomach clenched, and she thought she might throw up again. Bile slicked her throat, but she swallowed it down.

"I could use some water," said Lydia, wincing against the bitter aftertaste that lingered on her tongue.

"'Fraid we're fresh out," said Mars, a grim expression on his face as he helped Immy wrap Reid's wound.

Lydia sat up, pulling her hair back in a ponytail away from her face. She caught Maya watching her, concern knitting her brow together.

"You've never had a sensitive stomach before," she said, her voice low. "Are you okay?"

Swallowing, Lydia gave a sharp nod.

"Up ahead," Tommy called from the back of the rubber dinghy, where he'd been steering the motor. Their eyes followed his to see a village in the distance, a web of docks along the river where they'd be able to pull in.

Glancing behind, Lydia was relieved that she couldn't make out Orion's ship anymore, but she knew this dinghy wouldn't be able to get them a safe distance away. Wherever they made land, it would be temporary. They needed to keep moving.

"Orion's hot on our trail," Jude said. "We need to lie low."

"As low as seven Americans can lie, you mean," said Immy.

Jude cocked an eyebrow.

"What?" She grinned. "I'm Peruvian. At least *I* have a decent shot at blending in."

He smirked, waved her off.

Tommy steered the dinghy up to the shore, and Lydia absorbed the Egyptian landscape for the first time. Rows of smaller river boats lined the docks, bobbing and swaying in bright blue water that reflected a blue sky smattered with a handful of lone puffy clouds. Square buildings painted all shades of yellow, brown, and even blue dotted the tan, rocky hillside. In the distance, Lydia spotted tan mountains. Bright green trees – palms, citrus, and others Lydia didn't recognize – peppered the port village. A pair of herons flew overhead.

Under different circumstances, it would have been beautiful.

Lydia glanced back at Reid. Mars said it was a superficial wound. A through-and-through. They'd managed to stop the bleeding, but it would be a while before they could get him to a doctor. Lydia hoped they were nearing the end of… all this. She wanted the treasure. She wanted to take her uncle down. But more than anything, she was tired of the running, the almost dying. Of seeing her friends injured and beaten and taken. She was ready to put it all behind her and start building a life with Tommy.

Her eyes wandered to the arid landscape beyond the port village. There was a treasure out there waiting to be found, lost wonders waiting to be rediscovered, but Lydia had already found her prize. Against all the odds, in defiance of every expectation, she'd found a family in those the world had thrown away. This was enough.

The dinghy weaved between the docked river boats. Jude – Lydia's half-brother, to her constant surprise – stood to toss the rope around one of the mooring posts, pulling them up close to a ladder that dipped into the river below. Voices carried through the air. Fishermen and sailors, tourists and locals. Voices in all languages mingling to create a beautiful, multicultural symphony. People living their lives, completely unaware of the darkness that crouched at their door.

"Ladies first," Jude said, extending a hand to Lydia.

"This is because she's suddenly your sister, isn't it," Maya said with an amused look.

Immy crossed her arms. "The girl burned down a mansion, Jude. I think she can climb a ladder on her own."

"Hey now," said Lydia as she accepted Jude's hand and pulled herself onto the ladder. "We have a lot of lost time to make up for."

Her eyes briefly met Jude's. He smiled, squeezed her hand, then let go.

Lydia climbed up onto the dock, drinking in her surroundings as she waited for the others to join her. Tommy's hand slipped into hers.

"You okay?" he asked. She noticed the lines around his eyes

– exhaustion, stress, worry leaving a mark on the man she loved.

Lydia nodded, smiled, but nausea still bubbled in the pit of her stomach. "I'm fine."

"Alright," said Tommy glancing around at the Jailbirds, half of whom still wore the clothes they'd slept in last night. "We need to get out of these clothes. The Hunters will spot us a mile away like this."

The Jailbirds moved quickly down the docks, earning a few stares but otherwise unimpeded.

The village wasn't as small as it looked. It was tightly packed, and some of the square buildings were stacked on top of each other. Just past the port they found a bustling market. The sound of horns honking, animals braying, and people talking rose above the sounds of the dockworkers. Colorful textiles draped over clotheslines, and handwoven baskets piled up in corners as their sellers haggled them away one by one.

Jude was the first to spot someone selling clothes and waved the Jailbirds over. They pooled their cash together and managed to bargain for themselves clean pairs of jeans and linen button-downs, the girls opting for lighter, long-sleeved linen shirts. Tommy bought a canvas satchel off another seller and put the map, the keys, and the glass disc inside.

"We need food and water," Reid said. "Who knows when we'll find another settlement."

Another wave of nausea swelled in Lydia's stomach. She turned to Tommy. "Hey, I'm going to look for a pharmacy or something."

He frowned. "You okay?"

Smiling, she said, "Yes. Lady things."

"Okay. Take Maya with you."

"I can handle myself," said Lydia.

"I have no doubt about that, but it would set my mind at ease if I knew you weren't out there alone."

Lydia sighed. "Okay." She turned to Maya, who had been listening. She kissed Tommy's cheek, then headed off, Maya catching up to her.

"You want to tell me what's really going on?" Maya asked.

"It's probably nothing."

She pursed her lips but said nothing.

It took a while, but Lydia managed to find the closest thing to a pharmacy in the belly of the market. At least, it had pharmacy things in it. She headed for the feminine care section of the shop. When she found what she was looking for, Maya's eyes widened.

Lydia's face flamed red, but she ignored it and carried the item up to the merchant, paid in cash, and wandered off in search of a bathroom.

Maya waited outside. The door latched, locked.

Setting the item on the bathroom counter, Lydia straightened and caught herself in the mirror. She looked tired, her face dirty, her hair haggard and pulled in all directions. And she couldn't decide what she wanted, but she couldn't avoid the question that had been building in her heart forever.

Take it as it comes – that's what they had said, and that's what she would do.

Lydia opened the box and followed the instructions, and when she read the results, her heart stilled.

A knock on the door.

"You okay in there?"

"Fine," Lydia said, her voice half-sob.

"I'm coming in."

The lock wiggled, then snapped open. Maya forced her way inside and shut the door behind her, locking it again for all the good that apparently did.

She stared down at the pregnancy test in Lydia's hand, her face unreadable. "So…?"

Lydia met her friend's eye, blinking back tears. She smiled. "I'm pregnant."

And terrified.

SIXTY-THREE
TOMMY

The Jailbirds waited in the shade of a pomegranate tree for Lydia and Maya to return. The market was still bustling with life. Blue skies and puffy white clouds overhead. A warm breeze on the wind and the scent of spices in the air. The Jailbirds weren't the only tourists around, and every time Tommy spotted one, he briefly panicked until he realized they weren't Hunters in disguise. But it wouldn't be long before Orion caught up. Every second they spent here was a second that Orion gained on them.

Reid sat in the dirt, his back against a tan dirt-and-stone wall. Pain still registered on his face. Blood seeped through the makeshift bandage around his shoulder. He ran a hand over his chest, massaging it, his eyes closed. Immy sat beside him, cross-legged as she turned a stick over in her hands. She watched Reid, her eyes flicking between his face and the wound in his shoulder.

On the ground beside them sat a couple baskets of bread, cheese, and fruit, along with several gallons of water for their excursion into the Egyptian desert.

Mars and Lucy flipped through Moroccan-style rugs draped over clotheslines while Jude stood by Tommy's side, his eyes scanning their surroundings.

"We're going to need a car," he said.

"I'd thought of that."

"Come up with anything?"

Tommy shook his head.

"I mean, I suppose we could hike out into the desert, but we'd be risking dehydration and heatstroke. If the map and the glass disc are any indication, Cuvier's vault is in the middle of nowhere and miles from civilization."

"Hiking's not an option."

"I agree, so we need to figure something out."

Tommy opened his mouth but stopped when he spotted their girls through the crowd. They pushed through the shifting sea of bodies and made their way back to the Jailbirds. Lydia wrapped her arms around Tommy's middle, and he pulled her close.

"Get what you need?" he asked.

She pulled back, looked up at him, her eyes flicking between his. "Tommy, there's—"

Shouts rose above the sounds of the market, and Tommy's eyes flashed to the crowd. A pair of Toyota Land Cruisers pushed through the crowd, the passengers armed to the teeth. They spotted the Jailbirds and shouted through the windows. Pedestrians and cyclists moved out of the way as the Land Cruisers surged forward.

"Grab what you can," Tommy barked as he pivoted on his

heel, taking Lydia's hand in his. "We need to go."

The Jailbirds snatched up the jugs of water and baskets of food and darted in the opposite direction of Orion's men. Feet skidding in the dirt, Tommy's heart raced. They shouldn't have stopped. They should've kept moving.

No time for that now.

Up ahead, the road split into two directions. One led back to the river and their dinghy; the other led deeper into the city. A glance over his shoulder and he spotted the trucks gaining on them. He faced forward to see two more Land Cruisers coming from the road that led to the Nile River. Tommy dodged right, tripping over a bicyclist, who fell over, shouting something in Arabic. He scrambled upright as Lydia helped him back to his feet.

They surged forward, their feet pounding the earth beneath them, but they weren't fast enough. Not on the roads.

Tommy was about to shout at the others to head inside when one of the trucks tore through the Jailbirds. Tommy and Lydia dove out of the way, landing in the dirt, their friends on the other side of the truck. The men inside shouted, the doors opening.

"Split up!" Tommy shouted when he caught Jude's eye.

Jude gave a sharp nod and scrambled across the street in the other direction while Tommy regained his footing. He grabbed Lydia's hand, her head swiveling back behind them as the truck swung into reverse and then angled toward them.

"We can't outrun them!" she shouted, fear in her eyes.

Tommy's eyes searched the settlement for a way out, his mind racing. He spotted a stack of crates along a wall and pulled Lydia toward them.

"Then we go up," he said.

His lungs burned, his heart raced. They swung into the narrow gap between buildings just as the truck rolled up on them. Tommy shoved Lydia ahead of him. She climbed the crates, scrambling up onto the rooftop. Tommy climbed after her as the Hunters left their vehicle in pursuit. The truck drove forward, kicking up dust behind them, while the men on foot started for the crates.

Tommy and Lydia darted across the rooftop to the ledge and, with no time to waste, launched themselves over the alley and onto the open balcony of the next house. The door wide open, they ran inside to the surprise of its residents. A man jumped up from their dinner table. A woman screamed. A child cried. The man shouted something in Arabic, flailing his arms. Tommy and Lydia surged through the house to the open window on the other side. They climbed up onto the ledge, and Tommy reached for the nearby clothesline. He grabbed it and pulled it toward Lydia.

"You first," he said.

She wrapped both hands around the clothesline, then swung up her feet and began shimmying across to the next building over. Tommy glanced back to see the Hunters stopped at the door of the house. His stomach twisted as one of them brought the butt of his gun and struck the Egyptian man in the jaw. The man tumbled to the floor, his wife running to his side.

Tommy spun toward the clothesline. Lydia was almost across. He couldn't wait.

He pulled himself onto the clothesline and, as she had done, pulled his legs up and began to scoot along the cord, praying that it would hold both of their weight. The line slackened only slightly, and Tommy looked to see that Lydia had made it to the next rooftop. He glanced back, his hair falling past his eyes, to see one of the Hunters grinning at him. The man brandished a massive knife and brought the blade down on the clothesline.

A snap.

Tommy dropped.

He yelped as the clothesline grew taut, his body slamming against the wall of the next building.

Lydia shouted his name. Tommy's ears rang from the impact, but his hands still held the clothesline in a vise. The cord dug into the tender flesh of his palm, cutting deep. Blood dripped down his forearms as he pulled himself up, his feet kicking at the wall in desperate search for purchase.

A hand cinched around Tommy's forearm. Lydia. She helped pull him up and onto the roof. They fell onto the ground together, panting for breath. Tommy groaned, bruises already beginning to form on the side of his body that had struck the wall. He gaped at his hands, a straight gash through each palm, but there was no time to deal with that.

Lydia pulled at him, shouted something, but the ringing in his ears had yet to subside.

Wincing, Tommy managed to get to his feet, clinging to Lydia's arm for support. He staggered forward, then found his footing. Stumbling, then running toward the end of the roof. Behind them, the Hunters had been momentarily delayed as they had to fight off the angry Egyptian woman and find another way to get to Tommy and Lydia.

They made it to the end of the roof just as a Hunter appeared at the top of a set of stone stairs. Tommy didn't wait for the man to take aim. He surged forward with a cry, wrapping both hands around the barrel of the rifle. The two men wrestled for control.

Lydia shouted and swung a board through the air that made contact with the Hunter's side. The man buckled slightly but didn't fall. Lydia struck again, this time getting the man's arm. He cried out, his grip on the gun loosening. Tommy wrenched it free, but the strap was still around the Hunter's shoulder, so he pivoted. Twisted the rifle around the Hunter's neck and pulled his back against him. The Hunter's fingers clawed at the rifle's strap as he choked for breath.

Grinding his teeth, Tommy growled as he tightened his hold around the man's neck. In only seconds, the Hunter stopped struggling. His body sagged against Tommy's, and Tommy released the rifle, untwisting it from around the unconscious man's neck. He pulled it over his shoulder and, grabbing Lydia's hand, they bounded down the stairs.

Tommy and Lydia raced along the rooftops while the others bolted left, but there was more than one truck. They were closing in from all directions. Mars' head swiveled in every direction as he sought an escape route. But they were outnumbered.

An idea formed. He spun to Jude, his eyes wide.

"There's too many!" he shouted. "We've got to split up."

"What?" Jude said. "No way!"

"Divide and conquer, Jude," Mars said, willing Jude to trust the look in his eyes. Everything would be okay. They just needed to split up and divide Orion's forces so that they couldn't converge on the Jailbirds all at once.

Jude gave a sharp nod. "Okay," he said, grabbing Maya's hands and glancing at the others. "We *will* find each other."

They nodded, fear and adrenaline evident in their eyes. Jude and Maya sprinted away, side by side.

"We'll go south," said Reid, and before they could respond, he and Immy ran south, the direction they'd come. They dodged one of the oncoming trucks as it skidded to a stop, its brakes screeching. The driver spun the wheel and barely got enough traction in the dirt to turn around and go after them. Jude and Maya ran back toward the river, two trucks tailing them.

It only took a look from Mars for Lucy to understand. For now, they were on their own.

They took off to the east, diving into the alleyway between two buildings and heading deeper into the village. Behind them, a car stopped. Doors slammed. Boots hit the ground. They were being pursued on foot.

The streets zigzagged back and forth up the hillside. Shouts came from behind, and Mars risked a glance over his shoulder to see the Hunters bowling through a group of people, sending them flying. One of the men stopped, aimed his rifle.

Mars shoved Lucy to the right. "This way!"

Gunfire tore through the air, puncturing one of the trucks parked streetside right in front of where Mars and Lucy had just been. They barreled into a nearby shop, making a beeline for the back in search of another exit. Mars could practically feel the Hunters' breath on the back of his neck. They burst through the back door and out into an alleyway.

Mars ran right. A dead end. He pivoted the other direction and came to a gate, but it had been chained from the inside with a padlock. He growled and slammed the padlock against the wooden gate, glancing around for a way out. The roof was too high and the walls too smooth to scale. They were trapped.

His eyes met Lucy's. "How are you at hand-to-hand?"

She ran her fingers through her shoulder-length hair and steeled her gaze. "I manage."

"Good. Get on the other side of the door. They won't expect us to be waiting for them."

Mars and Lucy positioned themselves on either side of the door and waited. They had no weapons, no real fighting experience, but they did have the element of surprise.

The first Hunter burst through the door, and Mars kicked his feet out from under him. He slammed to the ground, and while Lucy struck out at the second Hunter, Mars dove into the dirt and grabbed for the first man's gun. Flat on his back, the Hunter brought his legs up and kicked Mars in the stomach. The breath expelled from his lungs in a wheeze, and he staggered back. The Hunter rolled onto his hands and knees, and Mars flung himself onto his back before the man could get his feet under him. He wrapped an arm around the Hunter's neck and pulled. The man elbowed him – once, twice, three times before Mars' grip loosened enough for him to fling Mars over his shoulder and onto the ground in front of him.

Mars' head spun. The man raised his boot and Mars rolled away just as he stomped his boot into the dirt where his head had been. Scrambling to his feet, Mars faced the irritated Hunter. The man aimed his rifle and fired.

Mars ducked beneath the spray of bullets and charged the man, his shoulder slamming into the Hunter's stomach as they went flying several feet before skidding into the dirt together. Mars managed to position himself on top of the Hunter, straddling him, too close for the Hunter's rifle to be any use.

The Hunter drew a large knife from a sheath on his belt and

raised it to stab Mars, but Mars grabbed his wrist with both hands and forced it to the side. He slammed the man's hand into the ground until the knife slipped free. Mars used his momentum to drive an elbow into the side of the Hunter's face.

While the man was stunned, Mars followed it up with a punch to the jaw. The Hunter writhed under him, struggling to get out from under Mars' weight. He clawed at Mars face and neck, and Mars pulled away, wrapping his hands around the Hunters throat. He squeezed and lifted the man's head slightly above the ground before slamming it back down again.

The Hunter stilled.

"Mars!" Mars whirled around to see Lucy being backed into a corner by the second Hunter. The man raised his rifle and aimed.

Mars scooped up the knife the first man had dropped and charged the second man. Startled, he spun his weapon away from Lucy and turned to Mars just as Mars' body collided with his. The knife found its mark through an opening in the man's tactical vest in his side. He cried out. Blood coated Mars' hand and spilled into the dust below as the man's body slumped.

Mars staggered backward, glancing down at the bloodied knife in his hand. It slipped from his fingers, clattered to the dirt. Blood stained his skin.

"Mars…" Lucy said.

He met her eye as she sidestepped the dead Hunter and rushed to Mars' side.

Mars glanced down at the man in the dirt and the knife at his feet, then back up at Lucy. She could have died. *He* could have died. And he hadn't even told her yet how he felt.

"Thank you," she said.

Mars took her face in his hands and pressed his lips to hers in a kiss. They fell back against the wall, her body sinking into his as adrenaline and emotion intertwined between them. He pulled back, his eyes searching hers. Her mouth hung open, breathless, surprised. A smile danced in her eyes.

He kissed her again as clarity settled over him. He didn't need to be Tommy to take care of the people he loved. He didn't need to be Jude to figure out how to express himself. Everything he needed to survive the world they'd stumbled into had been inside him all along.

"You're welcome," he said.

SIXTY-FIVE
MAYA

Up ahead, the bright blue surface of the Nile River glittered like a sea of diamonds. Sweat beaded into Maya's eyes, nearly blinding her as she sprinted across the dirt road, she and Jude heading back to the rubber dinghy – the only way they'd be able to outrun the Hunters.

Jude darted out into the road and Maya ran after him, but a black blur dove between them, separating them. The truck's doors swung open, and Maya backpedaled. On the other side of the truck, Jude skidded to a stop. The driver's side door opened, and he jumped forward, slamming the door on the driver's arm. The man's weapon dropped to the dirt, and Jude slammed it again against his head. He slumped back into the seat.

Maya ran around the front of the car, Jude grabbing her by the hand and pulling her away from the Hunters and through a bank of trees toward the river. Gunfire erupted over their heads. They dodged right. The docks appeared in the distance, and somewhere in that maze of boats was their dinghy – the only way to put permanent distance between themselves and their pursuers.

With a yelp as a bullet whizzed past her ear, Maya ducked and tripped on the dirt, pulling Jude with her. He managed to keep his footing and helped Maya back to her feet but not before one of the Hunters overtook them. Jude let go of Maya's hand and swung a fist at the Hunter. The man ducked, striking the butt of his rifle into Jude's ribs.

Jude cried out, doubling over.

Springing to her feet, Maya grabbed the man's gun and managed to wrench it from his grip. But he spun and kicked the weapon from Maya's hands. It tumbled through the air and landed on the ground too far to reach. Breathless, Maya dropped to a crouch, fists raised as Jude sidled up to her, one hand nursing his rib.

"You okay?" she asked, her eyes fixed on the Hunter as he unsheathed a giant tactical knife and flashed a sinister grin.

"Just dandy," Jude growled.

The Hunter lunged first, and Jude and Maya dove in opposite directions. Maya brought her knee up into the man's stomach while Jude brought his elbow down on the man's neck. The knife dropped as the man gasped for air. Jude swept the man's legs out from under him and he faceplanted in the dirt with a thud just as two more Hunters burst from the trees.

Maya lunged for the first Hunter's gun several feet away while Jude dove for the knife he'd dropped. He brandished the blade and Maya spun the rifle toward the Hunters, her aim going back and forth between the two men. The four opponents sized each other up for a split second before one of the Hunters raised his weapon.

Maya fired. Missed.

But the target dropped his own weapon as he dove out of the way, and she fired at the ground around him. Jude charged the second man, thrusting the knife out in front of him. The Hunter didn't have time to draw his gun, and so he blocked Jude's thrust by bringing an arm down on Jude's arm. The knife slipped from Jude's grasp.

Maya spun her weapon toward Jude's opponent, but the other Hunter managed to find his footing and charged her. She fired at him but missed again. His body slammed into hers and they flew backwards, skidding into the dirt. Maya whirled onto her belly, the gun just inches from her fingers. She crawled toward it. Hands grabbed her waist, hooked into the band of her jeans and dragged her away from the rifle.

Gritting her teeth, Maya spun back onto her back and gaped at the Hunter lying on top of her. She swung a fist, barely connecting with his temple. But it was enough to make him pull back. She brought her knees up to her chest and pushed him off her. He rolled to the side, and she spun to a crawl, scrambling for the rifle.

His hand cinched around her ankle, and she dropped onto her stomach. The breath hissed from her lungs as she flailed her legs, kicking at the Hunter behind her. Her boot connected with his shoulder, then his face. Blood spilled from his nose to the dirt below and he cried out, uttering a string of profanity.

Maya threw herself forward, her fingers hooking around the rifle's strap. She tugged it toward her, whirled onto her back just as the Hunter got to his feet, aimed the rifle at center mass, and fired.

A spray of bullets found their mark. The man gaped down at her in surprise, then down at the wounds in his chest and stomach. His eyes rolled back in his head, and he collapsed.

Panting for breath, Maya pulled herself onto her knees, then her feet. Twenty feet away, directly parallel to the Nile River, Jude and the third Hunter still fought, each having lost their weapons and now relying solely on brute strength. Blood spilled from a cut in Jude's lip as he stumbled away from the Hunter's kick. Bruises marked his arms and face.

With a growl, Maya aimed the rifle and fired again until the magazine ran empty. In seconds, the last Hunter was facedown in the dirt.

Dead.

Jude stopped, his chest heaving as he caught his breath, sweat and blood dripping from his face to the riverbed beneath his feet.

Maya tossed the empty rifle to the ground and staggered toward Jude.

He smiled, his teeth stained red, his wild blond hair glued to his forehead. Maya let out a shuddering sigh of relief.

Behind him, the surface of the water broke as something huge burst forth onto the riverbed and caught Jude by the ankle. Eyes flying wide in horror, Maya lunged for Jude as the massive crocodile's jaw snapped around his leg.

Jude cried out and fell to the ground. The crocodile tugged him back toward the water. He kicked its snout with his other foot, but the beast didn't relent. Maya grabbed the gun, fired.

Empty.

She panicked.

"The knife!" Jude shouted, still kicking the beast. Blood

spilled from the animal's mouth as it wrenched Jude back and forth, dragging his entire body across the riverbed.

Maya spotted the glint of the blade in the dirt. She sprinted forward and kicked it toward Jude while she searched for another gun. He wrapped his fist around the blade, turned toward the crocodile and released a primal cry as he brought it point first down into the animal's skull. Maya found a gun under the body of one of the dead Hunters and pulled it loose, spinning toward Jude and the crocodile. He stabbed the knife repeatedly into the animal's skull until the blade found purchase in its eye.

The crocodile released Jude's leg, then slithered backward into the water before going limp.

Maya ran to Jude's side. He clutched his leg, the jeans torn around two gashes in his flesh.

He groaned as Maya tore his jeans at the knee and wrapped the fabric around his leg. She helped drag him away from the water's edge. The collapsed to the ground in the shade of the bank of trees, gasping for breath as they stared out across the water.

Jude fell onto his back and stared up at the branches above. His head rolled to Maya. She frowned when she saw the grin on his face.

"What are you smiling about?" she asked.

"I just wrestled a crocodile," Jude said as though it were the coolest thing in the world.

Maya fell onto her back and laughed. They both laughed, the adrenaline seeping from their bones.

"Call me Steve Irwin and put me in a pair of khakis," said Jude, his voice a little too loud, "because I'm the Crocodile Hunter, baby!"

Maya patted him on the arm. "Don't get too excited. You have to walk on that leg."

But not even the wound in his leg could steal Jude's smile.

SIXTY-SIX

REID

Reid's feet pounded the dirt as he struggled to stay ahead of the Land Cruiser in pursuit. The bystanders had slowed the vehicle down as Reid and Immy ducked into a narrow street on the southern edge of the village. The horns honking pierced the air around them.

To Reid's surprise, Immy managed to match his pace. Life in the harsh jungles of South America had done more than leave her with a few scars – it had equipped her body for the fight of their lives. Did she realize how strong she truly was?

Up ahead, the street ended and opened out into the Egyptian desert. A camel pen set against a tan, stone building. Out there, Reid and Immy had no hope of outrunning the Hunters. They'd need to fight.

"Quick! In here!" He pointed to the camel's pen.

They banked right and threw themselves over the roughshod

wooden fencing and ducked under an awning. Reid savored the shade even as he heard the Land Cruiser fast approaching, the Hunters' shouts growing louder as they argued with the villagers.

Reid turned his head to Immy, sized her up. Sweat streamed down every inch of bear skin. Her clothes clung to her frame. She caught his eye.

"Be ready," he said.

Immy nodded.

The Land Cruiser burst through the end of the road. Brakes squealed as it screeched to a halt and idled there, engine humming. From behind, Reid watched through the windows as the Hunters scanned the desert. He snuck along the length of the wall and slipped back over the fencing, coming up behind the truck. Immy followed suit. He motioned with two fingers for Immy to take the right side of the truck. He took the left.

Crouched low enough they wouldn't see them through the windows, Reid focused on the rearview mirror.

"They can't have gotten far," said one of the Hunters.

"If they went out there," said the driver, gesturing toward the wide, open desert and the rolling dunes of sand, "they're dead already."

"Orion wants bodies," argued a third. "You saw what happened to Phil when they escaped the brig."

"Phil was an idiot."

Reid crawled through the dirt toward the first door. He reached a hand up to the handle and slowly released the latch as he sat back on his heels. In a single motion, Reid swung the door open and hurled a fist toward the man in the window seat. He yelped in surprise, his eyes wide as Reid dragged him out of the vehicle, dropped him to the dirt, and brought his boot down on the man's face.

On the other side of the truck, Immy had her arm around one of the Hunter's necks in a chokehold. Impressive.

Reid seized the unconscious Hunter's weapon and dove into the dirt as the driver unloaded his pistol on him. Tumbling into some bushes, he rolled to a crouch and aimed his own gun at the driver. A single shot pierced the man's midsection.

Immy had the passenger side door open and her fist around the last remaining Hunter's throat. He threw up his hands.

"Please, don't kill me," he said, eyes wide with fear.

Reid opened the driver's door and pulled the dead Hunter out, grabbing both his guns and the knife from his hip. He threw them into the seat, then turned to the unconscious man in the dirt.

"Is that what my parents said?" Immy seethed as she pressed the man against the side of the truck, tightening her grip around his throat.

Reid froze, eyes on Immy. "Be careful…" he warned.

Her eyes flicked to him, then back to the sniveling Hunter.

"Did they beg for their lives before you let Orion *execute* them?"

"I-I don't know anything about that. Honest. I'm new, okay?"

Immy's lips curled in a sneer as she brought her face inches from his. Her eyes shimmered with tears, her face lined with years of rage and grief and guilt all overflowing at once.

Reid almost thought she'd do it, kill the man with her bare hands. And he wouldn't blame her – part of him wanted to see her do it, avenge her family. But he knew what would happen if she did.

Rounding the front of the car, Reid settled a hand on Immy's shoulder.

"Killing him isn't worth what it'll do to you," he said.

"We've already killed," she replied. "What's one more death?"

"We kill to survive," said Reid. "That's the difference. But if we let ourselves *become* them, we'll never truly *beat* them."

The Hunter squeezed his eyes shut, snot and tears streaming down his face.

Immy released him and threw him to the ground.

Reid breathed a sigh of relief. "Help me gather their weapons. We need to go find the others."

Tossing guns and knives into the trunk of the Land Cruiser, Reid climbed into the driver's seat and Immy into the passenger. He shifted the truck into reverse, dodging the prone bodies of the fallen Hunters. Out of the corner of his eye, he watched Immy deflate, her head falling back against the head rest. After a second, she swiped at her eyes, inhaled, and pulled herself together – the kind of strength a man like Reid coveted.

Driving north on the road they'd been chased down, Reid scanned the village for any sign of the Jailbirds. He took a left toward the river – the direction he'd seen Jude and Maya go.

"There, there, there!" Immy shouted, pointing across the dash. Reid looked toward the river to see Jude limping away from the water, his arm around Maya's neck.

Slamming on the brakes, he jumped out and opened the back door. Jude crawled in, Maya after him.

"What happened?" Reid asked, glancing over his shoulder in the back seat.

For some reason, despite the blood staining the bandage around his leg, he was grinning ear to ear.

Maya rolled her eyes. "He wrestled a crocodile, so he's very pleased with himself."

"These scars'll give Immy's a run for their money," said Jude as the Land Cruiser bounced over the dirt road.

Immy laughed, gripping the console to keep from being tossed around. "You'll need to wrestle a few more crocodiles if you want to play catch-up."

Back on the main road, they found Mars and Lucy on foot, another truck in pursuit. Reid drove between them, the other truck slamming on their brakes to avoid a collision.

Through the window, Reid shouted, "Get in!"

Mars blinked, then dragged Lucy toward the open door.

Reid peeled away, kicking up a cloud of dust behind them. He spotted Tommy and Lydia up ahead, running toward the village's edge and the open desert. In his rearview mirror, he spotted the Hunters all converging in pursuit of them. Reid spun the wheel to the right, cutting off Tommy and Lydia. Maya swung the door open, and Tommy looked about ready to punch her in the face before he realized who it was. He dropped his fist, glanced over his shoulder at the three approaching vehicles, and shoved Lydia into the car ahead of him.

Once Tommy was inside, Reid didn't wait for the door to close before he took off, pressing the gas pedal to the floor as he aimed the truck toward the open desert.

SIXTY-SEVEN

IMMY

The Nile River shrank into the distance behind them, the village blending in with the dusty mountains. Plumes of dust rose to the sky, indicating the three trucks that sped across the desert to catch up with the Jailbirds.

"Can't this thing go any faster?" Jude shouted from the back seat.

"It's forty years old," Reid shouted back over the roar of the engine. "We're lucky it's not falling to pieces under our feet!"

"They're gaining on us," Maya warned as she glanced through the back window. Immy turned in her seat to see for herself.

One of the trucks was getting closer to the Jailbirds by the second, about to overtake them.

"I have an idea," said Immy. She cranked her window down.

"What are you doing?" Reid said, brow furrowed.

As the Hunters approached, Immy pulled herself out through the window. The truck rocked beneath her, but she managed to hold on. She turned to face the car that came up beside them, and as the Hunters veered toward them, Immy launched herself through the air. She landed on the hood of the truck. The driver swerved back and forth to try to shake her off, but she dug her fingers into the gap around the windshield wipers.

The Hunter in the passenger seat rolled down his window and reached his arm through, aiming his gun at Immy. Immy grabbed his wrist and pulled him halfway out the window. Still holding onto his wrist to keep her anchored, she turned to pull his arm up between her knees and kicked his shoulder. A pop as the shoulder dislocated. The man cried out in pain. The gun slipped from his grip and fell to the desert floor. She kicked again, this time aiming for his face. He yelped, and she used the distraction to pull him fully out of the truck. His body hit the sand and shrank behind the moving car.

Suddenly the truck jerked as the driver slammed on the brakes. Immy flew forward, grabbing hold of the hood with one hand, the rest of her body dangling down. She looked up and saw the driver through the windshield, anger burning his face red. She tried to crawl forward, but she couldn't get enough traction.

A thump.

Immy looked up to see Reid squatting on the roof of the truck, his head down to keep from being blown off even as he favored his wounded arm.

"What are you doing?" she shouted over the roar of the wind in her ears. "Who's driving?"

"Jude!"

"The wounded and maimed?"

"He's still got one good leg!"

Immy reached her other hand up to pull herself forward, but she couldn't latch on. "I've got this handled!"

"I can see that!"

The driver reached under his arm for his handgun and aimed it straight up at the underside roof to the truck. He fired. The bullet pierced metal. Reid dodged.

In the back seat, the third passenger rolled down his window and crawled out onto the roof behind Reid. Reid spun, bring up a leg just as the man found his footing. He dropped his gun and managed to pull himself to a crouch.

The Hunter swung first, and Reid ducked the blow. He struck a fist out, his punch landing on the Hunter's inner thigh. The man clutched his leg, and Reid took the opening, ramming the crown of his head against the man's jaw. Blood sprayed in the air.

On the hood, Immy struggled to hold on, but she finally managed to get her second hand hooked around the hood. She pulled herself up, locking eyes with the driver. The man aimed his gun at her through the windshield. Fired.

She rolled right.

He fired again, and she rolled in the other direction.

A third shot, and Immy used the momentum from her roll to the right to swing herself around, bringing her feet through the driver's window, her boots connecting with the driver's jaw. His head rolled back as Immy pulled herself the rest of the way into the truck's camp.

The truck lurched. She undid the driver's seatbelt, pushed his door open, and shoved his unconscious body out into the sand.

Slipping into the driver's seat and taking control of the wheel, Immy reached through the open window to adjust the side view mirror so that she could see Reid. The last Hunter managed to hold his own against Reid.

"Hold onto something!" Immy shouted. Reid glanced at the mirror, then threw his body down the roof the car, his arms stretching to hold onto the sides.

Immy slammed on the breaks, and the Hunter flew forward over the front of the car. He landed in the sand, unmoving.

Reid slipped through the passenger window and into the seat beside Immy. She stepped on the gas, swerving past the Hunter ahead of them.

"I told you, I had it handled," Immy said.

Reid grinned, a cut in his mouth lining his teeth with blood. "You're welcome."

SIXTY-EIGHT

JUDE

"They're gaining on us!" Tommy shouted over the roar of the engine from the passenger seat beside Jude.

Jude glanced over his shoulder. Sure enough.

One of the trucks came up beside them, and Jude about turned the wheel in the opposite direction until he realized Immy was driving. She gave a two-fingered salute.

"That girl's lost her mind," said Jude with a smile as he shook his head.

Maya leaned over the console between them. "What's that up ahead?"

Jude turned his eyes forward. His mouth fell open as he leaned forward, hunched over the steering wheel. A shadow fell over the vehicle as a massive wall of dust rose to blot out the sky ahead of them.

"Sandstorm," Mars said from the back seat.

Glancing in the rearview mirror, Jude saw the Hunters gaining on them. He looked back ahead at the sandstorm. Danger in both directions.

"Roll up the windows," said Jude as he pressed on the gas pedal. "Tell Immy."

Lydia shouted through her open window for Immy and Reid to roll up their windows. They nodded and followed suit.

"What are you going to do?" Tommy asked, bracing as though he already knew the answer.

The storm wall fast approached, and the winds began to rattle the truck. Jude glanced in the mirror again to see the Hunters turning their vehicles around and racing in the other direction, away from the sandstorm. Which was what Jude should have done.

"Hold onto something!" he shouted. White-knuckling the steering wheel, Jude sucked in a breath. "I'm going to drive us into that storm."

Seconds later, darkness swallowed them.

Episode Seven

THE LOST VAULT

"Hate is a cage, Tommy," she said, "and
when we forgive the people who hurt us,
we set ourselves free."

SIXTY-NINE

MARS

Howling winds buffeted the Land Cruiser. The truck swayed, the Jailbirds tucked inside as they waited out the sandstorm. They'd driven into the tempest as far as they'd dared but were forced to stop as they were enshrouded by darkness. Mars couldn't see past the windows, but he hoped Reid and Immy were somewhere nearby – and safe.

The Jailbirds passed the time in relative silence. Tommy had climbed into the middle seat with Lydia, and she'd fallen asleep in his shoulder. He'd rested his head on hers and fallen asleep soon after. Maya and Jude sat up front, Maya busying herself by worrying over Jude's wound. Mars almost couldn't believe the story that had come with the three long gashes in his leg – fortunately they'd not been deep. Technically, he probably needed stitches, but doctors were few and far between in the middle of the desert. They'd have to rely on Father Time to heal Jude's cuts.

Mars sat in the trunk, his back to the trunk door. Lucy lay on her side, using her arms as a pillow under her head. They'd shoved the pile of weapons out of the way to make room for the two of them. Mars had counted four rifles, six handguns, and three tactical knives. The Jailbirds had actually managed to chip away at Orion's forces, but there was no telling how many Hunters remained on their trail. At times, they seemed unending.

The threat loomed in the shadow of Mars' mind, and frustration brewed in his chest that all they could do was sit and wait. Every second that passed seemed to bring Orion closer than before. He could only hope the freak storm was enough to get the Wild Hunt off their trail.

Mars reached into his pocket to remove his wallet. Tucked beside a dollar bill, he pulled out a picture of his parents. An old photo, taken when Mars was just a kid – five or six, maybe. He tried not to think about how things might be in Mammoth. The city had been in uproar when they'd left. He could only imagine what it was like now, after they'd broken Reid out of police custody and fled the state. Were his parents okay? Was the city in ruins? They'd already lost so much.

But there was anger mixed with the sadness when Mars thought of his parents and of Mammoth. The Highlands had once had a chance to make things right once, but they'd failed to do so. Christopher Rhodes had reached out for help, and Mars' parents had ignored him. They'd turned their backs on their friend, and he'd died as a result. Mars had found the letter in his parents' safe – along with the crystal pendant they'd used to cover up the Titan in Peru. Years had gone by, and they'd never once tried to set things right. Orion had grown stronger for it, and now the Jailbirds suffered the consequences of their parents' inaction, and Mars carried the weight of his father's betrayal. Mars was not about to make the same mistake with Tommy or *any* of his friends. They would be better than their parents were, and they would put an end to this madness once and for all – whatever it cost.

"Tell me about them," Lucy said.

Mars glanced over at her to see her eyes opened and looking at the picture in his hands. Mars pinched the photo between his fingers, turning it so she could get a better look.

"My parents?" he asked.

"Mm-hmm."

Mars shrugged. "They made their fair share of mistakes, but they were good to me. For all the good it did them."

"What do you mean?"

"I was supposed to go to college, have a career, become a hero. Instead, my parents' entire lives burned to the ground, and their son's become an international fugitive."

"I don't know, 'international fugitive' sounds pretty impressive to me."

Mars smirked. "You'd think I was a James Bond villain or something."

"We're not the villains," she said, looking up at him, her eyes shimmering in the shifting shadows.

He angled his head toward her. "Are we the heroes?"

"I think… even if history doesn't get it right in the end, when it comes down to it, we'll know that we did what good we could with the time we had." She paused. "We can't blame ourselves for things we had no control over. Orion's killed and he's lied and he's stolen. He's chased us to the far corners of the earth, and in spite of all of that, we've managed to hold onto what makes us different than him."

"What's that?"

"You would fight to the death for each other," said Lucy as she sat upright, her shoulder brushing his. "The only person a man like Orion would die for is himself."

Mars nodded, tucking the photo away in his wallet.

"Seems like you've figured it out," Mars said with a smile. "That you fit with us, I mean."

She frowned, brushing her hair behind her ears.

"What's wrong?" asked Mars.

"Nothing, it's just…"

Mars waited for her to finish.

"I used to have these friends. Back in Mariner's Cove. We did everything together – we were practically inseparable."

"What changed?"

"We started keeping secrets and lying to each other and things happened, and it just… we fell apart." Lucy glanced up at him, eyes shimmering. "How can you say I fit with you when I lied to you about who I was and why I'd joined you guys?"

Mars couldn't imagine life without the Jailbirds. Their families' secrets had almost torn them apart when they were kids, but they'd managed to defy the odds and find each other despite their parents' best efforts. Maybe Lucy would get the chance to one day make things right with her friends, to fix what had broken between them. But for now, he was glad she was here. With him. And she didn't need to feel guilty for figuring things out in her own way and in her own time. "Can't say I blame you," he said. "I have my fair share of secrets. Besides, you needed to figure out if you could trust us."

"And can I?"

"I think I speak for all of us when I say welcome to the club."

"Oh, do I get a badge? Is there a secret handshake? What about a codeword?"

Mars chuckled. "No, the only thing you need to know is that once you're a bird-"

"You're always a bird," she finished.

Smiling, Mars tapped her leg with his knuckle. "See? You're a fast learner."

"Yeah, I know this guy, and he's really smart, so he's probably rubbing off on me." Even in the dark, Mars was certain he saw her cheeks tint red.

He found himself leaning toward her. "Oh, yeah? Anyone I know?"

The space between them thinned. "Yeah, you've met."

"Do I like him?"

"I don't know," said Lucy, "but I do."

Mars smiled, closing the gap between them. Lucy Adler, the first girl to make his stomach tangle in knots inside of him. The first girl to make him feel like the man he'd always wanted to be. The first girl he'd ever kissed.

Their lips met, and he drank her in. Warmth radiated between them. He held her face with his hand, memorized the dip in the skin behind her ears, desperate to learn everything he could about the one person in the world who made him feel invincible.

Lucy pulled away first, her forehead resting against his as she gasped for breath, licked her lips. "Mars…" she whispered.

"I know," he said. There were lines they couldn't – wouldn't – cross, places they wouldn't go. Not like this.

Lucy's fingers tightened around the front of his shirt. He wanted to give in, let her have it all. But he wouldn't allow temptation to poison this moment, so he pulled away and pressed a final kiss to the knuckles of her hand. His thumb brushed the skin of her fingers, savoring the way they felt in his hand.

Mars sat back against the trunk door, and only then did he realize that at some point the winds had stopped and the truck had stilled.

The storm had passed, and a sliver of light spilled through the sunroof.

"Guys," said Mars.

The others stirred at the sound of his voice. Tommy glanced back at him, then up at the light coming through the roof. "The storm's over?"

"Why's it so dark?" asked Jude.

Mars swallowed. "I think... we're buried in sand."

SEVENTY

TOMMY

Tommy squinted up at the shaft of light spilling through the sunroof. Lydia sat up in the middle seat, glancing at him.

"Is that… sand?"

"I think so." Tommy got onto his knees and came closer to the glass. Sure enough, sand covered the truck's roof. "Great."

"What is it?" asked Lucy from the back.

"If we break open this window, the sand'll come spilling in and probably faster than we can climb our way out."

Maya turned in the driver's side, her brow furrowed. "What are you saying?"

"I'm saying… we're trapped."

A pause.

"Well," said Jude, "at least Orion *definitely* won't find us now."

"That's the spirit," muttered Mars.

Something thumped overhead. A shadow blocked out the sun.

"Wait," said Tommy.

Suddenly, a face appeared on the other side of the sunroof. Reid smiled down at them.

"Need a hand?" he asked, Immy appearing over his shoulder.

Tommy let out a laugh. "We'll take what we can get!"

Reid and Immy stooped to scoop the sand away from the window, widening the shaft of light that spilled into the truck. Tommy turned to the others. "Grab what you can, and hand me my bag."

As Lucy gathered the weapons and passed them around to the others, Mars handed the rucksack to him. Tommy pulled it over his shoulder, patting it to make sure the map, the keys, and the glass disc were still inside.

"Move back," Reid shouted through the glass.

The Jailbirds scooted as far away from the sunroof as they could. Reid brought the butt of a rifle down against the glass, and it took three tries before the glass completely shattered. He dragged the rifle along the outside to break out any remaining shards. One by one, Reid and Immy helped the Jailbirds out of the truck. By the end, the bandage wrapped around the wound in his shoulder began to seep with fresh blood.

Tommy watched with concern as he clutched his arm, backing away. "Thanks," he said. "How's your arm?"

"Still in one piece," Reid said with a wince.

Tommy chose not to press as Reid turned away. He was glad to have the ground under his feet again, but as he looked around, the only thing he saw for miles was an ocean of sand.

"Why weren't you guys buried?" Lydia asked Immy.

"Reid got us to that outcropping of rocks over there." She putted to a stone formation that rose above the sand. "We parked behind it, and it protected us from the storm."

"The truck still run?" asked Tommy.

Reid nodded. "Far as I know."

They crossed the sand to the rock formation, tossing their weapons into the trunk. Tommy laid the map out on the hood of the truck as his friends gathered around. He pulled a compass from his pocket and set the glass disc over Egypt on the map, aligning the etchings with the curve of the Nile River. Glancing down at the compass, Tommy shifted on his feet until he got his bearings – a general idea of the direction they'd gone since fleeing into the storm.

He pointed westward. "We go this direction, and it should bring us in the general vicinity of Barnaby's destination here."

"That's a lot of ground to cover," said Reid.

"Safe to say we bought ourselves some time since the Hunters turned tail and ran," Jude added.

"Well," said Mars, "we better get going, then, before they figure out where we're headed."

Piling into the truck with Reid at the driver's seat and Tommy in the seat beside him to keep them on course, they pulled away from the safety of the rock outcropping and headed into the open desert.

Even with the windows open, as the hours wore on, the heat in the desert seemed inescapable. Tommy hadn't quite imagined it would be this bad. Every now and then, a gust of wind would shudder across the sand and cool the sweat that beaded on their skin.

It wasn't long before Land Cruiser's engine began to sputter, and when it died, the Jailbirds were forced to go the rest of the way on foot.

Tommy squinted up at the sun, wishing they'd thought to steal the Hunters' sunglasses along with their weapons. As they rose to the top of a dune, he turned in a circle, surveying their surroundings. Nothing to see for miles but sand and clear blue sky. Not a drop of water or a sliver of shade in sight.

But they kept going, because that's what they did. No matter what, the Jailbirds never stopped pushing forward.

SEVENTY-ONE

MAYA

aya drank the last few drops of the water jug Mars had passed to her, savoring the moisture before she swallowed. She scraped her tongue over her dry lips as she willed herself onward.

"Oh, look," said Jude as they rounded another dune. "More sand."

Falling behind, Maya focused her eyes on her friends in front of her. Tommy and Lydia off to the left, Tommy practically dragging Lydia by the hand. Lydia's eyes had grown listless, but she kept herself upright. Maya was more worried about the baby than anything. How long could a baby survive in the womb in these conditions? Had Lydia even told Tommy yet?

Ambling across the sand toward Lydia, Maya opened the last jug of water. "Here," she said, shoving the bottle toward Lydia. "Drink."

Lydia glanced at Maya, then the jug of water. She stopped in her tracks, took the water, and drank a sip.

"No," said Maya. "More."

Frowning, Lydia said, "I'm not going to hog the water."

Maya leaned in, whispering, "You *need* to drink *more*."

Lydia's eyes flicked back and forth. She relented and took a deeper swig of water before screwing the cap back on. She passed it to Tommy, who took a drink. Tommy's forehead flared pink from the sun exposure. They needed shade and water, and they needed it fast. The lack of wind these past few hours had only served to increase the temperature of the air around them. Every time Maya took a breath, it was like being smothered.

A few feet away, a rock jutted out from the sand. It would be nice to sit for a second. Maya drifted toward it and turned to sit, but Jude shouted something.

"What?" she asked, squinting against the setting sun behind Jude.

He darted toward her. "Watch out!"

Maya turned slowly and froze when she realized she had company. On the rock sat a scorpion, its wicked tail poised to strike. She backed away slowly, swallowing what moisture she had left in her mouth. Jude yanked her back further, grabbing her shoulders. "Did it get you? Are you okay?"

"Yeah, I'm fine." Her brain couldn't seem to keep up with what was happening. She was tired, so tired. She just needed to lie down for a second.

Jude was worried – she saw it in his face. He took her hand in his and said something, but Maya wasn't listening.

She stumbled away from the rock, following after Jude, forcing her brain to focus.

"May?"

"Hmm?"

"I said, you need to drink some water."

Without prompting, Tommy passed the jug to Jude, who opened it and put it to Maya's lips. Hadn't she just drank? How long ago was that?

Time seemed to slip by like sand in an hourglass. How long had they been wandering around out here? Were they even headed in the right direction?

The sky began to change colors. Bright blue morphed into orange and yellow, then purple and pink as the sun began to dip behind the horizon. With the dusk, the air began to cool, and at last the Jailbirds found some relief from the incessant heat.

"What I'd give to be back in Mammoth," said Tommy, his voice uneven as he trudged onward toward a goal that seemed somehow further now than it had an hour ago. "Taking the *Perdition* out on the water. The spray of the ocean. The call of seagulls. A simple, quiet, safe life."

"I'd kill for a burger from Darby's," Mars added.

"A chocolate shake and onion rings," Lydia added.

Maya's stomach grumbled in response. When had they last eaten?

"Tacos," Jude groaned. "A boatload of tacos…"

Lucy moaned. "Guys, you're killing me."

"Remember when we went swimming in Peru?" said Immy. "That water felt *amazing*."

Reid wiped the sweat off his brow, turning toward the last flicker of sunlight in the distance. "I could be shooting pucks at a net right now, but instead I'm in the middle of the desert about to die of heatstroke."

Jude shoved his shoulder. "Who you kidding, bro? This is better, and you know it."

"Better than hockey and my health? I'm not convinced."

Maya smirked. Laughter bubbled up her throat, and she couldn't hold it in. The others stopped and turned to her like she was a crazy person – and she probably was a little out of her mind right now.

"What are you laughing at?" Lucy asked.

She jutted a thumb at Reid and Jude. "I just remembered," she said, her stomach clenching as the laughter took over. "They're *brothers*."

Jude cocked an eyebrow. "And that's funny to you?"

"No, it's ridiculous!" Maya doubled over, clutching her stomach. "This whole thing is ridiculous! So ridiculous it's funny."

Lydia started to laugh, too.

"After all this time, you guys hating each other, only to find out you're actually related? Come on, you've got to find that at least a *little* funny."

Reid rubbed the back of his head. "Well, I mean, I guess it is… a little."

"And our parents? What a mess!"

Laughter began to spread like wildfire as the absurdity of it dawned on the Jailbirds. All of the sudden, the amusement seemed to wake them out of a slumber, and soon the Jailbirds found themselves more animated as they continued their trek into the desert. They were going to make it, and everything would be okay. Maya was certain of it.

SEVENTY-TWO

IMMY

It wasn't so much the heat that got to Immy – given she'd grown up south of the Equator. It was the sand. Everywhere. For miles and miles. The way it felt beneath her feet. Each step she took was a little like sinking. The sun's setting had taken the heat of day with it, but it hadn't relieved them of the exertion of walking endless miles. The only thing they had to distract themselves as the last water jug slowly ran out was each other.

Immy sidled up to Reid, her arm bumping his. "Thanks," she said.

Reid glanced down at her, his eye cocked. "What for?"

"For the help back there."

"Ah." He paused. "You would've been fine on your own."

"You're right," she said, lifting her chin a little, even though she knew she was wrong. "I would've been."

"Yeah, that's not why I did it for you."

"No?"

He shook his head, a smile tugging at this corner of his lips. "I just didn't want you to get all the glory."

Immy elbowed him.

He winced, rubbing his arm.

"Fine," she said, looking away. "I suppose I'd be willing to share the spotlight with you."

"So gracious."

She shot him a glare.

He held up his hands.

Overhead, the sky twirled hues of blue Immy hadn't seen since leaving Peru. The stars clear and bright – burning signal fires on the horizon. The moon big and full and round overhead, lighting the way before them as clearly as if they were walking streets lit by lamps.

"Last drink?" Jude said from somewhere behind Immy. She glanced over her shoulder to see him holding up the nearly empty jug of water, offering to any takers.

"Give it to Lydia," said Maya.

Lydia started to argue, but Maya shot her a glare.

Jude passed the jug to her, and she drank, then dropped the empty container.

"I hate that we're littering right now," she muttered.

"Are we even headed in the right direction?" Mars said, stopping in his tracks as he stretched. Lucy stopped just ahead of him, her eyes scanning their surroundings.

Tommy glanced at his compass. "Yep."

"And you're sure that thing's not broken?" Jude asked.

"As sure as I can be, but I guess we'll know for certain if we end up wandering across the border into Libya."

A groan arose from among the group, and Immy turned to force herself forward.

"If I never see another grain of sand after this, it'll be too soon," she muttered.

"Just keep moving," said Reid. "Try not to think too much about it."

"Oh, if only it were that easy, Clark."

He smirked. "What'll you do when all this is over?"

Immy stopped, cocked her head. She hadn't really thought it over. Her mind had been so focused on stopping Orion, on getting revenge for her parents and uncle that life after this didn't quite seem... real. "I don't know. I think... I think I'd like to go back home, at least for a while. I need to put my parents and uncle to rest once and for all. After that? Who knows."

Reid nodded. "Maybe I'll go with you."

"What? To Peru?"

"Sure. I'm a fugitive, after all. Besides, there's nothing for me in Mammoth anymore."

"A sister, a stepbrother, and a brother-in-law?" she offered.

"They're fugitives, too. I don't think *any* of us will be going back to Mammoth anytime soon."

"Well," she said, looking away, "you're welcome to come to Peru with me. If that's what you want, I mean."

"I can show you where he's buried," Reid said without looking.

Immy's heart sank at the reminder of Emilio. At least she wasn't angry at Reid anymore – no, she saw too much of herself in him to be angry with him for what had happened. "I'd like that."

Reid led the way up the next rise. He stopped at the top,

gaping at the distance. Immy's legs protested every upward step.

"Look," she said, "if you're going to keep stopping, then we might as well—"

Immy froze beside him, eyes wide. Her mouth fell open, and the words failed to come.

"Guys?" said Tommy. "What is it?"

"Is it Libya?" asked Jude.

"'Is it Libya?'" Mars repeated. "Really? As if there'd be a giant sign that reads, 'Welcome to Libya, Weary Travelers.'"

"There *could be.*"

Immy turned, the look in her eyes silencing them. Her gaping mouth morphed into a smile as she waved for them to come. "It's…"

"Real," Reid finished.

The rest of the Jailbirds joined them at the top of the dune, and Immy turned forward. There in the distance at the heart of a valley nestled between mountains of stone and sand, was a jungle of green palms and wild-grown citrus trees that encircled a large, glittering spring. An oasis, at the center of which was built a pyramid.

Cuvier's Lost Vault – they'd found it.

SEVENTY-THREE

JUDE

The breath escaped Jude's lungs in a hiss. Cast in moonlight, the oasis seemed almost too good to be true – a mirage.

"We made it," Tommy said, half-laughing.

Jude drank it in – the sight of trees and the pyramid and the sound of birds in the distance and *water*. He glanced at the others, a grin spreading across his face. "Race ya!"

He broke into a run down the hillside, the sand doing its level best to slow him down, but that fresh spring called to him. Behind him, he could hear the others laughing as they ran to catch up with him. Jude half-ran, half-rolled down the slope as the oasis grew nearer and larger all at once. The sand beneath his feet turned to dirt and stone and underbrush, and the solid ground felt jarring after so many hours spent trudging through desert dunes.

They'd made it. They really had. Despite the danger and the

opposition, despite their enemy's best efforts, the Jailbirds had found their way to Othniel Cuvier's lost vault of discoveries and treasures in the middle of the Egyptian desert. It didn't matter that they had no idea how they'd get it all home yet. It didn't matter that they may not be able to share their discoveries with the world yet. It didn't matter that they were still fugitives in their own hometown. The Jailbirds had won, for the first time in a long time. They'd defied the odds and broken through the barriers.

Jude swiped at the tears of joy that formed in his eyes as he raced across the dirt, the smell of water and wet earth wafting through the air toward him. And as he ran, he pulled his shirt over his head and tossed it to the ground, hopping on one foot at a time to remove his boots so that when he came to the water's edge, he could dive right in.

His entire body submerged in the cool water, he held himself below the surface as the water reached places long dried out. He flicked out his tongue to taste, the coolness sliding down his tongue to the back of his throat, reviving him. Shoving upward, Jude broke the surface with a laugh, staring back at the shore as the others caught up. They dove in after him, splashing around as they laughed.

"We did it!" Jude shouted, raising both fists in the air. He whooped as loud as he could, the others joining in.

Mars threw an arm around his shoulder, laughing as he dunked Jude below the surface, then swam away to find Lucy. Reid stood in the water up to his neck, and Immy splashed him with a mischievous look in her eye. He grinned and chased after her. Tommy held Lydia's hand as they waded through the water together, smiles bright on their faces, eyes shimmering with the same thousand emotions and thoughts that sparked through

Jude's own mind like electricity.

Jude searched for Maya and found her head emerging from the water, pulling her hair back from her face. He waded through the water over to her and wrapped his arms around her waist, pulling her body against his. She draped her arms around his neck as she looked up at him. Her eyes shimmered in the moonlight, her skin glittering like diamonds as droplets of water reflected the starry sky.

"What do you think, May?" he asked.

"I think there's no one I'd rather discover an oasis in the middle of a desert with than you, Jude Mayfield."

He grinned and pulled her into a kiss, slow and deep. Her fingers tangled in the waves of his hair as his hands studied the curve of her back. When he pulled away, he whispered promises and apologies, memories and hopes in the form of three words: "I love you."

As the night wore on and the Jailbirds drank deeply of the desert spring, savoring the coolness it brought to their tired, aching bodies, they dragged themselves back to shore and settled against the trees. Palm fronds fluttered in the breeze and branches swayed. Jude and Mars built a fire by the water and drank in the view of the spring with the pyramid reflected in its surface as it rose above the trees on the other side of the water.

"Why do you think Katherine Rhodes built a pyramid to store her father's discoveries?" Lucy asked.

"She probably hired local workers," Tommy offered, "and this is what they knew for something so big."

"You think it's rigged?" asked Jude.

"Oh, a hundred percent," Maya replied, her fingers tracing circles around his knee as she leaned against him. Jude sat back on his hands, the warmth of the fire washing over him, drying the moisture that still clung to his skin and soaked his trousers.

"I don't think we can afford to wait until morning to breach it – especially if Orion's men are still in pursuit," said Reid.

Tommy nodded. "We'll catch our breath, then when we're ready, we'll get moving."

Jude watched Tommy, the trepidation in his eyes as he stared into the fire. This was everything his father had been working toward until Orion murdered him in cold blood. Now that Tommy was about to finish what his father started, was he afraid it would mean losing him?

"He'd be so proud of you, Tommy," Jude said from across the fire.

His best friend met his eyes, tears brimming.

"You did it, man," he said. Tommy's eyes closed. "You *did it*."

SEVENTY-FOUR

LYDIA

The lapping of water against the shore of the spring filled the silence as the Jailbirds lounged by the fire. Ribbons of smoke drifted through the air. Twinkling stars stood watch above. If it were under any other circumstance, it would be perfect. The kind of romantic excursion she'd read about in novels. Instead, every time Lydia turned around, she expected Orion to be there. Fear had taken root in her heart, and she wasn't sure how to undo the damage it had done.

How was she going to bring a child into this? What kind of life would it have, always on the run with them? Tommy and Lydia were fugitives, even if they were innocent. She'd always wanted kids, and she knew Tommy would make a great dad, but… what a time to start a family.

She looked up to see Maya staring at her, concern written in the lines on her forehead.

"Tell him," she mouthed.

Now that they had their first free moment since she'd found it, she needed to tell Tommy. But the words seemed stuck in her throat.

Lydia turned to Tommy, and he met her eye, smiling.

"Hey, baby," he said, his voice soft, his breath warm on her face.

She grabbed his hand as she stood, pulling him with her. Tommy rose to his feet and followed her away from the campfire and the others gathered around it. She stopped when they were out of earshot, turning to face Tommy.

His brow dipped. "What is it? Is something wrong?"

Lydia shook her head. "Nothing's wrong. Um…"

He rubbed his hands up and down her arms, warming her. Lydia looked up, studied his face. The tint of pink on his skin from the sun exposure. The thin layer of dirt that covered him head to toe. The curl of his hair and the stubble along his jawline. For a moment, she was struck by the man he'd become. He wasn't the boy she'd named dinosaurs or run through the museum or played hide-and-seek or danced on rooftops with anymore. Suddenly, he was a man, with a heart that was good and with hands that were strong.

Lydia sucked in a breath and forced her eyes to meet his. In his gaze, she found the kind of love that silenced the voice of fear in her heart. "I'm pregnant."

Blinking once, then twice, Tommy's mouth fell open. Seconds passed before he spoke. "Are-are you sure? How do you know? How *long* have you known?"

"I'm sure," she said. "Back in the village, when we went looking for a restroom, it was because I wasn't feeling well. I found someplace that sells pregnancy tests, and it came back positive."

"So, you're going to… *we're* going to…"

Lydia nodded. "We're going to have a baby."

He mouthed the words back to her as he processed the news. Lydia startled when he through his fists into the air and shouted, "I'm going to be a dad!"

Lydia covered her mouth, laughing as he whooped and hollered, his eyes wide, her eyes brimming with tears. Her heart thrilled.

The Jailbirds jumped up from around the fire as he shouted.

"What?" Jude said. He looked to Lydia, then to her stomach. "You're pregnant?"

Lydia bit her lip, nodded.

Jude laughed, grinning. "I'm going to be an *uncle*!"

"All of you," said Lydia, nodding. "Aunts and uncles."

Jude hugged her tight and spun her around as he laughed. Maya laughed as she watched him from beside the fire.

"Did you know?" Jude asked her when he set Lydia back on the ground.

Maya nodded. "I did."

"What a secret to keep!" Mars exclaimed.

Lucy and Immy took turns hugging Lydia and congratulating her, then Tommy who paced back and forth, muttering excitedly about all the things he planned to do with the baby when it was born. All the games they would play and the fun they would have. The books they would read and the trips they would take.

A hand settled on Lydia's shoulder, and she turned to see Reid standing beside her. "I'm happy for you," he said, a tremor of emotion in his voice. "You deserve to be happy."

Tears threatened to blind Lydia, so instead she wrapped her

arms around her brother's midsection and buried her face into the crook of his neck. "I need you, Reid," she said. "You're my brother, and I need you with me."

Wrapping his own arms around her, he held her tight. "You have me."

When Reid released her and returned to the fireside, Tommy came back to Lydia, resting his hands on either side of her stomach. He looked down at her. "This baby's about to be the most loved kid on the planet," he said.

Lydia's gaze passed over the odd group that had come together in the middle of a desert oasis after being chased and shot at, after surviving a sandstorm and the threat of heatstroke – Tommy was right. But she realized this baby wasn't the start of their family – they'd already found family in each other. In the way Jude and Mars teased each other constantly. In the knowing looks Maya and Lydia exchanged. In the brotherly love that bound Tommy to Jude. In the newfound healing between Reid and all of them. In the way Immy fought for them. It was broken and it was messy and it was beautiful, but wasn't that what a family was?

This baby would be a gift for them all – a promise that no matter the loss, life could find a way to spring from the ashes.

SEVENTY-FIVE
REID

The early light of dawn began to streak across the sky in threads of pink against a backdrop of purples and blues. Sleep had come in waves for all the Jailbirds, and the fire had eventually been reduced to embers. Reid snuffed it out with the heel of his boot, then doused it with water from the spring. He turned his eyes toward the pyramid, the morning light making it appear almost golden amid the lingering shadow of night.

Set against the face of the pyramid that was angled toward the spring was a long, rectangular structure with a flat roof supported by rows of columns with two sets of stairs on either side that led to the roof. Reid was no Egyptologist, but he understood that pyramids were the tombs of pharaohs long dead – could this structure be a temple of some sort? A structure meant for a funeral procession, or sacrifices to ancient gods?

His linen shirt having dried overnight, Reid pulled it over his head. The fabric was light on his skin – perfect for the desert heat. He shoved one of the handguns in the waist of his trousers and pulled the strap of one of the rifles taken from the Hunters over his shoulder, holding it close. He didn't expect to find anything alive inside that tomb – this wasn't *The Mummy*, and he wasn't Rick O'Connell – but he felt more at ease knowing he could protect himself and his sister should something less-than-supernatural happen.

"Keep an eye out for traps," Lucy warned as she straightened, turning her eyes across the water toward the pyramid.

Mars smirked. "We are well-acquainted with those, I'm afraid."

Buttoning his shirt, Tommy came to stand beside Reid. He glanced at the weapons in Reid's hand, then back at the others. Reid noted the bulge of a handgun in the waist of Tommy's pants.

"Whatever it takes," he said, "we keep them safe."

Reid studied the look in his eyes. An intensity in the way he set his jaw, the way the veins in his neck seemed to flare as he swallowed. It reminded Reid of Spokane, of how far Tommy had shown he was willing to go to save Lydia. Reid had never thought much of Tommy before these last few months. Before Orion had turned him into an enemy, he had just been another Jailbird. A nobody. Now, Reid saw him for what he was: Tommy Rhodes was a force to be reckoned with. Funny thing was, Reid didn't think Tommy knew just how dangerous he really was.

It was no wonder Orion was hellbent on destroying him.

Reid nodded. Satisfied, Tommy turned to rejoin Lydia. With her, the intensity in his eyes turned gentle, attentive.

Glancing back at the others as they gathered themselves, and despite the steadily throbbing pain of the bullet wound in his shoulder Reid asked, "Ready?"

Tommy shrugged his backpack onto his shoulders and lifted his chin. "Let's do this."

Reid led the way around the spring toward the pyramid and the temple entrance. His eyes darted back and forth across their surroundings, watching for tripwires and traps waiting to spring. All was quiet and still.

They came to the entrance of the temple, the structure larger than it had appeared from a distance. There were images carved into the pillars in overlapping patterns, and faces etched from stone that looked down on any who dared step foot inside this tomb. But something was off.

"This doesn't make sense," said Mars as he gaped up at the structure. He reached out to touch a nearby pillar. "These aren't Egyptian hieroglyphs."

"No," Lucy said. "They're something else entirely…"

"That's because this place isn't Egyptian," said Tommy as he pointed up. "Look."

Carved into the face of the temple roof were three images all too familiar to Reid. They were the same images that had been carved into the three keys in Tommy's rucksack: a mammoth, a Titanosaur, and a Spinosaurus.

"A tomb of behemoths and tyrants who once ruled the world," Tommy muttered as his eyes flicked back and forth over the image.

"So, these inscriptions on the pillars," said Mars, "they're another language entirely? What language did Cuvier and his daughter speak?"

"They sometimes wrote in Latin, but I don't think they were

fluent in it," Lucy replied.

"Could it be some sort of warning?" asked Lydia.

Reid squinted at the pillars. He stepped closer, eyes darting over the inscriptions. "I don't think so. What's the name for a T-Rex in Latin?"

"That *is* the Latin name," said Mars. "Tyrannosaurus rex. It means 'tyrant lizard.'"

Reid's fingers tapped the word where it was inscribed in stone. "And the Titan?"

"Titanosaur," said Mars. "It means 'titanic lizard.'"

"Thank you, Encyclopedia Britannica," Jude muttered.

"This isn't a warning," said Reid as he found the word on the pillar. He glanced across at the pillar on the other side of the temple, where he found the word *Spinosaurus*.

Tommy's eyes widened. He crossed to the other side of the temple, searching the inscription. "*Aurum*," he said. "That's the Latin word for gold." He locked eyes with Reid. "You're right. It's not a warning, it's a record."

Reid took a step back as realization dawned on them one at a time.

"That means…" said Lydia.

"I count eight pillars on each side," Maya added.

Lucy ran her hands through her hair. "Katherine built this place to be more than just a vault to protect her father's discoveries." She paused. "She built it to be a *monument* to her father, so that if anything was ever stolen the proof would still be here."

"That's honestly genius," said Jude.

"Either way, Cuvier's legacy would be found out, one way or another." Tommy held his hands behind his head as he gaped up at the pillars.

"And all of this," Lydia pointed at the pillars, "is inside there?" She pointed to the pyramid.

Mars came to stand in the middle of the pathway into the temple. "The vault."

"Time to crack the code." Jude popped his knuckles and reached for Maya's hand.

Reid stared down the walkway to the ornate entrance into the pyramid. "Alright, then."

He took a step forward, the first to enter the temple. The shadows swallowed them. His eyes found the pockets in the walls where torches would have been lit, but they had long fallen to decay. Light filtered between the columns, guiding their path toward a large opening in the side of the pyramid framed with more inscriptions – these, images painted on the surface of the stone in hues of red, green, and blue. More depictions of dinosaurs and beasts from an ancient, primeval world. Not a warning, but a promise. A promise that even when men would try to steal and rob and plunder, the truth would never stay long buried. History would always belong to those who discovered, explored, and ventured.

There was no door on the entrance to the pyramid. Instead, it stood wide open. An invitation.

Or a trap.

Reid stepped into the long, wide corridor, and the others followed. They moved in silence, perhaps out of reverence for the man whose legacy had built this place. Reid couldn't imagine building a gravestone for his father, let alone an entire secret monument, but that's what Katherine Rhodes had done. She had kept her father's discoveries secret until the world was ready to acknowledge him for the man he was. Obadiah Hawthorne and Orion Clark, they may have tried to bury Othniel Cuvier, but they would fail. They would fall like giants toppled from the heights.

Something depressed beneath Reid's foot, and he froze. He pulled his foot back, and with the grinding of stone on stone, the tile slid back in place.

A thunderous groan surged from the heart of the pyramid. A gust of wind bore down the corridor, whipping dirt and sand into the air. Reid squinted, shielding his eyes with a hand.

"What was that?" Lucy said.

A slam. Darkness swallowed them.

Reid spun on his heel. The entrance had been shut. They'd lost their light and their exit.

The ground began to tremble. A light sparked behind Reid – Jude holding a lighter aloft. The Jailbirds' worried faces shone against the black. The light illuminated the stone walls on either side of them.

Reid's heart sank. The walls were moving, closing in on them.

"Run!" he shouted, pivoting on his heel, following the corridor deeper into the pyramid. The terrible sound of stone dragging, scraping, clawing against stone as the walls inched toward each other kept them moving. He bounded out into a wide open space, nearly tripping over his own feet in the darkness. One by one, as the walls came dangerously close to crushing them, the rest of the Jailbirds came running out after him. Mars was the last left behind, forced to run sideways as the gap narrowed.

Reid thrust his hand through the opening, grabbed Mars by the arm, and practically dragged him out of the corridor just as the two walls slammed together. A cloud of dust burst into the air around them, and the light went out.

SEVENTY-SIX
MARS

Heart racing, sweat dripping into his eyes, Mars felt around on the floor. Dirt, sand, and stone scraped against the flesh of his palms. Alive? Yes, alive.

"Hello?" Mars said into the dark, his voice still shaky from the surge of adrenaline at nearly being crushed to death.

A hand found Mars' shoulder.

"We're here," said Reid.

A light flicked on. Jude's lighter, casting an orange glow across a small, closed chamber. Mars yelped and jumped to his feet when the light landed on tangled, skeletal remains slumped against one of the walls. Gaping holes where eyes should be stared back at him. He shuddered.

"That's… unsettling," said Lydia.

Jude turned, carrying the light with him. Torches lined the

walls, and he lit them one at a time. Inside this chamber, they'd managed to survive the elements that those in the temple outside had succumbed to.

Tommy crouched in front of the remains, arms on his knees. He cocked his head, studying the skeleton. He'd seen that look before, only Christopher Rhodes had worn it last time. He was becoming more and more like his father by the day. Mars could only hope they wouldn't share the same fate.

Mars dared a step closer as Tommy reached for the tattered fabric that draped over the skeleton's rib cage. "What is it?" he asked.

"This uniform," said Tommy. "It's German."

"So?"

Tommy glanced up at Mars. "From the second World War."

"You're kidding," said Maya as she inched closer, peering over Tommy's shoulder.

Swallowing the bile that hovered on the back of his tongue, Mars decided he'd spent enough quality time with the former soldier. Something about seeing the bones of a person who had once lived as full and vibrant a life as Mars did now left him feeling… haunted.

He searched for Lucy and found her standing further back, her eyes wide. "You okay?" he whispered.

She nodded, though the whites of her eyes shone bright enough in the flickering torchlight to tell Mars how she really felt.

"You almost *died*," she hissed.

"But I didn't."

She nodded again, then wrapped her arms around his neck. Mars folded his arms around her middle, holding her close as she buried her face in the crook of his shoulder. She pulled away, swiping at her eyes. "What is this place?"

"Apparently, it's a trap," said Jude, glancing back at the skeleton. "Seems our pal Herr Schmidt here landed himself in a heap of trouble."

Reid stood to the side, studying the wall opposite the direction they'd come. "I think this is a door," he said.

Mars inched closer, ignoring the nearby skeleton. Reid was right. There were long seams around this section of stone that made it distinct from the rest of the room. He smiled as his eyes came to the center of the door. "Hey, Tommy. Looks like we can finally put those keys to some use."

Tommy straightened, coming to join Reid and Mars at the door. In the center of the stone panel were three holes – each shaped like a hexagon.

Smiling, Tommy slipped the rucksack over his head and reached inside to produce the three keys, each with a different image carved into its surface. "Here goes nothing," he said.

Reid and Mars took a step back while Tommy leaned forward. Mars held his breath. Lucy slipped her hand into his, and he gave it a reassuring squeeze. One at a time, Tommy inserted Cuvier's three keys into the holes in the middle of the door.

He stood back, waiting. Nothing.

Jude frowned. "Well, that was anticl–"

The wall to Mars' left exploded, sending fragments of stone through the air as water surged into the room, knocking the Jailbirds off their feet. Mars hit his head against the opposite wall. His ears rang as he struggled to get his feet under him. The Jailbirds moved frantically around the room as it began to fill up with water.

"Reid! Help me!" Jude called.

Mars whirled toward his voice, saw Jude on the other side of the room pulling at a mound of stone that had Tommy's arm pinned down. The water level began to rise rapidly. Mars splashed across the room to help. If they didn't get Tommy free, he'd drown before the room ever even filled.

"No, Mars," Jude said as he and Reid pulled at the stones, Reid ignoring the wound in his shoulder. "Get that door open!"

Mars' eyes flicked to Tommy, then Jude. He nodded, then turned on his heel and splashed over to the door. The water had risen to his knees, and Tommy was straining to keep his head above the water while everyone else worked to unbury him.

Mars studied the door. There were no inscriptions. No symbols. Nothing to tell him what they'd done wrong.

Three keys. Three locks. There must be a pattern.

Popping each of the keys back out, he studied the locks. They were lined up vertically, one keyhole on top of the other. He peered inside, but even if there was a marking on the inside of the keyhole to guide him, he couldn't see it in this darkness. Half the torches on the wall had gone out.

"Mars, hurry!" Maya shouted.

He risked a glance over his shoulder to see they'd almost gotten Tommy's arm free, but he was sputtering above the water. The water had risen to mid-thigh.

A pattern, he thought, forcing himself to concentrate. What kind of pattern? Maybe the keys were meant to be inserted in order of the time period the fossils came from. That would put the Mammoth at dead last, but which came first? Titan or Leviathan?

Not order of era. Order of discovery.

He turned around as the water rose to his stomach. The Jailbirds had Tommy free now, but the water gushing from the wall was filling the room up faster than he could think.

"Tommy!" he shouted over the roar of the water. "What was Cuvier's order of discovery?"

"What?" he shouted back.

"Which fossil did he find first?"

"The Leviathan!"

That's right.

"Okay, second?"

"Um… the Titan."

That made the Mammoth last.

Mars shoved the Leviathan in the bottom keyhole, the Titan in the middle keyhole, and the Mammoth in the top keyhole. Nothing happened.

Descending order.

As the water rose to his neck, covering the keyholes, Mars popped the three keys back out. His toes barely held onto the ground. He bounced in the water, and one of the keys slipped from his fingers.

"Mars!" they shouted at him. "Hurry up!"

Sucking in air, Mars dove beneath the surface. The light from the remaining torches wasn't bright enough to reach down here. He patted the bottom of the chamber floor, sifting through stone until he finally found the key. Pushing off from the floor, Mars surfaced for air to find the room nearly full. Head space only. Unintelligible shouts filled the shrinking space.

Mars sucked in another breath and dove toward the door. In the darkness, he fumbled to find the keyholes.

Leviathan, Titan, Mammoth in descending order.

They clicked, and the wall seemed to pull the three keys in further. A rumble pulsed through the water as the door burst open and Mars surged forward with the wave. His body scraped across the floor, and the water launched him off a ledge. He turned onto his stomach and clawed at the stone until his fingers found purchase, his lower half hanging over the ledge. The water swept Lucy past him, and Mars shot an arm out, barely catching her before she went flying over the edge of the platform. She cried out as her arm wrenched. Mars pulled himself up and her with him as the last of the water splashed over the edge.

He collapsed onto his back, gaping up at the darkness overhead, Lucy lying on his arm. His head rolled toward her.

She panted, her hair glued to her head, but she smiled.

Mars laughed, then glanced back to make sure the others had made it. He pulled himself onto his feet, helping Lucy to hers, and took stock. All eight Jailbirds lay on the stone floor, completely doused as they caught their breath.

Mars sighed and fell back against the floor, relief washing over him. It was all too clear to him that, had he taken even another second, the Jailbirds would have met the same fate as their German friend, washed away in the surge.

Closing his eyes, he offered a whispered prayer of gratitude.

SEVENTY-SEVEN
TOMMY

Tommy winced, folding his wounded arm against his chest as he sat up in the dark. Nothing felt broken. Just bruised or sprained at the most. But he couldn't see two inches past his face to be sure.

His eyes adjusted to the dark, and he glanced around, his legs sloshing in puddles of water that had yet to run off. He found Lydia lying a few feet away. He scrambled across the stone toward her, grabbing her shoulder and rolling her onto her back.

She groaned, her eyes fluttering open. "I'm getting tired of booby traps."

Tommy let out a laugh, his heart still racing. "You and me both, baby."

He helped her sit up, brushed her hair out of her face and tucked it behind her ears.

Lydia gasped. "Your arm!" She pulled it gently toward her,

and Tommy made out the dark spots where bruises had begun to form.

"I'm lucky it's not broken," he said. He glanced over his shoulder, his eyes searching the dark. "Everybody good? Call out."

One at a time, the Jailbirds responded. Everyone was okay. Bruised, wet, and tired, but okay.

Tommy let out a sigh of relief, then stood to his feet and pulled Lydia up with him.

"Tommy, check this out," said Jude.

Following his voice, Tommy found Jude at the far left edge of the platform. A stone trough lined the platform's edge, disappearing further into the darkness. Water shimmered in the shadows.

"What is it?" Tommy asked.

Jude dipped his fingers in the water and brought it to his nose. "Smell it. It's not water."

Tommy followed suit, his eyes widening at the smell. "It's oil." He paused, glancing around. "Light it up."

With a nod, Jude pulled his lighter from his pocket as Tommy stepped back. The lighter sparked, and Jude set the flame to the oil. Light exploded into the room as the fire rapidly spread, consuming the trough, then surging deeper into the darkness.

Tommy gaped as his eyes followed the trail of light that illuminated a narrow bridge connected to this platform and shone further to reveal a massive chamber. The light wound a maze through the room, exposing tall ceilings and deadly drop-offs. The smell of smoke and oil saturated the air.

The Jailbirds gathered on the platform to marvel at what the light revealed. It wasn't the size of the chamber that stole their breath away or the intricate pattern the fire began to weave across the room that caused them to marvel. It was what waited on the other side of the narrow bridge, just a few short steps away from the Jailbirds now stood.

Cuvier's hoard.

Frozen in place as though time itself had stopped, the Jailbirds stayed where they were even after the trail of light had halted. The flickering fire caused the room and all its contents to seem almost alive as the shadows shifted back and forth.

The first to take a step forward, Tommy made his way across the bridge, his friends – his family – following close behind. Nobody said a thing. No wisecracks. No clever jabs. As if they each understood that a moment like this required a reverence they didn't normally have to offer. After all these months, after nearly dying time and time again, after being chased across cities and shot at through jungles and mountains, after plane crashes and shipwrecks, after murders and riots, the Jailbirds had finally found their treasure.

On a massive circular platform wreathed in light in the heart of the pyramid sat mounds of treasure, and the Jailbirds now stood in the midst of it. Chests overflowing with gold. Platforms bearing the bones of ancient fossils out on display, as if waiting to be rediscovered. Crates filled with scrolls and tombs, untold stories, and histories long lost. Massive clay vases bearing swords and spears and bows belonging to civilizations now dead. And at the center of it all, mounted on bars of iron, were the massive, fossilized remains of the greatest dinosaur ever to walk the earth: *Tyrannosaurus rex*. The king of the prehistoric world. A tyrant among beasts.

Tommy gaped at the Tyrant, marveling at its condition despite the years. Its giant skull stared back at him, empty sockets where eyes once were, teeth still razor sharp and now turned to stone. He dared a step forward, struggling to take in everything around him. The gravity of the moment sat heavy on his shoulders. Everything his father had fought for, here now in front of him, a breath away.

Because of Tommy – because of his friends – Christopher Rhodes had not died in vain.

Feet shuffled over stone as the Jailbirds fanned out, gravitating toward the many marvels kept hidden in the chamber. Despite the heat of the desert outside, the air here was cool, even damp. Waves of warmth rippled from the flaming troughs that encircled the perimeter of the chamber.

He came to a crate, shoved the lid to the side. It hit the floor with a *thud*. A shield and gladius decorated with markings from Ancient Rome sat side by side in a bed of straw. Tommy moved to the next crate, upon which sat a stack of old tomes. He held in a sneeze as he picked one up and ran his hands over its aged, leather cover, sending a cloud of dust into the air. He lifted the cover. The letters written on parchment inside seemed Greek. He returned it to the stack as Lydia came up behind him.

Moving slowly, Tommy wound his way through the trove toward the center where the Tyrant stood surrounded by fossils of other kinds. Troglodytes imprinted in sheets of prehistoric stone. Teeth and claws piled together in baskets. Tommy reached for a Velociraptor claw where it rested in a crate among smaller bone fragments. His fingers traced the groves in the claw, the curve of the calcified bone.

Blinking back tears, Tommy whispered, "We did it, Dad."

Lydia's hand came to rest on his shoulder. He reached up to settle his hand over hers, drawing comfort from her nearness.

"He would be so proud of you," Lydia whispered.

Tommy squeezed his eyes shut, his lip quivering as he struggled to hold himself together. He wanted to feel happy, thrilled even, that he'd finally found this place, but somehow the grief seemed suddenly overwhelming. His father should be here, standing by his side, celebrating the restoration of their family's legacy with Tommy and with Lydia. Preparing to welcome his first grandchild into the world. Instead, he was gone. And it wasn't right. It wasn't fair. And the man responsible was still out there, free and unaffected as though he hadn't turned Tommy's entire world on its head.

"Hey," said Lydia, squeezing his shoulder. "What's going on?"

"I hate him." Tommy wiped at his nose with the back of his hand, tears slipping down his face to the stone floor below as he struggled to keep his composure.

"Who?"

"Orion. I hate him for what he's done, and I thought finding this place, proving my dad right, would somehow make things right in my own heart, but… it's somehow worse. I don't know if I could ever forgive him for what he's done."

Lydia forced Tommy to turn her way, taking his hands in hers as she looked up at him, eyes watery, gaze gentle. "Orion doesn't deserve our forgiveness," she said. "But forgiveness isn't for him. It's for us."

Tommy opened his mouth to reply, but a sob threatened to choke him. He looked away, tears blurring his vision completely.

"Hate is a cage, Tommy," she said, "and when we forgive the people who hurt us, we *set ourselves free.*"

He sucked in a shaky breath.

"It doesn't mean we forget, and it certainly doesn't mean we let them back in." She paused. "It means they don't own us anymore. When Orion kidnapped me, I wanted to kill him. I almost did, but I couldn't pull the trigger. Maybe I should've, but in that moment, it wasn't survival that made me grab the gun. It was hatred. And if I'd done it, he may have died, but he would've won. I won't let him have that, Tommy. I *won't let him have me.*"

"I don't know if I can do that," said Tommy, waves of grief and rage crashing on the rocky shores of a weathered heart. "I'm not strong enough."

Lydia reached up to cup the side of his face with her hand, her thumb brushing away a tear. "You're not. No one is." She smiled, tears shimmering in her eyes. "But, Tommy, you're not alone. This isn't a weight you'll have to carry or a road you'll have to travel by yourself. Look around you."

Tommy looked up, glancing to his right to see his friends gathered around him and Lydia, their eyes red as they stood in resolute silence, unmoving and undeterred.

"We carry each other when we can't carry ourselves," she said. "*That's* what makes us a family."

Folding his body against hers, Tommy wrapped his arms around her middle and buried his face in her neck. Memories flashed across his mind. His father, laughing and playing when Tommy was just a child. His mother, happy and healthy in the days before she was broken. The Jailbirds as kids long before they'd ever learned the truth about their parents or paid the price for their parents' failures. Happy memories. *Good* memories. The growing hate in Tommy's heart had tried to bury them, but Tommy wouldn't let it. Even if he had to decide day by day, again and again.

I won't let him have me.

SEVENTY-EIGHT
MAYA

L ook at this," said Jude as he plucked a sword from the ground and held it up, the fire reflecting on the broad side of the tarnished blade. He thrust it forward, piercing an invisible enemy, then lunged backward.

"Careful," Maya warned. "Don't cut yourself."

Jude straightened, considered the blade and testing its edge with his fingers. "Nah, this thing's dull as – *ow!*"

He winced, sticking the wounded finger in his mouth.

"Don't say I didn't warn ya," said Maya with a smirk. She turned around in circles as she took in her surroundings. She didn't know where to begin.

On one side of the platform, Reid lifted an old Renaissance painting, Immy at his side, telling him something as she gestured at another painting nearby. Tommy walked in circles around the vault's main attraction: the Tyrant on display, massive teeth and tiny arms with claws now dulled by the ages. Lydia sifted through a chest of gemstones and old jewelry.

"This is incredible," said Mars as he turned a dagger over in his hands. "It's more than fossils. It's an entire archive of lost history!"

Nearby, Lucy rifled through a crate of old scrolls. "I'd be willing to bet some of these are from the Library of Alexandria."

"Didn't that place burn down?" Tommy asked from the other side of the platform.

"Yeah, but no one really knows what was lost in the fire. Maybe some things were saved *then* only to be lost *later*."

Maya found Jude as he returned the sword where he'd found it. He snatched her hand up instead, smiling down at her. "Can you believe we're actually here right now?"

She smiled, but her stomach hadn't stopped doing somersaults since they'd stumbled into the vault. She couldn't escape this sense of… *foreboding*. Like she was just waiting for the pin to drop any second now. She'd become so accustomed to Orion swooping in at the last minute to thwart the Jailbirds that she half expected him to blow a hole in the side of the pyramid to get inside.

Which was exactly why they could never let him find this place. While the rest of her friends marveled at their discovery, Maya wondered how they were going to protect it. They had no power, no money, no influence. Meanwhile, Orion seemed to have the entire world in the palm of his hand. Maybe she gave him too much credit.

"What is it?" Jude asked.

Maya's eyes darted around the room. "Jude, we're *trapped* in here. I mean, I know I should probably be celebrating right now, but… how are we supposed to get out of here?"

"We'll cross that bridge when we get to it," said Jude. He pointed toward the bridge that spanned the chasm between this platform and the one they'd washed onto earlier. "Literally."

Maya rolled her eyes, punched him in the shoulder.

"Ouch!"

"Well, you deserved it."

Chuckling, Jude grabbed her by the waist and pulled her to himself. Maya hesitated, then met his gaze. "There's a way out of here. Trust me. Katherine Rhodes' goal was always for her devil-squid, octopus organization… secret society thing…"

"*Devilfish*," Lucy corrected from somewhere nearby.

"Yeah, that." Jude smiled, his arms threading around her waist to settle at the small of her back. She wrapped her arms around his neck. "Devilfish's goal was to protect what Othniel Cuvier discovered so that one day his legacy could be shared with the world, and everyone would see the man Katherine Rhodes' father *really* was. That means she intended for someone to be able to get inside *and* get back out."

"Right, but do you see a door?"

"What? Not like there's going to be a blinking EXIT light somewhere."

"No," said Mars, flipping through the pages of a tome, "but that would be helpful."

"Think like a Rhodes," Jude said.

Maya closed her eyes. "See the whole picture."

But she couldn't see the whole picture, because all the light in the room was concentrated around the central platform, sending everything else into pitch blackness. It was impossible to see anything beyond the wall of fire currently consuming the oil trough.

Maya broke from Jude's embrace and crossed the platform to the other side. She followed the ring of fire to the far end and smiled when she found a gap in the fire. A narrow stone bridge that had been obscured behind stacked crates and barrels and other artifacts and bones.

"Help me," she said when Jude came up behind her.

Together, they moved the crates aside and cleared a path to the bridge that arched over the wall of fire.

"See?" Jude said with a wide grin. "What'd I say?"

"Okay, *you* don't get to take the credit for this."

Tommy and Lydia came to join them. "What is it?" he asked.

Maya's eyes followed the narrow stone bridge that led away from the central platform, connecting to a ledge on the far wall of the chamber. The stone rose in a diagonal, zigzag pattern up the interior wall of the pyramid.

Jude's hand squeezed hers.

"A way out," she said.

SEVENTY-NINE

IMMY

"So, what's the plan?" Immy asked, turning to Tommy.

He blinked, looking around at the Jailbirds as they waited on him. He exchanged a glance with Lydia, who offered a smile.

"Alright," he started, "here's what we're going to do. We can't go public with this. Not yet. So we lay low for a while and we do what Katherine wanted – we protect this place. Mars, can you get the keys out of that door back there?"

Mars nodded. "On it." He darted across the platform to the door that hung ajar.

"The rest of us, we gather only what we can carry. Gold coins, jewels, smaller artifacts or fossils. Mine's the only bag, so everything else will have to fit in our pockets."

Immy grabbed a nearby crown and set it on her head, propping her fists on her hips as she smiled back at her friends.

"Or on our heads."

Tommy chuckled. "Whatever works."

"Where do we go from here?" asked Jude.

"Someplace far away, where Orion can't get to us. We keep the keys safe along with Captain Barnaby's map and the glass decoder disc. One day, when we clear our names and take Orion down, we'll come back here. We'll show the world who Othniel Cuvier and Katherine Rhodes really were." His eyes flicked to Jude's. "We see the devil out."

Jude nodded, arms crossed over his chest and jaw set.

"Until then, we stay hidden, and we stay quiet."

"Aye-aye, Cap'n." Jude feigned a salute, then they dispersed to fill their pockets with whatever they could.

Immy grabbed a nearby chest and set it on top of a crate, lifting the lid. Her eyes widened as the gold and jewels glittered back at her, glittering in the firelight as though on fire themselves. Plucking a diamond ring out from among the jewels, her gaze darted to Tommy, who was whispering something to Lydia as he helped her sift through a clay pot filled with teeth. Smiling as an idea formed, Immy dug through the chest until she found what she was looking for.

She carried both items over to Tommy, tapping him on the shoulder. He turned, his eyes meeting hers, then dropping to her outstretched hand. A smile stretched his lips, and he took both items from Immy and turned back to Lydia.

"What is—" Lydia stopped, gasping.

Immy watched over Tommy's shoulder, the others gathering around as Tommy slipped the diamond ring onto Lydia's finger alongside the bent and twisted key ring that had, until now, been the sole symbol of their vows before God.

"I'd marry you again and again for the rest of my life," he said.

Lydia took the other ring – a simple gold band with three smaller diamonds embedded within. She slid the ring in place, lifting onto the tips of her toes to kiss him. "I adore you, Thomas Bridger Rhodes."

"Well, well, if Immy Alvarez isn't quite the romantic," Jude said with a laugh.

Immy responded by hurling one of her daggers across the room at him. It lodged in a pile of crates by his head. Eyes wide, his Adam's apple bobbed up and down. "A deadly romantic," he corrected.

"And don't you forget it." But even her dangerous skillset couldn't bury the smile that tugged at her lips. She'd been with Tommy and Lydia the first time he'd almost lost her. He'd seen what it had done to him to watch her suffer. Tommy's love for that girl deserved a place in the pages of history, but Immy couldn't give him that. They may never have a big wedding with a preacher and wedding gifts, although to hear them talk, she knew they didn't care about that stuff. But this was something she could do for them. Because they had become the family she'd spent most of her life searching for, and she'd spend the rest of her life making sure they knew how much she cared about them.

Mars returned with the three keys as the door rumbled shut behind him. He shoved them into Tommy's rucksack alongside the map, the glass disc, and as much treasure is the bag could carry.

The Jailbirds' pockets full of coins and jewels, daggers tucked into their waistbands, they turned toward the stairs. One by one, they set out across the bridge. Immy forced herself to keep her eyes forward. The ground below disappeared into darkness, and there was no telling how deep it went. She wasn't about to find out.

They arrived at the stairs, which were little more than blocks of stone set into the wall, just wide enough for a single person to climb at once. Tommy went ahead, testing each step before putting his full weight on it. The Jailbirds followed one at a time, leaving Immy and Reid to take up the rear.

"Just don't look down," Reid said when she hesitated.

Immy nodded, forced her foot forward. Exhaling, she took another step, then another. Reid moved close behind her, prepared to catch her should she fall. Seconds later, she stepped out onto the stone landing with the others.

Mars clapped her on the back. "Ya did good, kid."

She smiled, exhaling in a puff of air. "Thanks, Martian."

She'd never really been bothered by heights before, but a lot had changed these recent months. Clearly her list of fears had not gone unaltered.

"Ready?" Tommy asked, glancing around at the others.

Jude nodded.

Tommy reached for the lever on the door and pulled. Stone ground against stone as the door popped open. A sliver of light appeared through a crack in the wall. Tommy pressed both hands against the stone and pushed, the crack widening as light spilled in. Momentarily blinded, they stepped through the door into a cleft on the outside of the pyramid.

Immy raised a hand to shield her eyes as a deafening *thump thump thump* rippled through the air. Gusts of wind gathered up her braid. Behind them, the door rumbled shut.

Immy's eyes adjusted to the daylight, and she took a step forward.

"Get down!" Reid grabbed her by the arm and pulled her back

against the wall. She blinked as a helicopter flew by, dust and debris whipping through the air in a whirlwind.

Immy's heart sank. Orion had found them… *again*.

"What do we do?" asked Lucy. "They're going to see us."

Immy reached for the dagger in her waistband, jaw set as she peeked around the angled pyramid wall. She spotted Orion's forces gathered around the entrance to the temple. Her fingers tightened around the hilt of the dagger as she slipped it free, sunlight glinting on the edge of its blade. She ground her teeth, glancing over her shoulder at the others. "It's long past time we take the fight to *him*."

Episode Eight

TAKE ME HOME

"Love was worth the cost."

EIGHTY
JUDE

They had a plan – a good one. Along with the element of surprise and the fact that they'd already taken down so many of Orion's men, they actually stood a chance this time. Orion wouldn't know what hit him.

The Jailbirds slithered down the side of the pyramid, careful not to be seen as they snuck behind it. They split up – Tommy, Lydia, Reid, and Immy went right, and Jude, Maya, Mars, and Lucy went left. Each knew the plan and the role they would play.

They would protect their discovery – and each other – at all costs. Orion Clark wanted a fight; it was time to bring him war.

Jude led the way into the trees. The heat of the day bore down on the oasis, but the trees offered plenty of shade and shelter from sight. They moved quickly and quietly, careful to watch where they stepped so as not to alert the Wild Hunt to their presence.

Unintelligible voices carried through the air. Seconds later,

Jude and the others came close enough to see the Hunters amassing at the entrance of the temple. A pair of black helicopters sat in the clearing by the spring while scattered trucks parked wherever they could find room. While the Hunters gathered like obedient toy soldiers, ready to do their master's bidding, Orion stood pacing at their head of the army. Arms crossed over his chest, one hand stroking his bearded chin, he fixated on the pyramid.

"We could blow it up," someone suggested.

Graham.

Jude glanced over his shoulder at Mars, who rolled his eyes at the sound of Graham's voice. Given that Graham had assaulted Mars unprovoked months ago, it was understandable that he didn't have much empathy for the Bluecoat who'd thrown in with Orion and the Wild Hunt. Graham Robinson was a sociopath. The Wild Hunt almost deserved him.

"Don't be ridiculous," Orion said, a sneer in his voice. "They'll have to come out eventually, and when they do, we'll kill them and take the treasure for ourselves."

"I still think we should just blow it up."

"You forget your place, Robinson."

That shut the kid up.

Jude smiled, turning in a crouch toward the others. "You guys remember the plan?"

"The one we just came up with five minutes ago?" Lucy asked. "Yeah, we remember the plan."

Maya chuckled.

"We'll go for the choppers," Mars said. "You provide the distraction."

Turning to Maya, he asked, "Ready?"

She nodded.

Jude held out a fist to Mars, who bumped it. "Good luck."

Smiling, Mars said, "I don't need luck."

Jude patted him on the shoulder and turned back toward the Hunters' encampment. With a sharp inhale, he crept forward through the ferns and shrubs, toward the vehicle nearest them. A lone Hunter stood at the back, his gun slung over his shoulder.

Jude glanced back at Maya, spotting Mars and Lucy further behind them, making their way toward the clearing with the helicopters. They waited for the signal.

Not even a minute later, a light glinted in the woods on the other side of the spring. They were in position.

Sucking in a breath, Jude lurched forward, keeping himself low as he snuck up behind the Hunter, wrapped one arm around the man's neck and clamped his other hand over the man's mouth. He let out a muffled scream. Jude kicked his legs out from under him, the dead weight carrying them both to the ground. The Hunter clawed at Jude's arms, but he'd already lost his advantage. In seconds, he was unconscious.

Jude eased the man's limp body off him, rolling it onto the ground. He snuck forward, Maya with him, and together they opened the driver's side door and the back passenger door, slipping inside. The key still in the ignition, Jude ignored his racing heart and the unease in his stomach, turned the key, and threw the truck into gear. He slammed on the gas, surging forward into the crowd of gathered Hunters. The truck plowed through them. They scattered in all directions.

Orion whipped his head toward the chaos, eyes locking with Jude's. They flew wide with rage, and he shouted something. Jude took great pleasure from seeing the vein in his neck bulging and his face going red. But the momentary shock passed, and the Hunters gathered their wits enough to open fire on Jude and Maya in the truck. Bullets struck the windows and the metal frame. Jude and Maya ducked as glass sprayed around them, cutting them.

On the other side of the spring, Tommy, Lydia, Reid, and Immy ran toward the chaos, firing their own weapons at the Hunters.

A bullet blew one of the tires, and the truck lurched. Jude slammed on the brakes. A hail of gunfire riddled the driver's side door with holes. He and Maya scooted across the seat and shoved the opposite doors open, falling out onto the ground and using the truck as a shield.

Orion shouted orders, but it was madness. Scattered Hunters fired at the Jailbirds, who fired back. Gun smoke filled the air. Footsteps pounded against the earth. The oasis had become a war zone, and the Jailbirds had the advantage.

A pair of Hunters ran around the front of the truck, angling their rifles toward Jude and Maya. They both sprang up at once. Jude ground his teeth as he grabbed the Hunter's rifle and wrenched it from his grasp. The strap still around the Hunter's neck, he stumbled forward, and Jude matched his momentum by striking the butt of the weapon against his nose. The man cried out, blood gushing from his face.

Maya ducked below the other Hunter's swipe of a large knife and threw her leg out to strike the man's knee. He buckled, and she followed it up with a punch to his temple. He dropped, unconscious. Jude kicked the man with the bloody nose in the chest, sending him back into the dirt and sand.

He turned to Maya, grinning. "I have never been more attracted to you."

She smiled back. "Focus."

Instead, he grabbed her by both sides of her face and kissed her, smiling against her lips.

The sound of gunfire brought him back to reality, and he turned, his back to Maya's as they watched their surroundings.

Jude pulled the rifle strap over Bloody Nose's neck, and Maya stole the other guys' knife. Back-to-back they stood, daring anyone to come at them.

Jude's eyes caught movement on the other side of the clearing – Orion and Graham running away from the fighting. They charged toward the helicopters where Mars and Lucy were. They were going to escape.

"Oh, *no*," said Jude.

EIGHTY-ONE
MARS

Do you even know how to fly a helicopter?" Lucy asked into her headset from the seat beside Mars. The pilot's unconscious body lay in the dirt and grass a few feet away. Ahead, the oasis had erupted in a firefight. Hunters ran in every direction while the Jailbirds played the offensive for once.

"In theory," said Mars over the whir of the helicopter's engine. "There's four primary flight controls: the cyclic, collective, antitorque pedals, and throttle. I just need to figure out how to get them all to work together."

"Work fast, then," urged Lucy.

Mars opened the throttle and pulled up on the collective, depressing the left foot pedal to counteract the torque. The helicopter shuddered and began to rise from the ground as the lift from the rotor began to exceed the chopper's overall weight. Mars had read enough about flying for a school project that he understood the basics, but putting it into practice was another matter altogether.

The collective goes up and down. The cyclic moves us around. The antitorque pedals control the tail rotor blades. Easy-peasy.

As the helicopter rose into the air, Mars shouted into his headset for Lucy to man the guns. She moved to the back of the chopper and grabbed the machine gun mounted to the landing gear. As they ascended higher into the air, she opened fire. Bullets pierced the dirt and the water, sending panicked Hunters in all directions.

The helicopter jerked to the right, and Mars used the pedals to steady it.

"Careful!" came Lucy's voice in his headset.

"Sorry!"

Mars grabbed the cyclic – the joystick between his knees – and used it to angle them toward the Hunters' cars. Lucy turned the machine gun on the vehicles, and they burst into balls of fire. Mars let out a whoop, but the celebration was cut short as something slammed into the side of the helicopter, jolting them to the right.

Mars struggled to regain control, but the impact had completely discombobulated him. He let up on the collective as the helicopter tossed back and forth, and they fell back to the ground. The landing gear struck the earth with a jolt. Mars' head struck the back of his seat. His ears rang, a bolt of pain piercing his temple.

"Lucy, you good?" he asked.

She didn't respond.

Mars unbuckled his seat belt and turned in his seat.

"Mars!"

Someone had her by the neck, was pulling her out of the helicopter. She kicked, clawing at her captor's arm, eyes wide.

Graham.

Mars lunged forward, threw himself out of the helicopter. He started toward Graham as he dragged Lucy backward toward the second helicopter. Behind Graham, the second helicopter's rotor blades began to spin, kicking dust into the air.

Something struck Mars in the stomach. He buckled over, gasping for breath. A hand grabbed the front of his shirt, wrenching him upright and slamming him against the helicopter's body.

Orion leaned in, bringing his face inches from Mars' as he growled, "Where are the Keys?"

"Find them yourself," Mars spat, his teeth clenched, heart racing.

The man punched Mars in the side, and he fell to the ground, grinding his teeth against the pain as he clutched the fresh bruise. Orion leaned over him, his breath hot on the side of Mars' face. "Tell me where they are, and I'll let him kill her quickly."

Mars' eyes flicked to Lucy. Graham held the edge of a blade to her throat. Her lips twitched. She forced her chin up in defiance, her jaw set despite the tears that welled in her eyes.

"Don't," she said. "Don't let him win."

Mind racing to form a plan, heart beating like a thunderhead in his chest, Mars met her gaze. "I can't."

"Running out of time, Highland," Graham snarled. He dragged the blade down Lucy's throat, a shallow cut drawing a slow thread of blood across her skin.

Mars had only seconds. Still doubled over on the ground, Mars' fist closed around sand and dirt. With a sharp inhale, he tossed the fistful into Orion's face.

The man let out a yelp of surprise, stumbling backward as he rubbed at his eyes. In that some second, Mars surged forward and grabbed Graham's arm, yanking it down. The knife fell to the ground, and Lucy broke free. Mars brought his leg up and kicked Graham in the stomach.

He staggered backward. Mars grabbed Lucy by the wrist and ran in the opposite direction, sliding behind one of the remaining trucks for cover as Orion opened fire.

Jude and Maya met them behind the truck, Mars pressing a piece of fabric from his shirt sleeve to the shallow wound in Lucy's neck.

Tommy came running up to them, a hand on Mars' shoulder. "You guys good?" he asked.

Mars gave a sharp nod, and Tommy darted off, toward the second helicopter. He glanced over the hood of the truck and gasped when he realized what Tommy was about to do.

EIGHTY-TWO
TOMMY

As the helicopter rose into the air with Orion and Graham onboard, Tommy threw himself headlong. His hands latched onto the landing gear, his feet dragging in the dirt until he no longer felt the ground beneath him. He pulled himself up, wrapping his arms around the landing gear. A downward glance turned his stomach as the ground shrank beneath him.

With a grunt, Tommy swung his leg up, missed the bar. He slipped. Below, his friends shouted at him. Gunfire burst through the air as Reid and Immy carved their way through the last of the Wild Hunt's ranks. Bodies lay strewn in the dirt, blood pooling around them.

Tommy's eyes found his friends, rallied around a wounded Lucy. He met Jude's gaze, who offered a nod of encouragement.

Grinding his teeth together, Tommy swung his leg a second

time, managing to hook his foot over the bar and pull himself up.

"Oh, no you don't."

A boot struck Tommy's shoulder, and he slipped but managed to keep himself upright, holding onto the bar that held the machine gun in place. Graham glared back at him, reaching for the handgun on his hip. Before he could grab it, Tommy launched his fist forward. It connected with Graham's jaw, sending him backwards while the impact rattled the bones in Tommy's arm. Knuckles bleeding, he pulled himself the rest of the way into the cabin.

He heard the sound of metal ringing as Graham unsheathed a large knife, holding it point down, his other hand balled into a fist. Crouching, Tommy held his fists out in front of him, shifting his feet so that he inched further inside the helicopter and away from the drop-off to certain death.

"You don't have to do this, Graham," said Tommy. "You don't know what you're getting yourself into."

Graham smeared. "I know *exactly* what I'm getting into. I killed my best friend to get here. What's to stop me from killing you and your friends too?"

Tommy's teeth ground together. "*You* killed Quincy?"

Shifting on his feet, Graham smiled. In the cockpit, Orion watched the two men with interest as the pilot steered the helicopter over the spring, toward the pyramid. This was a test, and he was waiting to see Tommy fail.

"*Why?*" Tommy asked. "You were never part of this. Orion, the Wild Hunt – *none* of this had anything to do with you!"

"Shut up!" Graham shouted, his face red, the veins in his neck flaring. "All you Jailbirds do is take and take what isn't yours. I'm here to fight for what's mine, for what I *deserve*."

"You got that backwards, Graham." Tommy clenched his fists. "You're the ones doing the taking. Orion *murdered* my father in cold blood! And he murdered Lydia's father and Maya's mother. Is this *really* who you want to side with?"

"You're wrong, Rhodes." Graham smirked. "Orion didn't kill Maya's mother. *I* did."

Tommy's fingernails bit the palm of his hand as his jaw clenched.

"History goes to the victor, Rhodes, and I intend to win." Graham struck out, the razor-sharp edge of the knife dragging down Tommy's forearm as he dodged right. He winced, pivoting on his heel.

With a smirk, Graham grabbed the machine gun and spun it inward, toward Tommy. He pulled the trigger just as Tommy ducked below the barrel. A spray of bullets tore through the glass and metal on the other side of the helicopter.

Tommy lunged for Graham, grabbing him by the feet and pulling them out from under him. Graham's back slammed into the floor of the cabin, the knife slipping from his grip. He retaliated with a punch that connected with Tommy's temple. Blood trickled into Tommy's eyes, but adrenaline muted the pain as he returned a punch to Graham's side.

Graham cried out in pain, bringing his knee to his chest and kicking the heel of his boot into Tommy's shoulder. Tommy fell backwards, the momentum carrying him through the opening Graham had blown in the helicopter's frame. Glass shattered and metal groaned as it gave way to his weight. At the last minute, he grabbed onto one of the bars, the rest of his body dangling in the open air.

Graham found his footing, tensing his shoulders and balling

his fists as he strode toward Tommy. Just then, the helicopter pitched to the right to dodge a spray of bullets, and Tommy used the momentum to launch his legs back through the hole, fragments of glass tearing at his clothes and skin as both feet planted into Graham's chest. Stunned, Graham staggered backward, his foot stepping out over the open air.

He dropped.

Tommy dove across the cabin to catch him. He stuck his upper body out over the edge and found Graham dangling from the landing gear.

"Rhodes!" he screamed, terror in his eyes. "Rhodes, help me!"

Silencing the voices of anger and hate that told him to leave him where he was, Tommy extended his arm as far as he could toward Graham. His fingers brushed Graham's knuckles. He ground his teeth as he stretched toward the man. Graham tried to lift a hand to meet Tommy's, barely making contact with Tommy's arm, but the constant swaying of the helicopter and the distance made it impossible.

"Don't let me fall!" Graham cried, spit flinging from his mouth.

"Just hang on, Graham," Tommy shouted over the roar of the helicopter blades. "I've got you, man."

With one hand, Tommy grabbed the bar that held the machine gun aloft and allowed himself to slide further out over the edge of the helicopter. If he slipped, they would both die. As he stretched his hand out, it connected with Graham's wrist, but a panicked Graham let go of the landing gear too early. Tommy didn't have a good enough grip.

In just a few excruciating seconds, Graham slipped from Tommy's grasp, and his other hand tore free of the landing gear.

Tommy watched in horror, the image of the terror on Graham's face forever burned into his mind, as Graham fell from the helicopter into the burning wreckage of tangled steel and gasoline down below, a terrible wail trailing behind him before he vanished into the inferno.

Tommy hung frozen over the edge of the helicopter, his left hand still cinched around the machine gun as time seemed to hold its breath with him. He blinked, jarring himself loose from the mixture of pity and guilt that gripped him. Pulling himself back into the helicopter, he sat back on his heels, remembering too late that he wasn't alone.

The cold steel of Orion's gun connected with the back of Tommy's head.

EIGHTY-THREE

LYDIA

Dear God…

Lydia stood frozen on the ground as the helicopter cut through the air, first trying to shake Tommy loose, then trying to dodge the hail of gunfire Jude had opened on the chopper. She stood powerless, both unable to help the man she loved and unable to stop the man who threatened to destroy everything that had ever mattered to her.

The Jailbirds had won the fight down here – the Hunters all either dead or unconscious – but there was nothing they could do for Tommy up there but watch in horror. He fought like a madman with everything to lose.

"He's going to be okay," Jude said, but she didn't know if it was for her benefit or his own.

"We've got to get up there," Mars said. "We can't just leave him without backup."

"What can we do?" asked Maya.

Their voices – the arguing, the planning, the fear, the adrenaline – faded into the background until all Lydia could hear was the rhythmic *thump thump thump* of the helicopter. She watched in horror as Graham fell out over the side. Tommy dove after him, reaching for him, trying desperately to pull Graham back inside.

And Lydia prayed. It was all she could do – a sling and stone against a giant. But it wasn't enough.

Gasping, her hands flew to her mouth as she watched him fall. Graham, swallowed by the fire that engulfed the wreckage of the Hunters' trucks. His cries cut short.

Lydia's ears rang. Her head spun. In seconds, she remembered everything Graham had ever been to her. And everything he'd allowed himself to become. But her grief was short-lived.

"*No.*" The words came out in an exhale as she watched Orion overpower Tommy, striking him on the back of his head.

Lydia was running before she knew what she was doing. Her feet carved a path through the dirt and the grass around the spring as she sprinted toward the temple. Voices called after her. Her friends. Her enemies. Telling her there was nothing she could do while the father of her baby fought alone inside that helicopter.

You cannot have him.

The vow branded itself upon her heart as she ran as fast as her legs would allow. She stooped to pull a rifle from the lifeless grip of one of the fallen Hunters. She came to the temple steps and bounded toward the roof. The pyramid shone in the sunlight. The helicopter danced in the sky. The smooth surface of the spring reflected the trail of smoke that split the otherwise blue sky in two.

So much death. So much destruction.

All because of one man's pride, his greed, his lust for power.

But it would end here. There would be no more running. No more hurting. No more losing. No more dying. They'd gone to the ends of the earth to bring Othniel Cuvier – to bring Christopher Rhodes – home, once and for all. Not even Orion could stop them. Lydia wouldn't let him.

She came to the rooftop of the temple, the pyramid at her back as she looked out over the water, the helicopter soaring toward her. Through the glass, she watched Tommy and Orion fight. Punching, kicking, shuffling, dodging. Tommy had Orion by the wrist. The gun went off, and a ring of blood appeared on the pilot's temple. His head lolled forward.

Lydia braced as the helicopter pitched sideways, the rotor blades cutting through the stairs the other side of the temple. She threw herself to the side, barely dodging the tail fin as it swung through the air where she'd stood a few seconds ago.

Tommy and Orion tumbled from the cabin of the helicopter onto the temple roof, a tangle of limbs twisting, clawing, and kicking before their momentum drove them apart – Orion sliding one direction and Tommy skidding across the stone in another. The helicopter skated across the roof before falling off the side of the temple and bursting into flame.

"Tommy!" Lydia cried as the helicopter's explosion rocked the temple. A crack cut across the roof, slithering between where Orion and Tommy each lay barely moving and covered in a layer of cuts and bruises.

She barreled forward, toward Tommy. But Orion was already on his feet. Lydia spun the rifle toward him, and in the fraction of a second it took for her to pull the trigger, she remembered the man across from her – who he had once been.

The uncle who had showered her with affection, who had

bought her every gift she had ever wanted, who had taken her to parks and zoos, who had praised her performances at school talent shows and bought her some of the earliest books she'd ever read. He was part of her and she was a part of him. There was a bond of blood between them.

A bond that he had severed by allowing himself to become this... *monster* at the other end of her gun.

So she did what she couldn't do before. She pulled the trigger.

But nothing happened. She tried again with the same results, then turned the gun to see that the magazine had already been emptied and she hadn't had the time to check.

Lydia's heart sank as her uncle smiled at her. In the corner of her eye, she saw Tommy start to move.

Orion raised his gun – the antique pistol that had been in Lydia's hands just weeks before, the one she could have used to end this long before he had driven them here – and aimed it at his niece. Blood stained his teeth and streamed from his brow to stain his beard – a beard that Lydia had stroked as a little girl while she sat in his lap and pleaded with him to tell her stories.

His lips parted, and his voice came out in a low growl. "This is *over.*"

He pulled the trigger. A shot like thunder rang out as the bullet cut through the air.

Lydia braced herself.

Someone shouted, and a blur shot out in front of her.

The sound of bullet meeting flesh, and a body crumpled in front of Lydia.

EIGHTY-FOUR
TOMMY

Time moved in slow motion.

Tommy reacted on instinct.

Lydia fired on Orion. Once, twice – both times, the gun was empty. She threw it to the ground.

Through eyes blurred by blood and vision spinning in circles, he watched her steel her gaze. Hands balled in defiant fists at her sides as she faced down the man with the gun. Orion held the wound in his side, wounded but not defeated. Tommy forced himself up by his hands. His body slow to respond. His ears ringing. Smoke billowed behind Orion, casting him in a sinister shadow. There were voices, people somewhere in the distance.

Lydia…

He pushed himself up, turning toward her.

Orion spoke, but the words were garbled in Tommy's ears. He tapped a finger to the side of his head – blood. Fingers dragging across stone, he found the large tactical knife he'd stolen from Graham and forced himself to stand, nearly falling on his backside before finding his footing. He broke into a run, feet racing across the roof of the temple. Lydia on one side. Orion on the other.

A blur of motion to Tommy's right. The thunderclap of a gunshot rang out just as Tommy threw himself forward. Knife in hand, he plunged the blade into Orion's chest, his momentum carrying them both over the edge of the temple.

"This is for my father," Tommy hissed through his teeth as the surprise registered in Orion's eyes.

And then they hit the ground.

The impact ricocheted through Tommy's bones as Orion's body crunched beneath his weight. The rattle of an exhale. A choke as blood spilled from Orion's lips. Tommy's face hovered over Orion's, his hands still wrapped around the hilt of the blade, and he watched as the life faded from the man's eyes.

Gasping for breath, Tommy rolled himself off Orion, falling onto his back in the grass. He gaped up at the sky, his lungs grasping for oxygen. Smoke whirled in the air. The heat of the helicopter's wreckage washed over Tommy. And somehow, despite the carnage, there was a bird. It darted across the sky as though none of this had ever happened. Tommy watched the bird dance, watched it twirl and flap its wings and thrust itself forward.

And then he got up, rolling onto his knees.

Someone somewhere let out a wail. A scream.

Thunder. The beat of a drum. The beat of a heart.

The blood of the man who had killed his father dripped from the knife in Tommy's hands. He dropped it, the point lodging in the ground at his feet as he forced a step forward, his body screaming in agony, his heart pounding inside his rib cage like an animal desperate to set itself free.

Another step. The stairs up ahead. Just a few feet of grass between them.

And another step.

He held out a hand to steady himself against the temple wall. He took the stairs as quickly as his body would allow. Through a wall of smoke from the wreckage to his right. Through the waves of heat radiating from the fire. Through the agonizing feeling of fractures in his arms and legs and ribs scraping against one another with every movement.

Tommy stepped out onto the roof, his gaze sweeping across the stone toward Lydia who sat on her knees, her body hunched over someone else's. She looked up, eyes red, tears streaming, cradling his head in her lap.

A sob escaped Tommy's mouth as he saw Mars lying there. He reached out, but he wasn't close enough. He nearly stumbled, picked himself up again.

Another step.

Tommy collapsed beside Mars, the others gathered around.

A pool of blood soaked the front of his shirt. A bullet hole in the center of his chest. Mars' breath came in gasps and hiccups as his eyes darted around, searching for his friends. Lydia stroked his hair. Lucy knelt on his other side, hunched over him. Jude and Maya stood behind her, Jude holding a sobbing Maya.

"He jumped in front of me," Lydia said, her voice a sob. "I didn't even… I couldn't…"

Tommy took Mars' hand. His friend's eyes flicked to him.

"Did… we…" Mars paused, sucked in a breath. "Get him?"

Tears blurred Tommy's vision. He swiped at his eyes, stinging from the smoke, the blood, and the heavy cloud of grief that suffocated him. "Yeah, Mars." He nodded. "We won."

Mars smiled, but the smile was cut short as he coughed, blood spraying from his mouth and dribbling down his chin. Tommy reached up to wipe the tear that slipped from his eye.

"My… pocket," he said. "There's… something."

"Shh, buddy," said Tommy. "Save your strength. I got it."

His hands trembling, he reached into the pocket of Mars' trousers, his fingers finding a piece of paper. He pulled the letter out, opened it. The letter his father had sent to Mars' father, asking for help before he died. The letter Mars' father had ignored.

Tommy frowned, chin quivering. He glanced up at Mars.

"I made…" He coughed. More blood. "I made things right."

Tommy nodded, grabbing hold of his friend's shoulder. "Yeah, buddy. Yeah. You did."

Mars' eyes flicked around, looking from one face to the next. He raised a fist toward Jude, who let out a strangled laugh as he bumped it with his own trembling fist, then wrapped his hand around Mars'.

"We were… always going to… win," said Mars, his voice soft. "As long as we… had each other." He rolled his eyes toward Reid, whose chin quivered, his eyes red, arms crossed over his chest. "Protect them," he said.

Reid nodded. "With my life."

Lydia hunched over, pressing a featherlight kiss to Mars' forehead. Immy sat on the ground beside Lucy, rubbing a hand up and down Mars' leg as she wept silently.

Brimming with tears, Mars' eyes found Tommy's again. He inhaled. "Take me home."

Seconds later, Marshall Highland was gone.

EIGHTY-FIVE
LYDIA

One week later...

Wind whipped across the tarmac. Lydia stepped down from the small commuter plane, eyes red and puffy, bracing for the wail of sirens and the flashes of light. Feet shuffled behind her – the Jailbirds, those who'd survived, following her out into the cold.

Lydia struggled to remember the days that had followed Mars' death. The memories felt distant, like scenes from a movie she'd only seen once many years ago. They'd sat for a long time on the temple roof in Egypt, grieving, holding Mars' body for the last time, desperately hoping beyond hope that he'd open his eyes and live again. It had been Reid who'd forced them to move. Jude had almost punched him for it, but Reid was right. If they hadn't moved then, Lydia wasn't sure they ever would have left that rooftop. It was his way of making good on the promise he'd made to Mars to protect them.

Tommy, Mars, and Maya had carried Mars' body down the stairs past the death and the destruction to the remaining helicopter. Some Hunters had lived, though injured or unconscious, but when they realized what had happened, they didn't try to attack again. Without Orion, they had no reason to fight. They ignored the Jailbirds, abandoned the bodies of their fellow Hunters, and fled on foot and in whatever cars had managed to remain undamaged in the firefight.

With Immy as his co-pilot, Reid flew them out, and they boarded a plane from Cairo back to the States two days later. Customs had been a mess – Egyptian law enforcement had heard about the chase in the riverside village, and Mars' body had raised a lot of questions – but they'd sorted everything out. Mars wanted to go home. That's all that had mattered. Even if home meant prison for the Jailbirds.

Lydia swallowed, blinking back the tears that threatened to spill over. It was only then that she realized the tarmac was quiet, save for the sound of the plane as the engine died down. She lifted her eyes, surprised to find there were no police cruisers waiting to carry her friends off to jail for crimes they hadn't committed. There were no photographers and journalists desperate to get a statement from the troublemakers that had caused citywide unrest. There, at the end of the tarmac beside the hangar of the modest, rural Washington airport, was a single black sedan.

Pausing, Lydia watched as the door opened and a woman stepped out. When she saw her face, the only thing Lydia could manage to say was a strangled, "Mom?"

She ran across the tarmac as Lorelai, eyes as red and puffy as Lydia's, straightened. Lydia threw herself into the woman's arms, burrowing her head in the crook of her neck as she wept. A dozen questions competed for preeminence on the tip of her tongue as her mind raced, her heart tumbling end over end inside her chest. "How…? Why…?"

Lorelai hushed her, smoothing the frayed ends of Lydia's hair down.

Eyes clamped shut, Lydia sobbed, "We lost him."

"Lost who?"

"Mars." Lydia sucked in a breath, a shadow falling over her from behind. In the corner of her eye, she saw Reid approach the two of them, his arm in a sling from the bullet wound in his shoulder. Lorelai looked from Lydia to Reid, her brow bent, her lips quivering. She reached a hand to cup Reid's face, pulling him closer.

"Oh, I'm so sorry," she said. "I'm so sorry."

Lydia pulled away. "I don't… I don't understand. Shouldn't the police…?"

Eyes shimmering, Lorelai dared a small smile as she held Lydia's and Reid's faces in her hands. And she told them what Mars had done, every word driving a stake into Lydia's heart. And when she was finished, now that the rest of the Jailbirds had gathered around to listen, Lydia felt a fresh wave of grief well up inside of her.

Reid's good arm fell over her shoulders. They stood there, the three surviving members of the Clark family. What had been built on a murder and a lie a hundred years ago had been whittled to nothing. But as new life bloomed in Lydia's womb, she hoped for the chance to chase away the ghosts that had haunted their family name for generations. The death of Marshall Highland would mean something; at least, to them.

EIGHTY-SIX
JUDE

Three weeks later...

There were things in this world worth dying for – Mars had proven that. Not treasure or fame, power or control. But the love of fathers and sons, husbands and wives, brothers and sisters. Love was worth the cost. Worth every scar and every bruise. Worth defending and fighting for. Worth the time and the effort.

Worth dying for.

February in Mammoth, Washington ended with the fresh fall of snow. Puffy gray clouds hovered in the air. Light white flakes drifted on the breeze, coming to rest on the boughs of cedars and pines, covering the heads of gravestones and mausoleums in Mammoth City Cemetery. The ground had turned white as the snow clung to the earth. Black umbrellas bobbed in the air as mourners surrounded the graveside, both seated in chairs and standing to the back. More than Jude would've imagined turning out to a Jailbird funeral.

Theo and Claire Highland sat in the front, right across from their son's casket as the pastor read from Scripture. Jude wasn't really listening. Not because he was angry, but because the only thing he could hear in the three weeks since Mars had died was the sound of his last breath leaving his body. He couldn't sleep without startling awake, that sound replaying in his head. He couldn't think without hearing Mars in his ear. Every time he turned around, he half expected to find Mars there with a sarcastic jab or some interesting fact to offer.

"Greater love hath no man than this…" the silver-haired pastor continued.

Maya's hand slipped into Jude's, her hands warm despite the cold. He turned his head toward her, placed a kiss on the crown of her head. She sniffed, eyes red and puffy. Around them stood the rest of the Jailbirds on the other side of Mars' casket, directly across from his parents. Jude watched them. He'd always known Theo as a stoic man, now broken under the weight of grief since the moment he'd found out about their son.

To their surprise, by the time their plane landed in Washington, they weren't met with handcuffs and flashing red-and-blue lights. Instead, Lorelai Clark had been there, waiting for them. That's when it had all become clear — Mars' final act of defiance against Orion's plan. The flash drive Maya's mother had died to get to her had contained hours of incriminating footage, including Alicia's bargain for Maya's life in exchange for her legal prowess. Alicia had sold her soul for her daughter's life. Jude knew Maya was still wrestling with how to come to terms with something like that. The mother that had never loved her had died for her.

Apparently, sometime after the Jailbirds had fled Mammoth, Mars had sent the files to Lorelai, giving her exactly what she needed to build the case she'd been working on for weeks. It wasn't long before the story had been broadcast. Not just to the entire city, but statewide. That on top of the crowbar – the one Reid had helped Jude and Maya recover off the pier, that had been used to murder Oliver Clark – had been enough to exonerate Reid and the rest of the Jailbirds and fully incriminate Orion in everything. As it turned out, when Reid had said he would give it to someone he could trust, that person had been the now deceased Sheriff Patterson. He'd sent the crowbar off for forensics, and the report had finally come back sometime after he'd died.

The Jailbirds' name had been cleared, and the story of their adventure, discovery, and triumph over Orion Clark and the Wild Hunt had made national news. Hundreds of people had gathered for Mars' funeral – more than had ever even known him in life – to honor the man who'd given up his life for his friends, for Lydia and her unborn baby. But they would never understand what it had cost them, or that, if he had to do it over again, maybe he never would have followed the clues they'd found in that secret room during the storm at Hollow Hill Lighthouse. Mars' death had earned his name a place beside Othniel Cuvier's, Katherine Rhodes', and Tommy's father in history books that had yet to be written.

As the pastor finished his sermon and committed Mars' soul to God, Jude swiped at the tears that fell from his eyes, watching the casket being lowered into the ground. Theo stood, holding Claire up as best he could. They wept their way to the grave and, scooping up fistfuls of dirt, tossed them onto the shiny black surface of Mars' casket.

Mars was only a few feet away from Jude, but it felt like an impassable distance.

Claire Highland let out a strangled sob, and Theo carried her away, strong arms around her shoulders. One by one, through tears and with trembling hands, the Jailbirds took their turn burying Mars beneath the earth a fistful of dirt at a time.

Jude paused over the grave, staring down into the hole but instead remembering the way Mars smiled, the sound of his voice, the feel of his hand on Jude's shoulder, the kindness in his eyes. That was how he wanted to remember his best friend. It was hard to imagine, but Jude knew in his heart that Mars was more alive now than he'd ever been. Though he grieved and wanted to rage against the world for taking Mars too soon, death was not without hope. It was not an end, but a new beginning.

It would take a while for Jude to get there, but there would come a time some distant day when he would remember his friend and the joy of having known him would outweigh the sorrow of losing him.

The mourners began to disperse, and through the crowds, a face appeared.

"Jude!"

Jude's eyes widened as he spotted his brother pushing through, shoving people aside as though he had no idea what was going on. "Henry?"

The boy practically leapt into Jude's arms. He caught him, wrapping his arms around his brother. He gasped, eyes filling with tears as he held his baby brother close. His eyes settled on his father, drifting through the crowd.

"You brought him here?" Jude said.

Eyes red, Jack nodded. "I knew you'd want to see him. Took some convincing, but his grandparents let me take him. For a little while, at least. I guess… there's some things I still need to work through. To make things right with us."

Jude sealed his eyes shut, struggling to hold himself together. He felt Maya's hand on his back. He inhaled, opened his eyes, and reached for his father, pulling him by the arm into a hug with Henry sandwiched between them. And suddenly Jude realized that he couldn't regret everything about these past few months. There were things he wouldn't go back to undo. Because for the first time in forever the Mayfields finally had the chance to be a family again.

"Jack."

Jude released his father at the sound of Theo's voice, heavy with emotion. Jack held out a hand, and he took it.

"I'm sorry for your loss, Theo," Jack said.

Theo's lip trembled. He opened his mouth to respond, then closed it again. He turned to Jude and the others gathered around. "I just… Claire and I, we wanted to thank you all."

"Thank us?" asked Tommy.

"For being our son's friend. For giving him a place where he could belong."

"He was more than our friend," Maya said. "He was family."

Theo blinked back tears, sniffed. "If only I'd been a better father. Maybe none of this…" He inhaled sharply, glancing off into the distance. "Thomas, I'm sorry I wasn't there for your father when he needed me. You kids… you proved that we were wrong. The secrets we kept, the lies we told. They only hurt us in the end. My son most of all."

The Jailbirds stayed silent.

"Your son didn't die *because of* you or anything you or anyone else did or didn't do," Lydia said, her voice watery. "He died *for* something. For *me*." She glanced at Tommy, a hand on her stomach. "For our baby."

Jude nodded. "That was the thing about Mars. He never lived his life like he was reacting to something; he lived his life like he had a mission."

"A purpose," added Immy.

Theo nodded, wiped his eyes. "Thank you, kids. I hope… I hope you'll come around every now and then."

Tommy reached forward, a hand on Theo's arm. "You can count on it."

With a nod, the man left. Jude set Henry on the ground, staring down into his brother's face. His eyes shone bright, his smile wide. Untouched by the harsh realities of the world that Jude had tried so hard to protect him from. Jude planted a kiss on the top of his head.

"Missed ya, kid," he said.

Henry wrapped his arms around Jude's waist.

Smiling, Jack tapped Henry on the shoulder. "Hey, buddy, let's let your brother breathe a minute, okay?"

Releasing Jude, Henry glanced back at his father. "Can we go get hot cocoa?"

Jack smiled. "Sure, kid." He caught Jude's eye. "Come by later?"

Jude nodded, and then they were off.

The Jailbirds lingered at the graveside until they were the only ones left. Jude's eyes traced the words engraved in the headstone. Mars' name. The day he was born, and the day he had died. The epitaph had not yet been engraved, and Jude wondered what Mars' parents would decide on.

It felt like a dream. But there was no waking from the reality of what had happened. The Jailbirds would be forced to learn to survive a life without one of their best friends – their brother. They would learn to *live* – because Mars hadn't just proven that love was worth dying for. He'd proven that, above all else, it was worth *living for*.

John McMill

EIGHTY-SEVEN
REID

It had been more than a decade since Reid stepped foot in a church, not including the hospital chapel he'd roughed up six weeks ago. Mammoth First Assembly was the last place he would've expected to find himself, but after the memorial service had long ended and the parishioners and funeral attendees were long gone, Reid couldn't bring himself to leave. Outside these walls was a world he didn't understand, a life he didn't recognize, and a future he had not planned for. But in here, all of that was held at bay.

The church was dimly lit, the light of dusk filtering through stained glass windows behind the pulpit and lining either side of the building. The wooden pews were hardly comfortable, and the checkboard floors seemed to reflect the cold. White walls held sconces between each window. Hymnals sat propped up in the backs of the pews. On the wooden altar, which looked to Reid to be little more than a bench, sat the golden platters meant to hold the emblems of Communion: bread and wine. Choir seats sat behind the pulpit below a stained-glass depiction of Jesus on the cross. An image Reid had not thought much about in a long time. A picture of Mars with his arms around Tommy, Maya, and Jude as they laughed in front of Hollow Hill Lighthouse sat propped up on an easel beside the pulpit.

The pastor had spent a good deal of time during the memorial service on the topic of sacrificial love. Reid couldn't remember all the Scriptures he'd quoted or much of anything about the sermon he'd shared, but one verse had stood out to him.

"Greater love hath no man than this, that a man lay down his life for his friends."

Reid had spent most of his life at the mercy of selfish men. First his father, then his uncle. He'd been abused, beaten down, and torn apart. Before he'd ever learned to ask a girl out or drive a car, he'd learned how to take a beating and survive without his father's approval. He'd seen other boys with their fathers and uncles, known in his head that there were good men out there even if his heart vehemently disagreed. Reid lived in a world where men asserted their dominance, vied for control, put their own needs and desires above all else. Where love was a fantasy and the only thing that truly mattered was oneself and one's own success. All the sudden, with a single bullet to the heart of a good man, the world had changed. Suddenly, there were men who would lay down their lives for those they loved. Not just Mars, but Tommy and Jude and the Man staring back at him from the stained-glass window, too.

He'd heard people call God their Father, and Reid didn't much know about that. What he did know, though, was that there was a sickness in his heart that went beyond the doctor's diagnosis. There was a kind of healing he could not find in the walls of a hospital; a healing that only the kind of God that Lydia prayed to could bring. What that looked like, only time would tell. Because of Mars, Reid had that kind of time. Lydia and the baby too. He didn't understand that kind of sacrifice – that kind of love – but he wanted to. Mars had made him promise to protect his friends, and Reid would make good on that promise. And, if he was lucky, maybe one day he'd become half the man Marshall Highland had been.

"I thought I'd find you here."

Reid glanced over his shoulder to see Immy walking down the aisle. She still wore the black dress she'd bought for the funeral, a black trench coat over top, cinched around her waist. She sat down in the empty space beside Reid, staring straight ahead.

"What are you doing here?" he asked.

"Looking for you."

"Me? What for?"

"Believe it or not, Reid, we're a lot alike." She angled her head toward him, her unbraided hair falling in waves down her back. "We're like animals; when we feel threatened, we retreat. Isolate."

"I don't feel threatened, and I'm not retreating."

"No?" Immy leaned forward, forcing him to meet her eyes. He found her crying. She swiped at the tears, but they kept coming. "You've hardly said a word since we landed."

"Not much to say." He shifted in his seat, fingers picking at the sleeve of his black blazer. His heart started to race, and a bolt of pain shot across his chest. He massaged the muscle with his hand, Immy's eyes watching with concern.

"Have you told anyone?"

Reid shook his head. "It's my burden to bear. Not theirs."

Immy smiled, bringing a hand to rest on the one massaging his chest. He stilled.

"You haven't figured it out by now?" she asked. "You're part of this family; we carry each other."

"There's just… so much pain already. I don't want to hurt them more by telling them what's going on with me, with my heart."

Immy squeezed his hand. "They won't be mad at you for letting them in."

"How do you know? You know the kind of man I was."

"Because *I* wasn't mad at you when you let *me* in, even though I knew the man you *once were*."

Reid inhaled, breath flooding his lungs.

"That's actually the reason I came looking for you."

His eyes flicked to hers. "What do you mean?

"I'm heading out tonight. I'm going back to Peru. Not forever – the only thing left for me there is a goodbye – but… I can't move on here until I let go of my life there."

Reid nodded, dropping his hands to his lap. He lowered his gaze, not sure how to take the news. Without their knowing it, Immy had become a sort of… anchor. Something solid to keep him grounded when the seas were raging.

"Reid, look at me."

He sighed, then lifted his eyes to hers, chewing the inside of his lip. "I'm happy for you," he said. "You deserve the chance to say goodbye the right way."

She reached out, her hand resting gently on the side of his face, her fingers slipping behind his ear. Unconsciously, he leaned into her, their eyes never breaking from each other's.

"I bought two tickets," she said. "I was… well, I was hoping that maybe you'd come with me."

He furrowed his brow. "Me?"

"For me, there are happy memories in Peru. Memories of my family, my parents… I need to go back to say goodbye. But here in Mammoth, with everything that happened with your parents and your uncle, maybe you need some time away to help you let go. When we're ready, we can both come back. Besides," she shrugged, "I don't know if I can handle being alone again."

Reid reached up, his hand on hers as he held it to his cheek, drawing strength from her presence, from the peace that a place like Mammoth First Assembly had to offer.

"I'll go," he said. "You're right. I could use some time away from this place. Besides… my mom's out there. Somewhere. Maybe I can find her."

"Maybe she doesn't want to be found," said Immy.

"Maybe I've already found something better." Reid risked a long look into her eyes.

She smiled, blinking back tears. "Come on. The others are waiting outside to say goodbye."

"The others?"

"Yeah," she said. "I wasn't the only one who came looking for you.

Taking him by the hand, Immy led him down the aisle of the church. As they came to the church doors, he glanced over his shoulder at the picture of Mars, then at the stained-glass image of Jesus. Mars would never know what his sacrifice had meant to Reid. But maybe one day, when all was said and done, Reid would get the chance to tell Mars himself.

EIGHTY-EIGHT
MAYA

The church doors opened, and Immy stepped out with Reid trailing behind her.

Maya waited, leaning against the passenger door of Tommy's Wrangler. Tommy sat in the driver's seat with Lydia beside him. Jude sat inside, the window opened as he popped his head out beside Maya's. Lucy stood on the sidewalk, hands shoved in the pockets of her puffy winter coat, her eyes distant.

"Picked up a stray," said Immy as she reached the bottom of the church steps.

Her door popping open, Lydia climbed out and threw her arms around Reid's neck. "I have seen you since the funeral," she said. "I was worried something had happened."

Reid gave a wry chuckle, rubbing an arm up and down her back. "No, nothing happened. Just needed to clear my head."

"Next time, clear your head somewhere we can find you," Maya said.

"Yeah," Jude added, "the church wasn't exactly our first guess."

"In that case," said Reid, glancing at Immy, "I should probably let you know I'm going to be out of town for a while."

Maya cocked an eyebrow. "Where are you going?"

Shoving his hands in his pockets, Reid shrugged against the cold, his breath puffing out in a cloud in front of him. "Immy's invited me to come to Peru with her. She has some things she needs to take care of, and she thought it might be good if I got some time away from this place. And I think she's right."

Maya glanced at Lydia, who looked like she was going to start crying. But instead she smiled. "As long as you're back for the birth of your niece."

"Or nephew," said Tommy as he rounded the front of the Wrangler, stepping onto the sidewalk with the rest of them.

Smiling, Reid said, "Wouldn't miss it for the world."

"When do you leave?" Maya asked.

"Tonight," said Immy. "We just need to pack, grab a few things, then we'll head to the airport."

Maya nodded. Silence drifted into the space between them, Mars' absence still so strong. He should be standing here with them. Instead all they had left were memories and pictures. Forced to plan futures that didn't include him. It was wrong, and every one of them knew it.

"I'm leaving, too."

Everyone turned to Lucy. The girl's eyes were still red and puffy, a bandage on her neck to cover the gash that Graham had given her, her raven black hair hanging down to her shoulders.

"Will you be back?" asked Lydia.

Lucy pursed her lips. To Maya, it looked like she was doing her best to hold herself together, to keep from completely falling apart.

"I don't know," she admitted. "I just know I can't be here. Not after…"

Maya closed the distance between them, folding her arms around Lucy. The girl stiffened.

"Don't run away from us, Lu," said Tommy, bringing a hand to rest on her shoulder. She wept quietly, rubbing at her eyes with the heels of her hand while the others gathered around to hug her all at once. Fresh snow drifted down from a somber sky, landing on their hair and the red tips of their noses, sticking to their jackets and melting on their hands.

Lucy was the first to break free of the hug. She sniffed, blinking rapidly as her gaze passed over each of them one at a time. "I think… I mean, I'll try to come back. I just don't know."

Maya smiled, nodded. She understood. Letting go of Lucy felt a little bit like letting go of a piece of Mars — of the man he could've become and the life he could've had with the girl he'd fallen fast in love with.

"You don't have to go, you know," Jude told her.

Lucy shook her head, eyes brimming with fresh tears. "I do. Everything here reminds me of him. *You* remind me of him."

Lydia reached out to take Lucy's hand, giving it a squeeze. "You will always have a place with us. Come back when you're ready."

With a nod, Lucy took in a sharp breath, turned on her heel, and walked in the other direction until she disappeared into the fog of snow.

"You sure you want to do this?" Jude asked.

Maya stood at the end of the sidewalk, hands in her pockets as she stared at her family's house. Her father's car was parked in the driveway. The lights were on inside. He was home. All she had to do was walk up to the door and knock.

What if he doesn't want to see me?

"I can go with you," Jude offered.

Maya smiled, turned to kiss him on the cheek. "I think I need to do this on my own."

He seemed unsure, but he nodded anyway.

With a sigh, Maya followed the sidewalk to the front porch. She reached out to knock, but the door was already ajar. Furrowing her brow, she pushed it open, leaned her head in. "Dad?"

There was no response.

She shoved the door open the rest of the way and stepped inside. She checked the kitchen first and nearly choked on the smell of spoiled food and alcohol even before she saw it scattered over the countertops. The kitchen was a disaster. Dirty dishes piled up in the sink. Empty beer cans crumpled up by the trash. Flies buzzing around. "Dad? Where are you?"

A thump upstairs.

Covering her nose, Maya left the kitchen and took the stairs slowly, nervous about what she might find. Her hand on the banister, she took the last step and turned into the hall. Her father lay sprawled on the floor between the hallway and his bedroom. She gasped. "Dad!"

Maya ran to his side, the smell of beer slamming into her. Her father moaned as she turned him over onto his back, plucking the half-empty can of beer from his hand.

"What are you doing?" she asked as she helped him sit up, leaned him against the hallway wall, slumped over.

His eyes fluttered open, darting every which way before they landed on her.

"*You*," he said, his voice an angry slur. "What are you doing here?"

"I came to see you, Dad."

The man laughed. "See me. You came to see me." He pointed a lazy finger at her. "Your mother's dead. Because of you."

Tears pricked Maya's eyes. "What? Dad, no. I-"

"Get out."

"Dad, please…"

"Get out!" he roared.

"May?" Jude called from downstairs.

Maya sniffed and wiped the tears from her eyes as she looked at her father, at the man he'd become in just a few short weeks. "I'm okay, Jude," she said, even though she was anything but.

She heard his footsteps as he climbed the stairs, rounded the corner, and saw Maya crouched next to her father, who mumbled under his breath, his head rolling back and forth.

Maya turned to him, stood, and stumbled toward him, folding herself into his arms.

"It's going to be okay," Jude said, holding her as she cried silently.

"He hates me," said Maya.

"No," Jude replied. "He hates himself."

"What do I do?"

Jude pulled back, glanced at her father, then back at her. "We can try to get him some help, but… he has to want it. It isn't your fault."

She knew that. Of course she knew that.

Consequences.

Their parents had long ago made the decision to let Orion get away with murder – literally. Their inaction regarding what Orion had done in Peru – along with the murder of their friend, Danny Dawson – had passed the burden of Orion's madness onto their children. They'd thought they could escape the consequences of what they had done, and part of Maya had thought that, now that he was dead and Cuvier's lost vault had been found, maybe things would get better, but actions always had consequences. Passivity in the face of evil would always exact a price from those who refused to fight.

"Let's go," Jude said, guiding her by the arm.

Maya nodded, followed him. She wouldn't give up on her father, but it would take time. For all of them, it would take time to heal. To learn to bear their burdens and each other's. To say goodbye to the people they had been. And to welcome a future they had not planned for. But Maya had faith that the Jailbirds would get there in the end. It would take a while, but Mars hadn't given up his life only for them to lose theirs, too.

They would live, and they would love. They would laugh, and they would explore. They would learn, and they would grow. They would fight for each other and carry each other and protect each other. That was how they would honor Mars' memory, his sacrifice. That was how they would keep him with them whatever oceans they crossed and whatever mountains they scaled.

EIGHTY-NINE
LYDIA

Four weeks later...

Lydia stood in the doorway of Hollow Hill Lighthouse, her gaze passing over the emptied room, a hand cradling the bump that her belly had become. As hard as it was to admit, life had kept moving. The baby inside Lydia's womb continued to grow. Thanks to the exposure that Orion's crimes had brought to the Jailbirds' discoveries, the requests for interviews still poured in. Though they hadn't responded to any of them. Tommy wasn't ready to tell their story. Not yet. The news stations and reporters could wait. There were more important things to worry about right now.

They'd sold off the treasure they'd brought back with them and given most of the money to Theo and Claire Highland to rebuild The Boathouse. What they'd kept, they split between the

Jailbirds. And after settling Tommy's mother's estate and selling off his childhood home, Lydia and Tommy had enough to buy a house of their own. But now that it was time to say goodbye to the lighthouse, Lydia felt unsure.

Tommy came up behind her, wrapped his arms around her middle. "It's still in the family," he said. "The Highlands still own this land. I heard they may even donate it to the city as a historical site now that it's part of my father's story."

"Speaking of… that professor called again," Lydia said, her hands over Tommy's arms, savoring the feel of his rough skin beneath her fingertips. The bruises had begun to heal, and the cuts had begun to scar. Even though the memories of that day nearly two months ago would not fade for a long time to come. "He really wants to meet with us. Says he can help us excavate the site in Egypt."

Tommy nuzzled her neck. "Mmm… I'll call him back when we're ready."

Lydia nodded, her eyes sweeping over the room. "A part of me wishes we didn't have to leave this place."

"Me, too. But I think… we need to stop living in the past. Start building a future." He paused. "That's what Mars would have wanted."

Closing her eyes, Lydia remembered that day when Mars threw himself in front of her, taking the bullet that had been meant to end her life — and her baby's. He had died so she could live, so she and Tommy could build a life together like they'd always planned, so they could grow old together and watch their child grow up.

"This place will always be part of us," Lydia agreed. "And so will Mars."

"I love you," said Tommy.

"I love you, too." She turned to face him, cupping his face in her hands. In the weeks since they'd returned to Mammoth, he'd grown a beard. More and more, he was looking less like the boy she'd known as a little girl and more like the man he was always meant to be – a leader, an explorer, a protector. But he would always be the boy who'd taught her to dance on rooftops, who'd named fossils with her and run through library aisles with her. Their life together would be built upon the foundation of the greatest love story Lydia had ever lived.

Tommy kissed her, then led her out the door. He turned to lock the door behind them and paused. Reaching into his pocket, he pulled out a picture – a smaller version of the one that had been used at Mars' memorial service. The four original Jailbirds, hanging onto each other, laughing and smiling. He slipped it into the doorjamb, smiling as their younger faces stared back at him.

Slipping her hand into Tommy's, Lydia leaned her head on his shoulder. They stood there for a while, saying goodbye in their hearts. And when they were ready, Tommy locked the door and they turned toward the car. Lydia glanced out at the ocean and the *Perdition* rocking in the water by the dock.

She smiled into the sunset as the last light of day faded over Hollow Hill.

NINETY

IMMY

A pair of pelicans called out as they flapped their wings, soaring over a bright blue ocean. Immy dug her feet into the sand, leaning back on her hands as she stared out at the water. The oranges and reds of the South American sunset exploded across the horizon. A warm breeze carried across the water, sending goosebumps across Immy's skin.

"For you," came a voice.

Immy glanced up to see Reid standing over her, holding a tall glass in each hand, his linen button-down flapping in the breeze. He looked good in shorts. But maybe it was less the clothes and more the fact that she'd never seen him so relaxed.

"Virgin piña colada," he said, handing one to her.

She took it, and he sat down in the sand beside her, crossing his legs. Immy squinted at him, smiling as she took a sip from the straw. "Never would've taken you as fruity drink kinda guy."

"Just because I gave up alcohol doesn't mean I'm no longer a fan of delicious flavor."

"Fair enough." She sat up, setting the glass in the sand in front of her. Behind them, the sounds of the coastal city felt distant. The beach was quieter. Less chaotic.

Reid had gone with her to visit the home she'd grown up in – one she hadn't set foot in since her parents had died. She'd gathered a few things to bring with her, but everything else… well, her parents weren't there anymore. They weren't in the things they owned or the house they'd built. They lived in her heart, and that's where she would carry them.

After that, Reid had taken her to where Emilio was buried. She finally got to say goodbye the right way. But she knew she'd see her family again. While her blood family may not be here anymore, she'd found another family. People she could walk through the rest of this life with. And she was grateful.

They'd stopped here a couple weeks ago. Neither of them were quite ready to go back to Mammoth, so they'd found a hotel and used the money Tommy had sent them for the treasure to enjoy a moment of peace and quiet.

But eventually it would end. They both knew it. The real world was still out there. A new adventure, new uncharted territory waiting to be mapped out in front of them. But for now, this was enough.

Immy's hand went subconsciously to the crystal pendant around her neck – the one Tommy's father had given her. It was funny how, for all she'd lost, she'd gained so much.

Her eyes flicked to Reid, who stared out at the water as he took a long drink through his straw. There was a funny side to him that Immy had never noticed before. Turns out, when you weren't running for your life or being hunted down like animals, you could actually have fun. And Immy really liked having fun with Reid. If Mars' death had taught her anything, it was that you never knew when it would end. You never knew how much longer you had left. All you could do was your best with the time you had now. No more second-guessing, no more what-ifs, no more hesitating.

So Immy did something she'd been thinking about for a while now. She leaned over and settled her head on Reid's shoulder and stared out at the water with him. He didn't pull away. He didn't stiffen. Instead he reached over and took her hand in his.

What happened next was an ocean yet to be crossed. But at least for now they knew they wouldn't be crossing it alone.

NINETY-ONE

TOMMY

Eleven months later...

Tommy adjusted his tie and straightened his blazer as he looked out over the group of middle school students. He smiled and shoved his hands in his pockets, standing beneath the shadow of Agatha and Bernie – the twin wooly mammoth fossils for which their town had been named.

The children listened in rapt attention as he told the story he'd only just begun to tell the world a few months ago – the story of Obadiah Hawthorne and Othniel Cuvier, of discovery and betrayal.

A hand shot in the air. "Why did Obadiah Hawthorne kill his friend?" a little girl asked."

"And for some dusty old bones?" added another student.

Tommy smiled. "You're not much into fossils, are you, kid?"

He shrugged but didn't say anything.

"That's okay," said Tommy, "I'll show you something else in just a minute that I think you'll like." He turned his attention back to the girl. "We can't know for certain what Hawthorne's true motives were, but we can guess that greed played a major role in his decision, and when Othniel Cuvier did not want to be a part of enslaving and slaughtering the natives who lived in this region back then, Hawthorne decided to remove Cuvier from the picture."

"But he managed to hide one of the tusks, right?" another student asked.

"That's right. Othniel Cuvier, with the help of his daughter, had already put a plan into motion to protect his discoveries from people like Hawthorne. As he was dying, and possibly with help, he hid Agatha's missing tusk in a cave on Apocalypse Island."

"Didn't you and your friends find the tusk, like, a year ago? I saw something about that in the newspaper, I think."

Tommy smiled. "We did. But that's not all we found. Follow me."

The group followed Tommy through the museum. It was field trip day, and groups from the elementary, middle, and high schools were all being led through Mammoth Museum of Natural History by other assistant curators – like Tommy. As it turned out, the paleontologist who had been trying to reach him had been selected to replace Orion Clark as head of the museum. And, after recovering Cuvier's hoard from Egypt, he wanted to offer Tommy a job as chief curator. Tommy had been skeptical at first, but the man wanted nothing in return – just the opportunity to help Tommy make things right. Apparently, he'd been a friend of his father's from college. So Tommy accepted the offer on the condition that he'd start at the bottom and work his way up. Tommy wasn't interested in handouts, but he wouldn't turn down the opportunity to get some hands-on experience now that he was going to school to become a paleontologist like his father.

They walked the length of the museum's main corridor, past bustling exhibits and glass cases filled with weapons from all eras of humanity's history. Before they even arrived, the kids started ooh-ing and ah-ing.

Tommy smiled, stared up at the massive *Tyrannosaurus rex* display. It had been propped up on a pedestal at the back of the museum's main corridor. They were preparing to move it toward the front, but the twin mammoths would always have chief position there.

"Can anyone tell me what kind of dinosaur this is?" asked Tommy.

The kid who'd pretended to be disinterested shot his hand up. "A T-Rex!" he blurted.

"Exactly right! This is an immaculately preserved fossil of *Tyrannosaurus rex,* and it was actually discovered by Othniel Cuvier himself. See, when Cuvier began to fear that his life – and his legacy – were at risk, he, with the help of his daughter, decided to build a vault to hold all of his discoveries and treasures until they could safely be shared with the world."

"Treasures?" a wide-eyed student asked with a toothy grin.

"That's right. This T-Rex wasn't the only thing my friends and I discovered when we traveled to Egypt a year ago. Over here," Tommy gestured to the exhibit hall just to the right of the T-Rex display, leading the kids into a darkened room, "is our new Othniel Cuvier exhibit."

"Wow," the kids said in unison as they walked into the room.

The walls had been painted black and the lights had been turned down low. Along all three walls were backlit glass cases filled with scrolls and tomes, weapons and fossils, pottery and primitive clothing, and – the coolest thing of all as far as the kids were concerned – gold coins and precious jewels.

Tommy walked to the center of the room, facing the group as they filed in through the door and fanned out to explore the displays. "While we did donate some of the relics we discovered to our sister museum in Mariner's Cove, Maine, most of Othniel Cuvier's discoveries have found a home here at the Mammoth Museum of Natural History."

His eyes flicked toward the back of the group when he saw his wife appear in the doorway with their friends. She smiled at him, their son propped up on her hip. Reid stood beside her, playing with the baby, with Immy beside him. Maya and Jude joined a second later, hand in hand. Waiting for him to finish his tour – they had plans today to honor the one year anniversary of Mars' death.

"How's that for lost treasure, huh?" Tommy asked, attention back on the group. His finger played with the gold band on his finger, stacked beside the old key ring. "But it looks like we have some visitors. Kids, I'd like to introduce you to my friends – the ones who discovered all of this right alongside me."

The kids turned toward the doorway, eyes going wide. The Jailbirds waved and smiled.

"Weren't there more of you?" one kid asked, looking at Tommy.

Tommy's heart lurched at the painful reminder. He glanced at Lydia who gave him a tender smile. Inhaling, he turned to the kid. "Yes, there were two more members of our group. Lucy Adler, whom we met in Mariner's Cove. And Marshall Highland, who actually died saving my wife's life and our baby."

"Aww, baby!" said one of the little girls. "Can I hold her?"

Lydia laughed. "Maybe later," she said. "And it's a boy."

"Cute! What's his name?"

Smiling, Lydia crouched so the little girl could get a better look at their son's happy face. "Christopher Marshall Highland," she said. "After Tommy's father, and after our best friend, Mars."

"What happened to Lucy?" a boy asked.

Tommy chuckled. The questions didn't stop with kids at this age, but he didn't mind. Telling their story was starting to get easier. Honestly, it helped. He didn't want to forget – not a single part of it. "Lucy went back to Maine. She took Mars' death really hard, and… well, we haven't been able to get in touch with her much since she left."

"If you had it to do over," one of the older boys asked, "would you do it again?"

Tommy paused, considered the question. "Yes and no. I believe in what we set out to do, but we were also, in a lot of ways, dumb kids who went into it without really knowing what we were getting into. We paid a heavy price for it, but we met some pretty incredible people along the way, and we've learned some pretty cool things about ourselves, too."

Lydia glanced at Jude, then Reid. They still hadn't quite gotten used to the fact they were all siblings now.

"My father was an explorer," Tommy continued. "And my great-great grandfather before him. It's in my blood, passed down to me going back nearly one hundred and fifty years." Tommy straightened, a hand coming to settle on the surface of one of the glass cases. He glanced at its contents – fossilized teeth and claws.

"We've been led to believe that the age of discovery has ended. But the truth is, there are just as many mysteries, perils, conspiracies, wonders, and secrets as ever. And as you grow up, you'll realize that none of us ever really knows anything at all. The world is so much *bigger* than they want you to think. Sometimes… you just have to see the whole picture."

EPILOGUE

A set of heavy doors swung open, slamming against the walls. Footsteps echoed across the stone floor as she stepped inside the room. Silence fell over those who had gathered, their arguments falling to the wayside. It made quite the picture, seeing rivals forced together into the same room. On one side, those who bore the mark of the Black Flag. On the other, those who bore the mark of the Wild Hunt. Separated only by the narrow path between them. She watched them as she passed, eyes falling on those whose fingers itched on the trigger, those who set their jaws in defiance of her presence here.

She did not belong, and half the room knew it. But when she was finished, they would bend their knee to her. Or they would suffer the consequences.

Moving swiftly, she kept her head up, staring down her nose at those around her before she fixed her gaze on the front of the room where a table had been set up. One chair recently empty. She rounded the table and claimed the empty chair despite the murmurs, the accusations and the whispers. Those who sat beside her shied away, glaring at her. She clasped her hands in front of her and stared out across the room. Hundreds of angry faces, scarred faces, confused faces. Wild horses in need of some breaking.

"Now that I have your attention," she said, "there is much to discuss."

"Why did you ask us here?" asked the man to her right.

"We demand answers," agreed the old woman to her left.

She had expected this – the opposition of those who fancied themselves leaders. But she wasn't here for them. Looking out over the crowd, she rose to her feet, fingers pressed to the surface of the table in front of her. Her eyes flicked to the cold stone walls where hung paintings of great discoveries and wars, portraits of generals and kings and queens – those who had gone before. "Look around you," she said. "There is a history in this place that we have long forgotten. It used to be that the Wild Hunt and the Black Flag rode at the helm of the age of discovery, and now what have you become? Orion Clark made you into goons and thugs for his own gain, but I would see you become something much more."

"You?" scoffed the man. "What have you to do with any of this?"

"Orion Clark named me his successor," she replied flatly.

To her left, the old woman's face twisted in a bitter scowl. "And I suppose to accomplish that, you showed him to your bed, hmm?"

Her hands balled into fists, knuckles pressed to the surface of the table. Despite the anger that coursed through her veins at the old woman's insinuation, she smiled.

The man grumbled, standing to his feet. "I've had quite enough of this nonsense. Orion Clark may be dead, but that does not give you license to come in and take over. This organization has existed long before Orion Clark, and it will exist long after."

"That is where you are mistaken," she said, turning to him. She raised her voice so that the others could hear. "You are just as responsible as Orion for the downfall of the Wild Hunt. By giving him total authority, you allowed him to effectively neuter one of the oldest organizations in the world – an organization responsible for the rise and fall of kingdoms and for some of the greatest discoveries and historic accomplishments that humanity has to offer. You stood by while Orion turned a thirst for knowledge into a quest for power, all because he promised to line your pockets."

"How dare you!" the old woman growled. "We will not stand here while you undermine our authority. This is *our* organization – not yours."

In a flash, she pulled the gun from her behind her waist and fired. The old woman hovered in place for a moment, a trickle of blood dribbling down her nose, then collapsed in a heap on the floor.

"If it isn't obvious," she said, blowing the smoke from the barrel of her gun, "I'm in charge now."

She turned to the man who had leapt to his feet, his face blanching. "Sit," she said.

He hesitated, then returned to his seat, gripping the arms of the chair like a vise.

Rounding the table, she came to stand before the silent crowd. All murmur and accusation had subsided. All eyes fixed on her.

"On their own, each of your organizations were successful in their own right, but you have lost your way. I intend to take what Orion Clark broke and do more than fix it. I intend to lead us into a new dawn of discovery and exploration. Join me, and we will become more than what we were – more than hunters and raiders."

Before she could even finish, the room erupted in cheers. Fists shot into the air. She smiled, blinded by visions of a future she had long worked in secret to build.

"From this moment on," she shouted over the crowd, "we will be called Pantheon, for we will become gods among men."

THE END

Lucy Adler will return in...

DEVILFISH

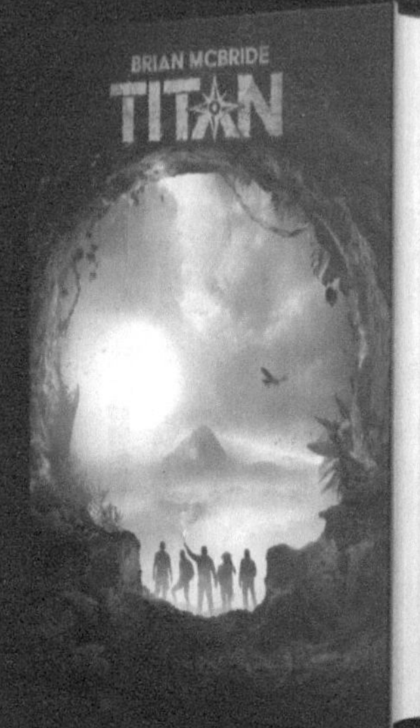

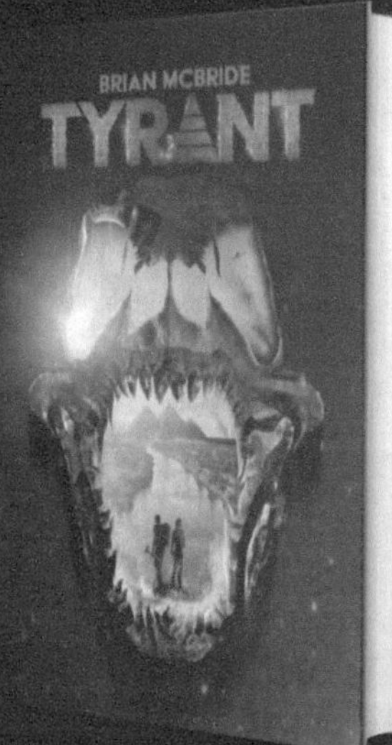

for more information, visit Irewolf.com

ACKNOWLEDGMENTS

We made it. When I began writing this series in the middle of the COVID-19 pandemic, I had no idea these characters, this story, and their world would capture my heart — or the hearts of readers all over — like they did. The Jailbirds are true friends, and their story is as much ours as it is theirs as we've shared in their triumphs and their losses, their joy and their sorrow. I owe them my gratitude; they have shaped me in ways so very unexpected, and I am grateful for their place in my heart. (And grateful that I don't have to say goodbye just yet.)

And, of course, I must thank my parents, Mark and Debbie. There has never been a time in my life where I haven't felt supported or believed in. While the Jailbirds may be lacking (for the most part) in the parent department, I have never lacked your love and support.

Thank you to my siblings, Michael and Eden, for listening to my endless ranting and brainstorming. They knew this story by heart before it ever hit the page.

Thank you to my grandparents for their constant support.

Thank you to my small community of fellow writers: Victoria M, Victoria L, Victoria D, Anna, Ariel, April, Robin, Kait, Wendy, Brigitte, Jaime, Hannah, Laurisa, Maria, and so many more. The names of all those who've championed this story could fill pages.

Thank you to JP for the breathtaking cover artistry, to Claire for untold hours spent catching all my grammatical errors, and to Laurisa for the beautiful map of Mammoth!

Above all, thank you, Jesus. My Champion and my Defender, the horn of my Salvation, and the Rock to which I cling. I am Yours and You are mine.

ABOUT THE AUTHOR

A winner of the 2016 Wattys Award, the 2019 Eric Hoffer Award, and a Finalist in the Readers' Favorite Book Awards, as well as a Readers' Favorite 5 Star recipient, Brian was born and raised in the misty mountains of Oregon until he moved to the San Francisco Bay Area at 16 years old. He's been writing since he was old enough to hold a pen and has been reading for even longer. Among other things he is passionate about his German Shepherd, Arlo, iced tea, and tropical getaways.

www.irewolf.com
www.instagram.com/brianmcbrideauthor
www.facebook.com/brianmcbrideauthor